The Manhattan Family Guide to Private Schools and Selective Public Schools

The Manhattan Family Guide to Private Schools and Selective Public Schools

Victoria Goldman and
Catherine Hausman

SOHO

Copyright © 1994, 1997, 1999, 2001 by Soho Press, Inc.
All rights reserved.

Published by
Soho Press, Inc.
853 Broadway
New York, NY 10003

Library of Congress Cataloging-in-Publication Data

Goldman, Victoria, 1958–
The Manhattan family guide to private schools and selective public schools /
Victoria Goldman and Catherine Hausman.
ISBN 1-56947-249-1

Fourth Edition

For Our Children

Acknowledgments

This book could not have been written without the help of many people in the independent school community: the parents, students and alumni who answered our extensive questionnaire and shared their experiences with us; the nursery school directors, heads of schools, admissions and development office personnel, educators and psychologists who offered their expertise and insight. And, of course, our editor, Laura Hruska, for her patience (and red pencil).

Authors' Note

As parents of young children (five between us at the moment), we had already been through the nursery school admissions process and found it daunting. When it came time to make applications for our children to ongoing (elementary or elementary/secondary) schools we again found ourselves overwhelmed by the number of choices and intimidated by the admissions process. We vowed that the next time around, we would know better—little did we know, however, that our research would lead to a multi-year project culminating in four editions of this book, the only guide to independent schools in New York City in which the text is *not* controlled by the schools.

We toured the schools and scrutinized brochures, annual reports, handbooks, curriculum guides and student publications. We interviewed admissions directors, heads of schools, educators, IQ test administrators, child psychologists, students, alumni and parents. Originally, we sent a letter and questionnaire to all of the heads of schools describing our project. Now, we ask for updated information.

It should not surprise parents that the schools that were most open to our questions are also the most secure about their missions and the new directions in which they are moving, and are the most welcoming to parents in general. While we can understand the reluctance of the schools to disclose the inner workings of their admissions decision-making processes, in the end, many heads of schools, admissions directors and administrators were very generous with their time and advice, and we thank them for their cheerful cooperation.

We hope that the fourth edition of *The Manhattan Family Guide to Private Schools* will serve the interests of families searching for the best school for their child.

Table of Contents

PRIVATE SCHOOL LOCATOR MAP

1. St. Bernard's School
2. Manhattan Country School
3. La Scuola
4. The Churchill School and Center
5. The Nightingale-Bamford School
6. Convent of the Sacred Heart
7. The Spence School
8. The Dalton School
   a. Little Dalton (K–3rd Grade)
   b. Big Dalton (4th Grade–12th Grade)
9. Horace Mann School
   a. Nursery Division
   b. Lower Division Bronx, NY
   c. Upper Division Bronx, NY
10. Trevor Day School
    a. East Side Campus
    b. West Side Campus
11. Saint David's School
12. Ramaz
    a. Lower School
    b. The Rabbi Joseph H. Lookstein Upper School
13. York Preparatory School
14. The Chapin School
15. Regis High School
16. Marymount School of New York
17. Loyola School
18. The Brearley School
19. The Brooklyn Heights Montessori School
20. The Caedmon School
21. The Rudolf Steiner School
    a. Elementary School
    b. High School

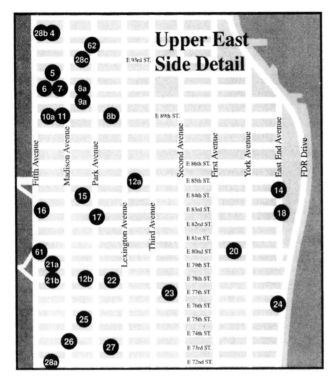

Upper East Side Detail

E 93rd ST.

E 89th ST.

Fifth Avenue
Madison Avenue
Park Avenue
Lexington Avenue
Third Avenue
Second Avenue
First Avenue
York Avenue
East End Avenue
FDR Drive

E 86th ST.
E 85th ST.
E 84th ST.
E 83rd ST.
E 82nd ST.
E 81st ST.
E 80nd ST.
E 79th ST.
E 78th ST.
E 77th ST.
E 76th ST.
E 75th ST.
E 74th ST.
E 73rd ST.
E 72nd ST.

22. The Allen-Stevenson School
23. The Birch Wathen Lenox School
24. The Town School
25. The Hewitt School
26. The Gateway School of New York
27. The Buckley School
28. Lycée Français
    a. N–5th Grade
    b. General Admissions Office 6th–10th Grade
    c. 11th–12th Grade
29. The Browning School
30. St. Hilda's & St. Hugh's School
31. Bank Street School for Children
32. The Cathedral School
33. Rabbi Arthur Schneier Park East Day School
34. Columbia Grammar and Preparatory School
35. Trinity School
36. The Abraham Joshua Heschel School
    a. 3's–5th Grade
    b. 6th–8th Grade
37. The Dwight Anglo-American International Schools
38. The Rodeph Sholom School
    a. N–1st Grade
    b. 2nd–6th Grade

39. The Calhoun School
    a. Lower, Middle, Upper Schools
    b. Lower School
40. Collegiate School
41. Stephen Gaynor School
42. West End Day School
43. The Ethical Culture Fieldston Schools
    a. Ethical Culture School (Midtown)
    b. Fieldston Lower School Bronx, NY
    c. The Fieldston School Bronx, NY
44. Professional Children's School
45. The Riverdale Country School
    a. Upper School Bronx, NY
    b. Lower School Bronx, NY
46. United Nations International School
47. Friends Seminary
48. Corlears School
49. The City & Country School
50. Grace Church School
51. Village Community School
52. a. Little Red School House and
    b. Elisabeth Irwin High School
53. St. Luke's School

54. Brooklyn Friends School Brooklyn, NY
55. The Packer Collegiate Institute Brooklyn, NY
56. Saint Ann's School Brooklyn, NY
57. Polytechnic Preparatory Country Day School Brooklyn, NY
58. The Berkeley Carroll School
    a. Lower School Brooklyn, NY
    b. Elementary School Brooklyn, NY
    c. Middle and Upper School Brooklyn, NY
59. The Children's Storefront
60. Alexander Robertson School
61. Abraham Lincoln School
62. The Gillen Brewer School
63. The Family Schools
64. The Modern School
65. Metropolitan Montessori School
66. The Solomon Schechter School
67. The Studio Elementary School
68. The Geneva School

WHAT'S SO PRIVATE ABOUT PRIVATE SCHOOLS?

INTRODUCTION

The "private"° school admissions season begins the day after Labor Day when New York City parents start to drag their children, barely out of diapers, through four months of touring and testing, then wait in a state of suspended animation until the middle of that bleak wintry day in February or March when a thick or thin envelope arrives in the mail. (Thick envelopes contain a contract; thin, a non-acceptance letter). Parental egos are either elated or deflated, but for those who are disappointed, it's still not too late to go house hunting in Westchester.

There are over seventy independent schools in the New York City area; these include some of the best schools in the nation. There are schools with religious affiliations, schools for children with learning disabilities, Montessori Schools and a Waldorf School: There really is an independent school for everyone, but it just might not be the one you have your heart set on. And though applying to New York City's independent schools has not gotten less stressful over the years, there have been important demographic changes in the city itself that have significantly altered the admissions game.

What Is an Independent School?

All of the member schools of the Independent Schools Admissions Association of Greater New York (ISAAGNY) are not for profit, racially nondiscriminatory, have their own board of trustees, are chartered by the New York State Board of Regents and accredited by the New York State Association of Independent Schools or the Middle-States Association of Colleges and Schools. Independent schools have six basic characteristics: 1) self-governance, 2) self-support, 3) self-defined curriculum, 4) self-selected students, 5) self-selected faculty, 6) small size.°° Private schools, on the other hand, are owned by individuals who may derive profits or incur losses from school operations.°°°

°In New York City most "private" schools are either "independent" (nonprofit) or privately owned and operated for profit. Most of the schools discussed in this book are actually independent schools.

°°*Independent Schools, Independent Thinkers,* edited by Pearl Rock Kane (Jossey-Bass Publishers, San Francisco, 1992), pp. 6–17.

°°°"Independent School Myths and Realities," a newsletter published by NAIS (National Association of Independent Schools), revised March 1994.

3

Teachers in these schools do not need to be certified by the state. They are, however, likely to be experts in their fields, for example, a historian teaching history or a drama department head who is a playwright and director when he's not teaching. Most independent school kindergarten teachers have a master's in early childhood education.

Perhaps the most important difference between independent and public schools is that the formers' "fundamental freedom from state and local governments' regulation has allowed independent schools to develop outside of the ferment that has rocked the public schools."[*] And, of course, public schools do not charge tuition and every child is entitled to placement in such a school (subject to residence requirements and other such prerequisites).

Each school has its own unique character, with a board of trustees that appoints the head of school, who ensures that the school fulfills its educational mission. The headmaster (in conjunction with the development office) assumes the role of CEO and major fund-raiser. Every independent school has its own philosophy of education, its "statement of mission" (the primary aims of the school). This mission statement is always included in the school's literature, but you sometimes have to read between the lines to find it. Each independent school is accountable to its students and their parents; if the parents are not happy with the fulfillment of the school's mission they can remove their children and find another that suits them better. If enough parents do so, the school will fail.

A good reputation is so vital to independent schools that although some myths about a school such as "having the brightest kids" or admitting "only the most terrific families" or "getting the most kids into the top Ivy League colleges" are misleading and often false, they do attract applicants. And some school admissions personnel, perhaps inadvertently, help perpetuate these "positive" myths. The fact is, independent schools are much more mixed than anyone admits. (We found that siblings and legacies were the great equalizers.) As the New York State Association of Independent Schools Guide to Choosing a School states, while SAT scores and college admissions records are "good indicators of the quality of the student body, not necessarily of the school . . . the schools of worth are those whose students, facile or not, are helped to realize their highest potential, develop a lifelong love of learning and forge good character."[**]

[*]*Independent Schools, Independent Thinkers, supra.*
[**]"Choosing a School-A Guide For Parents," a pamphlet published by the New York State Association of Independent Schools (NYSAIS), *infra* pp. 487–488.

4

The level of work, the pressure, pace of learning and challenge, hours of homework and amount of remedial support provided by the school all contribute to designation as "very selective." The qualities a child needs to get in and stay in one of these schools are strong academic potential, an outgoing nature, intensity, good self-esteem, independence, maturity and perseverance. A less competitive, more nurturing school would be better for a child with an average IQ, a known learning disability, a very creative or artistic nature or a nonconformist or shy personality. A desire not to subject a child to externally imposed requirements at an early age and a belief in a child's innate abilities, which, given time to flower, will lead him to a happier, more fulfilling life militate against the choice of a highly pressured school experience.

We believe that there truly is a school for your child, but it is not true that if you can pay, your child can go to the school of your choice. The apparent arbitrariness of admissions decisions is hard for "power-house parents" to accept. Said one admissions director: "After all, they got into an Ivy League school, joined the sorority/fraternity of their choice, landed the job of their dreams and they expect the same for their child too." The baby boom echo is making admissions at all levels very competitive. In response, many schools are expanding their lower schools, adding an extra kindergarten or first grade class that will continue up through the school.

In the past few years, schools that give preference to siblings and legacies (descendants of former students) have often had more applicants than places, and have been forced to make some difficult decisions. Your child's year might be a year in which many siblings apply at the school of your choice but take heart: If your child doesn't get into your first-choice school in kindergarten, you might try again in a few years, by which time attrition will probably have occurred due to divorce and families relocating to other cities and the suburbs. Because more families are now staying in the city, fewer places are available in first through fifth grades. Places do become available in sixth and seventh grades at most schools. (Another interesting trend is that of single, divorced parents moving back into the city with older children to enroll in independent schools.)

Changes in School Services

Gone are the days when women volunteers devoted their time exclusively to serving on school committees, chaperoning field trips and organizing fund-raisers. The two-career family is now the norm (and you are as likely to see a forty-five-year-old father attending the school play or walking afternoon safety patrol as a mother). There is an increased need for after-school, vacation and summer programs, and working parents are happiest if those programs are part of their children's own schools. Most schools now have after-school programs. Caedmon School was the first to introduce "child-minding" until 6:00 P.M. Even the Collegiate School and Brearley School finally added their own after-school programs, recognizing that working families depend on these services and if they want diversity in their schools they have to provide support for them. (Parents are also scheduling more after-school activities such as sports, music and religious instruction, in addition to playdates, for their children.)

One outcome of working parents' desire to have their children in school for longer hours is that the Guild of New York Independent Schools agreed to extend the independent school year from 160 days to 170 days (still ten days short of the public school schedule). Schools also agreed to open their doors earlier in the fall, closer to the Labor Day holiday weekend. A handful of schools still give "travel days" on either side of spring break, a vestige of the era in which families routinely packed a trunk for Europe. Now many of these families travel to snow country in Utah or Colorado.

Financial Pressures

The question of the affordability of private school education is becoming more acute as tuition for Manhattan day schools, which doubled in the past decade, continues to rise. Now parents can expect to pay about $14,000 and up for third-grade tuition. In addition, the gap between income generated by tuition and rising operating costs has widened and all schools count upon voluntary giving and annual fund-raising revenues. "Schools are under more pressure for outside fund-raising from corporate and private sources than at any time in the past," according to an administrator of educational grants at a prestigious foundation. "Capital campaigns seem to come around as often as White Sales these days," says one beleaguered family. We know a couple who received a solicitation letter from their son's school announcing a new capital campaign with a return card enclosed showing a suggested contribution of $10,000. The next day the couple marched into the development office and asked, "Do you expect this much every year?" They were informed that they could pay in monthly installments over a five year period. The pressure to give can be especially intense when the class representative tells you they are hoping for 100% participation. What most parents don't realize is that there is no threshold for annual giving. Parents are asked to give whatever they can; contributions within a given class may range from $5.00 to $25,000. Of course only a contribution of $10,000 and above will earn you inclusion in "The Headmaster's Circle"; the new millennium's equivalent of The Social Register.

The economic boom has allowed the independent schools to make capital improvements and raise the bar academically; tuitions have gone up as well. While endowments have doubled since the late 90's, a deep recession could strain a school's finances. (However, parents who are concerned about the financial health of a prospective school should not ask for the annual report until *after* their child has been accepted.) A healthy endowment shouldn't be the only reason to pick a school. But unless a school has a substantial endowment current parents will be the school's prime source of revenue.

Many parents do not know that tuition covers only about 80 percent of a school's operating expenses and budget, much of this going toward teacher salaries and fringe benefits. Capital improvements, new technology and science labs, and improvements and repairs to existing facilities, are necessary to keep the schools competitive. Adding to this pressure is the increased need for tuition assistance of parents whose children are already in the schools.* "A tremendous increase in the amount of money raised by annual giving and capital fund programs over the past decade" has helped schools make ends meet, according to Fred Calder, Executive Director of the New York State Association of Independent Schools. Thus it doesn't hurt to have families who manage charitable foundations in the parent body. As one admissions director confided, "We *are* a business, you know."

There is increased concern about socioeconomic stratification within school populations as many middle and upper middle income families find that they are unable or unwilling to pay approximately $150,000 for thirteen years of private school tuition. Most schools are

*See "Applying for Financial Aid," p. 49, *infra*.

seeing an increase in families with high income levels applying for financial aid. According to Meade Thayer, Director of Financial Aid Services at NAIS, "Families may well have financial need from their perspective, but does the school have the financial aid available to meet the needs of *all* families applying?" Schools are being forced to make tough decisions about which families to support. "The decisions they make illustrate the school's attitude toward socioeconomic diversity and their desire to have it," says Thayer.

Following the national trend towards eliminating junior high schools in favor of middle schools (serving grades 6-8), Community School Districts 2 and 3 on the Upper East and West sides of Manhattan recently decided to end their elementary schools at fifth grade. A number of very bright and highly motivated fifth grade public school students now apply to the private schools for entrance at sixth grade. Many of the top private schools are scrambling to make space for them, while at the same time, reserving places for Prep for Prep program graduates who enter at seventh grade. Some schools we surveyed, such as Riverdale Country Day School, and Trinity School, told us that because of the way their schools are structured (the lower school is comprised of kindergarten through sixth grade, for instance) and/or because of space restraints, openings in sixth grade at those schools would depend upon natural attrition. Others, including The Brearley School, Horace Mann and the Dalton School said they had already expanded their sixth grades to accommodate public school applicants.

As tuitions climb and the competition for places in the most exclusive schools becomes more intense, the private schools face growing resentment from full-tuition paying families who find that their hard earned tuition dollars are subsidizing increasing numbers of scholarship students. However, NAIS statistics reveal that the numbers of students receiving *full* scholarship is in fact declining. Schools find it is more cost effective to support two families on partial assistance (each paying $6,000 toward tuition, for example) thus achieving a greater diversity of families for the same investment. In another instance of how elementary and secondary private school admissions parallel admissions at the college level, some middle class families of color, Hispanic and Asian families, (all of whom are historically underrepresented in private schools), cognizant of their marketability, find that they are able to shop around for the best deal.

Parents should keep in mind that there is a significant difference between applying for financial assistance at the elementary and secondary levels and applying at the college level where federal assistance is available in addition to institutional assistance. Parents of elementary and secondary school age children also have another viable option—public school. More middle and upper middle class parents are considering select city public schools for a portion of their child's education. Although Hunter Elementary is under the aegis of Hunter College of the City of New York, acceptance to this highly selective tuition-free school is considered as desirable as acceptance to the most prestigious private school. The specialized high schools such as Stuyvesant, Bronx Science and Brooklyn Tech are still magnets for many private school students beginning in ninth grade.

Technology

At one independent school this spring, we watched as the "old" Macintosh computers went out the door and the "new" Dell computers came in. To remain competitive and up-to-the-minute, schools are under increasing pressure to spend more of their budget on technology. In addition, many schools are running "computer initiative" capital campaigns to further augment their technology programs. One school hosted a "cybercarnival" to give the school's technology program a boost.

Upgrading hardware, adding high speed connections to the Internet and buying the latest CD-ROMS and software is just a part of the expense. The best technology in the world is useless without people; almost every comprehensive independent school now has a Director of Technology. Many schools also find it essential to have a full-time "network administrator" to maintain the system.

And that's not all. A good educational technology program requires trained faculty to integrate all this "stuff" into the curriculum in meaningful ways. Staff training, whether through an outside workshop or an "in-house" technology coordinator, is fundamental—and expensive.

According to one technology seer, the day when "machines are the hand-maiden of cognition in the classroom" is not far off. Students at The Trevor Day School and at Hewitt tote Toshiba laptops to and from school in their backpacks and use the computer in every subject class as a "transparent tool"—as they would use pencil and paper. Students at many schools already have access to a school "intranet" or internal website that allows students to access homework assignments, read school notices, join in school conferences, communicate with faculty and send in their homework via e-mail.

The Internet has become a primary research tool and nearly every school library is now on-line. Schools subscribe to several services that allow students to search an extensive database of full-text articles from over 200 periodicals, including *The New York Times* and major magazines, via the World Wide Web. At The Nightingale-Bamford School, students in a Constitutional Law elective learn how to conduct keyword searches on these Web-based services for information related to their study of a particular amendment. Furthermore, students can use the Web to access legal cases that are currently before the Supreme Court. We saw an English teacher at York Prep using the Internet to look up the lyrics of Bob Dylan's songs for a course on the Romantic poets. Students in the 8-9's at Manhattan Country School communicate via e-mail with the Zuni Nation in New Mexico.

Desktop publishing gives students "ownership" of the publication process. For instance, The Brearley School offers desktop publishing workshops and an interactive design class for aspiring student editors. We saw tenth graders huddled around a monitor laying out an article for their class publication, *The Pulse*. Students in their own Student Publications Office also produce a literary magazine and The Brearley School Yearbook.

At Convent of the Sacred Heart we observed young women in a biology class use special motion, temperature, pH and pressure probes attached to laptop computers to record and graph their laboratory data, allowing them to fine-tune their experiments.

Learning literally "comes alive" when students create multimedia projects using ClarisWorks or Hyperstudio. At The Nightingale-Bamford School students created an interactive tour of a medieval village as part of a third grade social studies unit on the Middle Ages. This "virtual village" was then displayed on a touch-screen computer in the school's lobby. By clicking on different characters, such as "Minstrel Martin" or "Sir William," students could learn about that individual's role in society.

It is not enough that students acquire basic computing *skills* such as word-processing, computer graphics, desktop publishing, databases and simulation. "Computer literacy means knowing how to use the computer as a tool to help create and think, to manage information, to solve problems, to express ideas and to communicate with others."*

*Ibid.

10

Parents looking at a prospective school should ask:

- Does the school have a Technology Mission Statement?
- How much of the technology budget is devoted to faculty support and training?
- How is technology integrated into all subject areas, not just the obvious ones?

An educational technology consultant suggested parents look at how the computer is used. Does the school use the computer as an "electronic playbook" or as a creative tool involving high level thinking? Do students spend computer time visiting the computer lab to play games such as "Math-blaster" or do they create something of their own using a program such as Microworlds (LOGO)?

In the most developed programs the classroom teacher initiates projects using different applications to solve problems, so students think in new ways. As Michael Smith-Welch, a fifth grade homeroom teacher at Little Red Schoolhouse and Elisabeth Irwin High School told us, "All the hardware in the world can't beat a good curriculum idea." For a unit on the study of ancient civilizations, Smith-Welch created a project that looks at the problems faced by archeologists in the interpretation of artifacts. The project integrates science, math, writing, computer, history and art and culminates in the creation of a classroom museum of artifacts as well as a "computer museum."

Not all students have access to a home computer, and those who do may not have the latest software applications or a connection to the Internet. Schools are devising their own solutions to this issue of equity. Some have purchased computers for scholarship students, others are keeping their computer labs open and staffed until late afternoon. Some independent schools bridge the gap by opening the school to public school students on Saturdays. Most NYC public libraries provide Internet access free of charge.

Faculty

In addition to the composition of the student body, another essential component in measuring the quality of a school is the calibre of the faculty. Teachers in the independent schools do not have the bargaining power of a union and can be hired and fired at the will of the administration. However, teachers in independent schools do have the

11

ability to design the curriculum and have flexibility in their choice of approach to their subject, books and materials. The advantage for schools is that they can handpick teachers who conform to the school's philosophy and style.

In some cases independent school teachers receive pay parity with public school teachers; in some cases they are paid significantly less. For instance, the head of the English department at an independent school told us that she earns about $10,000 less than her suburban public school counterpart. The exact figures vary from school to school. Heads of schools contend that it is health and other benefits for staff that really eat into the budget. Still, in order to keep the best teachers, schools are under constant pressure to offer faculty inducements such as housing and stipends for study and travel. Many schools have named scholarship funds earmarked for this purpose.

Multiculturalism and Diversity

New York City is the most multicultural city in the country, and many parents and educators believe that its independent schools should reflect that "metropolitan mix" in their student bodies. Despite programs such as Early Steps, a program that promotes diversity at the kindergarten and first grade levels, and Prep for Prep, which prepares talented junior high school students of color for entrance into New York City's independent schools, as well as more abundant scholarship money in the upper schools, the lower schools (K–6) have remained remarkably homogeneous. The so-called "progressive" schools have always been in the vanguard of new thinking, while more "traditional" schools adapt at their own pace, especially regarding the thorny issues of diversity and multiculturalism. Schools such as The Ethical Culture Fieldston Schools, Friends Seminary and United Nations International School have always welcomed a diverse student body. Some of the older, more traditional schools did not always do so but many of these schools now actively recruit students of color. We know of two schools that do not yet give recognition to the Jewish holidays.

During the new millennium the pace of change is likely to become more rapid for two reasons: 1) The changing college admissions profile—in recent years, bright and able students of color have fared particularly well in gaining admissions to the elite Ivy League colleges and universities; since a large part of an independent school's status derives from the number of students they feed to the Ivy League, this trend has inevitably trickled down to kindergarten admissions. 2) the schools do not want to give the appearance of "elitism."

A faculty commitment to diversity is important. Diversity training for faculty is on the rise and many independent school teachers spend time at anti-bias retreats and conferences related to these themes. Adah Askew, Chairman of the Faculty Diversity Committee at Dalton, coordinates the student mentoring program there. Each year her high school students visit the traditional Southern black colleges ("where there are role models in every classroom") so that they might consider "The Harvard of the South" for instance, as an alternative to the Ivy League schools. The parent body also influences the pace of change. Many of the independent schools have a parent committee on diversity. Some parents prefer to have their children in a more homogeneous setting and therefore may choose a more "traditional" school.

Students at New York City's independent schools, along with the rest of the nation, are struggling with the issues of race and ethnicity and the meaning of "difference." Active recruiting and competition for children of color makes some educators uneasy, fanning fears of tokenism and concern for the schools' sensitivity to these students' needs once they are enrolled. A former Parents Association president illustrated this attitude by saying "We want to see our kids in a school with a healthy scholarship program, but of course, we will bring *them* up to our level." Support groups for families of color and students of color (some adopted students of color are not from families of color) abound. In addition, many schools now have anti-bias groups, Cultural Awareness Days and clubs such as Students Aware of Multicultural Ethics (S.A.M.E.). There is an Interschool Multicultural Coalition. The New York Diversity Resource Collaborative, comprised of twenty-eight independent schools, sponsors workshops for professionals and job fairs for people of color and provides information about diversity issues through its computer network, Diversity-On-Line. Even in schools with diverse student bodies there are problems. For example, younger children who commute from Upper Manhattan and the boroughs find it difficult to reciprocate playdates. In some instances parents have been mistaken for baby sitters. In the upper grades there are "scholarship cliques" and tensions have been aired in school assemblies or focus groups.

The independent schools, particularly the girls' schools, are also concerned about gender issues. A 1992 study commissioned by the American Association of University Women (AAUW) carried out by the Wellesley College Center for Research on Women, entitled "How Schools Shortchange Girls" documented the subtle gender bias in schools and how girls are steered away from pursuing careers in math, science and technology. The AAUW report showed that young women were not receiving the "same quality or quantity of education as their brothers."*

The AAUW issued a new report in 1998 which took a critical look at the value of single-sex education for girls and found no evidence that girls were better off in separate schools: "What the research shows is that separating by sex is not the solution to gender inequity in education. When elements of a good education are present, girls *and* boys succeed." In a press release from the AAUW, Sandy Bernard, president of AAUW says, "No learning environment, single-sex or coed, provides a sure escape from sexism. Sound teacher training is key to reducing sex stereotyping in both the coed and single-sex programs." Ninety-five per cent of America's schoolchildren attend coed public schools. The press release states that there is debate about whether the benefits of some single-sex programs (such as a heightened regard for math and science among girls) derive from factors unique to single-sex programs or factors that promote good education such as small classes and schools, intensive academic curriculum and a disciplined environment. (See also AAUW, *infra* p. 485).

Some independent schools have special programs to deal with sex bias. For example, the Dalton School has a parent-sponsored committee that reviews sex-equity issues in the school. The Berkeley Carroll School has a faculty sex-equity study group that meets regularly; Manhattan Country School received a five-year "gender equity grant" for $100,000 from a private family foundation in Washington; The Riverdale Country School held a series of parent education evenings on gender issues.

The AAUW Report states, "By the year 2000 two-thirds of the new entrants into the work force will be minorities and women." If these groups are shortchanged now, the future of our country will be compromised. In response, many schools have reevaluated their curricula, either adding or revising courses that include other perspectives including electives such as "Africa in America: an Examination of the Literature of the Men and Women Who Shaped Contemporary Black American Culture" and "Reform Movements: The Advent of Feminism, Black History and Civil Rights." Eighth graders at The Allen-Stevenson School study Asian, African and Latin American con-

---

The AAUW Report: How Schools Shortchange Girls, the AAUW Educational Foundation and the National Education Association, Washington, D.C., 1992 (p. v.).

tributions to Western civilization; eighth graders at The Nightingale-Bamford School study Islamic forms in math and art. Certainly there are still some schools where the DWEM (Dead White European Males) curriculum predominates, and for some parents a classic curriculum in a traditional setting (for example, Chapin, Buckley or Trinity) is just fine. That's what freedom of choice is about.

In recent years, single-sex, established, traditional schools (many of which have ample endowments) once again became very attractive to many well-to-do parents. Even though both parents might have high-powered careers, these "new traditionalists" are reassured by structured classrooms, the old-fashioned values and a traditional curriculum, as well as the status that acceptance into these schools still confers. But today even the so-called traditional schools are sometimes hard to tell apart from the progressive schools.° Some schools have a unique educational philosophy such as Bank Street School for Children, Fieldston Lower School, The Dalton School, The Rudolf Steiner School and The City & Country School; many traditional schools have incorporated what were once considered "progressive" approaches to elementary education into their curricula. Schools are moving away from teacher-directed classrooms and toward encouraging classrooms where collaborative learning is stressed and where different learning styles and different rates of development are accommodated. There is increased integration of subject matter; most elementary programs favor using the experiential or hands-on approach to learning for everything from science to social studies. Parents should be aware that it is in the middle and upper Schools that the schools are most different from one another. When they look at a kindergarten they should look at the upper School as well.

New York City's independent schools are not the ivory towers they once were. Although still exclusionary financially, certain schools are more inclusive in the makeup of their student bodies than they ever have been. When schools renovate, they must now make accommodations for the disabled. But as the former associate director of the Educational Records Bureau reminded us, "Private school education is still a privilege, not an entitlement." The private, independent schools of New York City are still distinguished by their ability to select . . . and exclude.

°We have noted the schools where uniforms are prescribed. This is often a clue for parents: it can be argued that uniforms diminish dress competition but usually coed progressive schools do not require them.

SELECTING A SCHOOL

Choosing an independent school in New York City is like dating. As one admissions director said, "The chemistry has to be right on both sides." Respect the judgment of the admissions personnel; they really know which children will be successful in their type of program. In making the final decision, a former Parents League president and leader of a toddler group advises, "There should be a commonality between home and school" and, in the final decision, "Use your gut feeling. The decision should be 98 percent stomach and heart and 2 percent head." Through it all remember that your child is unique. And be wary of the Trophy Child Syndrome. As David Elkind writes in *Miseducation: Preschoolers at Risk*, "The social pressure on contemporary parents to use their children as symbols of economic surplus and status is powerful, even if parents are not fully aware of it." Misguided parents believe that "a successful child is the ultimate proof of one's own success."* As one Director of Admissions advised us, "Consider your *child's* comfort level" when selecting a school.

Factors to consider

1. **Location: City or "Campus"**
   Note that a campus school (located outside of Manhattan) may require busing or other transportation, which can cost up to $2,800 annually. The child attending a school far from his immediate neighborhood spends many hours in travel over the course of his education. Parents of young children may choose a campus school so that they can experience a clean outdoor environment for relaxation and recreation daily, and so that, when they are older, they may enjoy grassy playing fields and tree-shaded quads. There is always a late bus to accommodate children enrolled in after-school activities. But for some children there may be better uses for this time. Many adjust with no problem, even in the early years; others find the extra travel draining.
2. **Single Sex or Coed****
   In the younger grades, many children do not seem to value friend-

---

Miseducation: Preschoolers at Risk, by David Elkind (Knopf, New York, 1987), p. 78
**Brearley, Browning, Chapin, Collegiate, Dalton, Nightingale-Bamford, Spence and Trinity are members of the coeducational Interschool Program. Students from member schools can participate in after-school activities, academic courses, intramural sports,

ships with members of the opposite sex. Later, this changes drastically. Parents sometimes prefer a single-sex school where girls may feel more encouraged to be leaders and where their competitive instincts may be less fettered.

3. **Philosophy of School (Educational Practices and Values)**

A school's goals are spelled out in its mission statement. Look at the history of the school, at its founder and his or her philosophy of education. Is the parents' association active and inclusive? Does the school strive for a diverse student body? Are multicultural perspectives included in the curriculum? Are classes formal or informal? How much homework is given? How much support is provided to students who are struggling? Is there enrichment for those who need it? Is community service required (or incorporated into the curriculum)? Perhaps the most important question parents of a kindergarten applicant can ask is "How are developmental differences handled in the early years?" Ask your nursery school teacher about your child's learning style to determine what type of learning environment would be best for him or her.

4. **Religious Affiliation**

Is the school presently affiliated with a religious institution? Many schools were founded in church buildings and later became independent entities, although they may retain the name of the church. In some cases, a representative of the church continues to serve on the board of trustees. Some Jewish schools are associated with a congregation. Is there mandatory prayer or chapel attendance? Which religious holidays are recognized on the school calendar?

5. **Parent Body**

How well will you fit in? Remember that you have to live with these people for the next eight or more years and their children will form your child's peer group.

6. **Size of School**

Consider your child's "comfort level." Will he or she fare better in a smaller, more nurturing environment? Are there programs a larger school may be able to offer that will be important to your child's fulfillment?

7. **After-School Programs, Early Bird Programs, Vacation Programs and Child Minding**

These programs are of particular interest to working parents.

---

community service projects and other activities and clubs. Weekend and holiday dances are an adjunct to single-sex schooling.

8. **Grade at Which School Ends (sixth, eighth, ninth or twelfth)**
   Pick the school that will be right for your child at the outset.
   Schools without a high school may put more emphasis on the
   lower grades and offer more leadership opportunities at an earlier
   age, such as student council president or editorship of the yearbook. Students say that exposure to the behavior of older adolescents, with the concomitant possibilities of experimentation with
   sex, drugs and alcohol, is more limited at a school without a high
   school. On the other hand, a parent may breathe a sigh of relief
   when his kindergartner begins at a school that continues through
   twelfth grade. But bear in mind that while the child *may* complete
   his or her education at this school that is frequently not the case.
   Further school applications may still lie in wait.

9. **Pace and Expectations of the Academic Program**
   How academic is the kindergarten? Certain New York City schools
   such as Horace Mann, Dalton, Trinity, Fieldston, Collegiate,
   Chapin, Brearley and Spence are considered the most demanding
   of their students and are sometimes categorized as "very selective." However, parents should note that the pace and expectations
   vary greatly amongst the lower schools at these "top tier" institutions. But a child develops at his or her own pace. Not every child
   who enters such a school is happy as it becomes more academically demanding; yet many who are not "ready" at the age of five
   blossom in the later years.

10. **Consider Your Own Family Pattern**
    If your family enjoys ski weekends be aware that some schools
    require more work on weekends and vacations than others. On the
    other hand, if your academic expectations are traditional you won't
    be comfortable waiting until your child *wants* to learn a subject
    you feel is important.

11. **Birthday Cut-Off**
    It's important to know whether your child is the appropriate age
    for entrance to the school.

Feeder Schools

Many New York City parents are concerned about getting their children onto the "Harvard Track"; they believe that if a child is accepted
into the right nursery school, then he/she will get into the right

ongoing school and will eventually be accepted at a prestigious Ivy League college. A "feeder school" is a nursery school that channels its graduates to a specific ongoing school. Twenty or more years ago, certain schools preselected their applicant bodies. When parents called a nursery school for an application, they would have a "chat" with the admissions director after which an application might or might not be forwarded.

Today, the reality is that each season, certain nursery schools have a large number of applicants to certain ongoing schools. Some are siblings of the students already enrolled, some live nearby, some are following the fashion at that nursery school. And over the years, certain nursery school directors have developed relationships with the admissions directors at the ongoing schools. They can communicate to those schools whether or not certain children would be good candidates for their programs. There is absolutely no guarantee that even at the "right" nursery school, your child will get into your number-one choice ongoing school. An educational consultant and former admissions director told us: "Kindergarten admissions have become terribly arbitrary over the past couple of years."

Even the most traditional schools, which used to take children predominantly from the Upper East Side or Upper West Side, now accept children from all parts of New York City. Admissions directors are having to go farther and farther afield to look at candidates these days. In a class of forty-four children at Collegiate School, twenty-six different preschool programs are represented. One year, The Chapin School had applicants from sixty nursery schools and enrolled children from twenty.

At nursery schools with a large number of applicants to a particular ongoing school, the director of admissions or a member of the admissions department of an ongoing school will go and observe the applicants in their nursery-school environment. This is an advantage because a child is more relaxed and natural when interacting with his peers in his own familiar classroom. (Most ongoing schools, however, still require that a parent bring the child in for additional testing at the school interview.)

Keep in mind that some ongoing schools have their own nursery or pre-K programs, most of which were originally set up as a service for the children of alumni. But Friends Seminary and Dalton recently dropped their pre-K programs, and Horace Mann dropped its youngest twos in response to limitations on classroom space and the recognition that it is too difficult to pick a two-year old who will ultimately succeed in a demanding academic environment.

The bottom line is, select a nursery school program based on proximity to your home and philosophy and schedule.

THE APPLICATION

Parents of kindergarten applicants should telephone to request school applications the week before or immediately after Labor Day of the year their child is four years old (applicants to the upper grades can wait a little longer). Applications should be filed no later than the first week of December. This deadline is getting earlier and earlier due to the huge number of applications that the schools have to process. Most New York City independent schools have a birthday cutoff date of September 1 (your child must turn five before entering kindergarten). But since the first step in the application process is to make tentative selections of the schools to which you may apply by consulting your nursery school director and other sources, you must start thinking about school far earlier. Some schools give spring tours.

If your child is in a nursery school program, the director will usually set up a meeting with each family to discuss proposed choices for further schooling. If you need more information than you have been able to obtain about a school or its suitability for your child, you should request a meeting with the director to further discuss ongoing schools.

In early October, the Parents League sponsors Independent School Day. Most of the New York City independent schools attend, staff a table and set out their literature. Usually a school's admissions director is there to answer brief questions. Be prepared: It's a little like Macy's at Christmastime. But going, picking up brochures and asking questions will save you a lot of time and phone calls.

Try to be organized. We recommend starting a file, with each school in a separate folder, to keep track of correspondence and appointments. Have some nice wallet-size photos on hand because some applications require a photograph. (Although one family that sent a nude photo of their toddler to a crusty but prestigious school received an acceptance.)

Type or write your application legibly. The sooner you return your application, the sooner you will get your appointments for tours and/or interviews. It's a good idea to seek an early appointment; in case your child is ill the day of the interview, you will still have time to reschedule.

Some applications, like those for Dalton and Friends, contain essay questions. Read the school catalog very carefully and be familiar with the program before you write your essay. But remember that the essay is about your child, not about your many accomplishments or great expectations. The most difficult part of the entire admissions process can be this essay, as it requires a real knowledge of your child, objectivity and verbal ability.

Don't send anything with the application except a letter(s) of recommendation if requested by the school. And if the school doesn't ask for an essay or photograph, don't send one unless you are a genuinely talented writer or photographer.

Early Notification

If your family is connected to a school (that is, if there is a sibling already enrolled, or if the child is a "legacy") then you are eligible for the Early Notification Program. These families will be notified approximately a month earlier than others not so connected. If your child is accepted and you accept the school, then you are required to withdraw your application to all other schools. You may wait until you have heard from all of the other schools on the regular ISAAGNY reply date, but you are not then guaranteed a place at the school that offered early admission.

A word of advice to parents of boys with spring or summer birthdays: There is a mistaken assumption that these boys are immature. As a result, many parents hold their boys back a year, so that quite a few boys turn seven during the kindergarten year. Discuss with your nursery school director whether or not it would be best to hold your son back. If you think he's ready, trust your instincts.

THE INTERVIEW

After the school receives your application you will be contacted to set up an appointment for your child's interview. Independent schools like to see both parents at tours and parent interviews as a demonstration of their commitment to their child's education. Parents usually meet with the head of school or the director of admissions. The requirements are different for every school so be sure to read the instructions on your admissions packet carefully.

The single-sex schools in particular like to meet with both parents together. At some schools, school personnel only meet parents as members of a tour group. Does this mean they are looking more carefully at the parents at some schools than others? Absolutely. Be prepared to talk in detail about your child. One mother was asked the following sequence of questions at a prestigious school, "When did you wean? When did he walk? When did he talk? Where do you go on weekends?" One admission director simply asks, "Tell me about your daughter." Parents have asked if it matters whether they are interviewed by the admissions director or a junior staff member or even a parent. The schools say it makes no difference who conducts the interview, the important thing is open and honest communication.

Nursery school and admissions directors say, "Dress your child comfortably" for the interview. If your child is fussing with his suspenders or playing with her hair it will detract from the interview. Long hair should be pulled back and off the child's face. And keep in the mind the style of the school—that is, whether or not there is a uniform or dress code. For example, when applying to Dalton, Ethical Culture, Riverdale, Friends Seminary, Village Community School or Calhoun, where most of the students will be casually dressed, play clothes are quite acceptable for your child. However, at Buckley, Chapin, St. Bernard's, Spence, or Convent of the Sacred Heart, children will be dressed more formally, and your child should be too: boys in a sports jacket or cardigan, collared shirt, slacks and leather shoes; girls in a dress. Parents should also consider the style of the school and dress accordingly.

For kindergarten admissions the interview may be conducted individually or in a group. The interview might be conducted by one of the following: the kindergarten teachers, the head of the Lower School or the director of admissions, who will record their observations of your child at play. At some schools your child will be asked to complete specific tasks, or take the school's own age-appropriate test. Children are frequently asked to draw a picture and we found that it does help if he/she can recognize and write his/her name.*

You can form an idea about whether or not the school is child-centered during the admissions process, says Grace Ball, an educa-

*See Test Preparation, *infra* p. 29.

tional consultant. "Who is the admissions director focusing on, you or your child? Is your child addressed by name? Are they really getting down to the child's level? After the interview is over do they give you any feedback about your child? Some admissions directors give parents a few minutes after the interview," she says.

How to Prepare Your Child For the Interview

The day or night before your child's interview is enough advance notice to give him or her. Don't communicate your anxiety to the child. Tell your child as specifically as possible what to expect; for example, if he or she will be accompanying you on a tour or will be joining a group, or will be meeting with a member of the admissions staff alone. The nature of the interview is usually described in the admissions packet but if you are not sure, call the school and ask so that you can prepare your child.

If your child wakes up with a runny nose, looking under the weather, it's a judgment call whether or not to cancel your interview. Some schools are so booked that you might not get another chance. But never miss your appointment without calling the school to notify them!

If you notice during the interview that your child is really feeling and behaving oddly, and later that day the child is diagnosed with a double ear infection, call the school and let them know. They might either invite you back or take it into consideration. These are teachers; they can tell when children are not up to par.

To Bribe or Not to Bribe

Parents who are desperate to get their child to perform well at an important interview may be tempted to use bribes. This can backfire. According to an early-childhood consultant, if you really want to offer an inducement to cooperate, promise your child quality time, such as playtime in the park with you, lunch with daddy at the office or a visit to grandma's, rather than a material reward like a trip to the toy store or that Perego jeep he's always wanted.

What if your child won't separate? We observed a fair amount of leg hanging and weeping at interviews. Please don't feel bad if your child won't go off willingly with a stranger, even though you've explained that it's a teacher. Remember he/she won't be going to kindergarten for another full year! How the school handles the separation is a good indicator of how much independence and maturity will be expected during the following year. For example, at one very selective school we were told if your child doesn't separate easily "it doesn't bode well." At other schools parents were invited to come and sit with their children during the group interview.

You should of course encourage and reassure your child that he or she is able to go with the teacher and that you'll be waiting right there for him or her to come back. The separation at the interview is the most anxiety-producing part of the touring/interviewing process. And don't pay attention to other parents who boast about their child's easy separation. This is only one of many factors, and we know plenty of leg hangers who went on to all of the best schools.

Letters of Recommendation/Thank You Notes/First Choice Letters

Directors of admissions at nearly every school advised us that letters of recommendation should be written by someone who really knows the family and the child. One admissions director said she could wallpaper her office with letters from celebrities and politicians. The most valuable recommendation comes from a parent of a child already in the school who knows you well. Never send more than two letters. But bear in mind, things can and do get lost in the shuffle. Always keep a copy on hand just in case.

If you know a trustee at the school, now may be the moment to let him know you have an applicant, but be advised that if your child is accepted at that school you are morally obliged to enroll the child there. You have asked for a favor and it would be rude to act otherwise.

After your interview, admissions directors agree that a thank you note is nice. "I keep it in the file; it never makes or breaks a decision; when we look back, after the child is in, it shows that this is a nice parent and we were right," says consultant Grace Ball. But one admissions director said she was already inundated with mail and didn't want any more! If *you* receive a nice note from a school after the interview don't necessarily think the school is recruiting your child. The Spence School sends handwritten thank you postcards to *everyone* who looks at the school, even if they don't apply.

If parents have a clear first choice they can convey this information to the school in several ways: 1) Write a *brief* note to the admissions director. 2) Tell your nursery school director, who will tell the school for you. 3) Have a friend, already in the school, write a first choice note for you. There is no consensus about the effectiveness of first choice letters. Some schools say it helps them calculate their yield, others say they don't pay any attention to them because some families have been known to write first choice notes to seven schools! That is unethical, as well as unwise, since schools do talk and you might need to apply to those schools again in the future.

THE ERB

The Educational Records Bureau
220 East 42nd Street (The Daily News Building)
Suite 100
(near Second Avenue)
New York, NY 10017
(212) 672-9800, FAX (212) 370-4096

Sharon Spotnitz, Executive Director
Mrs. Lucille S. Porter, Associate Director

If your child is applying for admission to an independent school, he or she will be asked to take the "ERB's". In fact, ERB is not the title of the admissions exam. It stands for the Educational Records Bureau, a national, nonprofit agency that serves approximately 1,350 independent and public schools nationally and internationally, which administers and interprets different types of tests for children from preschool all the way through high school. The ERB employs forty psychologists (examiners) during the admissions season. According to the ERB: "All of the examiners are at least Masters' level school or clinical psychologists, many of them are doctoral level candidates, and some are Ph.D's. They are all experienced examiners. The ERB has been under contract with ISAAGNY (Independent Schools Admissions Association of Greater New York) for over thirty years. For New York City independent schools, the ERB administers a collection of tests that sound like kitchen appliance attachments: the WPPSI-R (revised) for preschool through first grade; the WISC-III for grades two, three, four, and five; and the ISEE for applicants to grades six through twelve. The ISEE is administered in three levels. The lower level: entrance to sixth grade, the middle level: entrance to grades seven and eight, and the upper level: entrance to grades nine through twelve. Practice questions are included in the back of the student guide. The ISEE takes approximately three hours. The ERB tests on the premises of approximately fifty nursery schools. Tests are also administered at the ERB's offices, as well as at other locations throughout Manhattan. The cost of the WPPSI-R is $285. (There is an ISAAGNY Fee Waiver Program for students requiring financial aid.)

If you are considering applying to Hunter Elementary or a New York City public school program for gifted and talented you'll have to go to an approved testing service for Stanford-Binet testing (approximately $125). (See Programs for Gifted and Talented Students, page 466, *infra*.)

26

Having a central testing agency administer one test to all children is intended to "eliminate repetitive testing and thus minimize the strain on children and parents." Prior to the selection of the ERB, parents used to take their children for formal testing at each school to which they applied. However, many schools still require up to an hour of their own "informal testing," so you can still expect your child to be thoroughly scrutinized everywhere he or she goes. It seems to parents that it is the strain on the schools that has mostly been alleviated since they can now see many more than one child at a time.

At some nursery schools, says one parent, "the fall semester of the four-year-old group is like 'Stanley Kaplan' for the ERB." The students get worksheets for practicing matching skills, copying geometric shapes and tracking mazes. They are drilled in their colors, taught to write their names and play with parquetry blocks (for spatial relations). Some children even bring *Weekly Readers* home to work on.

The WPPSI-R determines strengths and weaknesses and where along the developmental scale a child falls. The head of a primary school described the ERB to touring parents as "a measuring stick against which all the children stand." The WPPSI-R was not devised as an admissions test, and a national sampling, not an independent school norm, is the measuring standard. It is an evaluation of the child's development in language and visual/motor skills. Like all standardized tests, it is a snapshot of the child's development taken on one day.

Children are compared with others their age; there is no advantage in holding off testing with the idea that "they will know more." In fact, they are expected to do more as they become older; in some cases the younger child may have a slight edge. Also, the later in the year it is, the more likely it is your child may have a cold or other illness. In fact, ERB introduced the option of spring testing in 1992. If your nursery school director thinks your child is ready "and your child is four years old by May 1st and, will separate readily" the spring might be better. Each report is individually written, carefully reviewed and mailed in the order of the test date. Remember to schedule well in advance of school deadlines. It usually takes 3 to 4 weeks to receive the ERB report.

Parents are sent a copy of the confidential ERB report. (See sample report on pages 30–31.) You can discuss the results with your nursery school director or you may schedule a private consultation with the ERB.

The WPPSI-R is composed of five verbal and five nonverbal (or performance) sections. Children *do not* have to read or write to take this test.

Verbal

Information: Breadth of general knowledge; alertness to environment; learning ability.

Comprehension: Commonsense judgment; social awareness; ability to evaluate in light of past experience.

Arithmetic: Ability to concentrate; skill in counting; ability to reason with numbers.

Vocabulary: Word knowledge; expressive skills; quality of thought processes; language background and development.

Similarities: Ability to perceive relationships between things and ideas; ability to generalize; maturity and logical thinking.

Performance

Object Assembly: Perceptual organization; recognition of part-whole relationships; visual-motor speed and accuracy.

Geometric Design: Visual memory; spatial visualization; development of fine motor control.

Block Design: Ability to perceive and analyze patterns; spatial visualization; visual-motor coordination.

Mazes: Planning ability; visual-motor speed and accuracy; ability to follow directions and work independently; level of impulsivity.

Picture Completion: Ability to differentiate essential from non-essential details; recognition of part-whole relationships; visual alertness.

It is common belief that some of the very selective schools have a fixed cutoff score below which they will not admit a candidate. This is simply not true. Admissions directors have said, "You wouldn't believe some of the scores we have here," and we know some children with astronomical scores who were not admitted. But some schools are more likely to take an "at-risk child" (with very scattered scores) than others.

Some directors of admission place more weight on the narrative portion of the test (the second page of the ERB report), which describes the child's test-taking behavior. One admissions director told us, "It's a personality thing."

The parent must fill out a form requesting that the test results be sent to the ongoing schools to which the parent has applied. There is a $6 additional charge for each school in excess of six. Be sure to follow up with the schools to make sure they received the results.

In sum, says an ERB administrator, "Have faith in your own child. You know him or her better than anybody else does. In the vast majority of cases your child will look on paper exactly as he or she actually is."

And remember, ERB reports are just one piece of your child's admissions application. Your child's interview, the evaluation form from your present school and the application are all given serious consideration.

Test Preparation

Don't say he or she is going to play games or be in a room with other children. Do tell your child, "You are going to work with someone like a teacher who wants to see the kinds of things you know. There'll be some new things and you'll get a chance to learn."

If your child attends one of the participating schools, the test is administered in the relaxed atmosphere of that school. Whenever possible, children should be tested in the familiar setting of their own school. The test is usually presented as enjoyable "special work." You might reinforce this gently beforehand if your child raises questions—but be light and casual.

You may use the same explanation if you are bringing your child to the ERB. Explain that he or she will do "special work" with someone like a teacher who is eager to see what 4, 5, or 6 year olds are able to do. Let your child know that you will be in the waiting room with other parents.

If the child is reluctant to separate from you, have your spouse or a caregiver bring him or her.

ERB will not test a child who is unhappy or reluctant. The anticipation of a pleasant experience is the best preparation for being tested.

Educational Records Bureau
220 East 42th Street
New York, NY 10017
(212) 672-9800

11/21/98

Student:	Test Date: 10/18/98	Test: WPPSI-R
School:	Birth Date: 03/14/98	Examiner:
Entering: K Sex: F	Age: 4 yrs 7 mo 4 days	Reviewer: _____

The Verbal subtests measure verbal comprehension and reflect skill in reasoning with words, learning verbal material, and processing verbal information. The Performance subtests measure perceptual organization and reflect skill in nonverbal reasoning, using visual images in thinking, and processing visual information.

Verbal	PR:			1	2	5	9	16	25	37	50	63	75	84	91	95	98	99		
Subtests	SS:	1	2	3	4	5	6	7	8	9	10	11	12	13	14	15	16	17	18	19
Information																X				
Comprehension														X						
Arithmetic															X					
Vocabulary																X				
Similarities																X				

Performance	PR:			1	2	5	9	16	25	37	50	63	75	84	91	95	98	99		
Subtests	SS:	1	2	3	4	5	6	7	8	9	10	11	12	13	14	15	16	17	18	19
Object Assembly													X							
Geometric Design												X								
Block Design														X						
Mazes												X								
Picture Completion																	X			

Percentile Rank (PR) is a number from 1 to 99 that shows how the student's test score compares to test scores earned by children of the same age in the U.S. general population. For example, a subtest scaled score (SS) of 11 has an equivalent percentile rank of 63, which means that the student performed as well as or better than 63 percent of a representative sample of children at that age level.

Scaled Scores that exceed the 75th percentile indicate strengths, whereas scores below the 25th percentile indicate weaknesses. Scaled scores on just one or two subtests ordinarily describe a child less reliably than the sum of the five scaled scores (Verbal or Performance). Please be aware that the sum of all ten scaled scores is not an IQ score. Also note that an overall percentile rank cannot be obtained by averaging the percentiles for the subtests.

Users of this report are reminded that test results need to be weighed in light of information gained from school records, parents and teachers, and student interviews.

Report Format Copyright © 1997 Educational Records Bureau

EDUCATIONAL RECORDS BUREAU

Student: Examiner:
Date of Birth: Date of Test:

Information on test-taking behavior frequently illuminates inconsistencies in the test performance and aids in judging how accurately the test results describe the student's abilities.

Comfort Level/Self-Confidence:
_____ a sweet, verbal child, easily interacted with the examiner, chatting about his calico cat named Carrot. Throughout the evaluation he was involved in tasks, appeared comfortable, was responsive and displayed excellent effort.

Understanding of Test Directions/Tasks:
Listened to directions and carefully observed all demonstrations. Easily understood what was being asked of him and followed through with purpose.

Language Skills:
Very verbal, easily expressed thoughts. Responses were direct and to the point. General language skills are very well developed. Vocabulary was very good and sentences were complex and filled with description.

Visual-Motor Skills:
Confidently reproduced simple geometric designs. _____ used his right hand; pencil grasp and control were good. Visual-motor integration is nicely developed. Materials were easily manipulated.

Work Traits/Motivation:
Attention and cooperation were very good. Motivated, able to persevere as items increased in difficulty. Responses were thoughtful. Used nice trial-and-error approach on difficult items, which then helped him to understand the more complex block patterns.

Contributing factors:
_____ really enjoyed discovering missing parts of familiar objects (picture completion) and worked with facility, determination and perseverance as items increased in difficulty, clearly enjoying the challenge. Was somewhat uncomfortable with the pictorial part of the similarities subtest and guessed at some of the items. However, when asked to verbalize relationships he had no difficulty, and responses were direct and to the point.

Overall Impressions:
_____ is an independent, verbal child who was comfortable with the examiner and the activities. He took great pleasure in his performance and it was a pleasure to work with him. Both verbal and nonverbal skills are extremely well developed at this time.

The all-important question facing anxious parents is whether and how much to prepare (or coach) their child for intelligence testing. Administrators at the ERB, say emphatically, "Don't do it!" If your child has been coached, it is immediately apparent. One four year old walked into the tester's office and blurted, "I forgot it all!" The tester is looking for how spontaneous the child is in responding to a question never heard before, and for his problem-solving strategy as well as level of information. The authors also believe that tutoring 4 year olds for ERB testing is futile and perhaps counter productive.

Admissions directors at the on-going schools have their antennae out for any signs of familiarity with the test and if they suspect that your child has been coached; if, for instance, all of the scores are very high and this performance does not match the nursery school report or the informal testing done at the school, then the application will be compromised. There are plenty of other families about whom they do not have ethical qualms.

We are sympathetic to parents who feel they have to do something, to prepare their child, if only to ease their own anxiety, so we have listed below some age-appropriate activities that you and your child can enjoy doing together. Remember to keep it fun and it will be a treat for your child to have Mom or Dad's individual attention. When your child gets tired or fidgety, stop.

Playing with wooden blocks, LEGO blocks, connect-the-dot books and puzzles strengthen children's visual spatial abilities. Tessellation puzzles are fun and challenging—one version is called "Mighty Mind." You can make your own unusual cutout images, and then ask your child to reassemble them.

Tic-Tac-Toe, "Quick Chess" (simple three-minute chess games for the super intelligent 4-year-old) and strategic board games also enhance visual spatial coordination (Keep in mind that some preschoolers get very upset if they lose—this is normal—and it's okay to let them win now; they'll learn about sportsmanship later.) The Ravensburger series includes all sorts of puzzles and games for preschool-age children (2- to 5-years old).

Reading aloud to your child increases his vocabulary and develops his pictorial imagination. There are poetry and non-fiction books that are appropriate for preschoolers, in addition to picture books. While you are reading ask your child questions based on the content, such as, "What do you think he's feeling?" "Where are they going?" "What do you think is going to happen next?" After you finish a simple story, ask your child to "tell" it back to you. Help him to put the events in order. Draw a simple picture story, or have him dictate his own stories to you. Another way to increase a child's vocabulary is to ask, "What do you call . . .(name things/identify objects)," also ask, "What do you do if . . . ?"

Incentive Publications, booklets that are available at Barnes & Noble, tap into preschoolers' verbal and math skills. *Scholastic* also publishes games for preschool children in reading, writing, learning and math. Phonemic-based books like Dr. Seuss's "Hop on Pop," and most of his other books, correlate sounds with the shape of a word in a simple way. There are CD-ROMs that help develop early pre-reading skills like the Learning Company's "Reader Rabbit" series. But whatever you do, don't push the reading! Learning to decode occurs when the child's brain is ready, not before; it's a little like losing teeth.

Always have lots of art materials on hand—crayons, paint, pipe cleaners, beads, markers, clay, stickers, etc.—for open-ended play. Children should learn how to hold a pencil correctly (there are special soft grips you can buy at any stationery store) and use it to try to write their names, run mazes and connect the dots. *McGraw Hill Spectrum,* as well as other companies, publish workbooks that focus specifically on fine motor control. Also, sewing with yarn, threading a big needle and beading (threading large beads on a pipe cleaner, for instance) help preschoolers' fine motor control.

A field of mass media called "edutainment" began with the Learning Company's CD-ROMs, which include "Math Blaster," "Millie's Math House" and "Math Rabbit" (see also "Reader Rabbit" mentioned above) and bolster young childrens' math skills. Parents should ask their child to count, use flash cards, play board games (Sorry, Trouble, Candyland, Chutes and Ladders) and simple card games like preschool Uno. You can make up games too. Bake and cook with your child to increase his awareness of simple addition, subtraction, fractions and percentages.

There's no substitute for experience and a trip to a museum, lollipop concert, a farm, the children's zoo, the bakery and the grocery store, can all be opportunities for learning and will increase a child's general knowledge.

Many New York City parents do have their older children tutored, either privately or in a group, for the ISEE (Independent School Entrance Exam for grades 6-12), the Hunter High School Entrance Exam (sixth grade), the SSAT, the Specialized High Schools

Exam (Stuyvesant, Bronx Science, Brooklyn Tech) and the SAT I and II. *What to expect on the ISEE* is a review book published by the ERB that includes practice exams and exact directions for the test. The ERB does not encourage or sanction tutoring for any child who is going through the admissions process.

Candidates for grades six and above should begin to review and refresh their knowledge several months preceding the exam using either a review book and/or a suitable tutor or review class. At the very least, students should look at the sample questions included in the registration materials.

Ideally, tutoring should boost a child's confidence in his/her abilities, familiarize the student with the kind of questions he will find on the test (multiple choice or essay type), teach test taking strategies and hone essay writing skills. It should be preparation that enables students to go into the testing situation thinking, "Hey, I know this stuff, I can do my best." Cramming for any exam the week or two before only results in a sleep-deprived and anxious candidate. Make sure your child has a good night's sleep and something to eat/drink before the test, and because most of these tests are over two hours long, bring a drink and a snack that doesn't make crumbs.

The best way to find a tutor is through word-of-mouth, or though inquiries at the child's present school. In some cases the city offers review courses such as The Math/Science Institute (see pp. 476–477, *infra.*) National test preparation companies such as Princeton Review and Stanley Kaplan have offices in Manhattan. Parents have recommended the following resources to us; rates vary widely so be sure to ask how much it will cost before you sign up!

GRF Test Preparation, Richard Geller, (212) 864-1100, 50 West 97th Street, apt. 11T, New York, NY 10025. Test prep for the specialized science high school entrance exam (Stuyvesant, Bronx Science, Brooklyn Tech), ten three-hour sessions, offered at two locations in Manhattan, also in Riverdale and Queens. Cost: approximately $700.

S & S PREP, Alan Silver. (845) 634-3128, S&S PREP's large group review for the Hunter High School exam is offered at Wagner Middle School, 226 East 76th Street.

School Skills, Inc. (212) 861-5083, Dianne Karlstein DeVizcaino, "Mrs. D." 210 East 73rd Street. Maybe it's the airheads and pretzels she keeps on her desk, or her thirty-plus years experience in teaching, but many children we know enjoy going to "Mrs. D." In demand for ERB and Hunter test preparation, Mrs. D. also provides basic skills review, city-wide test preparation and college application essay writing.

Advantage Testing, (212) 744-8800, 300 East 85th Street. Individual tutoring in your home, Manhattan only. SSAT, ISEE and SAT specialists.

Inspirica, (formerly Stanford Coaching, Inc.) (212) 245-3888, website: www.inspirica.com, fax: (212) 245-3893, 850 Seventh Avenue. Inspirica provides one-on-one tutoring in most academic subjects, specialized programs for HSEE/ISEE, PSAT, SAT I and SAT II exams and other highly individualized programs, and also admissions consulting.

Retesting

"Schools, either nursery or ongoing, will know if a given test isn't reflective of their observations of the child, and if they determine it is necessary they can request a retest," says an administrator. Retesting is usually done at the request of the ongoing school. (But, of course, results of both tests will be under consideration by the school(s) to which application is being made.) It is rarely requested.

DO'S AND DON'TS

Do

1) The week after Labor Day start to make a list of schools in which you are interested. Call these schools for a brochure and application.
2) Give your current school director the school report form from the admissions packet. Note: Some schools send this form directly to the nursery school once they have received your completed application.
3) At the same time, make sure that you have requested the required admissions testing from the Educational Records Bureau; promptly fill out the form and return it to the ERB with your check.
4) Read the brochure before your tour and interview.

5) Call ASAP if you are going to miss an appointment, whether for a group tour or your child's interview.

6) Pose thoughtful, not provocative, questions, that show you've really read the material and know the school. Know at what grade the school ends.

7) Say something nice about the school during the parent interview, and turn off your cell phone or beeper.

8) Ask whom you might contact if you have any additional questions during the admissions process. Being able to call a parent in the school is very helpful.

9) Call the ERB to make sure your child's test scores have been sent to all of the schools to which you have applied, and call each school in early January to make sure your file is complete. The file should contain: 1) your completed application, 2) letters of reference if requested, 3) school report from your nursery school, 4) results of ERB testing.

10) Use discretion when discussing ERB testing results and acceptances. We've seen feelings get hurt and friendships ruined by boasting.

11) If you genuinely have a first-choice school, let your nursery school director know and let the school know (in writing from you or a parent in the school who knows you). But realize that if you are accepted, your child is morally obliged to attend.

12) Do use pull if you have it *before* completing the application process. Don't wait until after your child is rejected; negative decisions are rarely changed. But use discretion; the thicker the file, the thinner the candidate.

13) If you are totally bewildered use an advisory service, but be discreet about it—some schools frown on consultants.

14) After admissions decisions have been made, call or write every school at which you have been wait-listed to let them know: 1) that you are still very interested or 2) that you have accepted a place elsewhere.

15) Revisit the school after your child has been accepted, and have your child sit in on classes if you need more information before making a decision.

16) Ask for a copy of the school's annual report only after your child has been accepted.

17) Recognize that you have the right to call a school and (politely) find out why your child was not accepted.

18) Realize that kindergarten is a transition year, and reevaluate your choice of schools every three to five years.
19) Be a supportive parent, try to see your child realistically, know his strengths and weaknesses, be his advocate.
20) Remember that there is no such thing as a perfect parent, a perfect child *or* a perfect school.
21) Realize that you don't know how good a school really is until you have a problem.

Don't

1) Pick a school because your husband's law partner and/or your best friend send their children there.
2) Coach your child for the ERB (WPPSI-R). (You can prepare your child for upper-level testing (ISEE or SSAT.)
3) Be late or miss an appointment without calling.
4) Send a personal essay, photos or any more recommendations than the school requests.
5) Ask for special treatment during the admissions process. Even celebrities have to take the group tour.
6) Ask them to convince you as to why you should send your child to their school.
7) Stand out on the tour by asking too many questions or taking notes as if you were writing an article or a book.
8) Brag about your achievements.
9) Offer money to or otherwise try to bribe the admissions director.
10) Think that you can change the basic style of the school.
11) Tell a school that it's your first choice unless you intend to enroll your child there.
12) Make the elitist assumption that all students of color are on scholarship.
13) Select a school solely on the basis of how many children get into Ivy League colleges. Do look at the range of schools to which students are accepted.
14) Forget that you're an applicant, not a supplicant.

THICK OR THIN

Admissions decisions are usually made by committee (although the Director of Admissions acts alone at some schools.) The members of these committees vary from school to school. At some schools someone from the development office sits in, and sometimes parents of students are on these committees. There is usually a core group of children comprising siblings and legacies who are definite admissions and the committee tries to put together a balanced class around this core. Schools want a balance of personalities as well; they don't want all leaders or followers. If it is a coed school they need an equal number of boys and girls. So your chances vary from year to year depending on what kind of sibling year it is, or for unpredictable reasons. For example, in a recent year at Riverdale Country School, more applications were received than in any previous year, "over five hundred for approximately seventy spots," according to the Director of Lower School Admissions. So a rejection one year might well have been an acceptance the following year. Never take it as a judgment of your child.

Do admissions directors talk? The independent school world is small; admissions directors go to lunch and phone calls go back and forth during the admissions process. Usually, they will not talk about specific families. They will discuss whether the "pool" is up or down for girls or boys this year and so forth. But somehow, if you tell each school that it is your first choice, it will get around. So don't say it unless you mean it.

The yield figure is a mathematical formula, different at each school, which attempts to predict the number of children who, having been accepted to the school, will actually enroll. Anyone whose child is in an over-enrolled kindergarten class knows that this is an inexact method.

There are three elements that make up your child's file:
1) **ERB Testing Results**
   The examiner prepares an individual report for each child. Each report is carefully reviewed by a child psychologist for accuracy and clarity. Parents and schools receive the identical report.
2) **The Nursery School Report**
   A confidential report (parents never see it) that discusses your child in depth: his growth, maturity, strengths and weaknesses over the past (three) years as well as information about the

family such as how supportive the parents are, how promptly they pay tuition, if they have donor potential and so on. Nursery school directors have to be honest in this report; as a former Parents League president put it: "Report plus rapport equals respect." An honest report plus a relationship between the nursery school director and the director of admissions at the ongoing school equals respect for the nursery school director's recommendation. Admissions directors know how to read between the lines of these reports and the notation "Call me for additional information" implies there is more to the story than what's written on the page. An early-childhood consultant told us that "for an unconnected family without significant means, it's essential that your nursery school director have an established relationship with the admissions director at the ongoing school and be able to really go to bat for you." It certainly can't hurt to be active and involved in your nursery school, and if you're unsure whether to give time or money, give both.

3) **Child's Interview**

An admissions director who's been in the business for twenty-seven years says, "I never read a file until I meet the child." The child's profile should fit together like a jigsaw puzzle, says a representative from Ethical Culture admissions. "The nursery school report should correspond to behavior in the interview, the ERB reaffirms both. If a piece doesn't make sense, then we have to look further."

If you've got three out of three you're accepted (provided there's room), and a contract will usually be included with the acceptance letter (thick envelope). Two out of three and you might be accepted or wait-listed. One out of three is usually a nonacceptance (thin envelope containing only a nonacceptance letter). This is not gospel; there are mitigating factors and if the child is outstanding in some way that might outweigh one of the other factors.

What They're Looking For

Schools are looking for readiness, a term in dispute but basically a quality measured by strong academic potential (the mastery of certain skills and tasks such as ability to count to twenty, recognize the alphabet, draw geometric shapes, and so on), and socialization skills (ability to share and get along with others, form an appropriate relationship with the teacher, work independently and show "maturity"). In the past, kindergarten might be a child's first school experience, but today most children have been in a preschool program for two to three years and prior to that, countless "Mommy and Me" classes. "Kindergarten has become an experience for which children need to be ready when they arrive."[*] However, this does *not* mean that parents should teach their preschoolers to read. There are some children who will learn to read before kindergarten (you know who they are because parents of such children will invariably boast about their "little geniuses"). However, educators stress that the majority of children are ready for formal reading instruction in first grade or when they are approximately six and a half years old. Admissions directors do not expect candidates for kindergarten to read, nor should you.

A good evaluation of a child, in the words of one nursery school director, is "Verbal, curious, good self-esteem, ability to concentrate, not fidgety, has enough to give to others." Then there is an intangible measurement dubbed "the likability factor" by an early-childhood consultant we know. We'd all like to think our children have it—it's a personality thing.

ADVISORY SERVICES

Aside from this book and the director of your nursery school, there are other useful resources in Manhattan to help you select the right independent school for your family. Keep in mind that the best source of information is the school itself. Ask if the school you are interested in has spring tours. Perhaps you can rule out a school or take a second look in the fall when you apply. Once the fall admissions process gets rolling you will usually not be able to take a second look until your child is accepted to the school. Advisory services (or educational consultants) help parents approach the independent school admissions process in an organized manner and provide reassurance and advice to apprehensive parents.

Parents, whether you choose to use a consultant or not, please be advised that some independent schools admissions officers have

---

[*]*Kindergarten, It Isn't What It Used to Be,* by Susan Golant and Mitch Golant, Ph.D. (Lowell House, Los Angeles, 1990).

informed us that they do not look kindly on applicants who use the services of consultants. So if you choose to use one, don't broadcast it during your interview.

All except two of the services listed below require a fee.

1. THE PARENTS LEAGUE OF NEW YORK, INC., 115 East 82nd Street, New York, NY 10028 (212) 737-7385, website: www.parentsleague.org
Patricia Girardi, Executive Director

The Parents League was founded in 1913 and is a nonprofit organization of parents and independent schools. Annual membership fee: $75 for one year or $200 for three years. The Parents League offers a School Advisory Service for member parents who need advice about the process of applying to schools and information about the schools. Please call for an appointment. The advisors are volunteers who are trained in-house.

The Parents League distributes the *New York Independent Schools Directory*, published by the Independent Schools Admissions Association of Greater New York (ISAAGNY). Anybody can purchase the book for an additional $15.00 at the office, $17.00 by mail or online. *Please be aware that the entries in this book are written by the schools themselves.*

The Parents League sponsors Independent School Day, held in the fall, at which parents can pick up printed material, including brochures and applications, from various city independent schools; representatives from the independent schools are available to answer *brief* questions. Be prepared for a mob scene, but it will save you countless phone calls.

The Parents League sponsors a Forum on Admissions, at which admissions directors from five or six independent schools speak and then answer questions from the audience about the admissions process. It offers a summer advisory service and a special education advisory service. You must be a member of the Parents League to participate.

2. GRACE BALL & ASSOCIATES, 300 East 51st Street, Apt. 2E, New York, NY 10022, NYC (646) 497-0086 or Westchester (914) 793-5584.

As she has worked as Director of Lower School Admissions for twenty-seven years at Riverdale Country School, Ms.

Ball is well respected in her field. Her vast knowledge of the schools, the admissions directors and their admissions policies and procedures is practically unmatched. Ms. Ball charges approximately $250, which includes three consultations, first with the parents for one hour, then with the child for another hour and a final meeting with parents that lasts about an hour. Phone calls are included. Additional time is billed at $100 an hour. For a flat rate of $2500, Ms. Ball offers a September through June package that includes multiple consultations with parents and children as well as advice on how to adjust to a new school, appropriate parent involvement, and development and financial issues.

3. JOAN MILLER ADVISORY, 4 East 88th Street, New York, NY 10128, (212) 876-6314

Joan Miller, a former teacher and admissions director, offers a more personal approach. Ms. Miller meets with parents in the privacy of her home or yours. Specializing in nursery school and kindergarten admissions, Ms. Miller helps parents through the application and admissions process step by step. The fee is $200 for nursery, $200 for kindergarten and above.

4. LOIS BERMAN, Ph.D., 177 East 87th Street, Suite 502, New York, NY 10128, (212) 722-0250

Dr. Berman was the psychologist at Trinity School for seventeen years and has worked with many independent school families. Dr. Berman advises families on choosing the right independent school for their child (as well as those considering a change of schools, but not for kindergarten placement.). As a licensed psychologist, Dr. Berman can also administer a psychoeducational evaluation to children with suspected learning disabilities.

5. IVYWISE KIDS, Nina Bauer, MA, 140 West 57th Street, Suite 3D, New York, NY 10019, (212) 262-1200, website: *www.ivywise.com* email: *nbauer@ivywise.com*.

Ms. Bauer has a Masters in early childhood education and has taught in both public and private schools. She offers a very personalized service in families who have children applying to nursery, kindergarten and high schools in Manhattan, as well as students who wish to transfer schools. Ms. Bauer guides parents through every aspect of the admissions process while helping them choose the right school for their child. There is a range of fees; we were quoted $1500 for two 90-minute sessions and $300 an hour after that. Ms Bauer does pro bono work for eligible students. College and graduate school consulting is also provided by Dr. Katherine Cohen, Ph.D., (212)262-3500.

6. LANA F. MORROW, Ph.D., 58 West 88th Street, New York, NY 10024, (212) 595-1141

Dr. Morrow administers neuropsychological evaluations and remediates children who have learning disabilities. She advises families as to which independent school will be best suited for their child.

7. SMART CITY KIDS, Roxana Reid and Karen Quinn, 1 Irving Place, Suite P21F, New York, NY 10003, (212) 979-1829

Ms. Reid, a former kindergarten teacher with a Masters in social work, and Ms. Quinn, a psychologist and attorney, specialize in kindergarten admissions. They hold workshops and private sessions that prepare parents and children for every aspect of the kindergarten admissions process—how to handle interviews testing, skill requirements, applications and essays. They also offer a Caregiver Workshop that suggests activities for caregivers and their charges, ages 3 and 4 years old. Fees are approximately $150 an hour.

8. VIRGINIA J. BUSH & ASSOCIATES, 444 East 86th Street, New York, NY 10028 (212) 772-3244

Since 1975, Mrs. Bush has been advising families on secondary school and college options.

9. EDUCATIONAL DIRECTIONS, Jane Ellen Weltz, 360 East 72nd Street, New York, NY 10021, (212) 879-0287

Ms. Weltz, a nursery school teacher, has been advising parents about school admissions from nursery through Middle School for over fifteen years. Ms. Weltz offers support, reassurance and encouragement for children who may need it.

10. SCHOOLS & YOU, Sarah D. Meredith, 328 Flatbush Avenue, Suite 372, Brooklyn, NY 11238, (718) 230-8971, website: schoolsandyou.com

Ms. Meredith provides information and consultations on school choices from nursery through eighth grade for both public and private schools. She will consult at your home or workplace. Resource materials accompany every consultation.

11. HOWARD GREENE & ASSOCIATES, The Educational Consulting Centers, 39A East 72nd Street, New York, NY 10021, (212) 737-8866

    The Educational Consulting Center was founded in 1969 by Howard Greene, former admissions counselor at Princeton University. Known for their college admissions counseling, Howard Greene & Associates will also advise parents about elementary and secondary independent schools. There is a range of fees.

12. SCHOOL CONSULTANTS ON PRIVATE EDUCATION (SCOPE), 309 East 87th Street, New York, NY 10128, (212) 534-6531, or 1-888-214-6590 (toll free), e-mail address, camps4u@aol.com.

    Director Elaine Vipler, M.S.Ed., is the director of SCOPE, an advisory service that helps families select appropriate school and summer programs for their children.

13. THE INDEPENDENT EDUCATIONAL CONSUL-TANTS ASSOCIATION, 3251 Old Lee Highway, Suite 510, Fairfax, VA 22030 (703) 591-4850 or 1 800-808-IECA (4322) website: www.iecaanline.com

    The Independent Educational Consultants Association will send a directory of listings in the New York City area, free of charge.

14. GREENBERG EDUCATIONAL GROUP INC., 315 Central Park West Suite 3W, New York, N.Y. 10025, Tel (212) 787-6800 FAX (212) 579-8200

    Greenberg Educational Group, run by a Fieldston School and Wharton Business School graduate, Eric Greenberg, provides test preparation, tutoring and educational advising.

15. ABACUSGUIDE.COM provides listings and links for private, public, and parochial schools in the NYC area. You can e-mail questions about particular schools to info@abacusguide.com. Emily Glickman, founder and director of the Abacus Guide, helps families navigate the school selection and admissions process.

MULTICULTURAL/SCHOLARSHIP PROGRAMS

A Better Chance
City College
North Academic Center 3-208
West 138th Street & Convent Avenue
New York, NY 10031
(212) 926-0315 FAX (212) 694-1332

National Office
88 Black Falcon Avenue
Suite 250
Boston, MA 02210
(617) 421-0950 FAX (617) 421-0965
website: www.abetterchance.org

Founded in 1963 by twenty-three independent schools in the Northeast, A Better Chance, Inc. is the oldest national, nonprofit academic talent-search organization for minority secondary school students. The membership comprises approximately 200 independent day and boarding schools. Students are recruited and admitted to these schools on the basis of high academic achievement and personal initiative. The majority of students apply in the eighth or ninth grade. Applicants must take the SSAT or the ISEE. Financial aid is provided by the member schools. A Better Chance provides ongoing counseling and support. A Better Chance has an Affiliated Colleges Program of approximately 100 colleges and universities that have demonstrated a commitment to increase their minority enrollment.

The Albert G. Oliver Program
44 West 28th Street
New York, NY 10001
(212) 889-0244 FAX (212) 889-4978
website: albertgoliver.org

Ms. Lynn Harwell-Algrant, Executive Director

The Albert G. Oliver Program, named after an outstanding New York City educator, is a nonprofit organization founded in the 1980s to help talented black and Hispanic youngsters gain access to day and boarding schools at the high school level. The brochure says "A primary goal of the Oliver Program is to nurture the hearts of these gifted young people so they develop a sense of caring, love and responsibility that will make a positive impact on the lives of others." The Albert G. Oliver Program is unique in offering a mandatory community service program (40 hours per year) and a paying summer jobs program. Each year up to fifty black and Hispanic students are placed in independent day and boarding schools that offer strong support services including financial assistance. Oliver graduates attend many Ivy League colleges and top universities.

Member Day Schools:

The Brearley School
Brooklyn Friends School
Collegiate School
The Dalton School
Elisabeth Irwin High School
The Fieldston School
Friends Seminary
Horace Mann School

The Nightingale-Bamford
   School
The Packer Collegiate Institute
The Riverdale Country School
St. Bernard's School
The Spence School
Trevor Day School
Trinity School

Early Steps
540 East 76th Street
New York, NY 10021
(212) 288-9684 FAX (212) 288-0461

Ms. Jacqueline Y. Pelzer, Executive Director

Early Steps is a membership organization, created in August 1986, to increase the number of students of color in city independent day schools at the kindergarten and first grade levels. Early Steps was an outgrowth of an Independent Schools Admissions Association of Greater New York (ISAAGNY) Minority Affairs Committee study that identified the need for schools to pool resources for the recruitment of younger students of color.

Early Steps provides counseling and referral services for families of color looking for and enrolled in city independent schools. Financial aid is available but families should be prepared to pay a portion of the tuition. Some families pay full tuition.

Prep for Prep

328 West 71st Street
New York, NY 10023
(212) 579-1390 FAX (212) 579-1443
website: www.prepforprep.org

Mr. Gary Simons, Executive Director
Mr. Dominic Michel, Associate Executive Director

The Prep for Prep program is a nonprofit educational organization founded in 1978 by Gary Simons. Some of the original group of Prep for Prep students attended Trinity School. Today, Prep for Prep identifies academically talented students from minority group backgrounds, provides fourteen months of intensive academic preparation and places these students in leading city independent schools and boarding schools with scholarships that are based on financial need and academic performance. The program is highly selective and rigorous; in a typical year, approximately 3,500 qualified students applied, but only 156 fifth graders were admitted into Prep for Prep (day school placement) and sixty seventh graders into Prep 9 (boarding school placement). Once enrolled, students are provided with ongoing counseling and leadership development opportunities until high school graduation. The Prep for Prep community includes over 2,000 students and alumni.

The TEAK Fellowship

15 East 65th Street
New York, NY 10021
(212) 288-6678
Website: www.teakfellowship.org

Justine A. Stamen, Founder and Executive Director

The Teak Fellowship prepares talented students from low-income families for admission to top public, private, and parochial high schools. Teak has a colorblind admissions process and accepts 22 low income, high achieving students per year. The program begins in seventh grade and follows students through their high school graduation, providing personal as well as academic support through tutoring and mentoring, test preparation, internship opportunities, leadership training and community service.

The New York Diversity Resource Collaborative

Collegiate School
370 West End Avenue
New York, NY 10024
(212) 721-2300

Susan Hinkle, Director
Mercy Rodriguez, Executive Assistant

The Diversity Resource Collaborative is composed of member schools from the independent school community. According to their brochure, the DRC is dedicated to the promotion of diversity in school curriculum, faculty and student body: "The Collaborative is committed to embracing and disseminating those multicultural resources that are unique and special to this area, to making use of the area's diversity and to demonstrating the immediacy of multiculturalism in the greater New York area." The DRC addresses issues relating to race and ethnicity, gender, physical differences, sexual orientation, religion and class. The DRC is funded by grants from the Citizen's Committee for New York City, Inc., strengthening neighborhood assets program, Chase Manhattan Bank, and the Boston Foundation. Funding to establish the DRC was provided by the DeWitt Wallace-Reader's Digest Fund and the Booth Ferris Foundation.

The DRC sponsors workshops and conferences for professionals, and is the cosponsor of the People of Color Job Fair and is conducting a research study "to give clarity to the current status of diversity and multicultural education in our schools."

Information related to diversity issues in the independent schools is available through Diversity-On-Line, a website. (See also "Inter-school Faculty Diversity Search," pp. 485–486, *infra*.)

Member Schools:

The Allen-Stevenson School
Bank Street School for Children
The Berkeley Carroll School
Brick Church School
Brooklyn Heights Montessori
    School
The Caedmon School
The City & Country School
Collegiate School
The Episcopal School
The Ethical Culture Fieldston
    School
Friends Seminary
Grace Church School
Horace Mann School
Little Red School House and
    Elisabeth Irwin High School

Manhattan Country School
Marymount School of New York
The Masters School
The Packer Collegiate
    Institute
Pomfret School
Poughkeepsie School
Professional Children's School
The Rudolf Steiner School
Saint David's School
St. Luke's School
St. Thomas Choir School
The Spence School
Stevens Cooperative School
The Trevor Day School
Trinity School

APPLYING FOR FINANCIAL AID

The rigorous process of qualifying for private school tuition assistance makes kindergarten admissions look easy. After your child has been accepted to an independent school, or if your child is already enrolled in an independent school and you are requesting tuition assistance (such needs may arise because of a divorce or the loss of a spouse's job) your first step is to contact the financial aid administrator in your child's school. The financial aid officer will give you a Parent Financial Statement or PFS which you must complete. Be forewarned that the PFS asks applicants to list all of their assets and expenses, including their country house, boats, family car(s) club memberships, lessons, summer camp, and vacations. The completed form must be returned to the SSS—The School and Student Service for Financial Aid. The SSS, an affiliate of the National Association of Independent Schools, is

49

a nationwide service that assists independent schools in processing scholarship applications. The SSS is administered by the Educational Testing Service (ETS). Parents are usually asked to submit a copy of *both* parents' W-2 forms and the previous year's joint or separate Federal Income Tax returns in support of their application. If there are no young children at home, the SSS will impute an income for a non-working parent.

In processing the PFS the SSS uses national guidelines set for independent schools; families who live in one state might be applying for financial aid from a prep school which is located in another state. A copy of the PFS is then sent back to the school with a recommendation from the SSS of how much tuition that particular family can afford to pay. The school then recalculates; some use specific software for this purpose, taking into account the cost of living in Manhattan.°° The final decision rests with the school. Most schools have a scholarship committee which reviews each application and then makes "lifestyle recommendations to the family" as one administrator put it. It is up to each family to decide the financial sacrifices or lifestyle changes it is willing to make. Some families start out on financial aid and eventually become full-tuition paying families and vice versa. Some families choose to "live on peanut butter" and make other sacrifices, others will consider a move to the suburbs, or begin to look at public school options.

TRANSPORTATION

Once your child has been accepted into school, whether public or private, your next consideration is how to get him or her to school and back each day, safely and conveniently. If they live nearby, many parents walk their children to and from school. Those who live further away must rely on a bus service. There are three types of bus service, one is free and public, two are private and require a fee. Depending on the size of your child's school, you might have a limited choice of transportation services. Some parents combine services, depending on their needs.

    1. ATLANTIC EXPRESS SERVICE: (A/E or yellow school bus service):

        Administered through the office of pupil transportation within the Board of Education, (718) 585-8592.

        Atlantic Express has an excellent safety record and is free

to public school students within the district who attend a gifted or magnet program school, and private school students attending participating schools. Students must apply through their own school. To qualify, students in kindergarten through second grade must live ½ mile or more from school. Students in third through sixth grades must live 1 mile or more from school. In early September, the school provides students with a list of designated bus stops (usually along the avenues) and times for pick-up and drop-off. Students using A/E bus service *do not* receive a bus pass for use on city buses. Middle and high school students are provided with subway and bus passes.

2. PRIVATE VAN SERVICE: The private schools contract with a van service (such as Selby, Street Smart (718) 923-0900 or A&S) which provides door-to-door pickup and drop off at specific times. This service is the most convenient and also the most costly. Roundtrip with Street Smart costs approximately $2,750.00.

3. SCHOOL VAN: Various private schools run their own van service which usually picks up and drops off at designated bus stops. The cost is less than for private van service.

Students attending a regularly scheduled after-school program one or more times a week often arrange with their school for private van service for dropoff to these activities.

SOCIAL ORGANIZATIONS

Boys and girls who attend the traditional single sex schools have limited social contact with the opposite sex. This is somewhat ameliorated by coed theater and musical productions, interschool classes and activities. But what could be more fitting for the offspring of the socially prominent than charity dances for the pubescent set to introduce them not only to each other but to philanthropy as well? Miniature charity balls, sponsored by organizations such as Yorkville Common Pantry and Goddard Riverside Community Center, are usually held at one of the private schools and the money raised benefits a variety of local causes. These dances for young men and women attending Manhattan's exclusive schools are a quaint but benign form of organized dating for many 11 and 12 year olds as well as a time for parents to enjoy their last vestige of social control because before they know it their teenager will be "moshing" at the downtown clubs.

The "White Glove" social organizations listed below are traditionally "by invitation only." However, you no longer need the proper pedigree to participate; after all, good manners are for everyone.

The Barclay Classes are headquartered in Westfield, New Jersey, (908) 232–8370. For almost 70 years, the Barclay Series has offered classes to children in the social graces, proper party attire and ballroom dancing. The classes meet once weekly. Spit and polish is the order of the day and young ladies wear white gloves until sixth grade. There are real parties twice a year, usually with a theme. Children enjoy the classes because refreshments are served and prizes are awarded. You must contact the Barclay Series to request an invitation if one has not already been sent. There is a waiting list for girls and boys. There is a sibling policy as well.

Dancing lessons offered by **The Knickerbocker Cotillion** begin in fourth grade and children must be invited to attend; unlike the Barclay Series, The Knickerbocker Cotillion is a not-for-profit organization, an older and some say, more exclusive group. Mrs. Jacques Nordeman, the group's coordinator, who also serves as co-director of admissions at the St. Bernard's School, says that from time to time she forwards applications to those who call; however, it is the organization's policy to refrain from publicity.

The Knickerbocker Greys: An after-school cadet program for boys and girls. Contact: Rosemarie Connell, (212) 585-1881. Once upon a time children from Manhattan's best families bought their school uniforms at Alex Taylor and their other clothes at Best & Company; the girls took dancing classes at Mrs. DeRhams' Dancing School at the Colony Club or if you were Jewish, at Viola Wolfe's, while their brothers drilled with the Knickerbocker Greys at the 67th Street Armory. Originally linked with Patriotic and Historical Societies such as the National Society of Colonial Dames and the Society of Mayflower Descendants this organization appeals to any child who simply likes history and tin soldiers. Since 1881 the Knickerbocker Greys has offered boys (and now girls) ages 6–16 the opportunity to participate in parades, reviews and civic ceremonies in New York City. (Remember when you had to join the Girl Scouts just to march in the Memorial Day parade?) The Greys is not a military organization but they use precision drill and the "pomp and circumstance of beautiful old uniforms." Meetings are held twice a week, attendance is required only one of the two days.

GLOSSARY

Alternative Forms of Testing: Testing that is not standardized, but rather a measure of an individual child's capabilities and progress relative to himself, not to other children. The most popular trend in alternative testing is portfolio assessment: A child will select his best work from the whole semester or year, and submit this work instead of taking a standardized test. This gives the child's judges the ability to gauge the child's progress over the course of the term, and gives them a fuller picture of the child's abilities, rather than a brief snapshot from a test taken on one particular day.

Child-Centered Program: A program in which learning in the classroom is facilitated by the teacher and directed by the students. Activities require active learning and motivation on the part of the student; the teacher does not lecture to a passive class. The phrase "child-centered program" is also used to describe a program in which a child is presented with age-appropriate, meaningful curricula.

Chicago Math: Chicago Math is a program developed at the University of Chicago that teaches children to reason logically, see mathematical patterns and relationships, and understand the usefulness of math in everyday life. Manipulatives, math games and literature are woven into the curriculum to develop abstract mathematical thinking while reinforcing computational concepts.

Classic Curriculum: Featured in traditional schools. A classic curriculum always includes Shakespeare, Virgil and the Greeks. The goal is "a cultured mind nourished by the humanist tradition."

Collaborative Learning: In a classroom that subscribes to collaborative learning, the students work in groups. It is assumed an individual student will be motivated to work because he or she will feel responsible to the group, that a student will learn to clarify his thinking through the need to articulate and debate his ideas within the group, and further, that he will learn new ways of thinking when he analyzes the ideas of other group members.

Cum Laude Society: The Cum Laude Society is an honor society modeled on Phi Beta Kappa, which has member chapters in several New

York City independent high schools. The purpose of the Cum Laude Society is the encouragement and recognition of academic excellence. Many chapters (particularly at schools that no longer rank students or do not give grades) make selections by such criteria as character, honor and integrity. New York City independent schools with member chapters and year of induction are: Berkeley Carroll School, Brooklyn, 1989; Collegiate School, 1922; Horace Mann School, 1951; Packer Collegiate Institute, Brooklyn, 1976; Poly Prep Country Day School, Brooklyn, 1908; The Riverdale Country School, Bronx, 1922; Trinity School, 1934.

D'Nealian Handwriting Method: Using the D'Nealian method young children are taught to form print letters with loops and rounded angles so that the transition to cursive writing later on is easier and more natural.

Departmentalization: When students leave their homeroom classroom to go to specialists for different subjects.

Different Learning Styles: This phrase refers to the idea that students learn in different ways, and under different conditions. Some students learn best from reading in a quiet room; other students learn best when engaged in debate. Teachers who subscribe to this theory will try to provide experiences that will accommodate different kinds of learners.

Experiential Learning: Learning through hands-on activities and first-hand experiences.

Fisher-Landau Program: A multimillion-dollar grant program endowed by philanthropist Emily Fisher-Landau to identify and give support to young children with learning problems. The original grant was made to The Dalton School and the Collegiate School. Fisher-Landau specialists conduct workshops and consult at other independent schools.

Integrated Curriculum: A curriculum organized around a central theme. All areas of study (reading, writing, math, science, social studies, art and music) are used to investigate this theme. In this way, the children learn process and content within a unified context. "Core curriculum" is a term that is often used synonymously.

Interage, Mixed-Age or Flexible Class Grouping: Classes that are not grouped according to calendar age. There might be a two-year age span within the class composed of children with "a diversity of achievement, capacity, talent and style, but who have enough intellectual and social congruence to work well together" (Bank Street School for Children brochure).

International Baccalaureate: The I.B. is an internationally recognized curriculum and examination. The I.B. diploma is required for admission to many foreign universities. The I.B. program is administered from Geneva, Switzerland, and taught in over four hundred secondary schools in thirty-eight countries. It is a rigorous and demanding program; students must master a minimum of six subjects and demonstrate the ability to think clearly and communicate effectively. Many colleges and universities in the United States offer advanced placement and/or a year of college credit for superior performance on the I.B. The United Nations International School, Lycée Français and The Dwight/Anglo-American International Schools, all in Manhattan, offer an I.B. program.

Interschool: A consortium of eight New York City independent schools—Brearley, Chapin, Nightingale-Bamford, Spence (girls' schools); Browning and Collegiate (boys' schools); Dalton and Trinity (coed schools)—which share academic, extracurricular and administrative components.

Invented Spelling: What we all do when we try to spell a word: We make an educated guess. The use of this method allows children the freedom to write the words they may not know how to spell, instead of "dumbing down" their writing to avoid making mistakes. Invented spelling is used in a classroom for rough drafts; students must use the correct spellings of words for final copies.

ISAAGNY: Acronym for the Independent Schools Admissions Association of Greater New York. Composed of admissions directors and heads of early childhood programs, ISAAGNY was founded in 1965 in order to simplify and coordinate admissions procedures among independent schools in the New York Metropolitan area. It is now composed of 150 member schools. ISAAGNY contracted with the Educational Records Bureau to administer uniform admissions testing. ISAAGNY also developed a uniform school report form and sets common notification and reply dates.

Kwanzaa: A seven-day African-American cultural holiday similar to traditional African harvest festivals. Kwanzaa means "first fruits" in Swahili. Kwanzaa coincides with the celebration of Chanukah and Christmas.

Learning Disability, Learning Disorder (LD or Learning Difference): The term currently used to describe a handicap that is neurological in origin, which interferes with a person's ability to store, process or produce information. The impairment can be quite subtle and may go undetected throughout life. The primary characteristic of a learning disability is a significant difference between overall intelligence and achievement in some areas according to the National Center for Learning Disabilities. If you or a school suspects that your child has a learning problem, your child will probably be asked to get a four-hour psychoeducational evaluation.

Montessori Method of Education: Based on Dr. Maria Montessori's scientific observations of the behavior of young children who were orphaned, disadvantaged or, for other reasons, institutionalized. The Montessori approach encourages active, self-directed learning in a non-competitive environment. The Montessori classroom features multi-aged, multi-graded heterogenous groups and is based on the principle of freedom within limits. Children are free to work at their own pace with materials they have chosen, either alone or with others. Individual mastery is balanced with small group collaboration within the whole group community. The teacher relies on his or her observations of the children to determine which new activities and materials he may introduce to an individual child or to a small or large group. Several NYC Montessori schools use an "eclectic" or "modified" approach, a comfort to those who think "pure" Montessori is doctrinaire or rigid.

Multiculturalism: In the classroom, multiculturalism introduces subjects and authors that are not typically considered a part of the Western cultural canon. It is a theory of inclusion that allows many cultures a place in the curriculum, with the aim of increasing respect and understanding for the diverse populations of the world.

Multiple Intelligences: Intelligence is not restricted to a score on an I.Q. test but can encompass many areas of life. Some people may excel in music, some in leadership. These are not necessarily testable qualities, but they are forms of intelligence nonetheless.

People of Color (Children of Color): An inclusive term of respect agreed upon by the National Association of Independent Schools' Committee on Diversity for people usually described as non-white ethnic minorities, including: African-Americans, Latinos, Asian-Americans, Native Americans, Pacific Islanders and natives of Alaska.

Progressive vs. Traditional School: These terms are in disrepute these days. Many of the traditional schools have incorporated elements of progressive education into their elementary school classrooms. Progressive schools remain in the vanguard in their use of innovative educational practices. A traditional classroom may have a teacher at the front of the room lecturing to students sitting in rows; children are grouped homogeneously by ability level and generally work on the same material at the same time. A progressive school is more likely to have an informal or seminar-style classroom with more discussion and is one in which children work in small groups independently. We found that traditional schools tend to be the older, established single-sex schools, which have a Latin motto, concentrate on the Western or classical canon, have a dress code or uniform, a handbell choir and "quaint" traditions.

Revolving Loan: At a school without a significant endowment parents are asked to give an interest-free loan to the school, refundable when the student graduates or leaves for any reason.

Waldorf Education: The Waldorf method is based on the scientific observations and pedagogical insights derived by Rudolf Steiner (1861–1925), an Austrian scientist, philosopher, artist, and educator. At the heart of the Waldorf philosophy is the belief that education is an artistic process. Innovative teaching methods address the whole child, working to develop clarity in thought, balance in feeling, and conscience and initiative in action. In a pure Waldorf school, students stay with the same teacher from grades one through eight and create their own Main Lesson Books for their core subjects. Students create their own textbooks based on classroom instruction. There is an emphasis on using natural materials and the arts. The program includes knitting, folklore, crocheting and woodcarving usually reserved for the afternoons. A typical Waldorf curriculum offers phonics, grammar, English, two foreign languages (in many schools German is one of the languages), music, eurythmy (a form of music and movement), mythology, drama, art, crafts, science, math and world history. The school aims to encourage close human relationships that help students develop a strong sense of themselves and an awareness of others.

Whole Language: A practical body of ideas about education that originated in New Zealand with the seminal work of Sylvia Ashton-Warner. The connections between reading, writing and speaking are made complete in the Whole Language classroom. Students in a Whole Language classroom read literature (not basal readers) and write stories, plays and poems (instead of filling out workbooks). A Whole Language classroom uses an integrated curriculum, so learning centers around one subject. In this way, students learn both process (the mechanics of learning, like long division) and content (long division is used to answer a question about the subject under study) simultaneously. Learning becomes relevant to the student, and ceases to be an abstraction. There is some controversy surrounding Whole Language. Some educators would like to see more of the "old-fashioned methods," particularly an emphasis on phonics, included in any Whole Language program, and on drills for matters that must be remembered and reproduced quickly and accurately (such as multiplication tables, spelling, grammar).

Writing Across the Curriculum: Teachers who believe in writing across the curriculum will not confine writing to language arts; instead they will provide writing experiences throughout the curriculum. This will help students refine their writing and will demonstrate that writing can serve a variety of purposes and is used in many disciplines.

Writing Process or Writers' Workshop: The teaching of writing in which students are taught to discover what they think about the topic in question and to clarify those thoughts through the process of writing, editing, rewriting and publishing: 1) drafting (brain drain), 2) revising (sloppy copy), 3) editing (neat sheet), 4) finalizing (final fame). Grammar, usage and spelling are taught within the context of the individual student's writing needs rather than in isolation.

THE PRIVATE
SCHOOLS

The Abraham Joshua Heschel School

(Nursery–5th grade)
270 West 89th Street
New York, NY 10024
(212) 595-7087
website: www.heschel.org

(6th–8th grade)
314 West 91st Street
New York, NY 10024

Coed
Accessible

Ms. Roanna Shorofsky, Director
Ms. Marsha Feris, Director of Admissions

Birthday Cutoff   Children entering nursery school must be 3 by August 31
Children entering kindergarten must be 5 by August 31

Enrollment   Total enrollment: 490
Nursery 3's places: 25
Pre Kindergarten places: 16–18
Kindergarten places: 12–16
Graduating class 2000: 39

Tuition Range 2001–2002 $12,500 to $17,300, nursery 3's–8th grade
Additional fees: for student activities and supplies, are approximately $350 to $570
Capital fund contribution: $750

After-School Program   Heschel After-School Program: until 5:30 P.M.; creative and recreational activities; an additional payment is required

———

The Heschel School was founded in 1980 by a group of Jewish educators and laymen. Named for Rabbi Abraham Joshua Heschel, a prominent scholar, philosopher and colleague of Martin Luther King, the school is not affiliated with a synagogue. The student body is composed of a broad spectrum of families from unaffiliated reform to modern orthodox. "Heschel is a Jewish school as opposed to a religious school," we were told. The school has a "holistic, child-centered approach." Girls participate fully in all aspects of the school.

Interest in Heschel is increasing because, one parent surmised, "Heschel is the answer to the current quest for spiritual renewal without being doctrinaire or rigid." Heschel is committed to Jewish ethics and values. There are social action projects on every level throughout the year. For instance, Pre-K children participated in the Common Cents penny harvest for the homeless; seventh graders collected blankets and brought them to Hale House.

Parents: A parent told us: "Heschel has a very West Side feeling even to a West Sider." According to her, "There are many professionals and lots of academics with Ph.D's.—the type who subscribe to *Tikkun* magazine. Some of the men are bearded and some of the women have Julia-Louis Dreyfus hair." But as Heschel's popularity continues to grow, "You can expect to see more suits and soignée blondes," she said. Admissions looks for the child who is "bright, inquiring and verbal, who can contribute to the Heschel community." There is no dress code except for the yarmulke (or baseball cap) which must be worn during meals and Judaic studies. One parent described the typical student: "She wears hightops, leggings and a cool T-shirt from Mexico."

Program: The Heschel School is rigorous and structured. Each class has two teachers all the way through eighth grade, which is unique. Classes often break into many small groups. Formal Hebrew and Judaic studies begin in first grade. Heschel's dual curriculum is composed of Jewish history, culture, and Hebrew language integrated with secular studies. There is no other formal foreign language requirement. "The Jewish and secular curricula are intertwined in an organic and relevant way," parents say. Experiential learning is stressed: Students might map out the campaign for the battle of Sinai. There is an emphasis on creativity and the arts through cooking, drama and art: A scribal artist came in to work with fifth and sixth graders on an illuminated manuscript project.

The Middle School is housed in a fully renovated brownstone on 91st Street between West End Avenue and Riverside Drive. In addition to classrooms, the Middle School building has a library, computer room, science lab, greenhouse, chapel, gym, music room, art room and lunch room.

There are no prizes given out at graduation. The theme for commencement, "Journeys," is derived from the Hebrew "Prayer for Journeyers." After an opening homily and reflections by a member of the staff, students read selections from their poetry journals; choral selections weave the pieces together.

Graduates attend a variety of New York City independent schools (Riverdale, Dalton and Fieldston are popular), select public schools, and Jewish high schools.

The Abraham Lincoln School For Boys
The Abraham Lincoln School For Girls

12 East 79th Street
New York, NY 10021
(212) 744-7300, FAX (212) 744-5876
website: www.abrahamlincoln.org

Nursery–8th grade
partially accessible

Mr. Howard Schott, Headmaster
Mrs. Barbara Solowey, Headmistress
Mrs. Regina Flecha, Director of Admissions
Mrs. Kathleen Kigel, The Ark Nursery School, Director

Birthday Cutoff   Children entering nursery school must be 3 years old by October 31
Children entering kindergarten must be 4 years, 6 months by September 1

Enrollment   125 students through 7th grade

Grades   Anecdotal reports for kindergarten through 4th grade
Letter grades start in 5th grade

Tuition Range 2001–2002 $8,200 (Nursery) through $10,800 (7th grade)
There is a $1050 activity and lunch fee

Financial Aid/Scholarship   25% of the student body receives some form of aid

After-School Program   None

Summer Program

The Abraham Lincoln School is part of a worldwide group of associated schools that share the same values. The oldest of these is the St. James School in London, founded in 1975. The choice of name reflects a recognition of "the needs and traditions of America"

64

according to the school's literature. The school building is an elegant landmark limestone townhouse which houses The School of Practical Philosophy in the evening. According to the headmaster, "Academics alone will not produce men and women who can lead happy and useful lives. A finely developed intellect needs to be balanced by a heart educated in the virtues."

Like The Ark Nursery School, now under its aegis, The Abraham Lincoln School is closely connected to The School of Practical Philosophy (a non-profit organization chartered by the Board of Regents of the State of New York). According to the brochure, The School of Practical Philosophy "draws upon the timeless teachings of both Western and Eastern traditions to discover the unifying principles that underlie human existence. The emphasis is on the practical application of these teachings."

The teachers at the Abraham Lincoln School are all members of The School of Practical Philosophy: "All teachers have attended the School's teachers group for many years studying both teaching and their particular subject."

Many subjects are taught in separate boys and girls classes in the belief that boys and girls learn better when taught separately.

The daily schedule includes such traditional subjects as reading, writing, mathematics, science and history as well non-traditional areas: philosophy, scripture, and Sanskrit (the oldest extant language known to man and a model for the study of language in general.) The development of strong language skills is emphasized, with particular care given to the clear development of speech. Students examine the universal themes and principles found in the world's great philosophic and religious traditions in weekly philosophy classes.

Central Park is used for recreation and exercise.

The Alexander Robertson School

3 West 95th Street
New York, NY 10025
(212) 663-6441

Coed
Pre-1st–6th grade
Not accessible

Rev. Leslie Merlin, Head of School
Miss Barbara Winn, Director of Admissions

Birthday Cutoff   Flexible

Enrollment   Total enrollment: 60
Pre-1st places: 12
1st grade places: 3
Graduating class size: Approximately 6

Grades   Four terms
Letter grades begin in 4th grade

Tuition Range 2002–2002 $9,500
Additional fees

Financial Aid/Scholarship   Limited; there are no full scholarships
available

Endowment   N/A

After-School Program   A variety of creative and recreational activities from 3:00 P.M. until 5:30 P.M. Monday through Thursday open to Alexander Robertson students; a separate fee is required. Friday afternoons the Parents Association sponsors a smart games club chess and scrabble.

Summer Program   None

––––––––––

Founded in 1789, The Alexander Robertson School is one of the oldest coeducational schools in the city. The school is named for its founder, a prosperous Scottish businessman and member of the Second Presbyterian Church. Among the original students were immigrants and freed slaves. Although The Alexander Robertson School is still owned and operated by the Second Presbyterian Church, it is nonsectarian "while strongly espousing Judeo-Christian values and traditions." In 1998 the Reverend Leslie Merlin became Head of School. The Reverend Merlin was Associate Pastor of The Brick Presbyterian Church for eighteen years, and as such was closely associated with the Brick Church School. She taught in the U.S. and abroad before entering Princeton Seminary, where she received her Master of Divinity degree in 1976.

The student body represents the diversity of the surrounding neighborhood. The ERB is required for entering students. The style of the school is traditional and structured. The program follows a logical sequence through all grades with emphasis on basic skills and study habits.

The pre-first class focuses on socialization, exploration of the neighborhood and world, and beginning academic foundations. Reading through phonics is emphasized in first grade, with greater proficiency encouraged in second grade. Basic math skills are taught using traditional methods and manipulatives, progressing through the grades to mastery of sixth and seventh grade concepts. Creative and critical thinking and writing skills are introduced and cultivated in the middle grades leading to clear, concise, expository writing, including reports in social studies and science in the upper grades. ARS's art program has earned awards for its students both locally and nationally. The music program includes movement, instruments, theory, introduction to the classics and vocal training. French is offered in all grades. Students bring their own lunch. Central Park is used for gym, recreation and science study.

The Allen-Stevenson School

132 East 78th Street
New York, NY 10021
(212) 288-6710, FAX (212) 288-6802

All boys
Kindergarten–8th/9th grade
Not accessible

Mr. David R. Trower, Headmaster
Ms. Ronnie R. Jankoff, Director of Admissions

Uniform   Lower School: Allen-Stevenson polo shirt with emblem, pants (no jeans), sneakers allowed kindergarten–3, no sneakers grades 4–9
Middle and Upper Schools: blazer, dress shirts, tie and pants (no jeans)

Birthday Cutoff   Children entering kindergarten must be 5 by September 1
Children entering 1st grade must be 6 by September 1

Enrollment   Total enrollment: 370
Kindergarten places: approximately 40–42
Graduating class size: approximately 22–25

Grades   Semester system in the Lower School
Trimester system in the Middle and Upper Schools
Lower School students receive anecdotal reports and checklists
Letter grades begin in 5th grade
Departmentalization begins in 6th grade
Practice exam given in 6th grade
First final exam given in 7th grade

Tuition Range 2001–2002 $20,770 to $22,200, kindergarten–9th grade
All fees are included in the tuition
An alternative payment plan is offered through the Key Tuition Plan

Financial Aid/Scholarship Approximately 12%–14% of the student body receive some form of aid
$700,000 available

Endowment Approximately $7.5 million

Diversity 14 Prep for Prep students as of fall 2000
Multicultural Committee for parents
Multicultural elements are incorporated into the curriculum at all levels

Homework Kindergarten: none
1st–3rd: 15–30 minutes
4th–6th: 1 to 1¹/₂ hours
7th–9th: 2¹/₂ to 3 hours

After-School Program Alligator Soup: open to A-S students only, with selected classes offered to Nightingale-Bamford students; kindergarten through 6th graders, 3:30–5:00 P.M., fall, winter and spring; a variety of creative and recreational activities; an additional payment is required
Middle School and Upper School intramural program
Junior varsity and varsity sports

Summer Program June Club: A 2-week sports and trip program open to A-S students and siblings from other schools; last 2 weeks in June. The 6-week summer day camp program is for kindergarten through 3rd grades. Second and 3rd graders may participate in either June Club or Summer Day Camp. The camp program offers a variety of creative and recreational activities; an additional payment is required.

———

The Allen-Stevenson School was founded in 1883 by Mr. Francis Bellows Allen, who was later joined by Mr. Robert Alston Stevenson as administrative head of the school. Allen-Stevenson was originally located in a brownstone next door to The Chapin School on East 57th Street. During this time, a group of A-S boys once climbed across the roof of the building and into the proper girls' school next door and were severely punished. Perhaps to avoid unnecessary temptation, in 1924 the A-S school moved uptown to its present location on East

78th Street. In the 1920s A-S boys would roller skate and roll hoops to school whereas now they scooter. A-S is a traditional school with an emphasis on hands-on learning within a structured setting. A-S has always had an emphasis on physical hardiness, music and language arts. Parents say that A-S graduates are very well-rounded and well-mannered.

Allen-Stevenson is located on the Upper East Side. It has a neighborhood school character; parents say the school provides a small and warm community. A-S recently annexed the Brinckerhoff carriage house next door. The new facility increased A-S's physical plant by one-third, adding a new skylit, full-court gymnasium, art and shop facilities, computer lab, two new classrooms and music space. The lunchroom and lobby were also recently renovated.

Getting in: The number of applications to A-S has increased over the past few years resulting in a much more competitive admissions process. After an application has been filed, parents tour the school with a parent tour guide. Parents meet individually with the director of admissions, then parents are invited back with their sons for a small group visit (six to eight boys). While the boys are busy in a classroom with members of the admissions staff, parents are invited to the library to watch a video about the school and to talk with the headmaster and the head of the Lower School. The visit lasts about one hour. The school maintains an active wait list and there is a sibling and legacy policy, but admission is not automatic. The most important criteria for admission is a good fit between the school, the boy and the family.

Parents: Parents are very comfortable at A-S. One parent described it as "an open, warm environment, a wonderful place." She described the parent body as "low key, with a lot of professional people." Another parent said, "It's a normal cross-section of independent school families." Annual class cocktail parties are held in the fall at parents' apartments. Fund-raising events include a Holiday Raffle, Book Fair and spring fund-raiser. There are annual holiday and spring concerts. New parents are invited to an evening reception at the school to meet the Lower School teachers and administrators. The school has no religious affiliation.

Program: Headmaster David Trower, who came from the Collegiate School, is credited with revising and updating the curriculum and attracting good faculty. Parents say, "Mr. Trower's door is always open and he goes out of his way to know you and your son," "He shakes every parent's and boy's hand." In a recent issue of *The Lamp-*

lighter Mr. Trower is quoted on the tone of Allen-Stevenson: "Our strong academic expectations of the boys are set within a nurturing context. This combination makes Allen-Stevenson unique." The board president, Ron Rolfe, an alumnus, is quoted as saying A-S is "a progressive school with a terrific curriculum and great teachers . . . there is a creativity that abounds."

Allen-Stevenson has a very strong music program and boasts one of the finest elementary school orchestra programs in New York City. All students learn to sing and read music. The Middle School Chorus has sung on the White House Ellipse.

The Artist-in-Residence Program during Book Fair Week at A-S features an artist or writer with a specialty. One year while the kindergarten boys worked with a paper maker, older boys made beautiful bound-book covers. Artwork frequently coordinates with other subjects. For instance, fifth grade boys study ancient civilizations in history and in art class, reinterpreting the art of of ancient civilizations: they make ceramic vessels based on ancient Greek vases decorated with narrative scenes or patterns. Trips to the museums support the study of "Ancients" in both art and history. The shop program is extensive and combines art and math skills. Beginning in seventh grade students select an elective arts course during the three weekly "creative" periods.

Public speaking and the dramatic arts are also important at A-S. Upper School boys participate in the annual public speaking contest. Every year there is a Middle School play with a student cast and crew. The popular fifth through ninth grade annual Gilbert and Sullivan production often includes faculty in cameo roles or chorus. A classic American play is produced by seventh graders. Girls from the Nightingale-Bamford School play the female roles in the annual Upper School Shakespeare production as well as the sixth grade and seventh grade plays.

At A-S technology is used to enhance teaching and learning. Boys are taught how, when and why to use computer systems beginning in kindergarten and technological tools are appropriately used by teachers and students in every grade as aids for thinking, producing and presenting work in all areas of the curriculum.

The Lower School at A-S is composed of grades kindergarten through third. Parents say that the Lower School has a non-pressured approach to learning. The teachers employ an eclectic array of materials to teach basic concepts and skills. Reading, writing and math skills are taught in small, fluid groups. There are computers in all of the classrooms. In addition to their classroom teachers, boys interact regularly with a science specialist, art and music teachers, computer teachers and the Physical Education staff. Artwork displayed throughout the school reflects A-S's commitment to the integration of the art into the overall curriculum. At the first of many science fairs, Lower School boys participate in "The Invention Convention," an exercise in problem solving. One boy solved the problem of soap sinking in the bathtub (he inserted a cork), another solved the problem of the spoon sinking into the sauce pot with a magnetic spoon holder. Seventh through ninth graders participate in the annual Science Fair while fourth through sixth graders have their own Science Festival each winter.

Middle School at A-S is composed of grades fourth through sixth. The boys now wear navy blue blazers with the school emblem on the pocket, a dress shirt and tie. Toward the end of third grade, the boys are invited by the fourth grade to a special "tie ceremony" where they are taught how to knot a tie.

The goal of the Middle School program is to develop a student's abilities and self-confidence so that he can begin to take more responsibility for his own learning. Critical thinking is emphasized in English. Science instruction encourages investigation, observation and interpretation of information. In mathematics boys now explore conceptualization, problem solving and logical interpretation of math facts. Fourth graders study map skills and geography as it applies to explorers and exploration as well as current events. The fifth grade history program covers The "Ancients": Near East, Egypt, Greece and Rome, integrating art, music and literature. Sixth graders begin the study of American history which continues into seventh grade. The school library is completely computerized with CD-ROM, on-line access, and a variety of on-line data base subscriptions. Middle and Upper School boys use the computer for writing and research. The Learning Resource Center offers support to students needing extra help in acquiring study skills and strategies as well as enrichment at all levels.

The level of work becomes more demanding in the Upper School (grades seven through nine) as the boys prepare for secondary school admissions. Critical reading of both classical and contemporary literature is emphasized. The boys also complete large "theme projects" such as "Facing History," an inter-disciplinary program dealing with the social implications of the Holocaust. The history curriculum incorporates geography and covers the study of the U.S. and the world.

Upper School mathematics covers the study of algebra, geometry and introductory trigonometry. The science curriculum is designed to develop scientifically literate, independent researchers who are ecologically aware and informed about global issues. Weekly labs provide hands-on experience in life science, physical science and biology.

Foreign language is introduced in sixth grade with a choice between French or Spanish. Language fundamentals are made clear through the study of Latin, introduced in third grade. The Arts are taught by professional artists and musicians. Art and music courses are required through seventh grade; afterward they are offered as electives.

In keeping with the longstanding emphasis on physical hardiness at A-S, there is ample opportunity for exercise. Boys in Lower School go to Central Park for "field" three times a week. There is gym on the other days. "A certain level of fitness is expected," said one parent. Another parent said, "The A-S boys are sports-minded but it's not a jock school." A-S offers ice hockey at Chelsea Piers and swimming at the Asphalt Green Aquatic Center. Team sports begin in Middle School. Upper School boys go to Randalls Island four times a week in the spring and fall. School colors are blue and gold. One of Allen-Stevenson's big rivals is The Buckley School, just down the avenue.

Allen-Stevenson has traditional Lower School weekly assemblies that feature a variety of guest speakers, class performances, poetry readings and so forth. At Middle and Upper School weekly "morning meetings" a member of the faculty will discuss subjects of concern to the A-S community. Topics have included the AIDS epidemic, community service projects and alternatives to watching television.

Project Charlie, the anti-drug program, begins in first grade. Education about health issues is part of the curriculum in grades seventh through ninth, including AIDS prevention. Seventh through ninth graders attend an advisory period once a week to discuss a variety of issues.

Boys participate in special projects in community service throughout their years at A-S. Ninth graders hold Community Service Week and are required to perform twenty hours of community service.

Extracurricular activities in the Upper School include: orchestra, theatre, yearbook, chorus, photography, painting, woodworking, printmaking, newspaper and student council. (Music rehearsals are scheduled so that they don't interfere with other extracurricular activities.)

Special privileges for ninth graders include overnight trips, the use of the seminar room and permission to leave school for lunch once a week.

There are numerous awards in recognition of excellence at A-S. The Anthony G. Couloucoundis Memorial Award is presented to a sixth grader for "scholastic excellence; all-around participation in athletics, the arts and community service and above all, the gift of friendship." Other awards distributed on Prize Day include the Alumni Medal, DAR Medal, an athletic award, the Charles E. Horman Award for Independence of Spirit and for Citizenship as well as awards in many of the academic disciplines, creative writing, public speaking, Latin, music, shop, art and drama. Closing ceremonies are held in the upper gym.

Graduates attend boarding schools and a variety of New York City independent secondary schools.

Traditions Founders' Day, Grandparents' Day, Mother's Day Lunch, Father/Son Breakfast, Father/Son Dinner, Holiday Concert, Spring Concert, Headmaster for a Day, Dinosaur Parade, Field Day, Science Fair, Book Fair, Arts Festival, Middle and Upper School picnic, annual Gilbert and Sullivan production, annual Shakespeare play, Young Alumni Day

Publications Alumni publication: *The Lamplighter*
Lower School literary magazine: *Rabbit Pie*
Middle School literary magazine: *What We Write*
Upper School literary magazine: *Pages*
Newspaper: *The Allen-Stevenson Weekly*
Yearbook: *The Unicorn*

Community Service Requirement Special projects in Middle and Upper School; 20 hours in 9th grade; 9th grade Community Service Week

Hangout The steps outside school

Bank Street School For Children

610 West 112th Street
New York, NY 10025
(212) 875-4420 (main number)
(212) 875-4433 (admissions), FAX (212) 875-4454

Coed
3's–13's (interage groupings)
Accessible

Mr. Reuel Jordan, Dean of Children's Programs
Ms. Betsy Hall, Director of Admissions

Birthday Cutoff   September of the year of entry

Enrollment   Total enrollment: 430 in 2000–2001
Nursery 3's places: 16
4's places: 10–14
5's places: 16–20
Graduating class size: approximately 40–46

Grades   Semester system
No letter or numerical grades
Bi-yearly parent conferences and reports
Departmentalization begins in the 10's (beginning of Upper School)
No formal exams or testing but there are "curriculum tests" and standardized tests in the Upper School

Tuition Range 2001–2002 $15,500 to $17,750, 3's–13's
Tuition payment plan available

Financial Aid/Scholarship   Approximately 33% of the student body receive some form of aid

Endowment $846,200; Bank Street has a capital campaign underway

Diversity   Multicultural Committee of parents and teachers

2 Prep for Prep students enrolled as of Fall 2000
5–6 Early Steps students each fall

Homework   6/7's, 7/8's: 30–45 minutes
8/9's: 45 minutes–1 hour
9/10's: 1 hour
10/11's, 11/12's: 1½–2 hours
12/13's, 13/14's: 2–2½ hours
There are group and individual assignments

After-School Program   Bank Street After-School Program: for children ages 4 and up; 3:15–6:00 P.M.; five days a week
Children 5 years and older have a variety of activities to choose from including: sports, art, violin, woodworking, puppetmaking, theater, judo, flute and quilt making
An extended day program of supervised play is available from 4:30 P.M. until 6:00 P.M.
School vacation program: Bank Street operates a full day program of activities for children age 4 and older
These programs require an additional payment

Summer Program   Bank Street Summer Camp: during the last weeks of June and the month of July

The Bank Street School, a demonstration school for children, is part of the prestigious Bank Street College of Education which also includes an independent Graduate School of Education, a Division of Continuing Education and the Bank Street Bookstore. The Bank Street School uses the "developmental interaction" approach to education, which is based on the views of visionary educator Lucy Sprague Mitchell.

Lucy Sprague Mitchell, the founder of the Bureau of Educational Experiments (which later became Bank Street) was part of a group of educators in the 1920s who believed that children learn best "when they are involved in the process of learning, in a developmentally appropriate environment." Concurrent with this philosophy is the belief that children construct meaning out of interaction with the world—they learn best from direct experience. Mitchell's vision of the "classroom as a community" was very different from the nineteenth-century "factory worker model" for schools. Today at Bank Street these elements of "progressive" education are put into practice with a diverse group of children, backed up with a dedicated and highly skilled staff.

Lucy Sprague Mitchell also believed that when children learn to be members of classroom groups that work together and care about each other's welfare, this lesson will extend to caring about the welfare of the society in which we live. The Bank Street College of Education was involved in designing the Civil Rights Act of 1965 and the Head Start and Follow Through Programs.

Getting in: Parents should call for the dates of the Fall open houses and register for one. At the open house we attended in early November, the school's spacious auditorium was packed. Parents are shown a video that illustrates the philosophy of the school. This video was unique—not a public-relations tool but a real snapshot of classroom life. A tour of the school is given after the open house and parents sit in on classes as part of the admissions process once they apply. If you then decide that this school would be right for your family call for an application. The WPPSI-R is not required for admission to the Lower School but ERB testing is required for admission to the Upper School. Parents bring their child to Bank Street for a small group interview (approximately four to five children); separation is handled gently and a parent can stay with the child during the interview. Parents also can observe two classrooms for about ten to fifteen minutes. The final step in the process is the parent interview in which there is an exchange of information. The interviewer will share what she observed about your child. Parents might be asked "What are you looking for in the next twelve years?" In addition to a diverse student body, the brochure says the school "seeks children who give evidence of becoming adventurous learners and who will use the school experience well." An admissions committee of eight staff members makes the final decision.

Parents: Parents describe the atmosphere at Bank Street as informal: "Everyone is on a first-name basis." Many professors from nearby Barnard College and Columbia University send their children to Bank Street. Although one parent said, "There's more money at Bank Street now than there was before," Bank Street is committed to a diverse student body and 33 percent of the student body receive some form of financial aid. Parents are welcome everywhere in the school. "In Lower School you might see ten parents listening in at morning meeting or going out on the deck," a mother told us. The cafeteria is the gathering place for parents in the morning. Potluck breakfasts and dinners are held. Parents often serve on committees or task forces; for example, recently both the music curriculum and the Spanish program were reviewed. Parent education is an important component of Bank Street. One year a teacher conducted a series of evening classes for parents about how math was being taught to their children. Parents say that the administration is always "looking, questioning, improving" the school.

The Parents Association consists of four elected officers and a president and vice-president for each division (Lower, Middle and Upper). In addition, the class parents meet with the dean of children's programs. There are a number of fund-raising activities undertaken in an effort to boost teacher's salaries. Since holidays are not celebrated at Bank Street, the Bank Street Winter Fest is an eagerly anticipated community celebration. Each year a central theme is chosen for the event (a celebration of the winter solstice). One year it was "fire." The whole school gets involved by writing skits, creating scenery and costumes, and performing. Tickets are usually sold out for this three-night event. There is also a Fall Fair and Auction.

Program: The program at Bank Street requires a lot of student initiative but the teachers are there to back students up. "They have an amazing amount of energy for the children," a parent said. Graduate students from the Bank Street College of Education provide extra manpower within the classrooms. There are two teachers in every classroom until fifth grade. One-third of the teachers at Bank Street are men. A typical 4/5's classroom of twenty-one children has a head teacher (who holds a master's degree), a full-time assistant, one or two graduate assistants, lots of blocks, a live rabbit *and* a worm house recycling pot.

The teachers at Bank Street "lead from behind" rather than lecturing in front of the classroom. They are actively involved with the students, guiding them in their choices. "The teaching is always adapted to the child's style, that's what they pride themselves on," a parent told us. Teachers are encouraged to derive much of the curriculum from student interests and from the students' cultures or environments.

The Lower School is composed of ages three through six. Flexible or mixed-age groupings are used throughout Bank Street. In addition to the 3's, there are two 4/5's classrooms and two 5/6's classrooms. There is typically a 14 month age span within the classroom groupings. Smaller groups are formed for reading and math. Activities are geared to the appropriate developmental level of the child. For instance, "pre-operational" thinkers are not pushed to master a task that will come naturally at age seven. The brochure says "the creation of meaning is the central task of childhood." In practice, children make sense out of concrete experience using concrete materials. (Bank Street students were among the first to use the Cuisenaire rods, unifix cubes and pattern blocks that have become standard materials used to teach math in many elementary school classrooms.) These are noisy, productive classrooms—there is the time and space for exploration, and a forty-five minute "block-time" is built into each day. There is, however, an underlying structure. Each day begins with a meeting at which students exchange ideas and learn to listen to each other. All of the students have classroom "jobs" that they take very seriously. Parents say students learn organizational skills right from the beginning.

The daily schedule written on the blackboard usually includes reading, writing, math, music, movement, gym time and recess and Spanish exposure. (By sixth grade students choose Spanish or French.) The youngest children play on the deck for forty-five minutes each day. Older students use Riverside Park. In the Lower School, movement, gymnastics and imaginative improvisation are all part of the physical education program. Students ten and older participate in interschool teams in soccer, basketball and softball.

The writing program includes teaching of reading from a literature-based program and involves all areas associated with language: listening, speaking and writing. (The Bank Street Readers were the first multiracial readers geared to young children growing up in an urban environment.) Recently, a 4/5's class visited the Bank Street Bookstore and then made their own bookstore in the classroom that they ran for one week as a real store (using pretend money). They sold library books and homemade books and ordered books by telephone. Other classes and parents came in. The money they made was donated to a charity.

The Middle School at Bank Street comprises ages six through ten. Students leave the classroom for woodworking, art, music and gym. The class often breaks into half groups; one-half of the class will go to computer lab while the other half does math in the classroom. In these years, students make the connection between the use of the concrete materials (Cuisenaire rods, unifix cubes and blocks) and the use of symbols.

In science students conduct experiments with natural and synthetic matter; they learn about simple machines. They examine hermit crabs and salamanders, and they experiment with the Nile Delta Stream table.

By third grade the students break into student-led reading response groups in which four to five students read the same book and discuss it. Parents say, "At Bank Street the children's opinions are really valued." By the 7/8's "they're picking magnificent books to read by themselves." Students write and revise their own work with their peers acting as gentle "critics." Using the computer the students then "publish" their work, which becomes part of the classroom library. There are two computer labs with Macintosh and PC computers and students begin writing on the computer in the 7/8's. Parents say there is a lot of independent reading and writing under the watchful eye of the teacher(s). Because of the low student-teacher ratio, learning difficulties are recognized quickly and a reading specialist works with children in the classroom.

Field trips are often integrated into the writing program. All students write in notebooks every day.

Beginning with the 6's, students visit the art studio and woodworking shop. Students are introduced to many media including: sculpture, weaving, batiking and printmaking. Art is frequently integrated into the curriculum. Murals are done in collective groups—we saw an impressive "Egyptian" collaborative mural.

In the Lower School the social studies curriculum expands from the study of neighborhood and community to the study of how people work in New York City.

Middle Schoolers completed a core study of the Hudson River. A class of 6/7's studied buildings around the city and the students created their own neighborhood complete with video store, pizza shop, and grocery store, all made from wooden crates which they painted and furnished. This "crate city" was then peopled with handmade puppets.

A group of 7/8's studying the evolution of Central Park learned about the original design of the park, talked with the present day parks commissioner, and drew their own maps. The unit culminated in the creation of a huge papier-mâché model of Central Park displayed in the school's lobby.

The music program is multicultural and the Orff method is used. The 7/8's learn to play the recorder. There are instrumental ensembles and chorus in the Middle and Upper School.

The Upper School is composed of ages ten through thirteen.

In the Upper School the classroom teacher is a homeroom advisor and subject teacher. There is a core curriculum (organized around themes) in English language and literature and social studies. The 13's produce a musical in theatre; students also write and produce their own plays based upon themes learned in social studies. Students leave the classroom for specialists in math and science and beginning at age eleven for foreign language as well. Abstract ideas are explored through role playing in the Upper School: Students might conduct a mock Senate debate on the president's economic package. In social studies, students examine Europe and Africa in the Middle Ages. Algebra I is taught in the eighth grade. The 13's have the option to attend their parent-teacher conference.

The 13's may leave the school building for lunch only. The 13's also participate in the annual four-day trip to Washington, D.C. One student writing in *The Bank Street Bugle* reflected on "our debt to the Greeks" after her Washington trip. The *Bugle* is an impressive school publication; it is thoughtful, incisive and honest.

Bank Street graduates attend a variety of independent day schools (Fieldston and Dalton are popular choices) and New York City public schools.

Traditions   Fall Fair, potluck dinners and breakfasts, theatre party, parents' fund-raiser dance, Tuesday morning meetings, overnight class trips (beginning with the 9/10's), Washington, D.C., trip for 13's, Winter Fest (celebration of the winter solstice), 13's play/musical, Spring Concert, alumni reunions.

Publications   Newspaper: *The Cornucopia*
Newsletter: *School for Children Network*
Yearbook
Bank Street News Bulletin
Various publications of Bank Street College

Community Service Requirement   None; the Upper School students have community service projects within the school

Hangouts   Famiglia Pizza, Samud Deli, New Nacho, Columbia Bagel (students often bring back sandwiches to eat in the cafeteria)

The Berkeley Carroll School

Lower Division (Pre-Kindergarten–Grade 4)
701 Carroll Street
Brooklyn, NY 11215
(718) 638-1703

Middle and Upper Divisions (Grades 5–12)
181 Lincoln Place
Brooklyn, NY 11217
(718) 789-6060, FAX (718) 398-3640
website: www.berkeleycarroll.org
e-mail: infor@berkeley-carroll.org

Coed
Pre-Kindergarten–12th grade
Not accessible, Lower Division
Accessible for 5th–12th grade

Dr. Peter J. Kountz, Headmaster
Mr. Andrew Webster, Director/Upper School
Mr. Henry Trevor, Director/Middle School
Mrs. Margaret Granados, Director/Lower School
Ms. Judith Valdez, Director/Extended Day Programs
Mrs. Pamela Cunningham, Director of Admissions
for Lower Division
Mr. Chris Weeks, Director of Admissions for Middle
and Upper Division

Birthday Cutoff   Children entering kindergarten should be 5 by
September 30 but readiness is key

Enrollment   Total enrollment: 750
   Pre-K places: 40
   Kindergarten places: 15
   1st grade places: 5 or less
   6th grade places: 10
   9th grade places: 10–12
   Graduating class size 2001: 55
   1999: 50

Grades Trimester system, Pre-K through 12.

In all grades, extensive narrative written reports twice a year, as well as family conferences. Beginning in 7th grade, students accompany parents at conferences.

Letter grades and Honor Roll begin in 6th grade

Departmentalization in English, History and Math begins in 5th grade

Required foreign language study begins in 5th grade

First final exam begins in 8th grade

Tuition Range 2001–2002 $8,700 to $17,500, Pre-K–12th grade

Lunch fee for grades 5-11: $800

Financial Aid/Scholarship Approximately 25% of the student body receives some form of aid

Endowment $2.5 million

Diversity 12 Prep for Prep students as of fall 2000

Early Steps participant

Seeking Educational and Diversity Program: A reading and discussion group for faculty and parents

Perspectives on Diversity Committee of Parent Association: Sponsors cultural activities

Faculty Study Group on Equity & Diversity: Advises the school on ways to insure student gender equity in all disciplines, as well as multicultural studies; vigorous recruitment of faculty applicants of color

Homework Kindergarten: Begins in the spring with "think about" assignments one night per week

1st: Twice a week, 15–30 minutes

2nd–4th: nightly, Monday–Thursday, 30–60 minutes, lengthening as age increases.

4th: all assignments are given at the beginning of the week to facilitate longer-range planning. Longer term projects are added

5th/6th: 1½ hours per night

7th/8th: 2–2½ hours per night

9th/12th: 3 hours per night

After-School Program Extended day program and early morning (7:30 A.M.) for Berkeley Carroll students only: for Lower and

Elementary Divisions, from 3:00 P.M. until 6:00 P.M. A variety of academic, creative and recreational activities; an additional payment is required

Interscholastic and intramural athletic competition for Grades 5–12

Music and voice instruction available

Summer Program   The Berkeley Carroll Summer Programs run through mid-August and are open to students from other schools; an additional payment is required for all summer programs

Summer Day Camp: for Pre-K–4th graders; a variety of creative and recreational activities including swimming trips and weekly BBQ

Creative Arts Camp: for 8–14 year olds; a variety of creative and recreational activities with an emphasis on the performing and visual arts

---

The Berkeley Institute, named in honor of Bishop George Berkeley, was founded in 1886. Bishop Berkeley envisioned a white glove school in which the classics were taught along with the arts. One hundred and ten years later the Bishop's vision is only a tintype memory. In 1982 the institute merged with the Carroll Street School, a growing Montessori-based elementary school. In 1994, The Berkeley Carroll School was one of four independent schools in the NYC area to be designated a Blue Ribbon School by the U.S. Department of Education.

Tucked away in the heart of Brownstone Brooklyn, within walking distance of the Brooklyn Botanic Garden, the Brooklyn Museum and Prospect Park, the Berkeley Carroll School's four coed divisions are housed on two campuses only four blocks apart. "Class Links" programs provide opportunities for the youngest toddlers to mingle with senior students, for activities such as crafting pottery or a walk in the park.

A capital campaign completed in 1992 nearly doubled the space of the Lincoln Place (Middle and Upper School) campus and the award-winning classroom complex also houses administrative offices, a student commons, and floor-through Visual Arts Center. In 1994 a new Media Center was added. Another campaign for a new athletic center is underway, scheduled to open by fall 2001. BC just added a child care center for 1 to 3 year olds.

Getting in: Parents can attend one of the many open houses that are offered in the Fall which include a tour of the school and Q and A sessions with current parents. To accommodate Manhattan families, open houses are also held in downtown Brooklyn and Manhattan. The school's Parent Ambassador program links prospective families with other BC parents in their neighborhood.

All Lower School applicants are tested and interviewed on site by the Admissions Director. Candidates for grades one through four must be tested by the ERB. Berkeley Carroll looks for students who are a good match for the program, "A child who is bright and motivated and demonstrates an interest in learning and doing." Middle and Upper School Admissions Director Christopher Weeks told us: "Every student we enroll brings distinctive strengths so that students may excel in all areas—academics, the arts and athletics."

Parents: Parents automatically become members of the Parent Association. The PA sponsors parenting workshops and a speakers bureau to which two speakers are invited each year. Recent guests include Terry Anderson, Anna Quindlen, Terry McMillan and Jonathan Kozol. Parents are also welcome to assist in the classroom, serve on committees, volunteer at the library, and accompany children on trips. At BC parents have a real voice in how their school is run because they serve on the school's 25 member Board of Trustees where they comprise the majority of members. But Dr. Zubay, the former head, was quick to note that the school is "not a parent co-op." The Administration remains firmly in charge of academic direction, class placement and faculty appointments.

Parents who are also authors (and there are quite a few) sign their latest books at the two PA book fairs. Parents created the elementary divisions Law Day, helping students stage mock trials at one of which the appropriate sentence for the Wolf in Little Red Riding Hood was adjudicated. Parents also organize and participate in Career Day at which students have the opportunity to create architectural models, write legal briefs and so on. Parents are involved in the social life of the school from planning a year end trip for graduating seniors to organizing the fifth grade bowling party.

Program: Active hands-on learning is the credo of the Berkeley Carroll School and there is an emphasis on writing, both expository and creative. In a pre-school classroom you might see several children stroking the ears of the class rabbit while charting its growth with pencil and paper. Others will be working independently on a classic Montessori activity such as fitting cylindrical shapes into self-correcting slots or might be gathered around the head teacher, mastering the "M" sound by carefully tracing the shape of a sand-paper letter. "The operative word in our division is 'Discover,'" says Lower School division head Margaret Granados. There's also a good full physical education program for the kindergarten.

Reading activities begin in kindergarten in a self-paced instructional setting. Many learning styles are accommodated; worksheets are available for those children who gravitate to them. Phonics and whole-language approaches are used to teach reading and all children work one-on-one with the Head Teacher. To complete a book is more than an exercise in pronouncing the words: children master vocabulary and answer reading comprehension questions after which they are "given" the book as part of their personal "library." By the end of the year, some six-year-olds have acquired a library of 12 books or more, testament to their diligent efforts.

The Lower School at BC is housed in two buildings. There is a weekly assembly program. Students receive a solid grounding in the basics through an integrated approach to learning. A first-grade unit on "community" might include activities related to the history of the school, and include field trips to several social service organizations. Second grade students studying Native-American cultures might play Inuit games in physical education. Third graders studying China make Chinese puppets. Parents praise Miss Maxine Barnett, a third grade teacher, for her "incredible ability to reach all children, whether it's a child in the middle, lower or upper portion of the class. She excels with every child." According to tradition, fourth graders studying the history of the American experience in the Westward Expansion, transform their classroom into a 19th century schoolroom for Caddie Woodlawn Day.

The teaching of writing begins with journals in first grade and progresses to include the use of dialogue, appropriate punctuation and grammar skills. In science, Lower School students study the life cycle of myriad creatures, make life-sized models of the human body complete with all the internal organs, and create papier-mâché models of the solar system.

Field trips are an integral part of the curriculum beginning in pre-school with visits to pumpkin farms and to dramatic performances. Starting in fifth grade all students take a full-week trip away from the BC campus. Fifth-graders journey to Nature's Classroom in Rhode Island for an adventure in team-building, scientific exploration and dramatic play.

After-school programs in music includes instruction in virtually all instruments and voice. Older children can select from a large variety of mini-courses including: cooking, quilting, chess, puppet-making, fencing, and gardening. The Lower School division participates year-round in the nationally recognized Hands-on-Science program.

The Middle School program at BC "recognizes that children are going through major developmental hurdles. We watch and guide children in every aspect of this development." In fifth grade students have three teachers for the five major subjects, with English/history and science/math taught as core subjects. Mandatory foreign language, either French or Spanish is added. By sixth grade, students are grouped according to skill level in foreign language and math. English and history are still taught as "core" subjects. By seventh grade, the curriculum is entirely departmentalized. Subjects are explored in depth and often involve multi-week projects. Sixth graders, for example, stage a December Aztec Day, during which one classroom is turned into a marketplace and another becomes a temple. Visitors meet Montezuma and Cortez as well as a priestess who explains the unusual 20-month calendar. Eighth graders use a study of Robinson Crusoe to discuss use of natural resources. During a symposium on tropical rain forest supervision, students play the roles of farmer, rubber tapper, eco-tourism developers, miners and environmentalists, all struggling to co-exist. Historical novels supplement the curriculum. All eighth graders take a full-year geography course.

The fifth grade writing curriculum stresses the conventional five paragraph essay. Middle School students gradually master expository and creative writing. At all grade levels, revision is a major component of the writing process and there is extensive peer and teacher review. The foundation of the Middle School math curriculum is mastery of the basics with an emphasis on creative problem solving, such as finding the most efficient route for a city sanitation crew. Advanced students finish algebra by the end of eighth-grade—some more quickly than others. Seventh graders study tessellations and their relationship to Islamic art. Pi Day (not coincidentally on 3/14 of each year) allows students to derive an approximation of pi using a "human" circle chain.

Science courses in the Middle Division begin with general science in fifth grade, life science in sixth, physical science in seventh and earth science in eighth grade with lab work at the core of each year's curriculum. There are several computer labs at BC. All campuses are hooked up to the Internet and the school's e-mail system allows for virtual links among teachers and between teachers and parents. The libraries are fully automated and use CD-ROMs.

In the Upper Division students model calculus derivatives on state-of-the-art calculators and computers. In 1996 the Upper Division science curricula were redesigned to put greater emphasis on biochemistry in the mandatory biology course. As a result, physics is taught in ninth grade, chemistry in tenth, and biology in the junior year. More than three quarters of the students take AP courses.

Choice within structure best summarizes the Upper Division at BC and students have several options in arts and athletics. A highly motivated student might play varsity baseball in the afternoon and sing in the choir at night. From ninth through twelfth grades, students take five core academic courses: history, science, English, math and foreign language. They also enroll in two rotating semester electives. (Fifteen electives are offered in everything from chamber orchestra and jazz band to photography and ceramics.) There are often multiple ways of meeting the course requirements—some more rigorous, others explore an interesting aspect of a familiar subject. For instance, juniors may opt for AP American History or select a course on Democracy in America or American Social and Cultural History.

Freshmen take a three period a week mandatory writing course in addition to English class. Sophomores must enroll in a twice-weekly health course; juniors and seniors have a mandatory college counseling requirement. All seniors participate in an internship program to explore an area of professional interest. The school helps them with placement and contacts; internships range from finance and medicine to photography, music, fashion and advertising. Foreign exchange opportunities are available for those who prefer a more far-flung experience. Each spring students from a school outside Paris spend two weeks with Berkeley Carroll tenth graders. BC students make a return trip to France. A companion program with a Spanish institution is another option. BCS is the first independent day school in the metropolitan area to host a small group of international students who will be enrolled for a full year at the school and live with BC families.

Athletics are an important part of the program at BC but this is not your typical "jock" school. Berkeley Carroll has won first place for four of the past five years in the independent schools judo championship. In the Middle Division, interscholastic teams are fielded in coed soccer, coed track, cross country, girls volleyball, and there are strong boys' and girls' basketball teams. The girls' softball team posted undefeated seasons in recent years. Berkeley Carroll's varsity baseball team won the Baseball League of Independent Schools championship for five of the past six years.

Community service starts in the preschool years with food drives for Thanksgiving. Older children devise their own community service projects. By the time students reach the age of 18 they are volunteering in soup kitchens, geriatric centers or on park clean-up crews. Upper Schoolers are required to perform 50 hours of community service but many graduate with more than 200 hours.

Popular College Choices   Tufts, New York University, Cornell, Vassar, Syracuse, Columbia, Skidmore

Traditions   All-School Theme Write-In (recent topics include gender differences, justice and fairness, and leadership), Arch Day, Lower Division Spring Festival, Thanksgiving Sharing Assembly, Holiday Candle Lighting Ceremony, Middle and Upper Division Prize Day, Parent Association Speakers Bureau, Halloween Party, Sesame Place Trip and Annual Auction

Publications   Lower School quarterly creative-writing compendium: *Explorations*
Newspaper: *Blotter*
Literary magazine: *Reflections*
Yearbook: *The Lion*

Community Service Requirement   50 hours minimum for Upper Division students; all students participate

Hangout   Ozzie's Coffee Bar, Roma's Pizza, Prospect Park playing fields

The Birch Wathen Lenox School

210 East 77th Street
New York, NY 10021
(212) 861-0404
Website: www.bwl.org

Coed
Kindergarten–12th grade
Accessible-elevator

Mr. Frank J. Carnabuci, Headmaster
Ms. Nancy M. King, Director of Admissions
Ms. Julianne Kaplan, Co-Director of Admissions

Uniform   Lower School: *Boys* (grades K-5): Tan or gray trousers, white shirt with BWL logo; Wednesdays (dress-up day): dress tie and navy blazer with BWL logo; dress shoes. *Girls* (grades K-3): Early fall and spring, pink uniform jumper, white shirt with BWL logo, dress blouse or collared polo. Late fall and winter, dark blue and green plaid uniform jumper. *Girls* (grades 4 and 5): Early fall and spring, pink uniform skirt, white top with BWL logo; late fall and winter, dark green and blue plaid skirt, white top with BWL logo, dress shoes.

Middle School (grades 6-8): *Boys*: dress slacks or pants (not jeans), dress shoes, collared shirt or turtleneck; *Girls*: collared shirt or turtleneck, dress skirt (must be longer than fingers of extended arm) dress slacks or pants (no jeans); dress shoes, loafers, or docksiders.

Birthday Cutoff   No specific cutoff; most children entering kindergarten have turned 5 by the beginning of school

Enrollment   Total enrollment: 410
Kindergarten places: 30
Graduating class: approximately 35

Grades   Semester system in the Lower School and Upper Schools
Trimester system in the Middle School

Letter grades begin in 6th grade
Departmentalization begins in 6th grade

Tuition Range 2001–2002 $18,122 to $21,360, kindergarten–12th
grade Additional fees: for trips, books, lunch, PA dues, and
activity fees are approximately $1,200. Lunch program ($990) is
optional for 10th throuh 12th graders; there is a 12th-grade graduation fee of $585

Financial Aid/Scholarship   21% of the student body receive some
form of aid

Endowment $5 million

Diversity   18% children of color

Homework
1st: 15–30 minutes, increasing during the year
2nd: approximately 30–45 minutes per night
3rd: and 4th: approximately 1 hour per night
5th: 1½ hrs per night
6th–8th: 20 to 40 minutes per subject per night
9th–12th: 3–4 hrs per night

After-School Program   Open to Birch Wathen Lenox students
only; a variety of creative and recreational activities; extended day
until 6:00 P.M. daily for Lower School; an additional payment is
required
Junior varsity and varsity teams

Summer Program   none

In 1991, the Birch Wathen Lenox School was created by the merger
of two established schools: The Lenox School (founded 1916) and The
Birch Wathen School (founded 1921). The sale of the former Birch
Wathen and Lenox School buildings created a substantial endowment enabling the school to weather the transition. Headmaster Frank
Carnabuci, who had been the assistant head at The Dalton School for
eleven years, brings administrative skills and enthusiasm to the job.

He has been at the school for over nine years. Parents say he knows every student by name and has implemented interesting new programs such as the Russian exchange, the overseas study program, and yearly schoolwide themes such as "The Year of Mythology" and "The Year of the Headline.".

Getting In: The ERB is required for admission to the school. Parents tour and return on a separate date with their child for an interview.

The Birch Wathen Lenox school is a traditional school with a nurturing atmosphere.

Birch Wathen Lenox's strength is the ability to individualize the curriculum to fit the child. The student to teacher ratio is very small. Parents say, "Nobody falls through the cracks." Specialists work with tutors and parents to resolve learning difficulties.

The school has begun a $13 million expansion that includes a technologically advanced two-story theater, and a state-of-the-art bleacher seated gymnasium equipped with locker rooms, showers, and a weight room. An extra elevator will be installed and at least eight extra classrooms will be added to the school.

The BWL School offers a traditional, comprehensive academic program that features small classes (average of 12 students per class) and serves a range of students. The school is able to meet the needs of a wide range of abilities through the use of an academic tracking system that separates students into groups based on their ability levels in specific subject areas. Tracking is a method familiar to most baby boomers but has long been out of favor with educators and is considered by many to be "politically incorrect." BWL, bucking the trend, says, "An academic tracking system allows students to progress sat a pace that appropriately challenges them, while ensuring the greatest degree of success."

The school is fully networked, with a T1 connection to the Internet. Computers are introduced in kindergarten. Students begin the study of French language and culture in fourth grade. Departmentalization begins in sixth grades in Middle School, where a traditional core of studies, including English, mathematics, history and science, and foreign language, are rounded out with computer science, music and art. In the Upper School, a traditional college preparatory program allows students more choices and independent study opportunities.

BWL offers an overseas study program during spring break that enables students to go to France, Italy, Spain and Britain. Students have recently traveled to Alaska and Greece. The program is linked to the school curriculum; daily assignments and a travel journal are required.

The extra-curricular athletic program is broad and includes championship teams in girls' volleyball and tennis, and championship boys' basketball, softball and soccer teams. The Middle School athletic program offers soccer, softball, basketball, track and field, and tennis.

Popular College Choices Princeton, Dartmouth, Cornell, Columbia, Connecticut College, Emory, Harvard, Washington University, RISD

Traditions "Great food," Holiday Pageant at All Souls Church, Arch Day, Field Day, Spring Fair, "Year of" theme

Publications

Lower School newspaper:	*The Upbeat*
Middle School Newspaper:	*The Black and White Ledger*
Upper School newspaper:	*The Clarion*
Alumni Magazine:	*The Banner*

Community Service Requirement

Middle School:	Grades 6,7,8	30 hours
Upper School	Grades 9,10	30 hours
	Grades 11,12	30 hours

The Brearley School

610 East 83rd Street
New York, NY 10028
(212) 744-8582
website: www.brearley.org

All girls
Kindergarten–12th grade
Accessible–elevator

Dr. Priscilla M. Winn Barlow, Head of School
Elizabeth Manley Murray, Director of Admissions
Eileen Graham, Assistant Director of Admissions

Uniform   Lower School: navy blue jumper, socks and shirt can be any color, sneakers permitted but no clogs or boots
Middle School: navy-blue skirt, shirt or blouse (with sleeves), shoes or sneakers, sweat pants on cold days
Upper School: none

Birthday Cutoff   Girls entering kindergarten must have reached their 4th birthday on or before October 1 of the year in which they apply

Enrollment   Total enrollment: 680
Kindergarten places: 50
Graduating class size: approximately 45–50

Grades   Semester system
Kindergarten: parent conferences twice a year
Classes I–III: fall parent conference; spring narrative report
Class IV: fall parent conference; midyear and spring anecdotal reports with grades
Classes V–XII: marks are given in every subject with comments and suggestions
Classes V and VI: receive marks and comments four times a year
Classes VII and VIII: receive marks and comments three times a year
Departmentalization in science, music, physical education, library and art begins in Lower School; math departmentalization begins in class IV; computer departmentalization in Class III

Exams: below class VII, classroom tests are informal and marks are averaged with the term's work; once-a-year examinations begin in class VII and are held in March

Tuition Range 2001–2002 $19,000 to $19,100, K–12th grade, which includes: books, supplies, trips, food, physical education and activities
Fees range from $500 for K to $2,550 for 12th grade

Financial Aid Available to all who qualify

Endowment Market value as of June 30, 2000: $67,600,000

Diversity 30 Prep for Prep students enrolled as of fall 2000
Students of color are advised by faculty member of color. A math teacher of color serves as advisor to Lower School families of color Schoolwide Diversity Committee; a two-year Task Force ('00–'02) which meets monthly and sponsors the annual Festival of Cultures; student clubs and support groups include Umoja, The Asian Awareness Committee, ELLA, for Latina students, and the Gay and Straight Partnership, and The Miller Society, a new association of alumnae of African-American and Latina descent that funtions as a mentoring program for interested students. Parent Diversity Forum

Homework Lower School families are expected to read aloud with their children from kindergarten on; when girls have learned how to read they are expected to spend ½ hour per night reading, as well as being read to
Classes II and III: weekly spelling assignments, math facts and puzzles, 20–30 minutes, plus nightly reading
Class IV: 30 minutes on weekdays, 60 minutes over the weekend, plus nightly reading
Class V: 60 minutes daily, 90 minutes over the weekend
Class VI: 1½ hours daily
Classes VII and VIII: 1½–2 hours
Classes IX–XII: four 50-minute assignments daily

After-School Programs Afternoon program: *The Clubhouse,* a joint after-school program with Chapin for girls in Kindergarten through Class IV; a variety of activities including sports, crafts, homework

95

help from 2:30p.m.–5:45p.m., an additional payment is required, financial aid is available. There is also competition in 13 inter-scholastic athletic teams, some beginning in Middle School. Middle and Upper School dramatic activities including Fall Drama, Winter Musical, Spring Senior Drama, all including boys from neighboring schools; Class VII Gilbert and Sullivan, Class VIII Drama, technical and design work all year long afternoons and weekends. Additional activities for older students include work on the school newspaper, literary magazine, yearbook and 14 student-run clubs and committees

Summer Program SummerStart, for children grades K–6; 2 weeks in June; creative and recreational activities for an additional fee; open to children in the community
Basketball Camp for grades 5–12 held at the Field House at East 82nd Street
Upper School students are offered a summer study scholarship and exchange program and can choose from a range of study/travel programs in the U.S., Europe (including Turkey and Greece) and Asia.

Brearley was founded by Harvard and Oxford-educated Samuel A. Brearley, Jr. so that girls could receive an education comparable to that offered at the independent boys' schools. Brearley opened its doors in 1884, originally serving many of New York's socially prominent families, including the daughters of the German Jewish upper class. The enrollment has since broadened to include students from a diverse range of families. Many Brearley families exhibit a decidedly intellectual bent. Since 1930 the school has had only four heads: Millicent Carey McIntosh (who later became Barnard's first president); Jean Fair Mitchell, head of school for twenty-eight years, who guided the school through the turbulent sixties and early seventies; Evelyn J. Halpert, a Brearley alumna, who succeeded Miss Mitchell in 1975 and served until her retirement in 1997, and Dr. Priscilla Winn Barlow, Brearley's current head. "Brearley is producing young women who think creatively and quickly, young women with an ethical core, who are wonderful writers, have self-confidence and ask the right questions," says Barlow.

British born Dr. Winn Barlow earned a Ph.D. in Zoology from the University of Liverpool and spent a Fulbright year at Rutgers. She was most recently Head of Havergal College in Toronto, a girls' prep school known as the Brearley of Canada. Her sense of humor and warmth permeate the school. In a recent issue of *The Brearley Update*, Dr. Winn Barlow described the skills women will need for success in the next century: "They're really all thinking skills. Analysis, creativity, risk-taking, leadership; they've got to know how to run something, solve problems, ask the right questions, communicate both in writing and speaking . . . They should also be extremely comfortable with technology."

Sequestered from the hustle and bustle of the city, Brearley's twelve-story red brick building on East 83rd Street overlooks the East River. Two floors were added in 1995 providing 10 percent more space. In September 1997, Brearley opened a 12,000 square foot Field House on East 87th Street, a short walk from the school. From the windows of the newly refurbished library in the school building on East 83rd Street, you can watch the sailboats and barges slip through the waves. Although at first sight Brearley might appear staid, when the girls are bustling through the halls or speaking forthrightly in class, informality reigns. There are no bells to signal the changing of classes. The atmosphere has lightened and relaxed; as you walk down the halls you can feel it. At a recent Parents Association fund-raiser, a prominent author who is a parent at the school described Brearley as "an intensely democratic elitist school." Here girls receive a superb education in an environment characterized by intellectual rigor, tolerance and social activism. A parent characterized the school as being "like my kindergartner's indestructible Brearley tunic: sturdy, practical, and essential. It might come home encrusted with, flour, paint, or papier-mâché but it washes clean and ready to go the next day." Brearley is not, as rumored, all work and no play. Frivolity prevails at the annual Lower School family fun nights; at Middle School social events such as the Class VIII Carnival and Class VIII Dance and at many Upper School events that are sponsored by the Self-Government Association and student clubs and committees. Brearley girls are just as well bred as "the green and yellow 'ladies' down the street at Chapin," and also strong, brainy, confident, poised and prepared. "These aren't shrinking violets; everyone has a distinct personality," says a parent of the girls in her daughter's kindergarten class.

Getting in: Brearley's catalog is a very understated, small white book, whose only decoration is the Brearley school motto, "By Truth and Toil" emblazoned on the front cover. Since 1999, the catalog has been complemented by *Images*, an equally understated, but beautifully photographed view book of school life. Applications must be filed by December 1 for Lower School and December 15 for Middle and Upper School. It is not imperative to apply before you tour the school, but one parent advised that you make your tour appointment by early October. And both parents should come. Tours for Middle and Upper School applicants are given by Upper School students. Parents of Lower School applicants are given tours by admissions office personnel or by parents who work for the admissions office. One prospective parent said, "It looks like a school: wide hallways, bright classrooms and everything is up to date and spotless." After your tour you meet with the admissions director, Elizabeth Manley Murray, who has expanded the schedule to make sure there is ample time for conversation with parents. Parents are asked, "describe your daughter." Brearley attracts and enrolls candidates from a broad base; in a recent year the kindergarten class came from 28 different nursery programs. What are they looking for? "Eagerness to learn, a sense of curiosity and the willingness to take learning risks," says Murray. She adds, "We don't expect the girls to come to us as finished products. We nurture each girl in her individual development, while instilling values of simplicity, generosity of spirit and respect for others." During the child's visit, the school looks for the beginnings of critical thinking skills and at how the child approaches a challenge. "Above all," says Murray, "we want to be sure that students can take full and joyous advantage of all that Brearley has to offer."

Interview appointments for applicants are made from October until early February, and a very helpful letter is sent prior to the interview to describe the process in detail. When you arrive with your daughter there are children's books in the waiting room (no squirm test here) and the children go into a classroom with age-appropriate materials. Children might be asked to play a game, tell a story, complete a puzzle or draw a picture while chatting with a teacher. The parents retire to a room with the head of the Lower School, giving them an opportunity to learn more about the school. One parent inferred, "They are also looking at the parents." Brearley's admissions decisions are "need blind," and based solely on the merit of the individual candidate. Financial aid is available beginning in kindergarten and there are no "arbitrary cutoff levels." Preference is given to siblings and legacies, but they are not automatically accepted. There is a wait list.

For applicants to Class V, tours are for parents only and are given in the morning and last about an hour. After the admissions office has received a completed application, there is a small group interview for applicants, which includes an assessment of the student's academic abilities. For students applying to Class VI and above, tours are given to applicants and their parents by Upper School students and last about forty minutes. An admissions officer or division supervisor interviews applicants and parents also only after the admissions office has received a completed application. If a family submits an application before seeing the school, then the tour and interview can be scheduled on the same day. Multiple standardized tests, teacher references and transcripts are required.

After gaining admission to Brearley, parents are invited to a meeting to discuss the next year's program. They are asked to jot down any questions they might have on the back of an R.S.V.P. form. In May there is a late-afternoon school visit for the incoming girls and their parents.

Parents: The parent body at Brearley, according to one former teacher and alumna, is eclectic, including but not limited to the following types: "Wealthy Park and Fifth Avenue WASPs, Jewish intellectuals, families of color and a small arty group of eccentrics." "The Brearley community includes families from every part of the city, and all feel welcomed and comfortable," says a parent. There is an active parents' organization and a parents' newsletter and a new Brearley Family website.

The Parents Association benefits at Brearley are the best in the city. One year the benefit was held at City Center where some 1,000 Brearley alumnae, parents and friends joined honorary host and past parent Walter Cronkite and a panel of media luminaries (several of whom had daughters in the school) for a close-up look at press coverage of the 1996 presidential contest. In 1998 the Parents Association held a family-oriented CyberCarnival at the Javits Center to benefit the school's computer and technology program. In 1999, the benefit, "Brearley on Broadway," brought talent together for a nostalgic look at at the school via music by former Brearley fathers, Irving Berln, Leonard Bernstein, Frank Loesser and Richard Rodgers. Since 1997, the Parents Association has sponsored an annual Festival of Cultures for Brearley families, students, faculty and friends, celebrating the richness and variety of the cultures represented in the school community; it is an extremely popular event.

Over the years, Brearley has made connections to the families of the girls. "They know a tremendous amount about each girl, but they don't intrude, they feel that the school isn't a parent," said a former teacher. Beginning in Lower School, the girls learn to be their own advocates in social and academic matters, parents say. A parent said she was surprised "at how tremendously observant and psychologically astute the teachers and administration are about each girl."

Program: The Brearley kindergarten has fifteen to eighteen girls in each classroom. Separation is handled gradually. Beginning in 1992–1993 the kindergarten day was extended to 2:00 P.M. Monday through Thursday, with early dismissal at 12:30 on Fridays. Kindergarten girls have specialist teachers for library, music, science, dance and physical education. In music they sing, move and use percussion instruments. In Class III, girls are introduced to a stringed instrument or recorder and hand bells. Lower School girls sing together at Assembly each week and recorder and hand bells are played by Class IV girls at various assemblies as well as at the Winter Assembly and Last Day. Although not "academic" in the traditional sense, the kindergarten year at Brearley is rich with creative learning experiences incorporating art and crafts and nature (quilting, weaving, papier-mâché, hatching chicks, butterflies and so forth.) One of the three kindergarten classes studied breads from around the world, made flour from wheat stalks, baked bread and sold bread from their classroom "bakery." In another kindergarten class each girl had a chance to bring Paddington Bear (and his knapsack with pj's and toothbrush) home overnight along with a journal in which they recorded his every experience. During the year the girls get to know each other as they meet in half groups for gymnastics, PE, music, or play with balls, bikes and wagons on "the pier" or playroof and in Carl Schurz Park.

Formal academics begin in Class I and II. In Class I reading is taught in small groups. One parent said the atmosphere is more relaxed than at some of the other very selective schools and "There is free time in the morning to visit other grades and classrooms." The aim of these early years, according to the brochure, is to help each girl to "form good work habits and to encourage her to be adventurous, responsible and kind." Emphasis is on cooperation, not competition. In Lower School, there is also an emphasis on public speaking with opportunities to recite poems and act in plays. One parent said girls get the sense that "everyone is good at something and the school fosters a sense of security and independence."

In Classes II and III homework includes a "math puzzle of the week" and some spelling words as homework. Starting in Class IV homogeneous math groups are formed but there is movement between groups and the girls all learn the same material, albeit at different paces.

Lower School girls have their own science lab where members of the science department oversee a hands-on approach: To study aerodynamics girls make parachutes and paper helicopters. One of the strengths of Brearley is that all of the faculty teach across the grades so they get to know the girls as they grow.

In Class II, the girls are introduced to formal computer classes once a week, twice a week in Class III. The Lower School Computer Room is fully equipped and staffed by computer teachers. The girls learn how to keyboard, create graphics, do word processing and work in multimedia. Computer teachers work closely with homeroom teachers to integrate computer activities with other subjects. Students in Class IV visit the computer room twice a week for a Creative Writing Workshop that focuses on word processing, concept mapping, timelines, and creating a multimedia slide show.

French and Spanish begin in Class V and can be continued through the Upper School. One parent said, "When a girl is able, foreign language arts courses are offered; when a girl needs extra help, skills courses are offered." Latin is required in Classes VII and VIII and there are also introductory classes in modern languages or Asian languages offered at Class VII or IX for entering students.

The curriculum in the Lower School is integrated with close coordination between the subjects. Frequently, English readings are related to topics in history and geography. One parent gave an example: "For a unit on China they studied the music, language, history, culture, customs, arts and foods of that country. The walls of the Lower School were lined with all things Chinese."

The Music Department offers private instrumental study to students in Class II through XII on a variety of intruments. A girl may choose from almost any instrument, from the recorder to the double bass or harp. There is an additional fee, but financial aid is available for those who qualify.

Middle School at Brearley consists of Class V through Class VIII. A quaint tradition at Brearley is the stuffed animal mascot for each class handed down from Class XII to the upcoming Class V. (This is not to be confused with the official Brearley mascot, the beaver.) By

Class VI all subjects are fully departmentalized. Attention is still paid to individual learning styles, placement and pace. Some coordination of subject matter continues. In sixth grade English the girls study Greek mythology while in history they are studying Greek and Roman history as part of a broader course in the History of the Ancient World. In sixth and seventh grades, the work load increases. A parent said, "By seventh grade expectations are high and the girls are well aware of their strengths and weaknesses." The parent of a seventh grader said that "reading selections are two years ahead of other schools, and high-level, sophisticated written work is required. Papers are returned with many red lines, sometimes with comments as long as the paper, but their work is the better for it."

In Class VII the girls are reading Dickens and Shakespeare and studying European history from the fall of Rome to the late seventeenth century. In the spring term they perform a Gilbert and Sullivan operetta. Drama, music and studio art classes are held once or twice a week.

Girls in Class VI take human biology, in which they study all the systems of the body including reproductive, as well as nutrition, drugs, alcohol and cigarette use. Health issues are addressed again in class VIII to fulfill the New York state requirement. Discussion group sessions are held for Classes VII through IX. Students also take a one-semester community service course in Class IX, and volunteer in school or in the community throughout their Upper School years. Teams in gymnastics, volleyball, soccer, softball, basketball, swimming, track and lacrosse are formed at this point.

The Upper School: The catalog says that Brearley students need sixteen credits to graduate but most leave with twenty or more. Students have about four to five frees (free periods) a week. Homework now averages four lessons a day of fifty minutes to one hour each. Formal testing begins in Class VII.

Advanced Placement (AP) exams are usually offered in fourteen subjects. Almost no "AP" or "honors" courses are offered but most girls take a number of AP exams based on the preparation they get in regular Brearley courses. Math is required through Algebra II though most girls go on to Calculus, and most students take more than two Upper School lab science courses. Those with proficiency in science can participate in the Columbia Science Honors Program. Any student can choose from five science courses in Classes XI and XII.

As an example of how the spirit of intellectual inquiry thrives at Brearley, a 1996 spring science project presented a challenge:

"Identify a problem in the community and use science and technology to solve it." Two seventeen-year-old Brearley juniors focusing on the transmission of HIV by the sharing of infected hypodermic syringes, designed a non-reusable syringe. The Brearley students triumphed over 470 other student team projects at the NYNEX Science and Technology Awards in Boston and each girl was awarded a $15,000 scholarship and they became eligible for $250,000 in seed money to develop their invention.

Seventh graders learn LOGO-programming in computer; ninth graders are required to have access to a computer at home with Microsoft Office, Geometer's Sketchpad (provided by the school), and an Internet connection. Financial aid is available for this program. There is no computer science requirement as such, but keyboard proficiency is expected by eighth grade and computer use is an on-going component of Lower, Middle and Upper School math, science, history and language classes. The Upper School offers two computer electives for eleventh and twelfth grade students: "Design of Interactive Multimedia" and "Computer Programming" are offered in alternating years. Greek courses are offered as part of a Brearley/Chapin exchange.

Class IX English is devoted to close readings of complex texts. In addition to such classics as Jane Austen and Shakespeare, the girls explore their own voices as writers. All students take a course in Twentieth century World History. In Class X students take "American Literature From the Puritans to the Moderns" and "United States History Survey." Their studies culminate in a trip to Washington, D.C.

In Classes XI and XII there is a winter requirement of Sophocles' Theban tragedies and Shakespeare's *King Lear*. Spring electives in English are determined by student interest, but even when given a choice, Brearley girls don't seem to stray too far from the classics. Past choices include: Dostoyevsky, modern British fiction and Milton's *Paradise Lost*. More recent electives have been African-American fiction and Virginia Woolf. History electives in Class XI and XII include: "Comparative Political Systems," "History of China and Japan," "Political and Social Philosophy," and "Modern European History." (In the eighties Brearley taught an interdisciplinary course for Classes XI and XII on nuclear issues and nuclear disarmament.)

Students take art, music or drama throughout the Middle School and continue in one or more of these disciplines in the Upper School. Class VII performs an annual Gilbert & Sullivan operetta and Upper

School students perform in three main stage plays including a coeducational musical comedy production (*Anything Goes* in 1999, and *West Side Story* in 2000), and numerous class drama productions.

For students requiring special help there is the Reading and Testing Department. The Brearley Reading and Testing Department oversees the development of skills in writing and reading English. In addition to the Lower School's reading program, there are small classes in the Middle School for girls who need significant help in some aspect of language. In the Upper School, a few girls continue to benefit from the individual attention that is offered by this department. A faculty advisor system began in the Upper School in 1990. All students have a homeroom teacher and Brearley now has a full-time school counselor who with the school nurse and a part-time psychologist form the Brearley health team. There are Middle School discussion groups and a peer leadership program to keep a finger on the pulse of the student body. Seniors who have completed one trimester of training during their junior year serve as a resource for younger students under the supervision of the school counselor and school psychologist.

In the spring term seniors have several options. They can choose independent study—for example an extracurricular project, job or internship. A recent project was a student generated production of *The Belle of Amherst*. Girls are also encouraged throughout the Upper School to do volunteer work. Girls in Class IX have a yearlong community service requirement and select a project or agency they will work with for an entire year. One opportunity is "Bridges to Learning": a highly successful student-run effort that organizes five or six Saturday programs in the Spring for students from P.S. 102 who come to Brearley for a day of arts, crafts, carpentry, computer and other activities. In addition, there are numerous community service drives throughout the year at Brearley, including the Annual Mitten Drive in which mittens are bought and donated to a food pantry. Brearley supported and raised funds for the Asphalt Green AquaCenter.

There are opportunities to nurture the adventurous spirit of the Brearley girl. In addition to Mountain Day, a day of outdoor activities for Classes V through XII at Bear Mountain, Class XI girls may spend a semester at the Mountain School program of Milton Academy in Vermont, or attend the Maine Coast Semester program of the Chewonki Foundation. They can apply to spend a term at the John F. Kennedy Schule in Berlin or at the American International School in Vienna, a program arranged by Ambassador Ronald Lauder. Students may also apply to study in China, France, Spain or Italy under the School Year Abroad Program. In 1999–2000 two additional foreign exchanges were added: one for Class VIII students with a school in Toronto and another in which Brearley has been selected as one of three schools to participate in an exchange program sponsored by the Japan Society. Numerous scholarships for study and travel abroad are awarded to girls in the Upper School.

While academic pressure is a fact of life at Brearley, steps have been taken to ease some of the pressure and provide more support for students. Classes in the Middle School continue to run for 40 minutes, but the new schedule allows for flexibility in the way that class time is structured. Language classes in Classes IX and X continue to meet for 40 minute periods, but a Class IX history course will configure its classes to meet fewer times per week and for a longer period. In addition, the school has taken steps to help students manage their assignments. In the Upper School, there are only three "major assignments" (papers, tests) a week and only one on any given day.

Dr. Winn Barlow and the faculty evaluate the homework load and coordinate efforts throughout the school to ensure that the Brearley experience is as Dr. Winn Barlow says, "challenging, manageable and fulfilling."

The school has done a lot to ease the pressure in the last few years. "Because most of the students are so smart, there's not much of a range and you lose perspective on how smart you really are because you're judging yourself against impossible standards," says an alumna.

Course titles don't tell you everything. One alumna said that "there is an international excitement to classes, especially English and history. All subjects are thought through; there is no automatic conservatism. Courses are infused with political liberalism and teachers are sensitive to ethnic issues and awareness." Politically correct terms at Brearley are de rigueur. The goal of Brearley's multicultural efforts is to create an inclusive community, and to develop on-going programs to continue the process.

Students at Brearley are aware of gender issues, and most girls are appreciative of the manifold benefits of single-sex education. In one first grade class a mother who is a pilot for American Airlines came in to talk about her nontraditional occupation. At a Brearley's Parents Association benefit, columnist Anna Quindlen explained what she saw as one of the great strengths of a girls' school: "Because each day when they walk into class they see a smart woman at the front of the room and, on each side a smart girl, and that means that never in their lives will they be able to believe any of the nonsense about all the things girls can't do." The school's emphasis on the written word is evidenced by the thick Bibliography of Alumnae Authors.

Two hotly debated topics in recent years were diversity and leadership. Differences of opinion are respected at Brearley. There is a certain leveling of class differences at Brearley because of the emphasis on intellectual achievement. "Brearley girls never want to appear too rich, too social or too fancy. There's an inverse snobbism," says an alumna.

There is recognition that Brearley girls need to have more fun. As one parent said, "It's not a party school; your socializing is postponed for another time." The school arranges some activities with the opposite sex. Friday night dances start in Class VIII and The Middle School Orchestra performs with two local boys' schools during each year. Coeducational activities for the Upper School students include drama department productions, joint chorus concerts with a boys' school near Philadelphia, and events planned by various student clubs. There is a Holiday Semi-Formal in December and a junior/senior prom (held at the Mark Hotel in 1999 and 2000) to which girls can ask boys.

The Class X trip to Frost Valley with five other single-sex schools from Interschool, including boys' schools, is very popular. Also, Brearley is a member of Joint Schools, which plan co-ed activities including an art show, poetry readings and community service days.

Student government is called Self-Government. Two girls form a team and they run for the positions of co-presidents. There are at least fourteen school clubs, some for Class V and up, some only for Classes VII through XII. The Service Committee organizes toy, book and mitten drives, and sponsors a child. The Tech Club builds sets for plays. Other popular clubs include the Harvard Model U.N., Asian Awareness and Harvard Model Congress. The Brearley Environmental Action Committee is an active organization that is spearheading student involvement in the N.Y.C. Department of Sanitation's WasteLe$$ program in which Brearley was one of three schools invited to participate. The students have performed a vital role in data collection and focus the attention of the school community on environmental issues such as recycling.

Brearley has a solid AIDS curriculum, beginning in fifth grade, focusing on awareness and education. Many Brearley students participated in the AIDS Walk and many others were sponsors. There is an AIDS Awareness Society, SIDA.

Outstanding sports teams are tennis, cross country and the gymnastics team, which recently was undefeated for the season and won the AAIS championship. Soccer and track teams have captured AAIS championships five years in a row and the lacrosse team (a new sport) won its first AAIS championship in Spring 1998.

There is praise for an extraordinary faculty. A building was purchased in 1987 on East 77th Street for faculty housing. Appreciation for the gifted faculty is evident from the numerous (fifteen) chairs and faculty awards provided. The Jean Fair Mitchell Fund for faculty development has provided enrichment opportunities for faculty. One class bestowed the Faculty Award Fund (recipients nominated by the senior class) in recognition of "the extraordinary commitment of the Brearley faculty to their students and to the entire Brearley community." At the end of the year the students write thank-you notes to their teachers. As Dr. Winn Barlow notes, "Brearley has a faculty that is one of the most competent and caring I've known. They enable our students to be challenged in a safe and supportive environment which is where learning occurs best, especially for young women." A music faculty made up of approximately thirty outstanding performing musicians offer group and private lessons to Brearley students and performs regularly at the school throughout the year.

The school has continued its emphasis on providing a rigorous classical education while continually reviewing its academic and extracurricular offerings to keep them relevant. "Brearley's strong curriculum," says Winn Barlow, "provides a firm anchor from which to prepare our students for the future with great confidence."

Brearley makes use of many graceful euphemisms as noted by the co-presidents of the Self-Government in their "Last Days" speech: "We don't have AP courses—our courses are just impossible. We don't wear underwear—we wear bloomers. We don't get 91's—we get Very Good minus minus plus slash good plus plus minuses. And we don't graduate—we Last Day Exercise." White dresses are worn at Last Day. There is an Awards Assembly at which school prizes in all subjects and scholarships for study and travel are presented. Students are recognized for community service work, and artwork from each class is placed in the school's permanent Kunz Collection. There is now also a "Head's Award" for contributions to the school community.

In the late nineteenth century when college choices for women were extremely limited, Brearley prepared girls almost exclusively for

Bryn Mawr College. Since then, Brearley has been very successful over the years in matching its students with excellent colleges and universities. Ms. Elenor Reid became the college advisor in 1999.

Does Brearley churn out a yearly crop of super women? Former Head of School Evelyn Halpert had said that the school's objective is to "turn out young women who will be good citizens in a democratic society . . . whether successful by the standards of our society or not. It would be wrong, I think, to suggest that we want everybody who leaves this school to be a leader or a powerful person. We want all our students to leave this school happier and stronger because of the experiences they've had here and what they've learned."

Legacies say, "I'm Brearley born and Brearley bred"; "Alumnae gatherings are so exciting, there's never a boring person"; "College was disappointing after Brearley." An alumna writes in the Brearley Bulletin Magazine of her years at Brearley: "A superb classical education and a permanent love of learning." From the Last Day speech of 1992 by the co-heads of Self-Government: "This school puts the life of the mind above all else." The process of learning is lifelong and many Brearley girls become distinguished scholars and professionals. An alumna now heads The Ford Foundation and another is head of the Philadelphia Museum of Art.

Popular College Choices   Yale, Harvard/Radcliffe, Brown, Vassar, Princeton, Amherst, Stanford, Dartmouth, University of Chicago

Traditions   "The best food of all the independent schools," Field Day, Mountain Day, Father's Chorus Performing at Winter Assemblies, Junior and Senior Prom, seventh-grade Gilbert and Sullivan production, eighth-grade Carnival with a surprise theme, Book Fair, Brearley General Store, Lower School Family Nights, Last Day Exercises

Publications   Student Newspaper: *The Zephyr*
Literary Magazine: *The Beaver*
Yearbook
Various "underground" newspapers organized by class
The Brearley Bridge
Parents Association: *Happenings, The Brearley Bulletin, Brearley Update*

Community Service Requirement for Class IX only, a one-semester community service course Brearley's coordinator of community service helps Class IX students to secure a year-long community service commitment with various social service agencies

Hangouts The Mansion (a diner at 86th and York), libraries

Brooklyn Friends School

375 Pearl Street
Brooklyn, NY 11201
(718) 852-1029, FAX: (718) 643-4868
e-mail: bfs@brooklynfriends.org
website: www.brooklynfriends.org

Coed
Toddler–12th grade
Not accessible

Dr. Michael Nill, Head of School
Ms. Sara Soll, Director of Admissions, Preschool
Ms. Jennifer Knies, Director of Admissions, Kindergarten
through 12th grade

Birthday Cutoff   Children entering kindergarten must be 5 by December 31

Enrollment   Total enrollment: 580
Kindergarten places: approximately 15
Graduating class size: 35

Tuition Range 2001–2002   Preschool–12th grade $9,800 to $18,300
An optional hot lunch is available for an additional charge

After-School Program   Quality Day Care Program beginning at 15 months, open to Brooklyn Friends families; for older students, a variety of creative and recreational activities are offered from 3:00 to 6:00 P.M.; an additional payment is required
Friends After Three Program: For Middle School students offers workshops in computers, the arts, language, drama and sports
Spring and winter vacation programs available subject to demand; an additional payment is required
Additional program: the Family Center Program at Brooklyn Friends School is a full-day, 11-month program with flexible hours for infants from 15 months to 2.9 years old
Clubs, sports, private music instruction

Summer Program   Summer camp: From mid-June through Mid-August. Activities for the younger children include arts, crafts, sports, trips and swimming; Middle Schoolers can attend Summer Arts Program or Academic Skills enrichment camp. Open to children from other schools; an additional payment is required

———

Brooklyn Friends School is a Quaker college preparatory school founded in 1867 by the Brooklyn Meeting of the Society of Friends. The school is housed in a seven-story art deco building. When you enter through the brass doors you are greeted by lobby displays of student work, from digital photos to paper mâché. In addition to classrooms, four science labs and two libraries, the school boasts a darkroom, music, art, sculpting, ceramics and dance studios, a woodshop, three computer labs, a video production and editing room, two gyms, a roof top playground and a 300 seat theater. The style of the school is informal and there is no dress code.

Getting in: Open house tours give prospective applicants a chance to meet parents and faculty. A personal interview is required for all applicants. Screening by a member of the admissions staff is required for applicants to preschool through fifth grade. The ISEE is required for application to sixth through twelfth grades. One-third of the student body receives some form of financial assistance.

The school is guided by the ideals of tolerance, equality and non-violence. Although Quaker traditions permeate the school parents say that the school is not in the least sectarian. "It manages to provide an enriching academic experience while fostering the sense that there is not a dichotomy between the secular and spiritual aspects of our lives." Students meet in silence for weekly Quaker Meeting and courses in ethics and social justice are offered in the Upper School.

Head of School: Dr. Michael Nill is a graduate of Fordham, Johns Hopkins, Columbia University's Teachers College and the University of Texas at Austin.

Parents: The parents at Brooklyn Friends are an eclectic mix of artists, office workers, lawyers, educators, physicians and Wall Street professionals who share a common philosophical commitment. According to one parent: "We looked for a private school that reflected and fostered our moral values, where the students were aware of their advantages but were not elitist." The parents play an important role in the school as class parents, library volunteers, and as members of the PTA, they engage in fundraising and community building.

Program: Experiential learning is emphasized throughout. All classes are actively engaged in creating, hypothesizing and building. The pre-school curriculum is based on the idea of play as "the work of young children" and fosters independence and the development of language and self-expression through the arts, dance and music. In the Lower School (K–4) students work to develop and increase basic skills as well as taking part in art, dance, music, library and physical education. Computer science, woodworking and Japanese language and culture are also part of the Lower School program.

Fifth and sixth graders stay in the classroom for reading, language arts, and social studies. They see specialists for science, math and foreign language. Latin instruction begins in fifth grade; students can select from Spanish, French or Latin thereafter. Seventh and eighth grades are fully departmentalized. The humanities program includes ancient history, the Middle Ages, the Renaissance and the Age of Exploration and American history. Environmental studies and discussions of new technologies enrich the traditional science curriculum. The school has a newly expanded the math department and several new computer labs.

Upper Schoolers (grades 9–12) take four years of English, foreign language, social studies, mathematics, and physical education; three years of science and art; one each of computer literacy and application, and ethics. Computers are integrated into the classroom curriculum from the Lower School through Upper School. The school recently installed a T1 line for Internet access throughout the building. In addition to classroom computers, students have access to six computer labs with Dell Optiplex systems. Upper Schoolers edit, write and explore scientific and mathematical formulas through a number of software programs. Brooklyn Friends has a website that is up and running.

The math department offers Calculus AB and BC and electives in engineering, programming, applications and robotics, statistics, architecture, and geometry. There are AP's in biology, chemistry and physics. Humanities course offerings include: American literature, Japanese literature, and Latin American Studies. The arts program is outstanding and includes painting, sculpture, ceramics, woodshop, video production, music and drama. All seniors take part in six week internships in hospitals, community organizations, engineering firms, law offices and so on, depending on their career interests.

Two-thirds of the high school students play on a sports team. For a relatively small school, the teams are quite successful. BFS recently won the volleyball league championships and a New York State Independent School Soccer Championship title. Athletics are seen as an opportunity to build skills and develop good sportsmanship; despite their recent successes, BFS is not a "jock" school; sports are seen as an opportunity to do one's best.

From second grade through the Upper School, students take overnight trips to develop peer leadership skills, for academic study and for personal growth. In recent years, students participated in environmental studies on Cape Cod, astronomy explorations in Frost Valley, White House tours in Washington, D.C., rock climbing at Camp Vacamas, language and cultural trips to Italy, Mexico, France, Canada and Puerto Rico.

Popular College Choices   Barnard, Brown, Clark, Colgate, Connecticut College, Haverford, Wesleyan, NYU, Sarah Lawrence, Swarthmore, University of Pennsylvania, University of Rochester, Trinity, Vassar and Yale

Traditions: Fallfest, Holiday Crafts Fair, Dance Concert, Turkey Trot, All School Art Show, International Dinner, Middle School Sports Night, Drama Productions, Sports Dinner

Publications   Pre/Lower School Poetry Magazine; Middle School Poetry Magazine; Middle School Newsletter; Upper School Literary Magazine; Yearbook; School Newsletter, Parents Notes

Community Service Requirement: All students take part in community service from pre-school through Upper School. Upper Schoolers are required to complete 70 hours of community service in order to fulfill graduation requirements

The Brooklyn Heights Montessori School

185 Court Street
Brooklyn, NY 11201
(718) 858-5100, FAX (718) 858-0500

Coed
2-year-olds–8th Grade
Accessible

Head of School*
Ms. Susanne Peebles, Director of Preschool
Ms. Maggy Sears, Elementary and Middle School Director
Ms. Sonia Nachuk, Director of the Little Room

Birthday cutoff   For 2's Program child must be 2 by September 1 in year of entry

Enrollment   Total enrollment: 321
Pre-K and kindergarten places: 156
Grades 1–3: 48
Grades 4–6: 48
Grades 7 and 8: 32
Little Room: 33
Little Room Kindergarten: 10

Tuition Range   2001–2002 $4,050 to $15,800, Preschool–8th Grade

Financial Aid/Scholarship   7% of the preschool budget is allotted for scholarships
11% of the Elementary Middle School budget is allotted for scholarships
The Little Room is primarily funded by the Board of Education

Endowment   None

After-school Program   A variety of recreational and creative activities are offered including: origami, French, dance, soccer and more; additional payment is required.

---

* Not available at time of publication.

114

Summer Program   The summer program offers a wide range of creative and recreational activities, including weekly trips, overnight camping and beach days. Early morning drop off at 8:15 A.M. and "after camp" until 5:30; an additional payment is required

———

The Brooklyn Heights Montessori School opened its doors on October 1, 1965 with twenty children attending the one-room school in the First Presbyterian Church on Henry Street in Brooklyn Heights. Since then the school has expanded and moved to the Cobble Hill section of Brooklyn. The school recently completed an award winning 32,000 square foot expansion, which includes not only spacious light-filled classrooms, but also a library, gymnasium and a student-designed Middle School lounge.

Getting In: Parents are invited for personal tours of the school and a personal interview is required of all applicants. For the Preschool program, parents visit the school and children come for an interview. Lower Elementary students come for informal testing and a classroom visit. Upper Elementary and Middle School applicants must submit ERB scores and spend a day at the school.

Parents: Parents play an important role in the school's community. In fact, the school's board of trustees is primarily composed of parents. The Parents Association sponsors a Speakers Forum to which a number of speakers are invited each year. Topics include diversity, raising special needs children, raising boys and helping children develop organizational skills. There are morning coffees throughout the year, a harvest square dance, a bowling party, and a Valentine's Day card making event. Other activities help raise money to support special projects for the school. The PA also teams up with the diversity committee to sponsor an International Festival and Cultural Diversity Potluck.

Program: There are currently three divisions of BHMS: the Preschool, the Elementary and Middle School Program and the Little Room.

All learning at BHMS is designed to happen within the Montessori model of mixed-age classrooms which are carefully prepared environments organized to offer children a wide range of experience and to facilitate the growth of their skills and confidence. Independent work, depth of study, critical thinking, respect for and understanding of others, are all emphasized by a supportive and developmentally oriented staff at all age levels. At each stage of learning, technology is used to enhance skills, share creative ideas and communicate thoughts. BHMS emphasizes developing a sense of responsibility for the ethical considerations inherent in the use of new technology.

In the Preschool and kindergarten classrooms the environment is supportive. The educational philosophy and the teaching materials developed by Maria Montessori provide the underlying structure for the program. The BHMS faculty is concerned with the overall growth of each child, so teachers regard social, physical and emotional development as going hand in hand with intellectual growth.

In the Elementary Program, the curriculum integrates all subject areas. Studying other cultures and countries helps children to understand themselves and their community in relation to the larger world. Cultures are studied in a three-year cycle, and a unit related to the United States is included each year. Older elementary students expand the level of study by viewing cultures from a historical perspective. Problem solving provides a primary focus for the math and science programs.

The Middle School Program (grades seven and eight) focuses on historical themes like revolutions, building a democracy, exploration and conflict, while examining the impact on this country. Students deepen their exploration of math, science and technology, and apply what they have learned to real life projects such as the Middle School student lounge. Middle School students also explore ways that they can contribute to the larger community.

The Little Room is a special educational program (Preschool through First grade) which serves children with speech and learning difficulties. Housed in its own space at BHMS, the Little Room shares much of the Montessori educational philosophy and practices. Integral to the Little Room is a unique mainstreaming program (the oldest in the city for preschoolers) which has been extremely successful in helping students move on to "typical" class placements.

Students in the mainstream classrooms also gain an opportunity to become comfortable with differences in people. They participate in mainstreaming activities with the children in The Little Room Program.

Publications   Newsletter *Handprints*
Literary Magazine *The Dancing Pen*
Weekly Bulletin

Community Service Requirement The Upper Elementary and Middle School students perform community service each week. Assignments range from working with younger children in the classrooms, to writing articles for the school newsletter to planting trees in Prospect Park.

The Browning School

52 East 62nd Street
New York, NY 10021
(212)838-6280, FAX (212) 355-5602
website: www.browning.edu

All boys
Kindergarten–12th grade
Not accessible

Dr. Stephen M. Clement, III, Headmaster
Ms. Jackie Casey, Director of Admissions

Uniform   Dress code for all grades (coat and tie with an option of polo shirt or turtleneck shirt in the Lower School)

Birthday Cutoff   Boys entering Kindergarten must be 5 by September 1

Enrollment   Total enrollment: 350
Kindergarten places: 30
Graduating class 2000: 25
12 Prep for Prep students as of Fall 2000

Grades   Trimester system
Letter grades begin in 5th grade
Departmentalization begins in 7th grade
Two reports per trimester

Tuition Range 2001–2002 $18,675 to $19,750, kindergarten–12th grade
Additional fees: for books and lunch and PE uniforms approximately $1,565
Tuition payment plan available

Financial Aid/Scholarship   Approximately 15% of the student body receives some form of aid

Endowment $3 million

Homework   Kindergarten: approximately 10 minutes each night
Lower School: increases to 1 hour each night
Middle School: about 2 hours each night
Upper School: about 3 hours each night

After-School Program   The Browning After-School Encore Program offers a wide variety of creative and recreational activities for boys in Kindergarten through sixth grades until 5:00 P.M. Popular activities include chess, computer, science, after-school study

The Browning Sports Club (Intramurals)

Junior varsity and varsity athletic competition

Summer Program   There is a three week recreational program available for the Lower School in June

---

The Browning School was founded with five boys as a college preparatory school in 1888 by John A. Browning. It is a traditional school, at one time very socially exclusive in its student body. Today, Browning boys are culled from a more diverse population but they still mind their manners—a group recently went to tea at the Macklowe Hotel. Parents say Browning offers a small, nurturing, supportive environment. "They are extraordinarily understanding and caring about the development of boys," said a parent of a first grader. "It's a gem that people haven't discovered." There is a formal dress code and every morning Browning boys are greeted with a handshake. Browning stresses "the importance of developing well-rounded gentlemen." Browning recently completed a $1.5 million renovation to create a new library, two new science labs and more office space.

Getting in: Parents should call the school and schedule a tour. You can tour without applying. Parents of kindergarten applicants take a tour of the school while their child is being interviewed. Applicants for first through third grades are scheduled depending on how many places are available. For Middle and Upper School applicants and their parents, small group tours are given and applicants return for half a day and a formal interview.

Parents: "I thought it would be very Muffy and Buffy, which it is," said a parent. "But, in my son's class of fifteen children there's a family from England, one from Thailand and one African-American. In the other class, there's a South American family and an Italian family." Parents can volunteer for the Parents Association and sponsor Book Fairs, Auctions, Sports Events and Workshops. The Parents Association also offers summer study stipends to support professional development.

Program: Browning is composed of three divisions: Lower

119

School (kindergarten through Fourth), Middle School (fifth through Form II)and Upper School (Form III [ninth grade] through Form VI [twelfth grade]). Foreign language begins in fifth grade with a choice of French or Spanish. Latin is offered in seventh and eighth grades. There is an annual Shakespeare play and public speaking contest. Browning fields strong teams in soccer, cross country, track, basketball, baseball and tennis. Field Day is a popular annual event.

The Lower School at Browning "lets boys be boys, and is structured, but nurturing. My son needed the structure and the small classes. I am beyond thrilled with the school," one parent said. The program is integrated; there are computers in every classroom. Formal reading instruction begins in first grade.

The Middle School program focuses on strengthening study and organizational skills. By fifth grade or Form I the program is fully departmentalized and a foreign language is introduced. Boys in Forms I and II study Latin in addition to French or Spanish. In music, boys are invited to sing in the Middle School choir.

In the Upper School, there are required classes in English, math, history, science, computer science, art, music and physical education. Advanced placement courses are offered in all subjects.

Browning is a member of Interschool and beginning in fifth grade Browning boys participate in a variety of activities with a number of girls' schools including exchange days, field trips, concerts, joint assemblies, dramatic productions and community service projects.

College advising begins in Form IV (grade 10) and Forms V and VI (grades 11 and 12) take an annual trip to visit a broad selection of colleges and universities. Personalized guidance enables each student to maximize his college potential.

Hot lunch is served daily in "Ruby's kitchen"—the school cafeteria.

Popular College Choices: Columbia, Cornell, Vanderbilt, Connecticut College, Boston College, George Washington University, Hamilton College

Traditions: Father/Son Dinner, Public Speaking Competition, Brother's Breakfast and Picture, New Parent Dinner, Book Fair, Field Days, Grandparents Days, Annual Art Show, Middle School Shakespeare play, Upper School play, Three Day College Trip, annual fundraising auction, Alumni Day, Middle School Overnight trips.

The Buckley School

113 East 73rd Street
New York, NY 10021
(212) 535-8787
website: www.buckleyschool.nyc.org

All boys
Kindergarten–8th/9th grade
Not accessible

Mr. Gregory J. O'Melia, Headmaster
Mrs. Jo Ann E. Lynch, Director of Admissions

Uniform Beginners (Kindergarten): prescribed knit blue or white Buckley polo shirt, pants (no jeans), leather shoes, no sneakers
Grades I–IX: jacket, tie, slacks and leather shoes

Birthday Cutoff Children entering kindergarten must be 5 by September 1

Enrollment Total enrollment: approximately 350
Kindergarten places: 40
8th grade graduating class size: approximately 18; more than half will attend New York City independent day schools, the rest will attend boarding schools
9th grade graduating class size: approximately 15–17; most will attend boarding schools

Grades Trimester system
Kindergarten through 3rd grade students receive anecdotal reports and checklists
Letter grades begin in 4th grade (3 times a year)
Departmentalization begins in 6th grade
First final exam given in 7th grade

Tuition Range 2001–2002 $17,700 to $18,100, Kindergarten–9th grade
Additional fees: for textbooks, classroom supplies, athletic fees, publications, lunch and snack, approximately $2,100
Fee for class IX out-of-town field trips approximately $580

Financial Aid/Scholarship 10% of the student body receive some form of aid
$450,000 in financial aid was awarded in 2000–2001

Endowment   Capital fund valued at $14.5 million (as of January 2000)

Diversity   8 Prep for Prep students as of Fall 2000

Homework   Beginners: none
   Class I: approximately 20 minutes, weekly spelling tests
   Class II: approximately 1/2 hour
   Class III: 45 minutes–1 hour
   Class IV: approximately 1 1/2 hours
   Class V: approximately 2 hours
   Classes VI and VII: 2 1/2–3 hours
   Classes VIII and IX: 3–4 hours

After-School Program   Classes I through IX: required after-school sports at Ward's Island, fall and spring
   During winter term required after-school sports in the Hubball Building
   Interscholastic athletic competition in the Manhattan Private School League
   Friday Afternoon Lower School Gymnastics Club and Middle and Upper School Basketball Club
   Saturday Sports Club (10 A.M.–12 P.M. in the Buckley gym)
   Vacation Club (10 A.M.–12 P.M. in the Buckley gym)

Summer Program   The Buckley June Program; 2 weeks in June: swimming, computers, arts and crafts, games and sports at Buckley and Ward's Island; an additional payment is required

---

Founded in 1913 by educator B. Lord Buckley, historically The Buckley School has groomed the sons of New York's captains of industry (including a few Vanderbilts, Rockefellers and their latter-day counterparts) as well as the progeny of prominent politicians (mostly but not exclusively Republican) for the elite boarding schools. Today, "leadership, citizenship and academic excellence" are still valued at The Buckley School, which is traditional in every sense of the word, but the student body now includes children culled from a variety of socioeconomic backgrounds—more than a few from neighborhoods far beyond the tony Upper East Side. While most of the current graduates still go on to schools like Groton and Deerfield, many of the boys now attend New York City independent day schools.

Some elements of the past remain: Buckley still has "travel days" on either side of the spring vacation, a formal tea complete with finger sandwiches is served at Exhibition Day, the male teachers and athletic instructors are addressed as "Sir" and women classroom teachers (who do not wear slacks) are addressed as either Miss or Mrs. (never Ms.). The boys are served by the kitchen staff family-style (the rumored white-gloved waiters are merely an apparition of days gone by). Bush won a 2000 student election by a comfortable margin.

The Buckley School is far removed from the turmoil rocking the public schools. Prospective parents who have toured Buckley are impressed by the sense of clarity and order. Lower School Director Mrs. Sonja Robinson says, "Clear goals make clear kids." The emphasis on a classic curriculum, the strict dress code and unabashed respect for God and country have tremendous appeal to nineties parents dubbed "the new traditionalists." Applications to The Buckley School have been at record levels in recent years.

Is there a typical Buckley boy? Parents say: "A boy who is very interested in sports, very smart, follows directions." But athletic ability and blond hair are not a prerequisite for admission, and we know many boys with a creative bent who managed to find their niche here. What is most important is that the boy will be able to handle the work, because by fourth and fifth grades the curriculum is demanding. Buckley boys are well rounded: Touring parents might see boys with their ties tucked into their smocks painting in the airy art room with classical music playing in the background. First graders recite poetry, Lower School boys perform in the annual rhythm band assembly, all classes put on a class play (Buckley's drama program is outstanding). Unfortunately, parents don't tour Ward's Island, where the extensive outdoor afternoon sports program (fall and spring) harnesses the boys' more aggressive instincts.

Getting in: An important criterion is "a match in values between school and home." Although many of the boys (including legacies and siblings) still hail from nursery schools like Park Avenue Christian, Madison Avenue Presbyterian and Episcopal, the kindergarten class is composed of boys from many different nursery programs.

Admissions at Buckley consists of four components. After the application is received comes 1) the tour, which is led by the director of admissions, the assistant headmaster or the Lower School head, 2) the parents' interview with the director of admissions and the headmaster, 3) the applicant's group interview and 4) the ERB and nursery school report. Decisions are made on the basis of the group interview, observation at the child's preschool, ERB and school report. Both parents are requested to attend the interviews with the director of admissions and the headmaster; they will accommodate scheduling difficulties and meet with the parents separately, if necessary. Letters of recommendation from Buckley parents who know the family are welcome. The group interview is about one hour long (during which the boys are observed playing a variety of "games"). One mother said her son enjoyed the experience so much he drew a picture of himself going to Buckley while at his Trinity interview.

What are they looking for? According to Jo Ann Lynch, Director of Admissions, a boy with "a love of learning, good self-esteem, not a little old man, rather, a naive but curious child who is fun to be with." They are also looking at how the boy socializes in a group. According to Mrs. Robinson the ERB is "a measuring stick against which all the boys stand." And of course, they also look at the family. There is a sibling and legacy policy (some boys' grandfathers attended Buckley); however, the school will not automatically admit a child who they feel would not do well there. Buckley does maintain a wait list.

After nineteen years as Headmaster, Brian Walsh, the last of the old guard of New York City Heads of School, retired in 2001. During his tenure, the Buckley School became a kinder and gentler place while retaining all of the school's beloved traditions; including the spit and polish upon which Buckley prides itself. His commitment to the school was unwavering—even the threat of a hurricane could not keep him from the Father/Son Overnight. His legacy includes the purchase and renovation of the adjoining townhouse, enhancing the school's physical plant while preserving the intimate nature of a small school. Mr. Gregory J. O'Melia, a Boston-born Harvard man, succeeded Walsh as headmaster in July 2001. Mr. O'Melia, though young in age, has extensive experience teaching and coaching in a range of private schools, including the Brooks School in North Andover, Massachusetts.

When Mr. Walsh came to Buckley, boys were still being ranked academically and Middle School boys received pins for the highest grade point average. Middle School pins are now given largely for effort. It is acknowledged that Buckley boys are very competitive, but the belief is that this competitiveness can be positive (and a great motivator) if used appropriately. The highest awards at graduation exercises are for character, not the highest G.P.A. Of course, any school is only as good as its teachers, and at Buckley there is tremendous respect for teachers and teaching. Approximately 80 percent of tuition goes toward teachers' salaries and benefits (some of the highest among teachers in city independent schools). Teachers undergo an annual self-evaluation as well as a formal evaluation by the headmaster.

Parents: The first Buckley Parents' Committee was started (in 1982) for the purpose of "service and communication." There is only one officer—the president. Class representatives are selected by the homeroom teachers and division directors. The Parents' Committee meets once a month, in a closed meeting, and the minutes are distributed to all parents. Parents praise the Buckley mothers, who are "time givers to benefit the school, a cohesive group of women working towards a common goal." School benefits are well organized and well staffed.

The tone at Buckley is definitely formal and very Upper East Side. (The staff is reputed to be more liberal than the parent body.) The parents are Wall Street bankers, lawyers and doctors, with a sprinkling of writers and business people. But as one parent said, "It's a cosmopolitan mix of French, Chinese, Japanese, African-American, Jewish and Muslim." Another parent had a different perspective: "Boring, old money, coupon clipping . . . they are more dressed in the morning than Brearley parents are in the evening." Parents dress for all school events (don't even think about wearing blue jeans). The class cocktail party is usually held in a parent's elegant Upper East Side apartment.

The school has no formal religious affiliation—Christmas and Chanukah songs are sung at the Beginners' Christmas party. The nativity play for classes I and II is an annual event, and after the pledge of allegiance, everyone recites the Lord's Prayer at assemblies. However, families of many faiths are comfortable here; the commonality seems to be a basic conservatism.

Traditions are important at Buckley. The used clothing sale and preview party, where parents can purchase gently worn Brooks Brothers pants and blazers for their sons, is a popular event. The Father-Son Overnight (kindergarten through ninth grade) is an annual rite, and the Fathers' Committee selects the Saturday night entertainment. The boys have a marvelous time playing tennis, fishing, throwing a football with Dad (substitute dads are available). One father recalls his first overnight when bedded down in his tent well after midnight, he heard a group of fathers singing "Kumbaya" around a distant campfire. Older boys attend the annual Father-Son Adventure

Dinner, which features an explorer or adventurer as speaker. In addition, the annual Father-Son Day at Shea or Yankee Stadium and family skating party help to bond the Buckley community.

Programs: Buckley's main facility consists of two fully renovated connected buildings on East 73rd and East 74th Streets. The adjacent townhouse was purchased in 1996. It has been completely rebuilt to provide additional classroom space for small group instruction and technology. It will also house some of the facilities now in the 74th Street building which is to be renovated for additional classroom space. In addition, a new Assembly Room with a balcony has been constructed providing more seating space and doubling the stage area of the old facility. The Hubball Building, two blocks away, named for James M. Hubball, headmaster for thirty-two years, houses three full-size gymnasiums plus the two beginners' classrooms. Parents like the fact that the beginners have their own little world, although they travel to "Big Buckley" for Friday assemblies each week. There is a Big Brother Program to help integrate the boys into Big Buckley. Lower School boys write "fan mail" to boys in other grades after watching them perform in a school production.

The Lower School at Buckley is composed of kindergarten through grade 3. Each year the two classes are reshuffled so the boys relate to different friends. "Kindergarten at Buckley is a gentle transition into grade school," parents say. Mondays and Fridays are short days, so there is time for play dates and for just settling in. "Except for a few leftover nursery school cliques, friendships seem to shift weekly in the kindergarten year," said one parent. The Friday afternoon gymnastics and basketball clubs (for an additional charge) are "more social than athletic" and most of the boys attend. Boys who want to learn gymnastics routines can attend afternoon sessions at the school beginning in first grade. After school several boys attend art classes at the Metropolitan Museum of Art, others go to religious school, take Chinese, piano or karate, and if they haven't had enough sports already, some Lower School boys attend the Cavaliers after-school sports program.

The Beginners' classroom is traditional, with block and LEGO corners, listening center, library corner and an adjoining outdoor play roof. On three extended days (until 2:45 P.M.), the boys alternate among gym, creative movement and cooking, and science and library. The kindergarten day is organized but not overly structured. Parents say, "They are really tuned into the rates at which little boys develop. Throughout Buckley the boys are challenged, but they are given the skills to meet those challenges." Kindergartners end the year with the Teddy Bear Picnic, to which boys bring their favorite stuffed bear (or other well-worn animal).

Beginning in first grade boys wear a jacket and tie to school, changing into their "Buckley blues" for after-school sports each day. The day is structured and the boys leave the classroom for art, crafts, music, science and library. First through third graders go to the science lab twice a week. There is a recess in the mornings and in the afternoon an hour of sports. Project Charlie is an anti-drug program in the Lower School that fosters good self-esteem and responsible decision-making.

Each boy is challenged, basic skills are taught in small groups and there is never the expectation that all the boys are going to be doing the same thing at the same time. Homework is given to teach study skills and responsibility. Parents say that "by third grade the pace is quicker, there is serious traditional work, a certain amount of maturity is expected." Third grade boys know how to use the library, and also have access to the New York Society Library on East 79th Street.

The emphasis at Buckley has always been, and remains, on a "sound traditional curriculum." The Buckley School brochure is notable for its brevity regarding the yearly curriculum, but there is more here than meets the eye. Social studies in the Lower School incorporates multicultural viewpoints. Boys learn to work in collaborative groups as well as individually. There are workbooks that reinforce reading, math and handwriting skills. Journal writing begins in kindergarten and first graders write daily. Formal reading instruction begins in first grade—boys break into reading groups based on ability. There is a lot of movement between these groups. Lower School Head Mrs. Sonja Robinson explains that the reading program is literature based and includes the teaching of phonics. (Buckley has not been quick to jump on the Whole Language bandwagon.) Buckley is quick to identify learning problems before a boy's self-esteem is affected. The Skills and Language Arts Program (SLA) provides support where needed. There is a learning specialist for each division of the school. Cathy Bose, a popular teacher "who really taught the boys how to think," is now the Lower School math specialist and she is introducing new methods of teaching using manipulatives and a hands-on approach. There is a computer in the kindergarten classrooms that is used for games. Boys in the Lower School "publish" their own books using the computer and there is a Lower School literary magazine that is a desktop publication.

Computer in classes I and II is mainly for math and reading

games. Formal computer instruction begins in third grade with "Microworlds." LEGO LOGO (designing LEGO constructions and making them "work" with the computer) is very popular. In recognition of the fact that in the near future the older boys will probably be completing most of their homework and writing assignments on the computer, a computer enhancement project is under way at the school. In a third grade geography pilot program Macintosh laptops were used to create state itineraries. The library is automated and a T1 line was installed for a school network in 1998. All classes are wired for the Internet.

Throughout the Lower School art is frequently integrated into the curriculum. For a unit on the Middle Ages kindergarten boys went to the Arms and Armor Exhibit at the Met and to the Cathedral of St. John the Divine to see and sketch Gothic architecture. Kindergartners make stick puppets and papier-mâché masks. First graders study the cultures of ancient Mexico and Japan. They study Mayan culture, make their own pottery, pictographs, patterns and illustrated stories. (One drawing had the caption "I am going to sacrifice you"). After visiting the Brooklyn Botanic Garden, one class designed their own Japanese gardens. The Japan unit culminates in a visit to the Urasenke Center for a traditional tea ceremony. Second graders make papier-mâché skyscrapers, study immigration and make a map of Manhattan.

The range of the art program at Buckley is visible on Exhibition Day. Works range from terra-cotta dinosaurs to seascapes inspired by Monet, from jungles à la Rousseau to multimedia sculptures and computer projects. There are collaborative murals and freedom quilts. The older boys make actual-size self-portraits of what they would like to be when they grow up: professional basketball player, botanist, illustrator, writer, ski racer, lawyer. In crafts the boys make smooth polished wooden bowls, letter openers and toys.

Middle School at Buckley is composed of fourth grade through sixth grade. Fourth graders enter through the 74th Street door and on the first day mothers must say goodbye downstairs as their sons find their own classrooms. Homework requires more sophisticated thinking and time, parents say (between forty-five minutes and two hours). There are more long-term assignments. Letter grades begin in this year. Boys choose a book for their book report (one self-described nonconformist told us he chose Stephen King's *Nightshift*). The boys study the ancient world and write research reports. They have their own Olympic games. French and Spanish are offered; Latin is required beginning in seventh grade.

The fifth graders study the Middle Ages, culminating in a Medieval Feast. The boys dress in period costumes, speak Old English and make banners and shields. One parent said by fifth grade the work is more interesting and there is more discussion than in the Lower School. Middle Schoolers study earth science, physical science and human systems (including reproductive).

Buckley takes athletics seriously and offers a highly organized, competitive sports program. Blue championship banners line the walls of the Hubball Building and the trophy case is full. The brochure says: "Physical fitness and skill development are emphasized." Per von Scheele, the director of athletics at Buckley for over twenty years, rollerblades to school and leads ski trips to Italy during spring vacation. In fall and spring the boys travel to Ward's Island for field sports. Beginning in fourth grade boys have weekly tryouts for the Strength Club, the Super Strength Club or Gladiators in "recognition of achievement of athletic strength at a level several years beyond a boy's grade level." Those who qualify get a T-shirt. By seventh grade afternoon sports are seventy-five minutes long and one mother told us "the boys come home around 5:00 P.M., do a load of work and go to bed." Not every boy needs to be a jock but the boy who is totally uninterested in athletics will not be happy here (although the boys do receive an effort grade in athletics on their report cards). Boys who love to compete and are talented will thrive. Buckley gym birthday parties are popular and parents must book them about a year in advance.

There are Middle School intramural leagues and beginning in seventh grade there are Varsity A and B teams. All boys must participate in one sport each trimester. In fifth grade the boys begin playing football. The Buckley Blue Demons are a source of tremendous pride and school spirit, they score on almost every possession and have been league champions for over fifteen consecutive years. In addition to football, Buckley has championship teams in soccer, wrestling, gymnastics, baseball, lacrosse, and track and field. At the end of each season awards are given out recognizing outstanding individual and team achievement. Class champions are named for classes four and up.

At the Middle School closing assembly pins are awarded for achievement in the areas of French, athletics, English composition and positive attitude. The Gold Founder's Pin is awarded for the student who made the greatest progress during Middle School, and the George Lane Nichols Award is given for "courage, loyalty, helpfulness and reliability."

The Upper School at Buckley consists of grades seven through nine. In classes VII and VIII boys read *The Iliad*, tackle algebra and geometry, hone their lab skills and study American history. They continue their study of French and Latin. During the spring term seventh grade boys write a 2,000-plus-word research paper on a topic of their choice in American history (subject to teacher's approval). Classroom discussions in the Upper School become increasingly animated. In eighth grade the boys read more classics: Dickens, *Julius Caesar*, *To Kill a Mockingbird*; they complete another spring research paper and study modern European history up to the Franco-Prussian War.

According to the handbook, ninth grade "readings are chosen for their relevance to the student's developing sense of ethics and justice." They read *Catcher in the Rye*, *Cry the Beloved Country* and more Shakespeare. There is a weekly debating period. Boys study Euclidean geometry, physics and modern European history through the present. Ninth graders take trips to Boston and Washington, D.C. (where the boys visit the Lincoln and Jefferson Memorials and Arlington National Cemetery, as well as the Holocaust Museum). Ninth graders complete a major research paper during the fall term.

The annual class play, a tradition at Buckley, starts in kindergarten. The boys soon become very comfortable onstage. Every boy participates in making scenery and has a small speaking part. First graders perform in the Nativity play and a poetry recital. The annual class plays become more sophisticated in the Middle and Upper Schools; many of these productions offer a contemporary twist on the classics, for example: "A New York Yankee in King Arthur's Court" or "Sherlock Meets the Phantom." For the spring operetta, girls from one of the independent girls' schools often play the female roles. In the annual Jack Woodruff Public Memorial Speaking Contest for seventh and eighth graders boys must go through four rounds speaking from four to five minutes on controversial current issues. Recent topics have included the rise of democracy in Russia, educational vouchers and immigration restrictions. The boys are judged on delivery and content.

Ninth graders take a year-long class in debating and engage in a formal debate before the student body. There are two classes in the Upper School on current issues as well as a leadership class taught by Mr. Walsh. Ninth graders can drop one language and take only five academic courses. They have the privilege of leaving school for lunch on Wednesdays during winter term so that they can use local libraries to work on their term papers.

The student council for grades four through nine is elected by popular vote, with some officers appointed by faculty. Other extracurricular activities include the popular Glee Club, which gives three concerts a year including an operetta and an annual Middle School operetta. (Some years boys go behind the scenes at the Met.) Boys can elect to work on the literary magazine *The Dawn* (named by Mr. Buckley after *The Salutation of the Dawn*, from the Sanskrit), the Upper School newspaper *The Shield* or join the Environmental Club. Community service activities vary from year to year and there is no hourly requirement.

At Upper School closing exercises the Gold Pin is awarded for academic achievement. There is a first and second honor roll, a student athlete award, as well as individual awards in most subject areas. The Harrison S. Kravis Award is given by the Lewis Eisenberg family in recognition of "progress, citizenship, participation in school activities, generosity of spirit." Four major athletic awards, most of them emphasizing character, effort and sportsmanship, are given.

Every graduating Buckley boy carves his own wooden plaque, which is affixed to the school walls. On her tour one parent noticed that in the sixties the plaques featured the occasional *Playboy* Bunny or peace sign, but by the late seventies returned once again to traditional subjects like sailboats, horses, guns, golf clubs, and shields. Nineties plaques show more diverse interests.

Buckley boys have good manners, excel at sports and speak well in public. Parents say that they are well prepared for the most rigorous secondary schools in the nation: "Buckley is prepping our son for life, with high standards in many ways," an alumnus parent says. Whereas a decade ago nearly every Buckley boy went to boarding school, now almost half go to New York City–area day schools. Deerfield, Hotchkiss and Groton lead the recent boarding school choices; Riverdale, Horace Mann, Collegiate and Trinity are popular day school choices.

Traditions   Friday assemblies, Father-Son Overnight at Camp Sloane in Lakeville, Connecticut, Father-Son Beginners' Breakfast, Father-Son Adventure Dinner, A Day at Yankee Stadium, Grandparents' Day, Book Fair, Buckley Skating Party, fifth grade Medieval Feast, Rhythm Band Assembly, Spring Exhibition and Tea, Glee Club operetta, Field Day, Nativity play, Holiday Concert, Annual Jack Woodruff Memorial Public Speaking Contest, senior class trips to Boston and Washington, D.C., Fathers' Committee softball game vs. Class IX graduates, used clothing and book sale and preview party, Theatre Benefit, alumni party

Publications   Lower School literary magazine: *A World of Stories*
Literary magazine: *The Dawn* (since 1926)
Upper School newspaper: *The Shield*
Yearbook: *Horizons*
Annual report
School and alumni news: *The Buckley Letter*

Community Service Requirement   No hourly requirement; past activities have included volunteering at a food pantry, Clown Care Unit at New York Hospital, annual Central Park cleanup, Ronald McDonald House

Hangouts   The Buckley Gym, EJ's Luncheonette, Duane Reade

The Caedmon School

416 East 80th Street
New York, NY 10021
(212) 879-2296, FAX (212) 879-0627
website: www.caedmonschool.org

Coed
Nursery 2's–6th grade
Not accessible

Carol Gose DeVine, Head of School
Erica Lowen Pels, Co-Director of Admissions
Mary Ann Winograd, Co-Director of Admissions

Birthday Cutoff Children entering the beginners' group must be 3 by December 31
Children entering kindergarten must be 5 by November 1

Enrollment Total enrollment: 195
Nursery 3's places: 35–40, largest point of entry
Kindergarten places: 5–8
Graduating class 2000: 10

Grades Semester system
No letter grades; detailed anecdotal reports 2 times a year and portfolio conference once a year in Elementary; three conferences and one anecdotal report in Early Program (3–5 year olds)
Departmentalization begins in 5th grade

Tuition Range 2001–2002 $8,600 (1/2 day), $13,800 (full day), $16,500 for K–6th grade

Financial Aid/Scholarship 11% of the student body receive some form of aid

Endowment N/A

Diversity 20% students of color

Homework First grade, 20 minutes written work plus reading. Homework increases as children get older

After-School Program   An additional fee is required for all Caedmon after-school programs; open to Caedmon students only. Child minding is available Monday through Friday until 6:00 P.M. The after-school program for 4's–6th grade Monday through Thursday from 3:30 P.M. to 5:30 P.M.; a variety of creative and athletic activities

Clubs for 1st–6th graders meet every Wednesday until 5:30 P.M.

Afterschool instrumental music program: private lessons in piano, classical guitar, violin and voice are available Monday–Friday

Summer Program   None

The Caedmon School was founded in 1962 by a group of parents interested in the philosophy of Maria Montessori; Caedmon offers a "modified Montessori" program. The school is housed in a five-story building and classrooms are bright and airy. The outside courtyard, sheltered from the street, has a safety surface playground. There is a large lunchroom with a full kitchen, which serves hot lunch to everyone.

Head of School Carol DeVine points out that Caedmon differs from the classical Montessori mold in the Early Program because "Caedmon utilizes and provides materials for fantasy play and there is an emphasis on group work and relaxed socialization amongst the children. There are many more differences in the elementary program, especially in the materials used."

An "attitude of compassion," community service, multicultural respect and acceptance are woven into Caedmon's curriculum. Ms. DeVine stresses that "we teach the child, not just the curriculum." Twenty-five percent of the student body is international; many parents work at the U.N. missions. One parent said, "My husband is with the U.N.; we move constantly and coming to New York City was overwhelming. Caedmon became an oasis for our whole family." Parents say that Caedmon is "warm and accommodating; they are very responsive to children's differing rates of development." There is praise for an "experienced, superb teaching staff" and for the "creative, well thought out homework assignments." Caedmon has expanded enrollment in the lower grades; the school population is somewhat smaller in the upper grades.

Getting in: The school has a fall admissions procedure; the application deadline is in December. Applications are processed in the order in which they are received. The application fee is $40.00. Parents are welcome to attend one of the two evening Open Houses held in the fall, or they can attend a morning group tour. After the application is reviewed, a date is arranged for the child to visit the school. Children are seen individually, although parents can join their child in the classroom if separation is difficult. One parent said that the focus is on the child, not the accomplishments of the parents.

Parents: Caedmon parents range from artists to investment bankers. The Board of Trustees has seventeen members and five spaces are reserved for parents with children enrolled in the school. The Parents' Auxiliary is close knit and dedicated. The PA hosts a "Back to School" night at the beginning of the year to introduce parents to their children's teachers and provide an opportunity for new parents to meet each other. An auction fund-raiser is held in March every year. A wine-tasting party for international parents is held in the fall and another in the spring for in-coming parents. Early morning "Coffee and curriculum" workshops are held throughout the year. Parents are encouraged to talk to their child's teacher either directly or on the phone. Formal conferences are held three times each year.

Program: Classes are small and the overall student/teacher ratio is 8:1. The atmosphere is academic but nurturing. Beginners start at two years and nine months; the Early Program is composed of children two and three-quarter to five-years-old and the Elementary Program consists of kindergarten through sixth grade. Specialists work closely with classroom teachers balancing the curriculum with science, French, library/research skills, computer, music, art, gym and community service projects.

The Early Program utilizes mixed-age classrooms and children frequently work together in small groups. The modified Montessori approach emphasizes Montessori materials and activities but also encourages creativity. Children on a full-day schedule have lunch and a nap. The afternoon activities include visits to the science room and library.

In kindergarten, the focus is on language-rich reading and writing curriculum with particular emphasis on basic skills. The math program stresses the use of numbers, words (solving word problems) and graphic measurements. Using manipulatives the students learn concepts and establish a strong foundation for learning more complex skills. Transition prepares five-year-olds for the more teacher-directed and academic demands of Caedmon's Elementary Program. "The teacher really understands that my five-year-old is both a playful child and a budding student," observed one parent.

The Elementary Program offers an integrated curriculum. For example, a social studies class was studying immigration and the students' countries of origin. The music teacher, a former Broadway actor and choreographer, wrote a play along with his class called *Making Tracks in America* with jazz and blues music taken from eighteenth century African-American spirituals and other American musical traditions. In art class, the students created various immigration scenes for the set.

Math is also integrated with other subject matter. Every year, during National Mathematics Month, the entire staff puts together a special all-day math event for the children. A different theme is selected each year with a variety of activities that demonstrate the practical applications of math.

Computer skills begin in kindergarten and the children have access to computers in the computer lab, library and every classroom.

Art and Music at Caedmon are exceptionally strong. Artwork by Caedmon students has been exhibited in the Monmouth County Museum (New Jersey), the Manhattan Children's Museum, WNET Channel 13 Student Arts Festival, WNET Channel 13 Student Arts International Exchange, and many other places. Original musical productions are put on twice a year; children from kindergarten through sixth grade participate.

Popular Secondary School Choices: Brearley, Browning, Birch Wathen Lenox, Calhoun, Chapin, Collegiate, Columbia Grammar & Preparatory School, Convent of the Sacred Heart, Dalton, Dwight, Hewitt, Manhattan Country School, Marymount, New York City Museum School, Park East Middle School, Riverdale, St. David's, Salk School of Science, Trevor Day School, UNIS, York Prep

Traditions: Caedmon Meeting (weekly meeting of entire Elementary community), student musicales, Back to School Night, Elementary apple-picking trip, all-school picnic in Central Park, all-school Thanksgiving feast and the Thanksgiving Book, Caedmon Chorus holiday performance at Lord & Taylor, Holiday Assembly, international parent wine tasting party, fundraising auction, Grandparent/ Special Friend Day, Parent breakfasts, Mathland, upper level overnight trip, annual spring trip to Jones Beach (Elementary), annual spring park day and picnic (Early Program), and new parent cocktail party.

Community Service: Community service is an integral parent of the curriculum in fifth and sixth grades. Students explore issues related to their community service projects through interdisciplinary thematic units of study.

The Calhoun School

Robert L. Beir Lower School
160 West 74th Street
New York, NY 10023
(212) 497-6550 (main number)
(212) 497-6575 (admissions)
FAX (212) 497-6591
website: www.calhoun.org

(2nd grade–12th Grade)
433 West End Avenue
New York, NY 10024
(212) 497-6500 (main number)
(212) 497-6510 (admissions)
FAX (212) 497-6530
website: www.calhoun.org

Coed
Nursery–12th Grade
Not accessible at 160 West 74th Street;
Not fully accessible at 433 West End Avenue

Mr. Steven J. Nelson, Head of School
Ms. Nancy Sherman, Director of Admissions
Ms. Robin M. Otton, Director of Lower School Admissions

Birthday Cutoff   Children entering nursery 3's must be 3 by September 1
Children entering kindergarten must be 5 by September 1

Enrollment   Total enrollment: 570
Nursery 3's places: 46, largest point of entry
Kindergarten places: 12
Graduating class 2001: 35

Grades   Semester system
Letter and number grades begin in 8th grade
Foriegn language begins in 7th grade
Modified departmentalization begins in 2nd grade (2nd through

138

4th graders move in homeroom or "cluster" groups to specialists in science, the arts and physical education.) Full departmentalization begins in 7th grade

Timing of first midterm or final exam varies

Tuition Range   2001–2002 $14,000 to $21,500 nursery–12th grade (includes lunch for 2nd through 12th grades and all materials and books)

Additional fees: for trips (5th–9th grades range from $100–$400–$375)

Tuition plans of 10 monthly payments can be arranged

Financial Aid/Scholarship   20% of the student body receives financial aid

Endowment   N/A

Diversity   9 Prep for Prep students enrolled in 7th through 12th grades as of fall 2000; membership in Early Steps and Faculty Diversity Search; in 1996–98 DeWitt Wallace grant funds were directed to conflict resolution training through Educators for Social Responsibility and the addition of two interns of color to the staff.

Homework   Nursery–1st grade: none
2nd–4th: approximately 15–45 minutes
5th–8th: 1–3 hours
9th–12th: approximately 2–4 hours

After-School Program   Calhoun ASP: a variety of classes offered each school day in both buildings to Pre–K–8th grades from school closing hours until 4:30 P.M. (74th street), 4:45 P.M. (81th street), with an additional extended care option available until 5 P.M. (74th street), 6 P.M. (81st street); activities include karate, science, computer, woodworking, cooking; an additional payment is required

ASP also offers courses for adults including driver's education and CPR

Springdays: a full-day program for children ages 4s–1st grade; half-day for 2nd–4th grade, offered during spring recess

139

Summer Program   Summercare: a six-week day camp program for
children ages 3–7, directed and staffed by members of the Calhoun School faculty; from the third week in June through the
July, 8:30 A.M.–2:30 P.M.

———————

Founded in 1896 as the Jacobi School, Calhoun soon became an
all girls school, and was renamed in 1924 for Head of School Mary
Edwards Calhoun. It became completely coeducational in 1971. Calhoun has always been a forward-looking institution known for its innovative curriculum, individualized attention and small class size. Within
each division of the school, there are few walls or doors and no rows of
desks, but rather areas assigned to each discipline. Although the tone
is informal, there is a strong underlying academic structure. Parents
say, "Calhoun prepares students well for college because they have
learned how to be independent thinkers and achievers."

Calhoun has two locations: Since 1989, preschool through first
grade have been housed in the Robert L. Beir Building on West 74th
street. Since 1975 grades two through twelve have been located in a
modern building at West 81st Street and West End Avenue. The
school is organized into four divisions, each with its own director.

Parents have a high regard for the teaching staff at Calhoun.
Parents describe Calhoun as a community consisting of administrators, teachers, children and parents. Teachers and administrators are
called by their first names. Under the inspired leadership of Dr. Neen
Hunt, a gifted educator and former head of school, Calhoun attracted
a dedicated and caring staff, some of whom have developed its innovative award-winning curriculum. Faculty incentives such as the Professional Development Program, a grant from the Edward Ford
Foundation and the Faculty Enrichment Grant allow teachers at Calhoun to continue to grow and learn. Parents say, "At Calhoun children
see good values that are reinforced by example." Current Head of
School, Steven J. Nelson, came to Calhoun with experience in a
variety of private school and college settings, and with a deep belief in
the value of a progressive education. In describing his philosophy, Mr.
Nelson says, "We need to think about education in America in a new
way . . . We should identify and nurture the rich mix of intelligences
that accompany each child through the schoolhouse door. We should
value the abstract painting as much as we value the calculation of com-
pound interest."

Getting in: Parents interested in learning more about Calhoun can attend an open house in the fall before applying. The application fee is $45. There are some short essay questions on the application, such as "Briefly describe your child's personality . . . distinctive qualities, temperament . . . special interests." The school views the ERB as just one component used to evaluate the match between the child and the school. Calhoun selects students with a broad range of interests and talents who have the potential to be focused and self-motivated and the intelligence necessary to meet the demands of their program. A kindergarten applicant's school visit is low-keyed, its aim is to get a sense of the child's personality and interests and to assess facility with basic skills and concepts. Parents meet with admissions personnel to see if Calhoun's philosophy and parental expectations for their child's education are compatible. The preschool program is very popular and the largest point of entry. There are some spaces each year for new four year olds, and space also opens up at the kindergarten level. Calhoun maintains a strong sibling policy.

Parents: Socially, Calhoun is low-key. The primary focus is always on the child, not the parent or social scene. Calhoun counts on parents to be active in their child's educational life, and the school in turn is very supportive of parents. There are frequent conferences, and parents are invited to call or visit when they need to. Annual Parents Association activities include the Lower School Halloween Fest Book Fair at Barnes & Noble, the PA Spring Carnival and an evening lecture series. Some of the more informal events for parents include Wednesday evening volleyball games and theatre parties, some of which, like *The Nutcracker*, are for families. Many parents say they feel a connection to Calhoun even after their children have graduated, and they continue to attend school events.

Program: At the Robert L. Beir Lower School building (preschool through first grade), classrooms are bright and airy. A strong, cohesive team of teachers collaborate to create an impressive curriculum which fully integrates art, music, theater, science, computers, and physical education. The collaborative, interactive model of education is stressed, the goal is the development of each student's self-esteem through validation of efforts and achievement. Lower School Director Kathleen Clinesmith has worked with young children for many years and is a strong proponent of Calhoun's collaborative learning philosophy.

Separation is handled gently on an individual basis: All children have a homeroom "cluster" area and a primary or "cluster" teacher; they travel from this cluster area to other rooms and specialists for certain subjects, depending on their grade level. Children in kindergarten and first grade have language arts, math, science, social studies, block building, cooking, art, music, shop, library, computer, drama, physical education, theater and creative movement. Children take recess on the terrace or go to the park each day. Parents say, "Creativity and socialization and the three R's are all stressed in the Lower School." Discipline is recognized as an inner process that is developed with the aid of adults. Calhoun teachers are sensitive to the differing rates of social and emotional development in children. A parent said, "Many are creative kids who march to their own tune."

A broad based approach to teaching reading is employed, making use of Whole Language, phonics, and skill-based instruction techniques. In addition, an innovative program integrates children's creative writing and music. First graders, whose classrooms are on the top two floors of the Beir building, continue to gain spelling skills while given the freedom to use invented spelling. Throughout the school year, first through fourth graders proudly publish their own original books and research papers, handbound and illustrated by the author, with all spelling corrected. First graders continue to follow a curriculum stressing hands-on learning, problem-solving and teamwork. Students begin a year-long study of Central Park. Weekly visits to the park provide experiences which are further developed back in the classroom, including detailed topographical maps of the park, observational drawings of its plants, animals, statues and structures, and classification of the various leaves and rocks that are collected.

Second through twelfth grades are located in the West End Avenue and 81st Street building, where each of the three divisions has its own floor. Second through fourth graders (the elementary school at 81st Street) are divided by grade level into groups or clusters of twelve to fifteen students, and assigned an advisor. They travel as a cluster, to other classroom and activity areas within the school. (Calhoun's cluster advisory system changes somewhat in the Middle and Upper Schools, where clusters are formed across the grades and students follow increasingly individualized schedules.) In keeping with Calhoun's philosophy of learning as a shared, connected experience, there are few high walls or doors separating cluster areas. Table groupings replace the traditional desks in rows.

Joyce Blyn, Elementary School Director, has more than twenty years of experience as a teacher and administrator. In her view, the teacher is the facilitator, motivating children and providing them with the tools they will need to become lifelong learners.

Once again an eclectic approach is used to improve reading skills. Small reading groups are the norm. A reading specialist and a part-time learning consultant are on staff. Students engage in creative and journal writing and learn the writing process. Research writing skills are introduced in first grade and developed further in successive grades. In third grade students complete a paper on a chosen topic. By the end of the eighth grade, students are expected to have strong skills in research writing. They choose topics and write individual formal thesis papers.

Math skills in mechanics and abstract thinking are taught in creative hands-on classes in which students participate fully, even writing their own math word problems to share with other math students. Homework assignments reinforce skills as well as challenge students. Critical thinking and problem solving encourage divergent thinking.

The school recognizes the different talents, abilities and learning styles of individual children. The curriculum is flexible enough to address itself to varying developmental needs. Parents say there is always an appropriate level of challenge. A parent with a child whose reading level in kindergarten was at least three years above that of his classmates spoke of the expert and sensitive way in which that child was always challenged and excited by the work he was given while never having to be isolated from his peers.

Though present in the earlier grade levels, Calhoun's interdisciplinary approach is most clearly obvious, beginning at the elementary level, when the Lower School literature is integrated with social studies, science and other subjects. The artful interweaving of different subjects into a cohesive whole is the hallmark of the program, evident at each grade level.

Second graders learn about the settlement of Manhattan through a special project with the New York Historical Society. Multicultural contributions of early settlers are demonstrated through literature, art, music and cooking. The "Connections" curriculum takes third graders on a year-long study their of contemporary urban environment, covering four basic areas of transportation, city geology-geography, methods of communication, and neighborhoods. Further connections are made with "sister cities" throughout the world. From reading *The*

Cricket in Times Square to visiting the Transit Museum, learning is always experiential and interdisciplinary. As they read *Coming to the Americas as a Slave, Letters from Rifka, All of a Kind Family* and *African American Folktales*, fourth graders learn why we are called "a nation of immigrants." Children enjoy modeling the designs and pottery of Native Americas and preparing and eating Pilgrim recipes. Dramatic presentations, trips to the Tenement Museum and to Ellis Island, guest speakers and the creation of a mural depicting contributions of numerous immigrant groups both past and present are but some of the year's highlights.

Terry Costin, Middle School Director, came to Calhoun after twenty-two years at Horace Mann School and has spent his entire career working with Middle School age children. Terry "grew up" as an educator in the early '70's progressive era in education. He describes the process at Calhoun as "intimate in nature," and he values "the school's commitment to the individual child, to community and to diversity."

The Middle School at Calhoun is composed of grades five through eight. The integrated English and social studies curriculum for fifth and sixth graders was developed by two Calhoun teachers and won recognition from the National Conference of Teachers of English. "Tapping Our Roots" and "Stories Old and New" represent the two-year cycle in which students examine the roots of Western civilization and read the literature of different ethnic groups, including Greek, Roman, Egyptian and Islamic. The course description says "Students discover similar motifs, plot devices and types of characters that reappear in old and new literature, no matter what its cultural origin." Units are enhanced by related activities: art, music, drama, creative writing, library assignments and/or computer study. For instance, the art program, complementing English and social studies curricula, structures projects in stained glass and illumination (fifth/sixth grade medieval studies) and impressionistic landscapes (seventh grade European history).

Eighth graders write a formal thesis. Each part of the research process is graded, and after the finished product is presented, further revision may be done. An alumna who went on to Stanford University says that papers at college are easier than those at Calhoun. The Middle School math curriculum is viewed as a process that extends over the four years of the division. At the eighth grade level, homogeneous or ability grouping begins. Advanced math students are given first year algebra. Two math/science teachers at Calhoun have won recognition: Middle/Upper School science teacher John Roeder, who has been at Calhoun for twenty-five years, won the National Tandy Technology Scholar award for excellence in science teaching. Middle School math teacher Phil Bender earns praise for his innovative conceptual math program. One project in applied math involves baseball statistics; another uses a trip to the Bronx Zoo as an opportunity to collect and process data. Each year a number of Calhoun students are accepted to the specialized math and science public high schools (see pages 476–478, *infra*).

Students begin formal instruction in modern language, electing either French or Spanish in the fifth grade. The program continues into the Upper School through advanced literature, AP and conversation courses.

Calhoun's computer program spans all grade levels. In the Lower School, students use graphics and word processing programs, in addition to educational games which reinforce math, language, and problem solving skills. Elementary school students (grades 2–4) use the computer as a tool to enhance the curriculum in all subject areas. Children create their own multimedia projects and interactive programs, using HyperStudio and Microworlds (LOGO programming) By the end of fourth grade all children complete a keyboarding program. All fifth and sixth graders continue with keyboarding, application software and LOGO programming. Sixth graders are introduced to PhotoShop. Projects, including multimedia presentations, remain integrated with the interdisciplinary social studies/English curriculum. Seventh graders learn Excel and advanced programming skills with LEGO LOGO Robotics. All eighth graders complete a basic Upper School course, which includes word processing, database, spreadsheet, desktop publishing and image scanning. Upper School students can choose from many advanced electives including multimedia programming, desktop publishing and designing and creating Web pages. Several Calhoun Upper School students have parlayed their computer expertise into well-paying summer jobs.

The Upper School at Calhoun consists of grades nine through twelve. Parents describe the Upper School student body at Calhoun as diverse; students with different strengths and interests as well as different backgrounds make up the relatively small classes.

Loretta Ryan, Upper School Director, has been at Calhoun for fifteen years. An anthropologist and formerly a member of the social studies department, she has promoted diversity of all kinds and introduced an inclusive two-year world history program in the Upper

145

School. As Academic Dean for the school, she works to preserve the school's long-standing goal of offering students a strong academic program and personal support.

Early fall activities for all ninth graders include an orientation day prior to the official beginning of classes, and a two-day overnight with peer leaders and faculty in late September. Peer leaders, specially chosen and trained seniors, also lead weekly discussions with small groups of ninth graders throughout the year, in a course called Life Skills.

The cluster advisory system continues in the Upper School. Parents find that it is an excellent and easy way to keep communication open and consistent. Beginning in the Middle School and continuing through the senior year students are scheduled once a week to meet individually with their cluster advisors. For graduation, 21 credits are required, including three in science, one-half in computer science and three in modern language. There are, in addition, the following non-credit requirements: four years of physical education and sixty hours of community service.

Classes are mostly discussion-based seminars. Parents say it is impossible for students to be lost in the shuffle because classes are small (an average of fifteen per class), and students are always active participants. Parents praised the exceptional English and social studies departments. Qualified students are invited to do Honors projects or participate in weekly Honors discussion groups. The school offers AP English, Biology and Spanish classes, and teachers assist students preparing to take AP Calculus and U.S. History.

A Senior Masterworks Program allows students to design their own projects for half or one credit in the subject of their choice, culminating in an oral or written presentation or performance before a Masterworks Committee. Sample projects have included play directing, a personal family history of the Holocaust, a collection of short stories, a sculpture, a dance demonstration/performance and vocal recital.

Calhoun participates in the Network of Complementary Schools, which offers a three-week exchange program for students as well as faculty at other innovative schools throughout the United States and Canada. For example, students may attend a school on a Navajo reservation in Arizona, an arts program in Interlochen, Michigan, or Oklahoma, an outdoor survival program in the Colorado mountains, or they can study architecture in a San Francisco school. Through Network, select students are also given the opportunity to attend a Multicultural

Leadership Workshop in Toronto. In the past, Calhoun has been host to students from the Navajo reservation, from Seattle, Washington and from a small rural town in Kansas. While on an exchange visit at a school in San Francisco, an Upper School English teacher developed a curriculum in Latino literature, now used at Calhoun.

Upper School students have a student lounge and, from tenth grade on, may leave school during a free period or during lunch. An active Student Government Executive Council is made up of class officers from each class and the elected president, vice-president, secretary and treasurer. The student government has, among its many activities, sponsored students at the AIDS Dance-a-thon and raised money for UNICEF.

The MCC (Multicultural Committee) organizes assemblies and discussions on cross-cultural issues. The Queer-Straight Partnership and the AIDS Awareness Committee also raises consciousness about social concerns. The school has an environmental concerns club: SAFE; the Umbrella Club, where political and philosophical issues are discussed, and a film club. Calhoun also has a forensics team whose members compete at the state and national levels each year in solo/duet acting or public-speaking formats.

There are two Upper Middle School drama productions each year held in the auditorium at the Robert L. Beir building. Café Calhoun, sponsored by student government, is a showcase for Upper School student talent. Students may work on the staffs of the school newspaper, literary magazine or yearbook.

Varsity sports include league-winning volleyball basketball and soccer teams, in addition to softball, tennis and sailing.

In their weekly College Seminar, second semester juniors begin discussing the process of choosing and applying to colleges. This seminar continues through the middle of the senior year, and individual consultation continues until acceptances are received and final choices must be made.

Calhoun is a charter member of the Cum Laude Society and annually elects outstanding seniors for membership. Numerous awards are presented at Class Day, Athletic Awards Assembly and Commencement. There are named memorial awards in many subject areas as well as athletic awards. Awards recognize academic strengths, character, integrity, maturity and service. Students can also graduate with distinction in given disciplines. Calhoun graduates go on to a variety of colleges, reflecting the diversity within the graduating class.

Popular College Choices   Brown University, Wesleyan University, Colgate, Kenyon, Skidmore, New York University, Vassar College, Boston University, Cornell and Sarah Lawrence.

Traditions   Harvest Festival (annual school Thanksgiving celebration with activities organized around a common theme), Fall and Spring MS/US dramatic productions. Café Calhoun (Upper School talent show), Book Fair, Spring Carnival, Cluster and Grade Trip Days (special activities for grades 2–12), Wednesday evening volleyball for parents, alumni basketball (alternate Mondays), Speakers Program, artist-in-residence Program, annual trustees' fund-raising event, Curriculum Expo (which includes the Annual Arts Festival), Class Day, Athletic Awards Assembly, Commencement exercises

Community Service Requirement   60 hours

Publications   Newspaper: *The Issue*
Literary magazine: *Antithesis*
Newsletter/alumni publication: *Calhoun Chronicle*
Yearbook

Hangouts   Riverside Park, student lounge, the plaza on 81st Street outside Calhoun, neighborhood coffee and pizza shops, Barnes & Noble Bookstore

The Cathedral School

1047 Amsterdam Avenue
New York, NY 10025–1702
(212) 316-7500, FAX (212) 316-7558
www.cathedralnyc.org
e-mail: ethurber@cathedralnyc.org

Coed
Kindergarten–8th grade
Not accessible

Phillip G. Foote, Headmaster
Edith Thurber, Director of Admission

Uniform   Flexible dress code: white blouses/shirts, navy, khaki or gray skirts, pants, shorts (in warm weather)

Birthday Cutoff   Children entering kindergarten must be 5 by September 30

Enrollment   Total enrollment: 267
Kindergarten places: 24–28
Graduating class 2000: 22

Grades   The Lower School (kindergarten–grade 4) is on a semester system
The Upper School (grades 5–8) is on a trimester system
Letter grades begin in 5th grade
Full departmentalization begins in 5th grade

Tuition Range   2001–2002 $17,500 to $18,000, kindergarten–eighth grade
Fees are included in the tuition

Financial Aid/Scholarship   40% of the student body receive some form of aid based on financial need

Endowment $3,100,000

After-School Program   The school has an extended day enrichment program for Cathedral School Lower School students. In addition, the Cathedral of St. John the Divine's A.C.T. program, open to all students, offers after-school and holiday programs. A.C.T. is open to students from other schools but Cathedral students have priority when registering; an additional payment is required

Summer Program   A.C.T. uses the 13-acre Cathedral close for the summer program; a variety of creative and athletic activities are offered for an additional payment

---

The Cathedral School was founded in 1901 to provide choristers for the Cathedral of St. John the Divine. Now a fully coeducational independent school, the tradition of providing the choristers for the Cathedral is still one of the school's unique features. When the strains of evensong float out of the gothic cathedral over the 13-acre close of flowering shrubs and herb gardens, shade trees and strolling peacocks, Cathedral School seems like a place out of time, yet this school is very much in sync with modern life and the latest educational practices. One of the best kept secrets on the Upper West side, Cathedral School is a vibrant community. Its growing popularity is due to not only its extraordinary location but also a strong academic program, an enthusiastic new head of school, and a diverse and talented pool of students.

Phillip G. Foote, former headmaster of the Horace Mann School in New York and the Greenhill School in Dallas (which became the top school in Dallas during Mr. Foote's tenure), was appointed headmaster in 1995. It appears to be a good fit.

Getting in: Parents can attend information-gathering open houses in the fall. They have ample opportunity to observe classes, and special events and ask questions of school administrators and parents. The School retains an affiliation with the Episcopal Church but admits students of all faiths. The ERB is required for admission. Parents come for a tour and applicants are interviewed individually at the school. Cathedral School has always valued diversity and a full 40% of students receive financial aid. The school roster reads like a mellifluous mix of nationalities. Entering kindergarten and first grade students visit the school in late May. All new students attend a one-day orientation at school before opening day.

Parents: The parent body at Cathedral School represents a hip cross-section of city life and includes some prominent writer/editors, well-known actors, academics from Columbia University, professionals, musicians, and artists. Parents value the inclusiveness of the community and everyone is made to feel welcome. Though most parents work, the Parents Association is very active and sponsors fundraisers, book fairs, class dinners, workshops, picnics and produces an impressively literate monthly newsletter.

Program: Classes throughout the school are small. The atmosphere is academic but nurturing and the curriculum is multicultural and experience-based. The Lower School is composed of grades kindergarten through four, and the Upper School is composed of grades five through eight. Each division has its own academic director, faculty, schedule and special facilities. Lower School students, working in a self-contained classroom setting, master basic skills in the three R's and science. French or Spanish is introduced in kindergarten. Whenever possible, teachers in different departments join together to write and teach an interdisciplinary curriculum so that students see connections between subject areas. For example, when Lower School students study the history and culture of Native Americans in social studies, they visit Manitoga in Garrison, New York, a living archeological site replicating an Indian village. They read Native American myths and folk tales and create their own, make Indian artifacts in art, write and perform original plays in music class and study indigenous animals in science.

Cathedral School is currently implementing a $500,000 technology initiative creating a technological structure that is curriculum driven and promotes active learning and critical thinking. The school has a T1 line and a new school-wide computer network. All classrooms have at least one computer and printer. The computer lab has 16 networked Power PC's; the library has five networked computers. The Upper School science lab is equipped with four networked Power-Book computers and one desktop computer. Recent projects include: a multimedia research project on ancient Rome, The International Children's Literature Project, the Glove Science Environment Project, and the Mighty Math M&M Internet Project.

Art is integrated into the curriculum wherever possible and student artwork is prominently displayed throughout the school. Students work in traditional media as well as nontraditional art forms like mosaic, architecture, and book-making. For good reason, the Medieval Studies curriculum at Cathedral School is the best in the city. Students tour every inch of the Cathedral and seventh graders celebrate the period's art, music, English and Latin in a Medieval

Evensong, held in the Great Choir of the Cathedral of St. John the Divine. They carry personal coat-of-arms banners and cardboard gargoyles, wear period costumes, recite original sonnets of courtly love, and sing and perform a regal dance that they choreograph themselves.

The interdisciplinary music curriculum emphasizes fun and appreciation. Children learn musical concepts, songs, instruments, movement, and the music of different cultures. The Suzuki method of violin instruction begins in first grade. Approximately 25 fifth through eighth grade boys and girls are choristers. All fourth graders are auditioned for the choir, a very selective process; however, joining the choir is optional. Choristers receive superior musical training, a stipend towards tuition and a wealth of performing experience. Student choristers recently performed at Shea Stadium for the opening game, at Harvard University, and at the memorial services for Jim Henson, creator of the Muppets, and jazz-great Louis Armstrong.

The physical education department uses Cathedral School's two gymnasiums and two outdoor playgrounds, as well as the adjacent playing fields in Morningside Park. Major playground and library renovations were recently completed. Intramural and varsity sports, both single-sex and coed, include basketball, soccer, softball and volleyball.

Hot lunch (a salad bar and sandwiches are also available) is served family style with mixed age groupings at tables; grace is led by student volunteers, including kindergartners, and sung by all. Older students take turns as waiters and servers, helping the younger students. On specific days throughout the year lunch features traditional ethnic cuisines such as African-American, Caribbean, Chinese, Greek and Jewish.

Every Friday morning Lower School assembly is held in the Common Room. One parent said assembly reminds him of why he chose Cathedral School in the first place: "The spirit, the mix of interests, the obvious involvement of the teachers." The assembly room overflows with parents who act as both audience and participants, we were told.

The Upper School at Cathedral (grades 5–8) is departmentalized. Each student carries a full program in English, social studies, math, science, French or Spanish and Latin. Latin is required in the seventh and eighth grades in addition to French or Spanish. For the last few years, Cathedral School's top Latin students have won first place in a New York City public and private school competition. In the Cathedral School Newsletter, Latin teacher Dr. John Vitale wrote a compelling treatise about the relevance of studying classical Latin today (and not just as a vocabulary booster for the SAT's).

Students visit the cathedral twice each week for services led by the chaplain. While the services concentrate on stories, feasts and values derived from the Judaeo-Christian tradition in the West, students are also exposed to the world's great religious traditions. For example, first graders and their parents built a succah for the Jewish holiday of Succoth and celebrated a multiethnic Passover seder. Students at the school represent a variety of religious traditions, including Buddhist and Muslim, or atheist. "The goal is to affirm the religious tradition of every child." Parents praise the spirituality which infuses learning at Cathedral School. Each fifth grade student works with the Chaplain in an experiential course called "Introduction to Spirituality" which is intentionally non-denominational.

Students say they wish the school had a high school so they could stay on another four years.

High school placement counseling emphasizes self-awareness and a search for a school that would be appropriate for each individual's talents and interests.

Popular Secondary School Choices   Friends Seminary, Trinity School, Riverdale Country Day School, Horace Mann School, Stuyvesant High School, LaGuardia High School of Music and Art and the Performing Arts, Fieldston School

Community Service Requirement   Students develop projects to support Cathedral outreach and environmental programs care for Cathedral Close or raise funds for outside organizations; Inspired by the twentieth anniversary of Earth Day in 1990, sixth grade students formed an environmental group called L.I.S.T.E.N. (Loving Interest to Save the Environment) which emphasizes recycling

Traditions   New parent dinners, all-school picnic on the grounds, class dinners, an annual fundraising auction, theater parties, Arts Festival, Earth Day, Alumni Day, Grandparents Day, Class Reps, Spring Fair, Field Day, Upper School Camp Trip, Chorister Tours, Peace Tree Ceremony, Passover Seder, Kwaanza Assembly, Eighth Grade Musical, Eighth Grade Pinning Ceremony, Eighth Grade Class Day, Chorister Divestiture and graduation

The Chapin School

100 East End Avenue
New York, NY 10028
(212) 744-2335
website: www.chapin.edu

All girls
Kindergarten–12th grade
Limited accessibility (elevators and stairs)

Ms. Sandra Theunick, Head of School
Mrs. Nicole Donnelly, Director of Upper School Admissions
Ms. Elizabeth Ferenzi, Director of Lower School Admissions

Uniform   Lower School: light green or dark green jumper, white blouse
Middle School: dark green pleated skirt with white shirt, khaki pants
Upper School: dress Gordon or dark green kilt or skirt, white shirt or blouse, khaki pants
Uniforms can be purchased from the Corey Uniform Exchange

Birthday Cutoff   Children entering kindergarten must be 5 by October 1

Enrollment   Total enrollment: 660
Kindergarten places: 50
Graduating class 2000: 39

Grades   Semester system in the Lower and Middle School
Trimester system in the Upper School
Kindergarten–3rd grade: detailed progress reports
Classes 4–12: letter grades and comments
Departmentalization begins in 4th grade
First final exam in 7th grade

Tuition Range   2001–2002 $18,600 to $19,300, kindergarten–12th grade
Additional fees: for books, lunch and school bus, approximately $700 to $1,800 (less for older students who no longer take the

154

school bus)
School bus available for K–6; cost depends on type of service

Financial Aid/Scholarship $1,270,975 in tuition aid for 16% of the
student body in school year 1999–2000

Endowment $34 million

Diversity   The school welcomes applications from Early Steps,
A Better Chance Students, Albert G. Oliver Program and Prep for
Prep

Homework   Class 1: 20 minutes 1–2 times per week
Class 2: 20–30 minutes
Class 3: 30–40 minutes
Class 4: 20 minutes per subject (average 3 subjects)
Classes 5–8: approximately 2–3 hours spent on an average of 4
subjects, depending on grade level
Classes 9–12: 3 hours

After-School Program   The Clubhouse is an after-school program
at the Brearley and Chapin Schools that provides a variety of
classes for students in kindergarten through third grade, Monday
through Friday. There is a play period before class when the girls
are given a snack or, on Friday, lunch.
The school oversees the organization of various activities in fine
arts, computer science and physical education for Middle and
Upper School students
Middle School intramural program
Green and Gold team competition (girls in classes 4–12 at Chapin
are either Green or Gold)
AAIS League interscholastic competition
Elective offerings in both the Middle and Upper Schools

Summer Program   June Jamboree, 2 week summer camp

The Chapin School was founded by Maria Bowen Chapin in 1901
as an elementary school called "Miss Chapin's School for Girls." After
the death of Miss Chapin, in 1934, it became The Chapin School, Ltd.

Throughout the years Chapin has had strong leadership: Miss Ethel Grey Stringfellow, headmistress for twenty-four years, was succeeded in 1959 by Mildred J. Berendsen, who, after leading Chapin into the nineties, retired after thirty-four years in 1993. Ms. Sandra Theunick was named head in July 1993.

In the 1920s and 30s, Miss Chapin's School groomed New York's young women to take their place in society. At that time, there were no afternoon classes. Some girls had great academic potential, and some less; classes were designated "general" or "college," depending on the aspirations of the individual.

Chapin in the nineties has an excellent academic reputation and sends its graduates on to the very top colleges throughout the country, but the tone of the school remains decidedly traditional. A parent told us "We wanted a place where our daughter would feel valued and loved. They care about keeping our girls sweet." And she added, "They highlight what she does well."

A major building program was recently completed. Improvements to the school included an additional gym, new science labs, more classroom space and new dance, art and computer facilities. Additional construction completed in 1998 includes: a two-floor library/multimedia center, a new gymnasium, a drama classroom/black box theatre and a foreign language lab. The greenhouse, outdoor play yard art studios and dining room were also renovated and a third kindergarten space was added.

Sandra Theunick, current Head of School was formerly head of school at the Stuart Country Day School in Princeton, N.J. Parents find Ms. Theunick a mix of the traditional and contemporary, committed to women's studies, forward thinking, but very academic, not trendy. When asked about the importance of single sex education Mrs. Theunick responded: "It's not yet an even playing field for women . . . We give them [girls] experience and strength; nobody can tell you 'You can't do it' if you've done it before."

Spring 1998 marked the official opening of the new library called The Annenberg Center for Learning and Research. An outdoor play-roof was converted to create this "Titanic" space which features port-hole windows and a grand staircase. The library has a multi-media center with capabilities for video-conferencing, private study rooms and in one section—plush purple armchairs! On previous tours The Chapin School felt like a renovated mansion; the effect of the current renovation is like taking down the heavy drapery and letting in the light.

Modernization is underway in other areas of the school as well: In 1998 the Upper School at Chapin voted to add Gap khaki pants to the school uniform, supplanting the Gordon Plaid kilt. The traditional Friday Morning Prayers have been updated to include recognition of other cultures, while retaining the name "Prayers." The girls now have a part in designing the program on Fridays which reflects the diversity within the school community.

One result of a wide scale strategic planning initiative to re-evaluate Chapin's mission for its graduates was a mandate to create a comprehensive Life Skills program. In addition to a rigorous academic focus, students in kindergarten through twelfth grade now address such issues as effective communication and leadership, self-awareness, respect for differences, and personal wellness.

Extensive research that included a review of existing data as well as input from students, alumnae, faculty and parents, launched the Life Skills Committee which has begun a successful process of reshaping life at the school. Two outgrowths of this committee are 1) Appointment of a full time coordinator of counseling services and life skills education who oversees the social and emotional growth and health of the school. 2) The introduction of a Peer Leadership program which prepares a select group of twelfth graders to counsel ninth graders.

Getting In: Parents don't have to apply in order to tour Chapin. Prospective kindergarten parents meet in a group with the Lower School head in the Reception Room for a short talk. Each family is given the tour individually by a parent tour guide and interviewed by the Director of Lower School Admissions. Parents return with their child for a play group interview during which Ms. Theunick and an Upper School student answer questions. Every applicant receives a plant from Chapin's greenhouse. After admissions decisions have been made, a wait list is maintained. The wait-list letter informs parents how to notify the admissions office of their continued interest in The Chapin School.

Parent body: The Chapin parent body is very involved and supportive of the school. The school, in turn, is supportive of parents: "There is total emphasis on the whole child; kindness and warmth pervade the Lower School. They are sensitive to individual needs and are concerned when there is a divorce or sickness in a family," parents say. "They are interested in making life easier for parents."

Chapin is also social in the traditional sense. "You would never dress informally for a school event," we were told although we noted that khakis and hair clips have replaced suits and headbands at drop-off and pick-up. The school now hosts a reception in the fall for parents in each division with faculty attending.

Parent involvement is welcomed. Parents with a particular skill or interest are invited to share it with the class. In one kindergarten class, for instance, parents were invited to celebrate the Japanese holiday "Girls Day" with rice cookies and tea.

Program: The Lower School consists of kindergarten through class 3. Separation is handled gradually. By the second week the whole kindergarten group is staying until 2 P.M. Monday through Thursday and until 12:45 on Friday. Parents had praise for the kindergarten teachers' warmth and skill. The days have a predictable structure, which gives the girls a sense of security: They know what to expect. Attention is paid to students' different learning styles. Although traditional in tone, there is a lot of creativity in the classroom. Art projects are used to enhance units of study. For example, a kindergarten group built its own solar system with tinfoil stars and plaster of Paris planets. As one parent said, "These are sophisticated projects; there's no macaroni and glue here." Another commented, "It's very well rounded. Activities are transformed; the doll corner or blocks might be changed into a restaurant or doctor's office for dramatic play." The Macmillian/McGraw Hill Program (with workbooks) focuses on both expressive and receptive language as well as reading and writing readiness. Each letter sound is reinforced in other activities: art, cooking, literature. Independent decision making is fostered.

Manipulative materials and everyday experiences are used to teach math concepts. Girls go out of their homerooms for music, dance, science, computer and library, as well as physical education including gymnastics.

Classes 1 through 3 stay until 3:00 P.M. each day except Friday when dismissal is at 12:50. The curriculum is a continuum, each year building upon previous experiences. In Class 1 reading, writing, spelling and oral expression are emphasized using both phonetic and sight word instruction. Creative writing begins with the girls keeping journals in which they record their poems and stories. Class 2 and 3 students begin expository writing and research. Work is published, bound and illustrated. Class 3 girls participate in a strong writing program emphasizing creativity and clarity of expression as well as reading with an emphasis on critical inferential thinking and critical analysis.

Where possible social studies is integrated with language and performing arts. Social studies in Class 1 includes a unit on Women in Herstory in which role models who have faced challenges and been successful are studied. Second graders studying India visited a Hindu temple, made curry and had lunch at an Indian restaurant. Another unit in Class 2 focuses on China, integrating many disciplines. The girls read Chinese folk tales and try their hand at writing in a similar style. A visit to The China Institute corresponded with Chinese New Year. A Chinese watercolorist and calligrapher taught her skills to the class. Symmetry was studied in mathematics using Chinese paper cutouts. In Class 3 the girls construct a Mayan town and sew cross-stitch pillows, write diaries, and visit the Tenement Museum and a Victorian brownstone. Class 3 girls also work under the guidance of members of the staff of the Metropolitan Opera to write, compose and perform an original opera.

Throughout classes in the Lower School, mathematics continues to be taught using an array of manipulatives and concrete objects, and focusing on basic operations and problem solving. The students practice many life skills such as measurement, time-telling and understanding money. Homework begins in Class 1. Multiplication, division and fractions are studied in Class 3. Use of the computer lab is an integral component of the curriculum with lessons in a new computer lab as well as the availability of computers in each classroom. The students learn keyboarding, to create a database, to word-process, to program, and to illustrate/animate.

Traditions that persist in the Lower School are Teddy Bear Day, Hat Day and Sock Day: You bring your own from home or make one.

Middle School at Chapin includes Class 4 through Class 7. Again, the English and history/geography curricula are coordinated where possible, and studio art is integrated with other subject areas. Clear and expressive writing is stressed, and writing skills are reinforced. Classes 4 through 7 meet weekly to put out one annual edition of the Middle School literary magazine, which is called *The Cog*. Class 7 is introduced to Shakespeare with *A Midsummer Night's Dream*. The study of foreign language begins in Class 5 with French or Spanish. Latin is introduced in Class 7. Social studies units in Middle School cover U.S. geography and Native Americans, a study of ancient and medieval civilizations and American history. In Class 7 there is an immigration project in which each student does individual research on a specific country.

Science highlights: Several classes at Chapin work in the greenhouse and Class 4 does a project on weather using Chapin's weather station. Formal health education begins in Class 1 with a unit on nutrition. Class 6 offers an introduction to biology that covers all the systems of the body, including reproductive, and the effects of drugs, alcohol and tobacco on the human body. At the end of Class 6 students go on "an intensive three-day field trip, an experience that focuses on environmental science."

Beginning in Class 5 girls go to nearby Asphalt Green for outdoor sports once a week. Field hockey, soccer, softball, track and swimming are offered. Afternoon electives in physical education are available for Classes 5–7 including fencing and gymnastics. Chapin girls are separated into the Green and Gold teams for intramural competition culminating in an entire day of competition at Bear Mountain in May known as Field Day. Interscholastic competition begins in Class 5 with gymnastics, in Class 6 with soccer, track and swimming, and broadens in Class 7 to include basketball, fencing and volleyball. The number of different sports offered and access to outdoor playing fields increases in the Upper School, and Chapin has several strong interscholastic teams.

Extracurricular activities in the Middle School include chess club, computer club, intramural and interscholastic sports teams, model rocketry, the literary magazine, readers' club, puppetry, art, drama, dance, music, debating and science. In addition, self-government begins in the Middle School.

The Upper School at Chapin consists of Classes 8–12. Chapin's Upper School remains "a caring, close-knit community" with "a shift in ninth and tenth grades as some girls leave for boarding schools or coed schools." Sixteen academic credits are required for graduation. Most students complete more than twenty-two. There are sixteen AP's offered, including art history, French literature, calculus I and II and physics. For Upper School students the Individual Study Option, Interschool courses and a residential term away (abroad, Vermont, or Maine) add breadth as well as depth to Chapin's curriculum.

Multicultural perspectives are explored in the Class 8 Asian and African History which covers the cultures of Japan, China, India and Africa and the Americas. English students contrast and compare a Japanese novel to Shakespeare's *Romeo and Juliet*. A new elective called The African-American Experience is offered.

Tenth graders are required to take an English course called "Self Discovery: a Thematic Approach to Literature and Writing" in which students read literature from many different cultures. Juniors and seniors can choose from a variety of English electives including "Southern Voices" (Toni Morrison, Josephine Humphreys, *et al.*), "The Urban Scene" and "The Lost Eden." History electives include "Women of the World," an introduction to comparative religion. and "European History."

The Upper School curriculum includes a Class 9 unit entitled "Urban Study." Class 10 attends an Interschool conference on environmental issues. Class 11 travels to Washington, D.C., where they visit the Holocaust Museum in addition to the usual sites, and Class 12 explores the New York City art world.

Physics, chemistry and biology are offered in the Upper School, with AP courses available for juniors and seniors. Students in the Upper School take algebra, geometry and trigonometry with calculus A and B offered to juniors and seniors.

In the Upper School, Chapin students continue active participation in studio art, dance, drama and music with opportunity for advanced work along with a wide variety of electives. For serious artists there is a portfolio course in preparation for the AP Studio Art Program, and there are courses in photography and multimedia studies as well. For drama students there is a playwright's workshop for Classes 10–12, and a course called "The Uses of Enchantment." The Drama Club involves all areas of theatre production. A Choral Club performs at holiday time as well as throughout the year. Dance Club members choreograph and perform their works in an annual performance. Club Night is a unique tradition in the Upper School. The Halloween Club gives a party for the Lower School girls; Dance and Drama Clubs put on student performances at night; and Holiday Club in December provides an evening for students, faculty and parents to join in singing together.

Upper School girls can participate in the student Self-Government (established in 1909), Science Club, S.A.V.E., an environmental organization, Amnesty International, Volunteer Community Activities, the Cultural Awareness Project, Model U.N., French, Latin, Spanish/Latin American Club, Literary Magazine, Yearbook, and *Limelight*, the school newspaper.

One parent says, "The curriculum is geared for the above-average girl." A former teacher says that "honor, achievement and academic rigor are valued at Chapin and that adds up to competition." But nobody describes Chapin as a "pressure cooker." "Chapin never gives up on a child," one former teacher said. "People seem to hop out of

161

the woodwork to help each other, there's lots of cooperation and teamwork." Individual attention and concern for the development of the individual are hallmarks of a Chapin education. One parent described Chapin as "the most well-rounded girls' school." Another parent said that although "nastiness is discouraged, cliques form early." One parent described a common scenario (seen in one form or another at all schools): "Cliques form between third and seventh grades. Seventh-and eighth-grade cliques form around physical development and looks and competition for clubs and boys." The parent of an alumna said that the girls "individualize their uniforms and can frequently be heard chatting away about the latest party." The net result of all this sociability is a boon for the school. Chapin's alumnae remain connected to the school long after they have left. The alumnae bulletin is bulging with notes and snapshots as if this were the largest extended family on the East Coast, and perhaps it is. It's no wonder that Chapin has had great success in fund-raising.

Chapin is working had to overcome the White Glove image. (The school used to emphasize "good form" in everything from dress to term papers, an alumna recalls.) Today, the rigor of the curriculum and the variety of cultural perspectives cater to the interests of a more diverse student body. One parent said, "People don't know what a jewel Chapin is except for the Chapin parent."

The day before commencement for the Middle and Upper Schools there is a final assembly at which awards are given for achievement in athletics, fine arts and academics. Chapin commencement is held at the school. The girls graduate as a class with no special recognition for any individual student.

Popular College Choices   Barnard, Brown, Dartmouth, Duke, Harvard-Radcliffe, Middlebury, Princeton, Stanford, University of Pennsylvania, Yale

Traditions   Fall Book Fair, Club Nights, Grandparents' Day, Lower School Halloween party, Holiday Program, Field Day, Chapin Spring Benefit (Family Night at Tavern on the Green or The Puck Building, etc.)

Publications   Upper School literary magazine: *The Wheel* (since 1917)
Middle School literary magazine: *The Cog*
Newspaper: *Limelight*

Computer news publication: *The Chapin Chip*
Yearbook
Alumnae Bulletin

Community Service Requirement   Community service is encouraged but there is no specific requirement

Hangouts   The purple chairs in The Annenberg Center for Learning and Research, student lounge, coffee shop on 84th Street and Second Avenue

The Children's Storefront

P.O. Box 1313
70 East 129th Street
New York, NY 10035
(212) 427-7900

Coed
Nursery 2's–8th grade
Accessible only at 70 East 129th Street

Mark H. Tashjian, Head of School

Birthday Cutoff   Children must be 2.9 years old by September 1st

Enrollment   Total enrollment: approximately 165
Preschool places: approximately 15
Graduating class size: approximately 10–15

Tuition Range   Tuition free

Financial Aid   100% of the student body

Endowment $3.9 million

After-School Program   After-school programs in music from 3:30
P.M. to 5:00 P.M.; free of charge

Summer Program   July preschool drop-off from 8:00 A.M. until
noon
Six-week (beginning of July til mid-August) summer camp in
Lyme, Connecticut
A 6-week academic summer program for children in grades
5 through 8

––––––––––

Ned O'Gorman came to Harlem in 1966 and opened a "grass-roots school" in a storefront on Madison Avenue. The school subsequently moved into four converted brownstones. The Children's Storefront is one of a few private schools that are tuition free. The Storefront receives the bulk of its funding from foundations, corporations and individuals. The Children's Storefront's annual fundraiser attracts many of New York's "A-list" partygoers. The school is accredited by The New York State Association of Independent Schools. There is a broad range of ability within the student body. There are children with learning disabilities, gifted children and average children. O'Gorman retired in June 1999; he was replaced by Mark H. Tashjian who holds an MBA. He decided after a 13-year career as a management consultant to dedicate his time to educating children. Average class size is fifteen, providing students with the attention they need to succeed. There is a waiting list of approximately five hundred students.

City & Country School

146 West 13th Street
New York, NY 10011
(212) 242-7802, FAX (212) 242-7996
website: www.cityandcountry.org

Coed
Nursery–8th grade (ages 2–13)
Not accessible

Ms. Kate Turley, Principal
Ms. Lisa Baker Horner, Director of Admissions

Birthday Cutoff   November 1

Enrollment   Total enrollment: 240
Nursery 2's places: 29
Nursery 3's places: 5
Nursery 4's places: 5
Kindergarten (5's) places: 8–10
Graduating class 2000: 10

Grades   No grades; detailed narrative reports, at mid and end-of-year

Tuition Range   2001–2002 $10,100 to $18,300, nursery–8th grade
Additional fees: $200 enrollment fee. II's and III's pay $700 building fee; IV's to XIII's have a $1200 building fee.

Financial Aid/Scholarship   20% of the student body receive partial financial aid

Endowment   None

After-School Program   Open only to City & Country students; a variety of creative and recreational activities and sports programs from 3:00 P.M. until 5:45 P.M.
Extra charge for 3–7 year olds; no extra charge for 8–13 year olds
Specialty classes for all groups, including: chess, dance, music, art, foriegn language, cooking; additional fee required

166

Summer Program   June group: two-week camp for 8–13 year olds; week-long courses in video, journalism, bookmaking and dance; museum trips

Summer day camp at The City & Country School: for ages 3–7; from mid-June until the end of July

These programs require an additional payment

City & Country School, founded in 1914, is one of the oldest progressive elementary schools in the United States. Located on a historic block in Greenwich Village, the school occupies three adjoining brownstones on 13th street and three floors in a brownstone on 12th street; the brownstones are connected by courtyards.

Getting In: Parents may tour the school and attend the open house before submitting an application. The ERB is not required for admissions but a screening is done of each applicant for kindergarten and of older applicants. Younger children come for a group visit (about an hour) and are observed at work and play in a classroom by teachers and the director of admissions. In addition, applicants are often observed in their nursery schools. Older applicants spend a day with a group of their peers and are observed by the group teacher and special teachers. A general skills assessment is administered during the visit.

Parents: The parent body runs the gamut from "corporate lawyers, bankers and doctors to writers and illustrators." What they have in common is that they want their children in "a quintessential progressive school."

Program: Visionary educator and founder Caroline Pratt believed children learn best through practical and meaningful experiences. The process of education and the tools of learning are important here. The kindergarten usually consists of two groups of sixteen to twenty students each. From the earliest years, students work with open-ended materials: blocks, water, paint, clay, and wood. Vs through VIIs plan their work as groups, which they sustain for a week or longer, creating cities with building blocks, wooden people, handmade signs, fabric and plasticine items and even electricity and running water. Frequent trips to observe the community at work are an important part of the program. In the outdoor yards, students create their own play environment each day with large boxes, blocks, boards, ladders and sawhorses. Older groups use the yard for running and ball games and team sports. Students bring their own lunch, and milk is provided as is midmorning juice and snack.

Reading and writing begin with frequent exposure to literature, experience charts, language arts games and activities, and early story-writing. Spanish is taught, beginning with the X's or fifth grade. From grades VII to XIII, all students have half an hour of independent reading in the library every day.

As a practical application of their academic skills and to develop self-esteem and responsibility, older children participate in the Jobs Program—running the school post office or store, operating printing presses, working with younger children, writing and publishing the school newspaper. Group and individual research using primary and secondary sources, literature, and trips rather than textbooks to study a civilization, time period, or major issue forms the core of the Middle and Upper School curriculum. This curriculum is integrated with the Special Subjects and Jobs Program for the VIIIs through XIIIs for instance, a study of "living documents" of the Revolutionary period in American history is coordinated with the older children's job of running the school newspaper. The annual IX's week-long country trip to Connecticut is a highlight. After completing a unit on the Oregon Trail, the students reenact everything they have learned. For example, they maneuver a covered wagon through the countryside, construct trailside rock-heated "ovens" and cook and eat real buffalo meat. Parents say the trip "really bonds the group; they come back changed."

All students participate in Rhythms (the music and movement program), and older children use the fully equipped woodshop, the art room, the science lab and the technology center. The music program includes a singing and instruction in recorder and stringed instruments. Chorus and orchestra are required in the upper grades.

Parents whose children have been in the school for several years note several changes which indicate that City & Country is not the bastion of progressive education it once was: "Traditionally each class has a job in the school but because the school has nearly doubled in size in the last 8 years there is less opportunity for children to actually take part in running the school."

Popular Secondary School Choices Stuyvesant High School, Fiorello LaGuardia High School of Music and Art and Performing Arts, The Trevor Day School, The Fieldston School, Friends Seminary, Packer Collegiate Institute, Bronx Science, Marymount, Dalton

Collegiate School

260 West 78th Street
New York, NY 10024
Tel (212) 812-8500 Admissions x552
FAX (212) 812-8547
website: www.collegiateschool.org

All boys
K–12th grade
Accessible

Mr. Kerry P. Brennan, Headmaster
Mrs. Joanne P. Heyman, Director of Admissions and Financial Aid

Uniform   Kindergarten and Lower School: long pants and a shirt
with a collar
Middle and Upper School: grades 5–12, collared shirt and tie,
long pants, shoes or sneakers,

Birthday Cutoff   It is recommended that boys be 5 by the start of
Kindergarten

Enrollment   Total enrollment: approzimately 600
Kindergarten places: approximately 40
6th grade places: approximately 4
7th grade places: approximately 4–6
9th grade places: approximately 6–10
Graduating class size: approximately 50

Grades   Trimester system (Lower and Middle School), Semester
system (Upper School)
Grades Kindergarten–4: detailed anecdotal reports and conferences
Letter grades begin in 6th grade
Departmentalization begins in 5th grade
First final exam is given in 7th grade

Tuition Range 2001–2002 $19,700 to $20,950, Kindergarten–
12th grade
Tuition at Collegiate includes lunch, books, fees overnight trips,
and most additional costs, but not athletic equipment or special
functions

169

There is an alternative payment plan through Academic Management Services

Financial Aid/Scholarship   Approximately 20% of the student body receive financial assistance

Endowment   Approximately $42 million

Diversity   Approximately 20% children of color
28 Prep for Prep students enrolled as of fall 2000
Collegiate has a Diversity Office
JAMAA: an organization for students families, alumni and faculty of color founded in the 1960s
Collegiate Teaching Institute for prospective teachers of color

Homework   Classes I and II: 1/2 hour reading every night
Classes III and IV: approximately 45 minutes plus reading
Classes V and VI: approximately 2 hours
Classes VII and VIII: approximately 2 1/2 hours
Classes IX–XII: 2–3 hours

After-School Program   In-house after-school activities program available for Kindergarten–6. Collegiate boys participate in various sports programs; Athletic teams practice after school

Summer Program   Two-week June basketball clinic for Lower and Middle School boys
For older boys there are exchange programs in Europe, China and Latin America

———

Collegiate is the oldest independent school in the United States. It marked its 370th year in 1998. The school maintains a continuing relationship with the Dutch Reformed Church. Collegiate's strength is an emphasis on classical education combined with modern innovations. Collegiate is a well-rounded, academically rigorous school with a superior college placement record.

Headmaster Kerry P. Brennan came to Collegiate in 2000 from University School, a kindergarten through twelfth grade boys day school in Cleveland, Ohio. He is also an accomplished musician.

Collegiate has had a long-standing relationship with the West End

Collegiate Church. In 1940 the church and school separated but they still share some facilities. The "Moving Up" ceremonies for the Lower and Middle School are held at the West End Collegiate Church, as is graduation. There is a school chaplain who is also an Upper School advisor. The Holiday program, held in the church, includes various religious traditions. Seventh grade students study world religions. In the Upper School, students must choose two three-credit religion courses.

All Collegiate students benefit from a recently completed series of renovation and building projects. In 1990, the school added a fabulous new gym and weight room, two new art rooms, a black box theater, a photography lab and a music room. In September 1997, Collegiate opened a kindergarten in the West End Plaza building of the school. Two spacious classrooms with an adjoining playroom provide room for academic centers, computers, creative movement, music, blocks and art projects. In the same year, the new science laboratories were installed for Lower and Middle School students. In 1998, a roof-top play area opened on top of the school's new six-story structure. The school's dining facilities were expanded, a two-story Middle School center was completed and state-of-the-art biology, chemistry and physics laboratories were built for Upper School students.

Getting In: The application fee is $40. Parents are encouraged to tour when their sons are eligible for kindergarten. Once parents have applied, they bring their son to the school. Kindergarten applicants visit in small groups with members of the faculty. Middle and Upper School applicants have interviews and guided tours of the school. Parents of applicants are interviewed on an individual family basis. There is a policy favoring siblings and legacies but admission is not automatic. Is there a typical Collegiate Boy? An alumni said, "He is self-confident, slightly preppie, a social, smart kid."

Parents: The parent body at Collegiate runs the gamut: Academics, artists, writers, professionals, musicians, and some Wall Street types mingle comfortably in what most say is an intellectual atmosphere. About half come from the East side and half from the West side. "It is a fun loving group, easy to connect with," said one parent. Another told us, "The parent body at Collegiate is tremendously diverse and not stuffy; cocktail parties might be held in an apartment in the Village with people eating cross-legged on a futon or in a Park or Fifth Avenue apartment." Jewish parents have long been comfortable at Collegiate. There are many Jewish legacies attending Collegiate and school is closed on the major Jewish holidays. Parents

Association meetings are scheduled on the school calendar and all parents are invited to attend.

Program: Academically, the early years at Collegiate are "challenging, yet comfortable." Learning is developmental and low-key. A former Lower School teacher said the style of the school "is not extreme, not too traditional or informal, but they've borrowed what's best and held onto the things that have worked." Throughout the kindergarten and Lower School there is the understanding that boys develop at different rates. Table groupings in classrooms are informal; no rows. The heterogeneous classrooms (approximately 20 boys in each with one teacher and a full-time assistant) often break into small groups for activities. There is an eclectic approach to reading instruction: some boys come in reading and some don't, it's not an admissions requirement. There is recognition of different learning styles.

First grade homework is approached with the attitude that parents are partners. Parents are encouraged to come in to the classroom to share their skills and talents, or to simply read to the boys during library time.

Lower School boys leave their homerooms to go to specialists in art, music, physical education and science. Kindergarten boys have science in their classroom while all Lower School students go to a specially designed new Lower School science lab. Through second grade there is a teacher and an assistant for each class. All kindergarten and Lower School students have access to computers in the classrooms. The boys have regularly scheduled classes in the new Lower School technology lab. The full-time Lower School technology coordinator works closely with teachers to support computer-related activities. In the Lower School, boys learn keyboarding, basic computer skills and begin to use computers as tools to create documents and multimedia presentations.

In the early grades reading and math are "geared to the individual." The Fisher Landau department consisting of learning specialists provides support and enrichment.

In memory of the founders, third graders celebrate Dutch Day. In social studies, third graders study immigration and learn about the Dutch settlers of New Amsterdam. One year, third graders doing a unit on Japan studied haiku, learned calligraphy and made kimonos in art, read Japanese fables, and went to a tea ceremony. They clipped articles about modern Japan and read them aloud to the class.

The music program at Collegiate is very strong; renowned pianist Emanuel Ax is a former trustee and parent of an alumnus. Lower

School boys have music twice a week. In fourth grade recorder is introduced; in fifth and sixth grades students study a stringed instrument; in seventh grade guitar is required. Each year students are given an instrument for use at school or practice at home. On our tour we saw eight boys playing their violins in a practice room. Private and semi-private instruction is available and music theory is taught. Third and fourth graders have a string ensemble and chorus. One year, the fifth and sixth grade chorus sang at Carnegie Hall as part of the Canterbury Choral Society's Fortieth Anniversary Celebration. Eighth graders are introduced to music technology and composition. The boys explore music and creativity through the use of computers and synthesizers.

In fourth grade the work load is stepped up and letter grades begin in sixth grade. Parents stressed, however, that "Nobody is pressured at Collegiate, the boys are encouraged to do their best."

The Middle School at Collegiate consists of grades five through eight. According to parents, Middle School demands a greater amount of independence. In fifth grade, departmentalization has begun. Fifth graders get lockers; desks are still organized in groups, not rows. There are regular forty minute periods. The Middle School technology lab is easily accessible and often used. Technology skills are put to use as boys write papers, examine data and learn to use digital information sources for research. Students use computer-generated graphic materials in oral presentations in many of their classes. Fifth graders select either French or Spanish which they can take through high school. They can also begin Latin in eighth grade.

Beginning in fifth grade, students are given long term assignments. Students learn to plan their weeks and organize their time. At Collegiate, students really know how to think. "My fifth grader was asked to write a paper about one of Robert Louis Stevenson's books from the point of view of a minor character," a parent told us. Another fifth grade assignment was to write a piece of historical fiction. One student wrote a piece on a Vietnamese teenager and the assignment was graded by both the history and English teachers.

Fifth through eighth graders take regular tests during the school year. At the end of seventh and eighth grades there is a formal exam period.

The social studies curriculum begins in the Lower School with the study of families and communities, and expands in the upper grades to include the wider world. Fifth graders study ancient civilizations and read Greek myths and English folktales. Sixth graders study the

Middle Ages, the exploration of the New World and the Cultures of the Americas and American colonial history. Seventh graders focus on American history from George Washington to the present. Eighth graders study World History (Asia, Africa, Islam and Europe). Research papers and projects are completed in all Middle School grades.

There is a non-academic elective and activities program for Middle Schoolers "to broaden and enrich the boys' experience." Course offerings include: community service projects, computer, photography, drama, architecture, student government, Middle School newspaper, literary magazine, and excursions away from school to take advantage of the urban setting.

Experience in public speaking is gained through weekly assemblies, morning meetings and many opportunities to perform in dramatic and musical productions. One trimester of drama is required in seventh and eighth grades. Arts for grades seven and eight includes the opportunity for the boys to play in a chamber music group, study photography, produce two dramatic pieces and learn musical composition using computerized synthesizers during the year.

Middle School boys can participate in coed afternoon activities that are occasionally held with girls schools.

Summer reading is required for grades five through ten. Most boys purchase their books at the Paperback Book Fair held in the Spring. They also gather books at the Annual Book Festival organized by the Parents Association in the fall. Guest authors often include Collegiate parents. Sixth graders produce their own anthology of original literature. Grades six through eight take a three-day trip to locations of interest. Sixth graders visit an environmental study center, and seventh graders begin the school year with a three day trip to Frost Valley. The eighth graders end their year with a trip to Washington, D.C.

Prep for Prep students usually enter in either sixth, seventh or eighth grades.

Interscholastic sports begin in seventh grade; participation is stressed over competition. After spring break, eighth graders can sign out for lunch and join their older peers at "Big Nick's Pizza." After school the courtyard handball court is the social gathering spot.

Upper School at Collegiate consists of grades nine through twelve. The Upper School curriculum, according to a trustee and former PA president, is both "traditional and innovative." The school is not rigid in its approach to education, though the backbone of the curriculum is classical. There is an academic core program with electives offered in eleventh and twelfth grades. Some readings focus on the classics. Other perspectives are explored in courses such as: Contemporary American Poetry, African and Caribbean Writers, and Women in Literature. In history, Civil Liberties, Civil Rights and Human Rights in a Wider Perspective, Modern China and Japan, Russian Civilization, History of Psychological Thought, and African History are offered in addition to the normal selection of required courses. In math and science, AB and BC Calculus, Statistical Modeling, Marine Biology and Astronomy are among the courses offered.

Parents say there is an emphasis in all grades on good writing and research skills. A former PA President told us that Verbal SAT scores are consistently high because of the emphasis on language arts and the academic core program. There is no summer reading list for grades nine through twelve. Summer reading is encouraged for pleasure at all grade levels.

The Technology Department offers an expanding program in computer and technology education and there are numerous opportunities for students to use computers in conjunction with course work in all disciplines. An academic local area network connects computers in the computer labs, the library, the science department and classrooms throughout the school Access to the network allows students to "plug-in" to the many resources available through the system, including the Internet, the library catalog and reference materials on CD-ROM.

In addition to the yearly course offerings, Collegiate students can design an Independent Study course in an area of interest, taken in addition to the minimum course load. A senior project in an area of the student's choice (often some form of internship) can be undertaken in the last semester of the senior year if all other requirements are completed.

"The faculty at Collegiate is extraordinary," says an alumnus. A parent said, "They are a very senior faculty. Teachers average ten to twelve years of experience and three-quarters have advanced degrees." There is an assistant teaching program in the Lower School in which less experienced teachers work with a mentor, eventually becoming head teachers. A big incentive to keep faculty is housing provided in a building connected to the school. A former PA President said, "Collegiate has one of the lowest tuitions yet offers the highest remuneration for independent school teachers which is why it keeps and attract good teachers." The faculty is part of the larger Collegiate community:

there is a parent/faculty chorus which performs yearly at a "Celebration of Music" event.

Student government at Collegiate consists of three representatives from each grade. The Middle School student government meets regularly and plans student programs and special events. Upper School student government has tackled furnishing the student center, finding summer jobs for students and relaxing the dress code.

Theater continues to be a strength in the Upper School at Collegiate. Upper School students put on two to three plays per semester, both in the school's two hundred and sixty-seven seat theater auditorium and in the recently enlarged "black box" theater.

Clubs at Collegiate are popular. The Model U.N. Club and JAMAA, an organization for students, families, alumni and faculty of color are among the more active ones.

There is a community service requirement at Collegiate of one hundred credit hours, twenty of which must be done outside of school. Programs include opportunities such as tutoring at IS 44 at 77th Street or the East Harlem School at Exodus House on East 103rd Street, working at the West End Avenue Collegiate Church soup kitchen, The Yorkville Common Pantry, or volunteering at various museums or hospitals throughout the city. There are special food drives each year and the proceeds are donated to various community programs. In-house tutoring performed at Collegiate is one way to fulfill the other half of the requirement.

As far as contact between grades, one alumnus said, "There's sports and chorus. It's too small a school for hazing." "Of course, you can only get a Collegiate varsity jacket if you play on a varsity team," an alum mentioned. The Dutchmen's colors are orange and blue, the same as the the Knicks and the Mets. Collegiate's biggest rivals are Trinity, Poly Prep, Riverdale and Fieldston. The traditional Friday night basketball games are popular. Collegiate also has a championship cross-country team that runs in Riverside Park as well as championship teams in soccer, basketball, track and wrestling.

A recent alumnus told us that more important than the traditions themselves is the sense of success you get at Collegiate: "When you've been there a long time, you begin to think 'I can do anything.' If anything, Collegiate boys spread themselves too thin." Another alumnus said, "Athletes are also actors or musicians too."

The school stresses values, particularly integrity. "They are sticklers for honor and principle; competition is stressed in a healthy way.

But it's tough and demanding," according to an alumnus. Collegiate is structured but students may choose from a growing number of electives from ninth grade on.

Collegiate enjoys great success at college placement. Mr. Bruce Breimer, Class of 1963, Director of College Guidance, who also teaches tenth grade history, is known in independent school circles as one of the most powerful figures in college admissions. Since the graduating class usually numbers about fifty, it not difficult for him to know each boy. Parents and alumni say Briemer is a strength of the school, as he has over twenty years experience. "It's a highly personalized process. He helps each senior take control of his own college search in an independent fashion and he encourages each boy to go beyond the obvious in the quest for the most felicitous match." A 1991 graduate told us, "He makes or breaks your career; he's the guy you want on your side."

There are no academic prizes at Collegiate. Seniors with outstanding grades are inducted into the Cum Laude Society (the secondary school equivalent of Phi Beta Kappa). The Collegiate faculty and graduating class vote for the Head Boy each year, a senior who shows a combination of leadership, sportsmanship and citizenship.

There is a genuine school spirit at Collegiate demonstrated at class dinners, the holiday assembly and at Moving Up Day. One parent said, "They all sing the school song and you cry no matter how many times you've seen it." A traditional graduation ceremony is held in the West End Collegiate Church. Cap and gown are worn and the alma mater is sung.

Popular College Choices   Yale, Harvard, Brown, Dartmouth, Princeton, University of Pennsylvania, Columbia, Wesleyan, Williams

Traditions   Library Week, Parents Association Book Festival, Paperback Book Fair, 2nd grade trip to Manhattan Country School Farm, 3rd grade trip to an outdoor environmental education center, 6th grade "Meet the Presidents Day," 7th grade trip to Frost Valley, 8th grade trip to Washington, DC, Middle School Special Days, 10th grade Interschool trip to Frost Valley, Lower and Middle School Field Day, 5th and 6th grade music evenings, Grandparents Day, Moving Up Days for Lower and Middle Schools, Athletic Banquet, graduation at Collegiate Church, alumni reception

Publications Newspaper: *The Collegiate Journal* (monthly)
Yearbook: *The Dutchman*
French publication: *Charabia*
Spanish publication: *La Herencia*
Literary magazine: *Prufrock*
Science and Technology publication: *Technically Speaking*
Opinion publication: *Issues*
Lower School: *Journal*
Middle School literary magazine: *Jabberwock*
Collegiate publication: *News From Collegiate, The Collegiate Review*
Alumni publication: *The Red Door*
Parents Association: *Newsletter*

Community Service Requirement Grades 9–12: 100 credits by graduation (40 minutes–1 hour = 1 credit)

Hangouts Collegiate cafeteria (the menu is in French, Spanish and English), the courtyard, library, Upper School student center, and technology labs

Columbia Grammar and Preparatory School
5 West 93rd Street
New York, NY 10025
(212) 749-6200
website: www.cgps.org

Coed
Pre-kindergarten–12th grade
Grades 7–12 accessible

Dr. Richard J. Soghoian, Headmaster
Ms. Simone Hristidis, Director of Admissions
(Pre-K–12)

Uniform   No torn jeans, sweatpants, T-shirts with inappropriate messages, tank tops, cutoffs, boxers, gym shorts or bicycle pants

Birthday Cutoff   September 1

Enrollment   Total enrollment: 820
  Pre-kindergarten places: 20
  Kindergarten places: 60
  7th grade places: 20
  9th grade places: approximately 20–30
  Graduating class size: approximately 60

Grades   Semester system
  Letter grades begin in 7th grade
  Departmentalization begins in 5th grade
  First final exam is given at the end of 7th grade

Tuition Range 2001–2002 $18,800 to $21,650, pre-kindergarten–12th grade
  There are no additional fees
  A revolving loan policy requires that each family make an interest-free loan ($1,500 for grades K–8, $1,000 for grades 9–12) to the school for each child enrolled
  A Tuition Refund Plan and a Student Accident Reimbursement Plan are available

Financial Aid/Scholarship   In 2000–2001, 14% of the students received aid totaling $1,368,669

179

Endowment $6,000,000

Diversity   13% students of color K–6,
18.5% students of color grades 7–12
58 families of color out of 113 received $924,525 (68%) of the
year's total aid in 2000–2001
MECA, Multi-Ethnic Cultural Awareness Club
12 Prep for Prep students enrolled as of Fall 2000
Focus, Families of Color United in Support

Homework   Kindergarten: none
1st: 20 minutes
2nd: 30–45 minutes
3rd, 4th: approximately 1 hour
5th–8th: 1½–2½ hours
9th–12th: approximately 3 hours

After-School Program   CGPS After-School Program for grades
K–4 offers a variety of creative and recreational activities until
4:30 P.M., Monday–Friday
Sunrise Club 7:45 A.M.–8:30 A.M.
Math Club for grades 1–4
Chess Club for grades K–6
Rollerblading for grades 2–6
Intramural and Interscholastic sports grades 5–12

Summer Program   CGS Summer Camp: for Pre-kindergarten–6
from the end of school until the end of July, staffed by CGS
teachers, an additional payment is required

Columbia Grammar School was founded in 1764 and functioned
as a feeder school for King's College (later, Columbia University).
Now CGPS graduates go on to a much wider range of universities and
colleges. CGPS became a nonprofit school in 1941 and merged with a
nearby girls' school. Since 1981 CGPS has been guided by Richard J.
Soghoian, who holds a Ph.D. in philosophy from Columbia University
and is also an International Fellow at the School for International
Affairs. His expertise is manifested in the innovative social studies,
history and geography programs throughout CGPS. Dr. Soghoian

recently guided the school through two major construction projects: a $6.5-million high school building completed in 1986 and a new $8.5 million building for grades 7–9 completed in 1996 which has five art studios, three science labs, a theatre and a new cafeteria. Recently, CGPS began construction on a new building located behind the high school at 4 West 93rd Street. This will be a $9 million facility with a second gym for students in grades five through eight. There will be three floors of classrooms above it and a 275-seat theater in the basement. The building is expected to open in the fall of 2001. The additional space will allow the school to increase the grade sizes to sixty students per grade in the Grammar School, and seventy-five in the Prep School. Individual class sizes will stay small, with twelve to fifteen students per class.

Columbia Grammar offers a well-rounded but structured program for able students. The Grammar School is now composed of pre-kindergarten through sixth grade (the first pre-kindergarten class of eighteen children was admitted in 1996–97.) The Prep School consists of seventh through twelfth grades.

The director of the Lower School, Stanley Seidman, was formerly head of Dalton's Lower School. Parents say Seidman is well-liked, knows all the children's names and is very accessible. Parents say they feel free to call the teachers at any time, and their calls will be taken even during classroom hours using the school's new voice mail system.

Getting in: The application is very straightforward. There are one or two essay questions. The ERB/ISEE is required. Please note that all applications for kindergarten and first grade must be filed by December 1. CGPS holds Friday afternoon teas for prospective applicants to pre-kindergarten and kindergarten. Dr. Soghoian as well as other representatives from the school are available to answer questions. Once an application has been filed, parents are taken on a more extensive tour of the school while their child is being interviewed (a small group interview of four children at a time, which lasts about one hour during which the child is observed by the Lower School head as well as admissions personnel). After the tour, parents meet with Mr. Seidman and Mrs. Hristidis over coffee. Parents say that the admissions process at CGPS is low-key and comfortable. "They are really interested in the child, not scrutinizing the parents," we heard. CGPS has not gone to their wait list in three years. What are they looking for? Hristidis told us, "A bright child who can handle an enriched curriculum, eager to learn; nice, well adjusted children; we're not looking for a type, a range of children would do well here but they must be academically inclined."

Prospective applicants to the Preparatory School attend one of several afternoon meetings in which the program is described followed by a tour. Tours are given by current Prep students. The application deadline is usually December 1st.

The typical CGPS student? "This is not a jock school," said one parent. "The typical student usually has some artistic bent." "The *atypical* student," one parent said, "is pushy, snotty or overly competitive." But, now that CGPS is growing, there are students who are getting more involved in a wide range of athletics.

Parents: The parent body at CGPS consists of many professionals. There is an equal division between West Siders and East Siders. Social competition is negligible. According to one mother, the parent body is "unpretentious, no limos or jewels, and if they have it, they leave it at home." "CGPS has a lot of generally liberal parents who might otherwise have sent their children to public school," said another. There are a number of Parents Association events such as the Skating Party, Theatre Party and Spring Benefit (held at Denim & Diamonds in 1996). They are fun, low-key events. At the annual holiday concert "First Noel" as well as "O Chanukah" are sung. "What you see is what you get," says one parent with two children at CGPS. "There are absolutely no surprises."

Program: The pre-kindergarten and kindergarten year begins with a fall picnic in Central Park, held before the beginning of school. The school provides a very informative handbook for each division (Lower and Upper). Parents say CGPS is supportive about separation when school actually begins.

All students have a well-rounded schedule, which includes a strong swimming program (required for grades kindergarten through fourth grade and optional for fifth grade.) Kindergartners swim twice a week for forty minutes, once a week in the middle grades) plus art, music and academics. CGPS swimming parties are a popular, inexpensive birthday party option; ice-skating and rollerblading parties are also in.

Presently, the Grammar School (composed of pre-kindergarten through sixth grades) is housed in five interconnected brownstones on West 94rd Street connected to the original school building on West 93rd Street (now housing grades five and six). Children and adults develop strong legs because of the many stairways in the school. The classroom space is long, with windows at either end, but well laid out and bright. There is a courtyard play area for recess. Parents say that the kindergarten teachers are warm, and make learning fun, although by third grade they get more serious. "The children respect the teachers," a parent commented.

Throughout the Grammar School learning is viewed as a progression, especially in math and reading. The brochure says: "Each grade's work builds on the work of previous years." Individual rates of learning in math and reading are accommodated. Wherever possible, art is coordinated with work in other subjects in the Grammar School. Pre-kindergarten and kindergarten have two teachers and one assistant. For first through third grades there are two teachers for approximately twenty to twenty-two children. Although it is considered a "structured school," the teaching at CGPS is flexible, "using a variety of approaches and techniques." Parents praise the well-paced reading program. In kindergarten reading readiness is the focus; in first grade "a phonics sequence is the basic method used for the teaching of reading." Whole Language literature based books are used. Math instruction in kindergarten stresses experiential learning through the use of manipulatives and games. There are at least three computers in all of the classrooms and LOGO and word processing are taught in the Grammar School. Fourth graders go out to the computer lab.

The extensive music program begins with the Kodaly and Orff methods, which are used for ear training. Second graders learn to play the recorder. Instrumental instruction begins in fourth grade and students are given an instrument to take home. Opportunities to perform include the third- and fourth-grade choir, a recorder ensemble for second and third graders, a string ensemble and a chamber music ensemble for more advanced students. In fifth grade students pick one instrument for further study.

The social studies curriculum for pre-kindergarten through fourth begins with families and community and broadens to include a study of ethnicity and immigration in second grade (including a trip to Ellis Island with students dressed as their immigrant forebears). Native Americans are the subject in third grade, explorers and Colonial America in fourth.

Fifth graders study the Revolutionary War and slavery. They use primary sources and read Early American folklore. Sixth graders study ancient civilizations and the Middle Ages and write a research paper.

The Writing Workshop is a standard part of the curriculum in which students practice the steps of good writing (see Glossary, p. 58, *supra*). Fifth and sixth graders also take public speaking, engage in debates and practice speech writing.

A highlight of the Grammar School is the Earth Fest in which mixed-age groups engage in a five-day study of an ecological or environmental topic. The unit concludes with a special assembly in the Upper School gym at which each group presents a project.

The approach to science in the Grammar School "is firmly experimental and based on the scientific method." Environmental awareness begins as early as first grade with a discussion about how waste leaves Manhattan island. First graders study endangered animals; second graders learn about water pollution and testing; third graders study air pollution; fourth graders examine wind and solar energy and travel to Nature's Classroom, an environmental study center in Connecticut. Sixth graders take a unit on environmental issues.

Parents say that by third grade the academic pace picks up and the work gets much more serious. Extra help is readily available. One mother said her daughter received extra help with reading during recess time.

Foreign language study begins in second grade with exposure to the Spanish language and culture, and is integrated with the social studies curriculum.

In mathematics, the focus is on problem-solving skills. There are enrichment topics in each grade. In fifth grade these are palindromic numbers, tangrams and hieroglyphics. Other enrichment projects include curve stitching and M.C. Escher's tessellations and participation in the Math Olympiad.

Reports and grades come home twice a year. The anecdotal reports in the Lower School are extensive and detailed. In addition, there is a checklist in each subject area showing that the student is either "progressing well," "developing" or "needs strengthening."

If a child has a learning deficiency, CGPS will "provide some degree of professional skills remediation on a temporary basis." CGPS also has a highly specific and intensive in-school treatment of learning disabilities called the Learning Resource Center, staffed by ten highly trained professionals. The program is limited to forty students, grades kindergarten through twelfth, who are otherwise fully mainstreamed students. There is an *additional* cost of approximately $15,000 per year. This program is an in-house program only. No outside applicants are admitted.

For physical exercise students play in the courtyard, on the roof turf playground or go to Central Park, which is located only a block from the school, weather permitting. Physical education is required in all grades. Intramural and interschool sports begin in fifth grade. After-school sports are available. A Field Day with games is held at the end of the year for each division.

The Prep School (grades seven through twelve) is on a semester system. Grades are issued quarterly, there are two parent conferences and two narrative report cards. The school day begins with a ten minute homeroom period and is divided into forty minute periods, ending at 2:55 P.M.

The new building housing grades seven through nine serves the "Middle Schoolers" exceptionally well; bright, and spacious, with special space for the arts: photo lab, filmmaking, jewelry-making and so on. The "underground" theatre holds 150. Stagecraft models (made by students) on display in the lobby are wonderful.

In seventh and eighth grades students are required to take English, science, social studies and math as well as art, music, computer and PE. Foreign language study begins with a two month sequence in each of four languages: French, Spanish, Latin and Japanese. In eighth grade students choose one of these languages for continued study.

Seventh graders are ready to think critically and express themselves clearly and sensitively on issues of social relevance. In history the horizons have broadened to include examination of the effect of historical policies such as apartheid and colonialism on emerging nations and current events. Seventh grade English is coordinated with the seventh grade history curriculum and covers the themes of prejudice, tolerance and freedom. Readings include *The Crucible* and *To Kill a Mockingbird*.

Latin America and African history, culture and geography are the focus of the history curriculum in eighth grade and students make African masks, symbolic flags and maps and graphs. The study of geography at CGPS is considered "essential to the appreciation of today's international interdependency." A unit on "the origins of the U.N. and the vital role it plays in the international environment" is included in the eighth grade year.

In grades nine through twelve students are required to complete four years of English, math and social studies, as well as three years of science. Foreign language must be studied through the end of eleventh grade. Other requirements include a course in computer literacy (there are two computer labs, one with Macs and the other with PC's) two of three offerings in the history of art, theater or music, and a community service requirement of one hundred hours to be completed by the end of the senior year. Electives are available in all the major subject areas. Six courses are the normal course load, except during the senior year when five are required. Students can arrange independent study projects in their final semester.

Ninth and tenth grades are assigned to full year English classes. In ninth grade, the class addresses the fundamental human theme of coming of age and exposes the students to a wide range of literature. In tenth grade the course focuses on the fundamentals of good writing, as well as a selection of British and American literature. Eleventh and twelfth graders choose from a variety of electives but they must take at least one course in each of the following: British literature, American literature, and pre-twentieth century literature.

When asked about a multicultural curriculum at CGPS, Dr. Soghoian responded that "CGPS has always emphasized Africa, China, Japan and South America on nearly an equal footing with the study of Europe in the preparatory school program." CGPS also uses its extensive assembly program to emphasize multicultural performers and themes.

The history sequence reads like a description of an advanced college history program. Students in ninth and tenth grades study Western Civilization, including European history from Greek and Roman times to the French Revolution and continuing through the Reactionary Era, Imperialism, World Wars I and II, and the Cold War. Eleventh graders study U.S. History, and juniors and seniors can choose from electives such as economics, philosophy, the Holocaust, and a course taught in conjunction with Tufts University as well as AP courses in comparative government, modern European history, and U.S. government.

Calculus BC and AB (college calculus and preparation for the AP exams) are offered by the math department, and graphing calculators are used in the calculus classes. At the annual Math/Science Fair, student teams present the results of their research on a variety of topics such as the mathematics of sound or an analysis of hurricane paths. The science department offers AP biology, chemistry and physics as well as electives in astronomy, consumer chemistry, human evolution, and a three year research course.

There is a great range of choice in the arts at CGPS. Photography, drama and filmmaking are popular. The ceramics room is full of inspired and beautiful work ready to be fired in the kiln. Wood shop and jewelry-making areas are busy places too.

The Prep School has its own Winter and Spring Concerts, (choral and instrumental) and a three day Arts Festival. There are several major theatre productions each year and at least one musical.

The student government, with elected representatives from each grade, helps coordinate activities such as the annual Field Day and fundraising for various causes. Clubs include MECA (the multicultural awareness group), Model U.N., Model SADD Congress, (Students Against Destructive Decisions) and Environmental Awareness.

At the Annual Social Issues Day a topic of importance is examined in depth through seminars and small group discussions. One year Gay Men's Health Crisis was invited to participate in small group question-and-answer sessions.

About 60 percent of the high school students participate in a varsity sport. The new spectator gym is large and cheerful with wooden bleachers. At the end-of-the-year Sports Award Banquet the year's outstanding teams and coaches are recognized and individual achievement is honored. CP has strong teams in soccer, cross-country and varsity basketball. There are trophy cases in the school lobby.

Moving Up Day at CGPS reinforces the feeling of a warm community. It is a special day when all the students from pre-kindergarten through twelfth grade, faculty and staff gather together in the gym to share awards for academic excellence, citizenship and character, success in sports and so on. Songs are sung and class banners are handed down from one class to another to signify graduation.

Alumni speak about fond memories of CGPS: "Reunions hold good memories," "CGPS was a little more laid-back and less pretentious than some of the other schools but we all did well there."

Popular College Choices   University of Wisconsin, Boston University, Brown, University of Michigan, Tufts, Cornell, Columbia, Vassar

Traditions   Grammar School Science Fair, Earth Fest, Field Day, Prep School Math/Science Fair class dinners, kindergarten Grandparents' Day, Holiday Concert, Skating Party, theatre benefit, Winter Concert, Spring Concert, Instrumental Concert, 4th-grade trip to Nature's Classroom, Gymnastics Week, Spirit

Week, Spring Benefit, The Reading Club, Operation Santa Claus, Social Issues Day, Sports Award Banquet, Moving Up Ceremony, Young Alumni Reunion

Publications   Alumni magazine: *Columbiana Today*
Literary, news and art magazine: *CPJ* (Columbia Prep Journal)
Yearbook
Newspaper

Community Service Requirement   Grades 9–12: one hundred hours, cumulative

Hangouts   McDonald's, deli around the corner

Convent Of The Sacred Heart

1 East 91st Street
New York, NY 10128
(212) 722-4745
website: www.cshnyc.org

All girls
Pre-kindergarten–12th grade
Not accessible

Mary Blake, Ed.D., Head of School
Mrs. Barbara S. Root, Director of Admissions

Uniform Pre-kindergarten: gray smock jumper or navy overalls; regulation sneakers and shoes must be purchased at East Side Kids (15% discount on sneakers when buying SH shoes *and* sneakers)

Grades K–4: gray jumper, white blouse with McMullen collar, white anklets (warm weather), red long-sleeved mock turtleneck shirt and medium gray knee highs (cool weather); red-and-white-check pinafore worn every day, navy stretch shorts worn every day under gray jumper

Grades 5–7: gray kilt, medium gray knee socks or white anklet socks, white long-sleeved blouse, oxford-collar or white polo shirt with collar or white turtleneck; tights must be white, black or beige and can be worn under knee socks; seventh-grade privilege: crew neck or cardigan sweater with detail or pattern may be worn except for formal occasions

Grades 8–12: blue pinstripe cotton kilt; solid blue or white blouse with collar or turtleneck (spring and fall); solid color tights, no long underwear or leggings; Coburn plaid kilt; white, red, yellow, or navy blouse or turtleneck; no oversized clothing; white, yellow, red, green, navy or black socks or tights; no sweat pants, long underwear or leggings

Birthday Cutoff Pre-kindergarten 3's applicants must be 3 by May/June before entering

Pre-kindergarten 4's applicants must be 4 by May/June before entering

Children entering kindergarten must be 5 by September 1

Enrollment   Total enrollment: 620
Pre-kindergarten 3's and 4's places: 28
Kindergarten places: approximately 35
Graduating class size 2000: 45

Grades   Trimester system
Letter grades begin in 5th grade
Departmentalization begins in 5th grade
First final exam is given in 8th grade

Tuition Range 2001–2002 $14,450 to $20,225, pre-kindergarten
3's –12th grade
There are some additional fees (*i.e.*, lunch, technology)

Financial Aid/Scholarship $1,392,957 (14.5% of the operating
budget)
24% of the student body receive some form of financial assistance

Endowment $7 million

Diversity   26% students of color
Women of Proud Heritage (founded 1991)
Women's History Assembly
7 Prep for Prep students enrolled as of 1998

Homework   1st: 15–20 minutes
2nd: 30 minutes
3rd and 4th: 45 minutes
5th–7th: 1–2 hours
8th–12th: 2–4 hours

After-School Program   All Lower School (K–4) after-school programs require an additional payment; ballet, ceramics, cooking,
dramatics, gymnastics, photography, violin, arts and crafts,
recorder, dance, tennis, sewing, puppets, computer, music, team
sports, stichery, math for fun, swimming, ice-skating, typing.
Private instruction in piano is available for students in kindergarten and up
Middle School: required Middle School electives are offered from
3:40–5:00 P.M. (the elective fee is included in the tuition); choices
include a variety of recreational and creative activities, gallery and
museum visits; sports activities and teams include: soccer, swim-

ming, volleyball, basketball, softball, track, running club, tennis
and gymnastics according to the season
Upper School: Junior Varsity and Varsity interscholastic athletic
competition in the Athletic Association of Independent Schools of
New York City and the Ivy League

Summer Program   Creative Arts Summer Program: a multi-arts
summer program for boys and girls ages 6–15 (junior program for
ages 6 and 7) offering instruction in art, drama, film, computer,
science and athletics; all-day arts festival at conclusion of the program; an additional payment is required (limited financial aid is
available)

———

Chartered by the International Society of the Sacred Heart in
1881, Convent of the Sacred Heart is the oldest independent girls'
school in Manhattan. Sacred Heart is housed in two magnificent landmarked buildings—the former Otto Kahn and James Burden mansions. The winding marble staircase leads from the vaulted lobby to
bright and spacious classrooms as well as banquet hall and ballroom
in the manner of Versailles complete with tapestry and marble. The
ballroom was a wedding gift to Adele Burden née Sloane (great-
granddaughter of Commodore Cornelius Vanderbilt) and the scene of
many splendid parties and dances in the 1890s. Today the ballroom is
used for Sacred Heart commencement, dance classes and assemblies,
and is rented out on the weekends for corporate and charitable events
and weddings, providing the school with additional income.

Sacred Heart, although a Catholic girls' school, is neither clois-
tered nor parochial in its outlook. Sacred Heart is governed by a lay
board of trustees and Miss Blake is the first lay head of the school; the
nuns are elegantly dressed (habits are not worn) and approximately
one-third of the students have a mixed religious background. As one
parent said, "It's a Christian school because Sacred Heart stresses how
you lead your life—there is an emphasis on ethics."

The idea of social service is built into a Sacred Heart education.
The catalog states: "A primary aim of a Sacred Heart education is the
development in each individual of a personal faith that impels to
action." All schools claim to care about every student as an individual;
at Sacred Heart, parents say, "They really mean it." Service begins
with age appropriate projects in the lowest grades and continues
through the Upper School where Sacred Heart has led other city

students in the Conference on Homelessness and intensive summer service programs.

Sacred Heart has enjoyed a decade of enrollment growth. Additional sections have been added in most Lower School grades, facilities have been upgraded, technology has been integrated into the curriculum; amenities have been added including a lunch program and cafeteria, weight-training room and exercise studio, automated library accessible via Internet, new science labs, upgraded libraries and renovated classrooms.

Off campus, Sacred Heart is experiencing a historic expansion of its recreational and athletic facilities. The school has joined the Black Rock Forest Consortium providing access to a forest and an environmental sciences center shared with several other independent schools. Sacred Heart has also endowed lanes at the Asphalt Green Aqua Center and it is one of the seven schools pioneering the renovation of sports fields on Randalls Island. Sacred Heart has committed to an extensive athletics rentals program to supplement its capabilities and 80% of the students participate in one or more JV or Varsity teams, often bringing home the championship trophies.

Getting in: Parents can request a tour of the school or attend one of the open houses before applying for their daughter. Largest points of entry are Pre-K, kindergarten and ninth grade. The application fee is $50, and the application asks for baptism, communion and confirmation dates, as well as parents' education and employment. After applying, parents come for their tour and interview on the same day. Brick Church, Park Avenue Christian, Episcopal, West Side Montessori, International Pre-school, and St. Thomas More Nursery School are all considered "feeders" to Sacred Heart. The admissions office is sensitive to the needs of parents: "They are very courteous," one parent said, "and particularly accommodating to families from abroad." A parent from abroad told us, "It's like going to a Hilton, you know what to expect." Sacred Heart provides an instant community for New York City parents: "When you're accepted at Sacred Heart you're accepted as part of a large international family," said a parent. Another parent said she found Sacred Heart's geographical and ethnic diversity "with a lot of families from Europe and Latin America," refreshing after her daughter's homogeneous nursery school.

Parents: Sacred Heart parents say that social competition is negligible. They don't need to dress up to pick up their daughters at school. Parents are considered partners in their daughters' education. Newsletters are sent home three times a year. Communication from teachers, the PA, and administration is frequent. There is a new parents' cocktail party and family dinner held in May for incoming families, as well as a welcoming party in September. The Parents Association consists of officers, school representatives and class representatives and hosts an annual spring meeting and cocktail party and the annual auction or benefit fund-raiser and family events. There are two or three dinner dances held each year including the bi-annual Spring Ball (held at the American Crafts Museum one year) and the Hatter's Ball featuring custom or homemade hats, "ostrich plumes à la *My Fair Lady*," which benefits the Creative Arts Summer Program Scholarship Fund. Other Parents Association functions include Christmas caroling, tree lighting and sale (neighbors are welcome) at which you can buy your tree as well as the ornaments and have a picture taken with Santa Claus by the Otto Kahn fireplace outside the former dining room where Enrico Caruso once sang.

Program: At a recent Upper School open house, five elements of a Sacred Heart education were delineated: 1) faith: You will learn "what you are going to be and give in this world"; 2) academic challenge: Sacred Heart's rigorous academic program will impart a love of learning and enable each girl to become an independent thinker and grow in her own particular gifts; 3) social awareness: Everyone does service at Sacred Heart, and "we do not count hours"; 4) growth as a community: There is a strong relationship between faculty and students, and a diverse student community; 5) personal growth: To recognize your strengths, gifts and limitations, "you come as you are and are loved into being the very best that you can be." A Lower School parent said that what she likes best about Sacred Heart is that the headmistress and the heads of the divisions "have a real concern for each and every family—people are what matters."

Religion and social service go hand in hand at Sacred Heart. According to the brochure, the "basic intent of the Lower School religious program is to build in each student a positive sense of herself in relation to God and to her community." Ethics and spirituality are stressed—the basic premise is "you have a friend in God." There is Mass once a week in the beautifully appointed chapel and parents are always welcome. In Middle School "the link between faith and action is forged by social action activities that reach out to communities beyond the school." Middle School service projects include working in a day care center and participation in walkathons, God's Love We Deliver (meals delivered to AIDS patients) and Amnesty International. In the Upper School community service is coordinated through the campus ministry and the Student Activities and Service Program. Students are expected to volunteer on a regular basis in a social service agency outside of school, keep a journal and share their experiences in a weekly meeting. Students in Class ten must complete a final project in which they examine a social issue in depth through academic research and field experience.

The Lower School at Sacred Heart is composed of grades pre-kindergarten through grade 4. In Lower School, the girls wear the signature Sacred Heart uniform: a gray jumper with a red-checked pinafore (both machine washable). Each Lower School girl has an "Angel" or "Big Sister" to guide her. The fourth graders are partners with seniors in the Upper School and Middle School girls read weekly to Lower School children. There are three kindergarten classes of approximately seventeen children each and two teachers in each classroom (plus a rabbit). Beginning in kindergarten the following subjects are taught: language arts, math, science, social studies and, in third grade onward, French. Students meet weekly for religion, art, music, library, gym and drama/movement. There are formal as well as informal assembly presentations. Exercise is taken on the two play terraces, which have views of the reservoir, or in Central Park across the street.

Parents say academics in the Lower School consists of "good old-fashioned teaching combined with some of the newer methods" and "there's a lot of structure." Conferences are held twice a year but parents say you can schedule one any time if necessary. A tone of "warmth and acceptance" prevails along with academic rigor. Director of Admissions Barbara Root describes Sacred Heart as "not overly pressured, but everyone is expected to do serious work." The mother of a third grader concurs: "Sacred Heart is competitive but each girl is encouraged to do her best." Collaborative learning is emphasized in the early years, and there are no individual desks until third grade.

The reading program begins in kindergarten and becomes more formal in Class one. Phonics is taught as an essential reading skill along with creative writing, Writers' Workshop, "whatever works." If a student is not progressing well she will begin working with a reading specialist. There is individual as well as small group instruction and basal texts are used. Girls are taught to experience mathematics "as an integral part of everyday life" through cooking, manipulatives and math games. For example, to learn the value of a million, one class is collecting and counting tea bag tags. The project is on display in the classroom.

Lower School science emphasizes the skills of observation and investigation. There is a two-day field trip to an environmental center in fourth grade. The social studies curriculum begins with a study of the students' own families, then extends to a study of the community. Students in Class three research topics such as the rain forest or deserts. Class four studies Early Explorers and American History.

Art is integrated into the science and social studies curriculum in many ways. Students in Class two pick an animal to study and model it in clay, then the entire class works together to create a Calderesque circus from wood, wire, foam and fabric. Students in class three made "incredible" papier-mâché vegetables in art and studied the growth of plants from seed through maturation in science. Fifth graders studying antiquity create a museum of ancient cultures.

Drama and movement activities are "designed to enhance the students' understanding of dance as a means of communication and expression." By Class four the girls create and perform their own original dance/drama pieces.

George Orio, Convent's Director of Technology, is credited with seamlessly integrating technology into the classrooms and curriculum. Formal computer instruction begins in first grade. The classes are team taught by a computer specialist and the classroom teacher and use multimedia CD-ROMS and related software. Fifth graders work with LEGO LOGO, a robotics application, and by sixth grade students and teachers use *Hyperstudio* to create multimedia research projects.

Study of the French language begins in Class three through songs and games to teach vocabulary and pronunciation.

A team of Lower School psychologists and learning specialists give additional help where necessary. Project Charlie, an anti-drug program that focuses on self-esteem, is taught in the Lower School. A comprehensive health program which focuses on nutrition begins in grade 2.

Birthdays in Lower School are special because the birthday girl can wear a party dress, bring in cupcakes or another sweet and can donate a book to the library in her name. Another fun event in Lower School is the Halloween costume party. The Lower School Christmas Pageant "can make you weep" it is so beautifully produced, parents say.

Middle School at Sacred Heart consists of Classes five through seven. All six Middle School homerooms are located on the fourth floor. Each new Middle School student has an "angel" for the first weeks of school. New students and their angels are invited to school for a luncheon and orientation day the week before school begins.

195

Flexible ability grouping in mathematics begins in Class six. French ability groups begin in Class seven. The first half of French I or Spanish I is offered to all seventh graders. The second half of this course is given in eighth grade. In Middle School, a study skills and research course and Latin (Class seven) and Spanish (Class seven) are added to the core curriculum of English, math, science, social studies, and religion. Students say there is an increased workload in Class six and the development of good study skills is emphasized.

By Class five, computer work is integrated into the English, math, social studies and science curricula. Fifth grade students explore the physical concepts of simple machines through LEGO LOGO. A unit in Class six on computer database filing uses *ClarisWorks*. Seventh grade students create multimedia presentations on the American Colonies using the *Hyperstudio* application.

Art continues to be integrated with the curriculum at many levels. Students in Class six studying Medieval and Renaissance Europe create family crests and banners, work on tapestry projects and make stained-glass windows. The study of South America in Class seven is supplemented by the creation of relief sculptures and the study of pre-Columbian art.

The Middle School elective program is a required weekly enrichment elective. Among the choices are sports, drama, literary magazine, photography, ice skating, swimming and ceramics.

There is a Middle School musical production in the fall as well as smaller productions in the winter and spring. Other highlights include the Class seven father/daughter volleyball game, the pancake breakfast and the mother/daughter liturgy.

The Middle School has its own student government, a Committee of Games, that oversees the sports competition between the Green and Buff teams. There is also a Big Sister Program. Each class takes an overnight trip, which is coordinated with the curriculum. Class five travels to Mystic, Connecticut, sixth graders to a Pennsylvania Renaissance Faire and seventh graders to Plymouth, Massachusetts.

Beginning in Middle School and continuing through Upper School, academic achievement awards are given to students who maintain an A average for the year in four or more academic subjects. At the end of the year there is a Sports Banquet to honor athletic achievement.

The Upper School at Sacred Heart consists of Classes eight through twelve. Class eight is a transition year at Sacred Heart. In

Class nine there is an influx of new students from parochial and independent schools in the New York City area while some of the students who have been at Sacred Heart since pre-kindergarten or kindergarten opt to leave for a coed or boarding school. Incoming ninth graders have an overnight immersion program and each new student in the Upper School has an "angel" for the first weeks. Upper School students at Sacred Heart say they feel they have more opportunity to take risks and to be more articulate in an all-girls school. (But we are told that the school continues to be strict about skirt length.)

Students say that the academic expectations are high—Sacred Heart was recognized by the U.S. Department of Education as a National School of Excellence. "The teachers work you hard, and honors courses are pushed," they say. The sense of community continues in the Upper School: "It's not so competitive because we're all friends and we help each other." There has been an enormous change in the emphasis on the sciences in the past four years—now 90 percent of the students take an advanced science course during their senior year. Students take six or seven academic subjects in Classes eight through ten and add electives in Classes eleven and twelve. A former Parents Association president told us, "The Upper School is rigorous but there is a lot of support." The study of religion includes textual study, literary exegesis, historical background, comparative religions, ethics and philosophy. In the eleventh grade the interdisciplinary approach culminates in a thirty-page baccalaureate level thesis and oral presentation of a topic combining Christology and the Arts. Recent topics have included examinations of the films of Fellini, the music of J.S. Bach, and Beguin lace makers.

Mrs. Price has been head of the Upper School for over seven years. Because the Upper School is small, the teachers know each girl very well. Teachers are approachable and there are peer tutors.

There is an intensive five-year writing program in the Upper School and students become familiar with all literary genres. Students are expected to write well in all disciplines. In Class nine there is an interdisciplinary social studies and English project that produces *Medieval Magazine* and culminates in a banquet. Juniors and seniors can choose from courses in Asian and African-American literature. The "Memoirs" course examines feminist thinking through the stories of women in a variety of cultures. For "New York City in Literature," students read the work of an author (such as Edith Wharton, who lived in New York City) and visit his or her home and/or sites in the novel.

Students who excel in mathematics can take calculus AB and BC. Members of the Mathematics Club compete with other Catholic high schoolers in the tristate area.

The school has a standing research internship program at Rockefeller University where several girls study each year. Students have also interned at the Museum of Natural History, the New York Academy of Sciences, the Cooper Union Engineering School, and the Columbia Science Honors Program. A lab science research internship is available to students in eleventh and twelfth grades. Interns spend six hours a week in a laboratory and write a research paper.

The art department has been expanded in recent years.

In May there is a three-week Festival of the Arts when students celebrate their accomplishments in many areas. Artwork is on display throughout the school, and there are dance recitals, as well as performances by the handbell choir and the Speech and Drama Clubs.

Many of the extracurricular activities in the Upper School are coed. There are Upper School dances in September and at Christmas each year, and Sacred Heart students can audition for roles in the Collegiate, Regis and Browning Schools' plays and musicals. At Sacred Heart the drama department produces one-act plays or Shakespeare in the fall and a musical in the spring in which boys play some parts. There are also Service Days together with neighboring boys' schools.

There is no Sacred Heart orchestra but students can join the Interschool Orchestra or the Sacred Heart Handbell Choir.

Other extracurricular opportunities include student government, Peer Support, Archeology Club, Drama Club, Environmental Club, yearbook, literary magazine, newspaper and Women of Proud Heritage. Sports are popular and plentiful: There are eighth grade teams, intramural clubs and eight varsity sports. Two of Sacred Heart's chief competitors are Trinity School and Brearley.

Sacred Heart students in Classes nine through twelve can participate in the exchange program at other Sacred Heart Schools either here or abroad. Students have studied in France, Belgium, Spain, California and Louisiana.

College guidance begins in Class nine, and there are assemblies with alumnae. Students say that because the teachers know and remember them so well it is easy to get recommendations. A young woman, a senior, who came to Sacred Heart from a public school, says she "holds school dear, it has molded me into what I am."

Popular College Choices Columbia, Georgetown, Harvard, Kenyon, Middlebury, Princeton, University of Pennsylvania, Vassar, Yale, Boston University

Traditions Big Sister/Little Sister Cookout, used uniform sale, class coffees, Middle School Mother/Daughter Liturgy, Upper School Mother/Daughter Tea, Senior Mother/Daughter Breakfast and induction into the Alumnae Association, tree sale and caroling party, Christmas Pageant, Sacred Heart Antiques Show, Father/Daughter Dinner Dance, Dad/Daughter boat cruise, Black History Month (February), Women's History Month (March), Ring Day, Sacred Heart Feast Days, First Communion, Confirmation, May Festival of the Arts, Spring Book Fair, Grandparents' Day, archeology trip, class nine Blairstown trip, class eleven retreat, Upper School service trip in March, Sports Banquets, Hatter's Ball, Senior Dinner Dance, alumnae mothers lunch, conge, Senior cut day, Spring Street Fair, Prize Day, Homecoming

Publications Newspaper: *Spirit*
Upper School Literary magazine: *Zenith*
Yearbook: *Cornerstone*
Women's issues: *Women of Proud Heritage*
French Literary Magazine: *Sous Presse* ⌐
Middle School Literary Magazine: *Millenium*
Annual report
Parent/Alumnae Newsletter
Alumae Magazine: *Les Amies*

Community Service Requirement Each student is expected to give of herself to the school community and to the community at large—hours are not counted

Hangouts Jackson Hole (hamburger restaurant), Million Dollar Deli (candy store on Madison), Timothy's, Pintaile's Pizza

199

Corlears School

324 West 15th Street
New York, NY 10011
Tel (212) 741-2800
FAX (212) 807-1550

Coed
Nursery–4th grade
Not accessible

Ms. Marion Greenwood, Head of School
Ms. Rorry Romeo, Director of Admissions

Birthday Cutoff   Children entering kindergarten should be 5 by September 1

Enrollment   Total enrollment: 170
Largest point of entry is 2/3's
Kindergarten places: varies from year to year
Graduating class 1999: 19
2000: 9, 2001: 16

Grades   Anecdotal reports and checklists

Tuition Range 2001–2002 $10,950 to $17,000, 3's–4th grade
Additional fees: $500 building fee; reduced to $300 for a second child in the school

Financial Aid/Scholarship   30% of the student body receive some form of aid

Endowment   None
Each family makes a non-interest-bearing loan of $1,000 per child
There is a 3-year staggered payment system for this loan

After-School Program   Child care available after school Monday–Friday until 5:45 P.M.
Corlears After-School Specialty Program: open to Corlears students only; weekdays from 3:15 P.M. to 4:15 P.M.; an additional fee required; activities include music, drama, sports, chess, gymnastics, chorus, Spanish, art and cooking

Summer Program Corlears Summer Program: six weeks from mid-June to the end of July for children ages nursery through 7; recreational and creative activities, swimming and trips; an additional payment is required

---

Corlears was founded in 1968 on the Lower East Side and moved to West 15th Street in 1971. Corlears has well-equipped classrooms, an art room, wood shop, library, two gyms and a lovely play yard. Children bring their own lunches. Admission is based on a personal interview and available school records. Corlears is small and nurturing and parents describe it as a neighborhood school. Corlears goes to fourth grade, specializing in the education of children in the early years. There are interage classroom groupings throughout. There is a supervised early-morning drop-off for children age four and older. Spanish is taught beginning with the 4/5's. Classroom computers are available for children six to nine years of age. Use of the computers is integrated into classwork. An extensive counseling placement program assists fourth grade graduates with entrance to Middle Schools.

The Dalton School

108 East 89th Street
New York, NY 10128-1599
Tel (212) 423-5200, FAX (212) 423-5259
website: www.dalton.org

Coed
Kindergarten–12th grade
Accessible

Ms. Ellen Stein, Head of School
Dr. Elisabeth Krents, Director of Admissions, Kindergarten–12
Ms. Eva Rado, Director of Middle School/High School Admissions
Dr. Lisa Waller, Associate Director of Admissions, Kindergarten–12

Birthday Cutoff   None (but prefer applicants to be 5 by September 1)

Enrollment   Total enrollment: 1,290
Kindergarten places: approximately 85–90
Graduating class size: approximately 100–115

Grades   Semester system
Letter grades begin in 8th grade
Full departmentalization by 6th grade
First midterm and final in 9th grade

Tuition Range 2001–2002 $20,520 to $22,280, kindergarten–12th grade
No additional fees other than minimal PTA and activities fees

Financial Aid/Scholarship   Approximately 21% of families receive some form of financial aid
$3.5 million available

Endowment   Approximately $15 million

Diversity   Approximately 16% children of color
29 Prep for Prep students enrolled as of fall 2000
Affiliated with Early Steps Program, A Better Chance, Albert G.

Oliver Scholarship Program for children of color, Faculty Diversity Committee, PTA Diversity Committee; Full Time Diversity Coordinator

Homework   Kindergarten: none
1st: none
2nd: ½ hour nightly (15 minutes of work, 15 minutes of reading, except for weekends or vacations) building to ½ hour of homework and minimum of 15 minutes of reading
3rd: 45 minutes plus reading (not on weekends)
4th–6th: 1–1½ hours
7th–9th: 2–3 hours
10th–12th: approximately 3 to 4 hours a night

After-School Program   The Dalton Serendipity Program: a variety of creative and recreational activities including computer, foreign language instruction (including French, Spanish, Chinese, and Japanese), newspaper, opera, ballet, cooking, cartooning, sports and games; an additional payment is required; Kids Club: after-school care daily on premises until 5:45 P.M.; an additional payment is required
The Dalton Chess Academy for all age students
Interscholastic athletic competition, clubs and committees for Middle and high school students

Summer Program   Summer camp for Lower School students, open to children from other schools; an additional payment is required

———

Since its founding in 1919 by visionary educator Helen Parkhurst, The Dalton School's mission has been the improvement of education. Dalton is often described as having "one foot in traditional education and one foot firmly planted in the progressive movement." Known for inculcating independence of thought combined with intellectual rigor and for having a plethora of innovative programs with an emphasis on the use of technology to enhance education, The Dalton School serves as a model for other schools around the world and Dalton clones can be found in England, the Netherlands, Australia, Korea and Japan. Dalton is a famous school well known for its philosophy and historically rich in people and programs.

The foundation of a Dalton education is still the Dalton Plan which is not as complicated in actuality as it appears in writing. It consists of *House* (the home base for each student); *The Assignment* (the work: a type of contract between student and teacher); the *Laboratory* (one-to-one or small group sessions between student and teacher that augment classroom work). Dalton is unique in that Lab time is built into each teacher's schedule and students say that teachers are very accommodating and Labs often take place on the same day they are requested. Throughout the First Program and the early years of Middle School, the House Advisor is also the classroom teacher. House groups change each year and are comprised of students of the same age until high school. Then there are mixed grade levels in each group and these students remain with the same House Advisor for four years. The role of the House Advisor is to act as an advocate for each child and as the key contact person for parents with the school. The Assignment is a document created by the individual teachers that covers a period of time and details the academic expectations in a unit of study. It is introduced at the First Program (Lower School) and increases through Middle and High School.

Getting in: Dr. Elisabeth Krents, a Dalton alumna with a doctorate in Education, is the Director of Admissions for kindergarten through twelfth grade. Parents describe her as "knowledgeable, enthusiastic and warm." She brings a welcome professionalism to the process. Parents interested in learning more about the school can attend spring tours conducted by Elisabeth Krents or attend open houses at both the First Program and Middle and High School in the fall before applying. Dalton now takes a close look at parents to make sure they have a clear understanding of the school's philosophy and to see if they have solid values. For First Program applicants, Dalton requires both a parent tour and a meeting with Elisabeth Krents or another senior admissions staff member. Children are either interviewed at Dalton in small groups or observed in their nursery schools. Letters of recommendation from Dalton parents who really know the applicant's family are helpful. Don't waste time with letters from every celebrity or politician you ever met unless they really know your child. This is true of admission to Middle and High School too. In the two upper divisions, Dalton is looking to admit students who seek an extremely challenging academic environment that also stresses a deep appreciation for the visual and performing arts.

Once an application is received, prospective students and their parents are invited for an individual family tour given by a member of the faculty or a senior. The tour is followed by a class visit for the student and a meeting with Eva Rado for the parents. Applicant families get a chance to meet Dalton students, teachers and administrators at each visit.

Dalton doesn't merely pay lip service to diversity. The school follows through with respect and support, providing an afterschool program for children whose parents work, anti-bias retreats for faculty, parent and student support groups and a superb mentoring program that pairs high school students of color with successful professionals of color. These high school students, in turn, mentor younger students coming up through the Middle School and in First Program. Beginning in 1996, high school students join with the PTA Diversity Committee to organize the First Program Cultural Festival featuring, art, food, music and storytelling.

What are they looking for? Elisabeth Krents told us "We are trying to get away from the myth that there is a 'Dalton type' of child. We look for *all* kinds of children. Helen Parkhurst's goal was to have a community of different individuals and to educate every type of child, preparing each for the real world. We want to admit students (and families) who reflect the diversity of the real world and that means geographic, socioeconomic, racial and religious diversity." Parents say that eccentricity and ethnicity are valued. The 2000 kindergarten class was composed of 25% children of color and of children from all over the city. One does not have to be a genius to be accepted to Dalton; a former admissions director told us they look for "the child who is not just a sponge, but who will contribute." Dalton has a policy of preferring, but not automatically admitting, siblings and children of alumni. Dalton will accept an "at risk" child and does mainstream children with moderate physical disabilities provided they can keep up academically.

Parents: The School views parents as partners in the education of their children and they are invited to be involved in many different ways: There are committees that focus on ethics, gender, community service, the Book Fair, safety, and children's entertainment. Ongoing parent dialogues are conducted at the First Program. Kindergarten to grade 12 parents are invited to "Rap sessions", meetings for parents and administrators to discuss developmental and social issues.

Dalton is working hard to eradicate its glamorous, materialistic image of the 1980's. In the past, students have been labeled "spoiled." A student described the problem as particularly acute in Middle School "where students are not as considerate of one another as they could be." The newly formed PTA Ethics Committee hopes to rectify all that. Values education is at the top of the school's agenda and an Ethics Task Force is at work to find ways to integrate ethics into the curriculum in a meaningful way.

Dalton families have changed over the years although Jewish families have long been comfortable at Dalton. The Downtowners Committee meets regularly since Dalton has an ever increasing number of children who live below 23rd Street. A three division PTA Diversity Committee exists to support families of color. If there's any question as to how Dalton families align themselves politically, just peek into the Lower School library where, instead of the chiseled faces of Dalton's former headmasters, you'll see portraits of John and Robert Kennedy and Martin Luther King. Dalton no longer has the monopoly on glitz which is spread more uniformly among the private schools today including those which were traditionally more staid such as Trinity and Spence. And according to a parent who is also a trustee: "In the nineties there's no fuss over famous families; it's old news." Still, with so many prominent families in the school, networking opportunities abound. For instance, a Dalton high schooler working on a journalism project was advised by a senior writer at *The New York Times* who has a child at the school. An alumna told us she landed her first fashion internship with Diana Vreeland at the Metropolitan Museum Costume Institute thanks to a Dalton connection.

Dalton parents have created an extensive internship program for students. Opportunities include working as an intern in the sciences, arts, publishing and politics. Recently, a senior developed a project through an internship that led to her winning the national Siemens/Westinghouse award.

Dalton parents are generous in their financial support of the school. A recently completed capital campaign funded major improvements in the school's facilities. A 32,000 square foot Physical Education Center was recently constructed at 200 East 87th Street with a spectator gym (the basketball team is a strong draw) and other amenities. A floor was added to the top of the 89th Street building that houses a visual arts center with seven skylit studios. A state-of-the-art 8,000 square foot science center was recently built increasing the space allocated to the science program by 25%.

Program: First Program (affectionately known as Little Dalton) consists of kindergarten through third grade. It is housed in three interconnected townhouses on East 91st Street. Recent renovations added 2,000 square feet of instructional space to the school which includes a new science center plus a spacious commons area used by all the grades. The children still find Little Dalton "cozy" and move about the building freely.

Ellen Stein, a Dalton alumna, and former vice principal at Friends Seminary, was the Director of the First Program for six years and is now Head of School, after serving for two years as Associate Head of School. The lower division went through a series of directors during the early 1990's and Ms. Stein's arrival in 1994 brought a much needed stability to the school. Parents speak highly of her commitment to ethics and the establishment of a strong sense of community in the school. "While Dalton is noted for its individualization, we also want to develop children's senses of their responsibility as members of the school and to the community at large." Since Ms. Stein's arrival, parents note that the First Program has tightened the kindergarten through third grade curriculum to create a more even balance between rigorous skills and "process learning." Janet Stark, an educator from Boston, who worked closely with Howard Gardiner at Harvard University and directed the Lab School at Tufts University, is the Director of the First Program.

Academics are approached in a structured but relaxed setting. In kindergarten the school becomes acquainted with a child's learning style. Instruction is individualized, some parents say "to a fault." While the day is highly organized, children are encouraged to proceed at their own pace within the context of curricular goals for the year that are consistent across the grade levels. "The children learn how to think, how to take risks and how to make mistakes," according to a parent. Children are not expected to read by the end of kindergarten but if they do, individualized work is planned for them. Careful attention is paid to the placement of each student with the right teacher and right class.

From the very beginning of the learning process at Dalton, young students are actively and creatively involved in what they study. Dalton is historically known for its strength in the arts which are integrated into the curriculum. Dalton's First Program is based upon a social studies "core" where language arts, math, science, music and art are directly related to the core study. Second graders focus on New York City. The children create a model city which reflects what they have learned about city needs and urban design. They write and revise written reports about landmark buildings on the computer. In music classes the children put their own city poems into song and in art they paint murals of city scenes. In science class while studying animals, specifically birds, they dissected owl pellets classifying the excreted bones and formed hypotheses about what type of prey the owl had consumed. In addition, second graders created their own multi-media magazine on the theme of "diversity in the city." One class photographed neighborhoods, buildings and faces, another class focused on jobs and workers, interviewing parents in their workplaces and analyzing the data they collected, creating graphs (and posting data on the Internet). Another class concentrated on schools, foods and neighborhoods.

Former art teacher Sheila Lamb, a Dalton institution and now its "Artist in Residence," has guided the creative work of First Program students for thirty-one years. "I treat every child like an artist," she says. Her approach "is to be with the children with their imaginations . . . nurturers of their visual language." First Program art integrates all forms of arts and crafts. Creativity carries over to the sciences as well. One of our favorites is a third grade unit in which students study the unusual properties of planet "Oobleckia" (the name is based on a Dr. Seuss book, the planet is made of cornstarch, water and food coloring). Students must come up with solutions to problems such as "How would you land a spaceship on Oobleckia?" They work in groups and make a final report at a mock conference.

Dalton is at the forefront of independent schools for its commitment (both financial and philosophical) to technology and education. The school has maintained a high-speed connection to the Internet since 1994. Under the Dalton Technology Plan, faculty have designed projects and curricula that utilize advanced multimedia technology. According to a former headmaster, technology does not replace traditional educational methods: "It allows us to deliver the Dalton plan more powerfully than ever and is consistent with Dalton's individualized approach, sense of community and mission to prepare students for life after Dalton. Technology shifts education from adults giving answers to students seeking answers to their own meaningful questions."

Walking through the halls one can see kindergarten children making their own interactive counting slide shows, sixth grade students being introduced to history and scientific principles through simulated excavations of Assyria and Greece, high school students participating in advanced astronomy simulation, and English students exploring the ideas of Shakespeare's *Macbeth* through online resources, including digitized versions of scenes from the play by three different repertory companies.

Specialists enrich the Dalton experience. It's the only school we know of with an archeologist in residence who spends six weeks with each third grade class excavating a dig set up in the backyard. Sixth graders participate in the Archaeotype program, "a computer-based, integrated curriculum unit" developed by Dalton faculty in which they examine artifacts from ancient Greece and Assyria, conduct their own research and discuss their findings. It is also the only school in the city to have a special lecturer who teaches Dalton classes at the American Museum of Natural History. Chess is taught to kindergartners and first graders by a Yugoslavian chess master. A story teller works with kindergarten children using a multicultural and gender sensitive approach to teaching fairy tales.

Don't worry if your child is fidgety—there's plenty of opportunity for the children to stretch their limbs as well as their minds here. In addition to daily play on the two play roofs and at gym several times a week, beginning in second grade students use Dalton's newly constructed Physical Education Center.

At the end of third grade the children at Little Dalton pass through the arch during the traditional Arch Day Ceremony in June and move on to Big Dalton. Before they do, each makes his or her own colorful ceramic tile that is permanently mounted in a hallway of Little Dalton. The transition to Big Dalton seems to be an easy one since the children have frequently visited "buddy Houses" and attended a variety of events at the ivy-covered 89th Street building.

In Middle School, fourth and fifth graders are taught in self-contained classrooms in which the House Advisor teaches most subjects. Departmentalization begins in sixth grade and all students in sixth through eighth grades are taught math, social studies and English by a core group of three teachers who work together. The core groups make Big Dalton seem small and provide a comfortable transition to the more demanding high school. Each core teacher is an advisor and each student has a sense of belonging to a particular core. Students are placed in different core and House groups every year. Individual differences in levels or skills are recognized by grouping within the classroom, by the individualized assignments and by the enrichment and support provided in the classes and in Labs.

Student life at Dalton's high school is informal. There are no bells and the dress code is relaxed. "There's a small grunge element," said a student, Starting in late spring ninth grade students can sign out and leave school during a Lab period. Students who serve as peer leaders or peer tutors are involved with faculty in programs for incoming freshmen. A parent told us, "They do a superb job to ensure that the transition is smooth."

There is no Dalton "type" per se; there are jocks and artists and techies, and cliques form around interests. There is a strong drama group, a newspaper group, and athletic teams. Dalton students have embraced the new technology and communicate through Forum, an active e-mail message system. Amusing top ten lists are popular, we were told. Students also discuss community and current events online. Contrary to what's been written about Dalton students, most do not carry cell phones although the beeper has become something of a fashion accessory. With the new ethics task force in place, students are paying more attention to how they treat one another, including keeping the cafeteria clean.

Community Service is one avenue for teaching ethics and values and it is integrated into the curriculum at every grade level. A recent project brought senior citizens from a local center to Dalton for computer lessons. Paired together with individual Dalton children, seniors learned how to operate a mouse and access the Internet. The students, in turn, learned about life in the city before the advent of television. Other community service projects occur throughout the year: making bread for a homeless shelter to distribute, or First Program parents and children getting together to decorate bags for the God's Love We Deliver Program for homebound patients with AIDS.

In the High School, Community Service is required and viewed as an opportunity for students to learn through interaction with the world beyond the school. The service program encourages students to assume an active civic role. Recently, Dalton students worked with such agencies as Each Teach by establishing an after-school program for students of ages five through eight from Harlem and they are working on a project with Habitat for Humanity.

Dalton students are politically savvy. During the war in Iraq, they held town meetings, and during the presidential election, students had an electoral college discussion and expressed their views through political videos, radio ads and cartoons. Dalton students have created their own video news program modeled on CNN and do not shy away from open and difficult discussions concerning race and gender. There are diversity groups such as: DAALAS (Dalton Alliance of African-American and Latino Students) and the more inclusive group, Another Perspective. A discussion might be sponsored by Another

Perspective, or Gender Issues or Human Rights or by the Exploration Committee and speakers such as Ralph Nader and Katie Roiphe are invited to address the students in groups both large and small. Environmental issues are important to the community and the student government instituted a recycling program and convinced the cafeteria to stop using styrofoam products.

In general, teachers are addressed formally (Mr. Smith, Mrs. Brown) but it depends on the teacher. Students describe the staff as "relaxed, intense, knowledgeable." And because of Lab time, students have the opportunity to develop close relationships with their teachers. Dalton nurtures its faculty providing some of the highest salary and fringe benefit programs offered by the independent schools. The school takes special pride in recruiting and retaining a talented, caring and charismatic faculty.

Faculty are encouraged to take advantage of sabbaticals, travel grants, workshops and funded summer curriculum grants. During one recent summer teams of Dalton apostles were abroad in Taiwan, Turkey and Australia to spread the word about the Dalton Plan and the use of technology in education. Among members of the high school faculty are published historians, writers and artists. They can be characterized as committed to creating a classroom environment that challenges students to pose compelling questions and to analyze and interpret texts and data. In addition, during lab, when students work one on one with faculty, the faculty validates students' academic work and their creativity in a tutorial mode. Students emerge as independent and confident thinkers.

Dalton's requirements and course offerings in the high school seem quite traditional in scope. Freshmen, sophmores and juniors have to take at least five major courses. Core courses are English, history, languages, math and science. Students take elective courses as juniors and seniors. A junior can choose among five different courses in American literature, each with a different focus and reading list. A senior can choose among such humanities courses as "Asian Literature: East Meets West" and "Postmodern America," or "All the News That's Fit: The Press and the Public Interest." AP level courses are offered in many subjects.

Personal exploration is also provided in Lab Time throughout the students' years and particularly in the high school as students become increasingly independent learners. "It's not an easy school to go to," said a junior, "because you can't squander your free time—you do have to go to Lab." The Assignment might be a month long project; for instance, students studying the pre-Civil War years might write a newspaper typical of the period.

In keeping with the emphasis on creative expression and intellectual pursuit, many students elect to produce senior projects in which they demonstrate their abilities to work as visual and performing artists, historians, scientists and writers. Recently, a senior initiative program, promoted through the student government, was established. During the final month of senior year, students focused on scholarly, creative and service work and presented their results to an audience of faculty, students and parents.

At Dalton, there is tremendous support and encouragement for students seeking their own personal vision in the arts. Whether developing an energetically choreographed piece set to hip hop, studying the complexities of a Schubert Mass, designing an original set for Stephen Sondheim's *Company* or studying life drawing for three consecutive years, a Dalton student is guided by professional artists who are committed to teaching. One student described his experience this way, "If you're interested in a certain area, you are given a great deal of support and encouragement to pursue it in depth." According to a senior art teacher, "The new skylit art center has become a place where everyone uses every inch of space for the creation and consideration of art."

Dalton students display an array of musical gifts. There are two orchestras for the Middle and Upper School, a wind ensemble, a percussion ensemble, and a jazz-rock ensemble; a high school chorus and madrigal group. And all groups perform at the Annual Spring Concert.

While Dalton High School students are serious in their endeavors and ambitions, they also embrace opportunities for poking fun at themselves and the school community. A humor magazine, *"Liquid Smoke"* and Phase, a student cabaret replete with spoofs, give the students an avenue for expressions of irreverence.

Dalton's logo shows a child confidently leaving a mother's embrace. After thirteen years of self-discovery and academic adventure, Dalton's graduating seniors sing the words of the school motto: "Here we have learned to go forth unafraid."

After you read this entry you can visit The Dalton School Home Page on the World Wide Web. And don't forget to sign the Dalton-Web Guestbook.

Popular College Choices Brown, Harvard, Cornell, Yale, University of Pennsylvania, Wesleyan, Amherst, Williams

Traditions Greek Festival, Candlelighting, Arch Day, Dance Theater Workshop Concert, Spring Concert, parent discussion days, annual trips beginning in Little Dalton and throughout Middle School, school street fair on 91st Street, high school prom

Publications Monthly student newspaper: *The Daltonian*
Literary Magazine: *The Blue Flag*
Middle School Literary Magazine: *Whispers*
Art, photography: *Fine Arts Magazine*
Public Affairs Journal: *Macrocosm*
Science publication: *Quantum Leaps*
Yearbook

Community Service Requirement 90 hours over four years

Hangouts Starbucks, Stargate, The Bagelry, the gym

The Dwight and the Anglo-American International Schools

291 Central Park West
New York, NY 10024
(212) 724-2146 ext. 1
website: www.ingress.com/~dwight/
e-mail: admissions@server.dwight.edu

Coed
K–12th Grade
Not Accessible

Mr. Stephen H. Spahn, Chancellor
Dr. Joyce Robinson, Head of School
Miss Susan George, Dean of Admissions, K–8
Miss Alexandra Mustonen, Director of Admissions, 9–12

Uniform   K–8 boys: khaki or gray slacks, blue blazer or sweater with Dwight crest, collared shirts or turtlenecks
K–8 girls: jumpers, gray or dark blue skirts, white collared shirts and blazers or sweaters
9–12 boys: collared shirt with tie, no denim or turtlenecks
9–12 girls: skirt or slacks (not denim), collared shirt, or turtleneck

Birthday Cutoff   Children entering Kindergarten must be 5 by December 31

Enrollment   Total enrollment: 400
K places: 20
1st grade places: 20
Graduating class approximately 70

Grades   Trimester system
Letter grades begin in 5th grade
Departmentalization begins in 5th grade and is completed by 7th grade
First final exam is offered in 5th grade

Tuition Range 2001–2002 $18,500 to $20,400, K–12th grade
Additional fees for registration, graduation and support activities

range from $900 to $1500
A tuition payment plan is available for families

Financial Aid/Scholarship $800,000 in financial aid is available
30% of students receive some form of financial assistance

Endowment $4 million

Diversity   15% students of color
35% of the students were born in a foreign country
The International Baccalaureate (IB) is offered
English as a Second Language (ESL) instruction is available
Dwight has an expanded language program offering French,
Spanish, Italian for native speakers, Japanese, Hebrew and Chinese

Homework   K: 15–20 minutes
1st and 2nd: 1/2 hour
3rd and 4th: 45 minutes
5th and 6th: 1–2 hours
7th and 8th: 2–3 hours
9th–12th: 3–4 hours

After-School Program   Dwight's After-School Program is open to
students from other schools
Grades K–4: creative and recreational activities for an additional fee
Grades 5–12: there are approximately 37 clubs and activities
offered before and after school, including an after-school study
program; Minivarsity, junior varsity and varsity sports beginning
in 5th grade

Summer Program   The Dwight Intensive Review Program is an
academic summer program for students who need extra support
or wish to accelerate; the program runs from mid-June through
the end of July; an additional payment is required
An intensive ESL summer program is offered to current and
incoming students; there is an additional charge for this program

The Dwight School was founded in 1880 as an academy of classical studies, became coed in 1967 and added a London campus in

1972. Dwight merged with the Anglo-American International School in 1993 and is now a comprehensive school which also offers the option of study for the International Baccalaureate (IB) Diploma. This consortium works out very well because the Spahn family has had a long association with both schools. Stephen Spahn, the chancellor of The Dwight School, attended Anglo-American and his father headed that school for more than thirty years. The Dwight School retains its identity as "a small traditional school" while adding the international elements of the Anglo-American School. The Dwight School follows the International Baccalaureate Curriculum from kindergarten through twelfth grade. The Dwight School also offers a fully main-streamed program for children with mild learning difficulties (the Quest program).

The school occupies three buildings—a five story building on 89th Street, a brownstone on 88th Street and a new space on Central Park West. In addition to classrooms these buildings contain a pho-tography darkroom, two computer centers, a theater space, and two gymnasiums.

With students and faculty from over thirty nations, the school has a unique social as well as academic environment. Multiculturalism has been a natural part of the curriculum for many years. Students learn that there are many ways to celebrate and observe holidays. One of the highlights of the primary school is the annual holiday show. Each grade selects a country (often the country of origin of a classmate) and celebrates the country's most important holiday. Middle and Upper School students attend and some are involved in production and musical elements.

The Dwight School is one of the few New York area schools to offer the International Baccalaureate diploma. As described in the brochure, "eleventh grade students may enroll in this challenging cur-riculum in six subjects requiring solid academic skills and the ability to think clearly and communicate effectively. The IB curriculum is a deliberate compromise between the specialization required in some national systems and the breadth preferred in others." Foreign stu-dents planning to return to their countries of origin are often required to have passed the "bac." The IB program is acknowledged as an excellent preparation for the more competitive U.S. colleges and can often represent a year's college credit.

The school believes that everyone has the capacity to excel at some endeavor. The curriculum that Dwight has used in the Lower and Middle Schools for over twenty years, relates to Dr. Howard

Gardner's theories of "Multiple Intelligence." (See *Glossary*). The Dwight School also appreciates the differences in students' learning styles and utilizes a "multi-sensory" approach.

In addition, the low student/teacher ratio (12:1) allows for small classes and individual attention. The faculty create many of the imaginative programs that prepare students to think critically while demonstrating common sense, the ability to work with others and manage time, people and information.

"Any child can succeed here," says Mr. Spahn. "We can take an average youngster and motivate him, provide positive reinforcement and transform him into a learner." There is nearly constant communication between the school and the families. "We welcome comments," Mr. Spahn says. "We have an open door policy." Parents say the warm, dedicated faculty come in early and leave late—help is there when help is needed. Student progress is monitored through standardized tests including the SATs. Grades are given on most work in the upper houses (grades). Parents meet with teachers three times a year.

Some students who are really struggling in the fast-paced, highly competitive independent middle and high schools transfer to Dwight, resulting not only in better grades, but improved self-esteem as well. A student who transferred into Dwight from Dalton said, "At Dwight teachers and peers give you lots of attention; everybody knows your name. Dwight has a traditional curriculum. They don't offer as many courses, but there is more structure." One mother said her daughter went from "just keeping up" at her old school to "doing very well at Dwight." The amount of homework was the same, about two to three hours, but she made honor roll. "She got so much out of it," says her mother, "real values and friendships." One parent whose child had a vision problem said it was handled so that her child never felt bad about herself.

Getting in: Upon request, parents can tour The Dwight School before filing an application. Once an application is filed the child's current transcripts are requested. The school will call the parents to arrange dates for their child's interview. Parents say the setting is relaxed. All applicants have a one-on-one interview. Applicants spend part of the day visiting classes.

Program: Dwight is described as "a family school" with many siblings in attendance. The Lower School is small; all of the primary schoolchildren know each other and the teachers. However, some European formality prevails, as the teachers are addressed as "Mr. Jones" or "Miss Smith." In the after-school clubs a first grader can get to know a fourth grader. Because reading and math are taught on an individual basis, a child can advance at his or her own pace.

Perhaps the most distinctive feature of The Dwight School, in the words of a student, is that "there is no norm here." The student body is composed of children from diverse cultural, religious and geographic backgrounds. There is also a broad spectrum of academic ability at Dwight: a talented and superior group of international students who take advantage of a well-arranged ESL program and the opportunity to take the rigorous International Baccalaureate; average students taking the regular college preparatory curriculum and students with mild learning difficulties who are taking regular college prep with the support of the Quest program. There is a positive emphasis on differences. But all see themselves as part of the school.

The Quest program was started at Anglo-American in 1976 to provide additional support for children with minor learning problems (not behavior problems) so that they could participate in a full college preparatory curriculum without having to go to a tutor every day after school. All Dwight students are expected to develop a solid foundation of basic skills but the teachers at Dwight understand that children learn differently. Quest teachers provide extra support outside and within the classroom allowing students to be part of the group. Approximately 10 percent of the school is involved in the Quest program and parents must pay an additional fee for Quest program specialists. A parent said, "The teacher-student relationships are very personal and caring. The individuality of the students is stressed." Parents say that the program instills confidence: "My child thinks that he's a good learner now," said one parent. Parents with children enrolled in the Quest program say that reports are informative and elaborate with over thirty categories. Parents also learn the results of special testing in speech, reading and hearing.

The Quest program can serve students with mixed abilities; for instance, one student who is in the Quest program for science takes the International Baccalaureate course in history. Quest teachers also provide enrichment in English during the schoolday. Foreign students taking English as a second language often need assistance in certain subject areas.

The Timothy House students (grades K–4) play in Central Park or the gym every day. Reading is taught using an individualized eclectic approach. A combination of literature, phonetics and basal readers is used through third grade. First graders use invented spelling but the work we saw on display was corrected. There are spelling tests every Friday in first grade. Lower School students have computers in their classrooms. Writing is incorporated into all areas of the curriculum: In addition to science and social studies reports, daily diaries are kept. Second through fourth graders use Writers Workshop, in which they learn the steps for effective essay writing: brainstorming, first draft, editing, final draft. Timothy House students study French.

Lower School students go to the art and music rooms twice a week. There is a darkroom, a music room and a painting annex.

Dwight's Middle and Upper Schools are divided into three houses. Each house has its own Dean. The first class period is a House Community meeting. Advisors are selected by matching students and teachers.

Bentley House is composed of grades five through eight. Average class size is fourteen to fifteen students. Study skills are taught in fourth and fifth grades. Students learn how to prepare for tests and quizzes. In addition to the usual academic offerings, all students take art and music. Fifth graders study ancient Egypt and Greece. They read such classic children's literature as *Charlotte's Web* and *Treasure Island*. They are introduced to LOGO and word processing on the computer. (Spahn says that when handwriting is a problem, the student can write on a word processor and the ideas flow.) Spanish and French conversation and culture are introduced.

Sixth graders study the history of Europe from ancient Rome until the early eighteenth century. Latin is introduced in this year. Hebrew is offered after school. Seventh graders read *Of Mice and Men* and *Animal Farm*. In mathematics they study pre-algebra and algebra I. Native Americans and American history as well as geography are part of the curriculum. Life science and the environment are part of the science curriculum along with a health course.

There is an honor roll. There are intramural and mini-junior varsity teams. Extracurricular activities include Photography, Riding, Drama, Chorus, Newspaper, Yearbook, and the Dwight Environmental Action Committee.

Franklin House is composed of grades nine and ten. Students learn computer programming—Hypercard and Pascal. A course is offered in world cultures, "a thematic study of global diversity: Latin America, Africa and Asia." Tenth graders write a weekly essay in English class and complete a research paper. There is an honors humanities course in which students do readings in historical and political classics. The study of foreign language in Franklin House expands to include Spanish, French, Italian for native speakers, Latin, Japanese and Hebrew.

The ninth grade human relations course covers the issues of substance abuse and AIDS awareness. Counselors will not break a confidence if a student wishes to discuss a personal issue.

Anglo House is composed of grades eleven and twelve. Students are prepared for the SAT and achievement tests in English, mathematics, history and language. In response to student interest Dwight has added courses in constitutional law, military history, psychology, sports medicine and physiology and filmmaking. There are AP and/or IB courses in computer science, chemistry, physics, biology, art, English, Drama, music and foreign languages.

For students interested in science and the study of medicine, Dwight offers internships and courses at Memorial Sloan-Kettering Hospital and Rockefeller University. In a recent year a group of students worked in a cancer research laboratory. One student participated in the creation of the shark exhibit at the American Museum of Natural History.

The Adventure-Based Curriculum for grades five through twelve offers various outdoor experiences including orienteering, whitewater rafting, backpacking and caving. The Adventure-Based Curriculum has a three-part goal: 1. To develop the student's maturity and ability to interact with groups; 2. To impart key academic concepts in new and innovative ways; 3. To familiarize and acclimatize a primarily urban group of young people to the natural world.

The school considers building character an important part of its mission through community service, extracurricular activities, and sports. The Dwight Sports Institute works with students who have the talent and determination to become potential world class athletes and provides them with a flexible academic program combined with superior coaching. Self-esteem is bolstered through participation in athletics, and Dwight's trophy case is full. Dwight has a championship boys basketball team and championship soccer and softball teams as well as strong girls volleyball and basketball teams. The track and baseball programs are being expanded. Scholar-athletes at Dwight have included six ranked tennis players and a women's U.S. Sailing champion. Students can play on mini-junior varsity, junior varsity or varsity teams.

Students are encouraged to participate in extracurricular activities including the Model U.N., Newspaper, yearbook, Inward and Outward Bound, the literary magazine and social service.

Popular College Choices   Brown, Columbia, Dartmouth, Bowdoin, Boston University, Ithaca College, Cornell, Georgetown, Miami University, MIT, Northwestern, NYU, Syracuse University

Traditions   Science Fair, History Research Paper Competition, Art Exhibition, Camerer Essay Writing Contest, Shakespeare Competition, Doris Post Oratory Competition, annual Benefit Gala, Bronx Zoo trips, assemblies with guest speakers, International Food Fair, International Street Fair, Inward and Outward Bound, Model U.N., Spring Arts Festival, holiday show

Publications   *Camerer Essays* (winning essays from the Camerer Essay Writing Contest)
Yearbook
Literary magazine
Dwight School newspaper: *Dwightonian*

Community Service Requirement   All students are required to do community service; in addition to the Community Service Club, Dwight students volunteer in soup kitchens, Dwight Environmental Action Committee, Make-A-Wish Foundation, tutoring, SAVE THE CHILDREN

Hangouts   Micro Grill, Columbus Star, McDonald's

The Ethical Culture Fieldston School

The Ethical Culture Fieldston School encompasses three divisions: Ethical Culture, Fieldston Lower, and Fieldston. Each division has its own principal and there is a central Administrative Council, consisting of the head of school, the principals and the heads of centralized administrative offices.

Ethical Culture

**33 Central Park West
(at 63rd Street)
New York, NY 10023
(212) 712-6220 (main number)
(212) 712-8451 (admissions)
FAX (212) 712-8441
main website: www.ecfs.org**

Fieldston Lower

**Fieldston Road
Bronx, NY 10471
(718) 329-7310 (main number)
(718) 329-7313 (admissions)
FAX (718) 329-7337**

Fieldston

**Fieldston Road
Bronx, NY 10471
(718) 329-7300 (main number)
(718) 329-7306 (admissions)
FAX (718) 329-7302**

Coed
Pre-kindergarten–12th Grade
Elevator at Ethical Culture
Fieldston Lower and Fieldston partially accessible

Dr. Joseph P. Healey, Head of School
James C. Thompson, Assistant Head of School for
Admissions and Financial Aid
Ms. Soraya Diaz, Admissions Ethical Culture
Mr. George Burns, Principal Fieldston Lower
Ms. Rita McRedmond, Admissions Fieldston Lower
Ms. Rachel Friis Stettler, Principal Fieldston
Ms. Taisha Thompson, Admissions Fieldston

Birthday Cutoff   Children entering pre-kindergarten must be 4 before the day school starts

Enrollment   Combined enrollment: 1,597
Total enrollment Midtown: 514
Total enrollment Fieldston Lower: 312
Total enrollment Fieldston: 771
Kindergarten places: approximately 36 at Ethical Culture and 18 at Fieldston Lower
Size of graduating class: approximately 130

Grades   Semester system
Scheduled parent-teacher conferences pre-kindergarten through Form VI (12th grade)
Kindergarten–6: detailed anecdotal reports and checklists of skills
Letter grades begin in Form I (7th grade)
Forms I-VI (Grades 7–12): letter grades with teacher's comments; first final exam given in Form IV (10th grade)
Students taking accelerated science have a final exam in Form III (9th grade)

Tuition Range   2001–2002 $18,675 to $20,675, pre-kindergarten–Form VI (12th grade)
Additional Fees: books, supplies and other course-related expenses are approximately $250 for grades 7–12 only; lunch and yearbook are included in the tuition

Financial Aid/Scholarship   The Ethical Culture Fieldston School has one of the largest financial assistance programs of any independent day school in the country. Four and a half million was granted in 2000–2001

21% of the students schoolwide receive some form of financial aid in 1999–2000.

Monthly payment plan with no interest charges available to all enrolled families.

Endowment $54 million

Diversity   22% students of color throughout ECFS
28 Prep for Prep students enrolled at Fieldston School as of fall 2000
Fieldston enrolls students in the Early Steps, Albert Oliver and Summerbridge programs.
Multicultural Concerns Committee for parents and faculty at all campuses, student clubs include: S.U.M.E. (Students United for Multicultural Efforts) Asian Alliance, Gay/Straight Alliance, Interfaith, Social Justice Watch, Women's Issues, and *Kaleidoscope*, a multicultural club and magazine at Fieldston

Homework   Kindergarten and 1st: no homework
2nd: varies from 10 minutes to ½ hour and 15 to 30 minutes reading
3rd and 4th: varies from 15 minutes–one hour plus additional ½ hour of reading each night
5th, 6th: 1–2 hours
7th and 8th: no more than 3 hours
9th–12th: 3½–4½ hours a night

After-School Program   At ECS and Fieldston Lower: after-school program for kindergarten–6 with some mixed-age groups; selections include sports, dance, music, cooking, drama, arts and chess (for fun) for an additional payment; classes meet from 3:30–5 P.M., Monday through Thursday; Friday after-school programs begin and end earlier. Drop off and extended hours options at EC and Fieldston Lower. "Good Deeds Bandits" for grades 1–2, and "Cookies and Dreams," for grades 3–5 at EC introduce children to community service; Before School Music at EC is small group instruction in instrumental music for grades 4–5;
7th and 8th: intramural sports, extracurricular clubs, Middle School newspaper and musical

9th–12th: interscholastic sports, extracurricular clubs, newspapers (3), literary magazines and yearbook, two theatrical productions, jazz, chorus, and orchestra and several student-written and produced plays

Summer Program Weeks of Discovery: at EC, Winter vacation and June Weeks: a variety of creative and recreational activities pre-K–3 are offered for an additional payment
Compuart and Design Camp a June weeks program at Ethical Culture: Lego building programming and web design and animation are offered for grades 3–8, for an additional payment.
Sports Break a June weeks program at Fieldston Lower and Fieldston: all sports/learn to swim program for Kindergarten–grade 6, basketball camp for grades 3–9, for an additional payment
Fieldston Outdoors Day Camp: for ages 5–12, at Riverdale campus, full activities including swim instruction; focus on nature, environment and Hudson River region; trips. Head counselors are experienced teachers, an additional payment is required
Fieldston Summer Service Institute: The summer program of a year-round academic enrichment program for public middle-school students taught by Fieldston juniors and seniors under the supervision of Fieldston faculty.
Fieldston Enrichment Program (FEP): A four-week program on the Fieldston campus for public school students in grades 7–8, beginning in July, offering rigorous academic classes and team-centered recreational activities; field trips, students who complete the program are invited back for school year Saturday sessions.
Young Dancemakers Company: a tuition-free project for public high school students, performances are open to the public and the schedule is posted on the school website

The Ethical Culture Fieldston School was started in 1878 by Felix Adler, the founder of the Society for Ethical Culture. The school was tuition free only until 1890, but continues to follow many aspects of Adler's original vision of active learning. The school has always been diverse ethnically, racially, and financially. In ECFS's recent strategic plan, the school restated its commitment to the original mission of the school: to ethical education as a foundation, to diversity in all its manifest aspects, and to being a "beacon for progressive education." A $24 million capital campaign in progress will address the school's desire for more space, an enhanced Middle School program, facility upgrades, and so on. ECFS is already among the top three in faculty compensation. In 1994–1995 an agreement was reached separating the schools from the Society, but ECFS continues to offer nonsectarian ethical training beginning in second grade. ECF backs up its values with financial support and personal commitment. The school gives out more financial aid than most other independent day schools in the country.

Today many schools boast about "educating the whole child"; it is in vogue to have a child-centered curriculum. The Ethical Culture Fieldston school has been doing this from its inception, and is way out front in developing an integrated curriculum that emphasizes experiential learning. Children are active participants in their education here. Head of School, Dr. Joseph P. Healey writes, "Schools, such as ours, that nurture in their teachers and students a passion for questioning and inquiry coupled with a sense of balance between the given and the possible, produce dedicated life-long learners and strong analytic minds."

Getting in: Don't be intimidated by the imposing turn-of-the-century stone edifice on Central Park West; Ethical Culture (EC) is a warm and friendly place. One parent described the admissions process at ECS as "humane." Parents bring their child for a group interview. The interviewer asks, "Who's ready to come and play?" "Whose name begins with A?" and so on. After some leg hanging, all the children go off to play while the parents tour the school and ask questions of the admissions personnel and/or parent guides.

What are they looking for in a candidate? A child who feels good about him/herself, who is enthusiastic, who enjoys being part of a group (there's an emphasis on collaborative learning). The child should enjoy his visit. If your child was unusually cranky at the interview and you go home that night and he's got a full-blown ear infection, let them know. "We look at all the measures of a child to make sure we have an accurate picture of each applicant," say Director of Admissions James Thompson. After admissions decisions have been made, the wait list is active. There is no typical student, but one parent said the children are "bright, and laid-back yet outgoing."

Parents: The parents are "a low-key mix" of West and East Side professionals, artists and media people "but without the pretentiousness you find at other schools," parents say. Perhaps there is a larger percentage of working mothers. There is an acknowledged association between Ethical Culture, liberal thinking and progressive education.

There are many opportunities to socialize, and interesting lectures are offered for parents on child-related, nonacademic topics such as discipline and allowance. There is often a Fathers' Forum. Class dinners are potluck, usually at a family's apartment. Social competition is minimized and celebrity parents (there are a few) enjoy their anonymity. Parents get involved in the school in the early years and stay involved. Parent volunteers help with awards dinners, book sales and the Parent-Teacher newsletters, for instance. Here, you can have lunch with your child (K–2). School events include plays. concerts, picnics in the park, carnivals and auctions. Birthday parties run the gamut. Three-fourths of the parents are in town over vacations or weekends, one mother said.

Program: An awareness of ethics is implicit from the moment children begin their Ethical Culture Fieldston education. Formal ethics instruction begins in second grade with community responsibility and decision making. The emphasis is on ethics in action. The million-penny drive began as a math exercise at Fieldston Lower, then quickly expanded to include all three schools. The goal was to collect a million pennies, or ten thousand dollars, to give to the homeless. Children in both Lower Schools helped collect, sort and count. Once they'd reached their goal they had to find a bank that would take a million pennies, which they did. A committee of fourth, fifth and sixth grade students, with teacher supervision, researched the many homeless organizations and chose to give the money to three that they believed would most directly serve the people in need. Community service is part of the ECF experience, from fifth grade editors assisting first grade authors to Fieldston high school students giving a party for a local community center.

One parent described her daughter's move from nursery school to Ethical as a "warm to warm transition." Pre-kindergarten and kindergarten separation is handled gradually; parents can stay for the first week if necessary. There is a staggered schedule. Under the guidance of two full-time teachers, children often work on group projects. For instance, one kindergarten class created a school-wide post office, complete with student designed stamps and mailboxes, with daily pick up and delivery of internal mail.

In pre-kindergarten, children begin going out to specialists in half groups but are not fully departmentalized until sixth grade. Most "specials" (library, movement, music, computer, social studies workshop and so on) are taught by the specialist in half classes. The other half of the class either attends another special class or remains in the classroom, allowing the core teacher to work with small groups in math and writing.

Parents say there's a new emphasis on building a collaborative approach between child/faculty and parents, as well as a greater openness at EC. The most noticeable change is improved articulation of the curriculum through the grades. The emphasis is still on full mastery and competence with awareness that children work at different paces. Students with exceptional talents receive an additional level of challenge and those who need extra help receive it. (Remediation and enrichment are always provided within the classroom.) "The focus is still on what's developmentally appropriate," with much "horizontal enrichment."

During the elementary years, students learn how to gather, organize, analyze, evaluate and communicate information. The work load increases appropriately as children are guided toward internalizing the learning process and becoming independent learners.

Ethical Culture has resisted pressure from high-powered parents to "hurry" the curriculum. Departmentalization doesn't begin until sixth grade, and no final exam is given until tenth grade. (Most schools start these in seventh grade.) Parents say, "Children at Ethical Culture develop a positive attitude about learning, which prepares them for the academically demanding high school." Proof that children with different learning styles can find success here is that more than 95 percent go on to the Fieldston School, which is considered a "very selective" high school. It is one of the three "hill" schools (along with Riverdale Country School and Horace Mann School) located in Riverdale, New York, just north of the city proper—a twenty minute drive that might take forty-five minutes at some hours.

The catalog describing the curriculum in the early years states, "Our first aim is to provide an anxiety-free environment"; the development of self-esteem is as important to the later learning process as the acquisition of skills. Every activity in the Lower School is coed. No basal textbooks are used in the first years. Homework is given in appropriate amounts, not as busywork or evidence of academic rigor. Some parents, who grew up in schools that stressed rote memorization and drill, are a little perplexed by these methods and a commonly voiced concern is, "Is my child learning enough?" They can be reassured that standardized diagnostic and achievement tests are given and regular assessments are made, so the school knows exactly where ECF students stand in relation to their peers at other schools.

While there is a definite curriculum for each grade, Ethical's developmental approach to learning anticipates that not everyone will get to the same place at the same time. Children learn at their own pace. Emphasis is placed on conceptual development in tandem with building skills in reading, writing and math." Because the program is responsive to children's needs and interests, it varies from year to year. Most of the children will learn to read in the first grade. From pre-kindergarten on, you see words all over the classroom. There is mixed-ability grouping throughout the school and at various times throughout the week students break into half groups. Ethical Culture and Fieldston Lower each have math consultants, and have recently adapted a new problem-solving based math program, *Investigations in Number and Data and Space*. There is a math lab. On one blackboard was written: "Fifteen Reasons to Learn Math" (practical applications suggested by the children).

Ethical Culture has three science centers: one is a fully equipped laboratory with sinks, microscopes and computers. Wherever possible, science is hands-on and the scientific process is stressed: collect data, analyze it, construct a hypothesis, test it, reach a conclusion. In one classroom the students were studying the use of earthworms for indoor composting. On visiting day parents can crawl through a tunnel into the Star Lab, an inflatable planetarium brought into the classroom that illustrates the constellations. Fifth and sixth grade students chart the constellations on the computer. ECFS has completed a four year plan to enhance the level of technology in the classrooms, establishing common areas for the use of technology, and creating "libraries without walls," i.e., information network accessibility to and from classrooms, homes, major universities, as well as the Library of Congress. The computer curriculum focus on computers as tools to expand thinking and problem solving skills. Each of the school's divisions has a computer coordinator who helps the teachers integrate technology into the curriculum. In grades 4–6 children are introduced to Ethics of the Computer, LOGO, use of spreadsheets, databases, word processing, graphics, and on-line and multimedia presentation tools.

Ethical says it educates the "whole child," bringing out his or her natural creativity and encouraging its expression. The creative arts are considered intellectual disciplines; it follows that the arts at Ethical are strong. Four full-time are and workshop teachers are available at EC; there is an art studio with a pottery center equipped with a kiln. Art is integrated into the curriculum at many points. "Social Studies Workshop," a hands-on program relating to the social studies core, includes woodworking, sewing and cooking.

A hallmark of education at the ECS is an integrated curriculum, with subject areas overlapping in many different ways. Creativity and writing ability are also fostered. These elements combine in dramatic play. As part of the kindergarten curriculum, children learn that people live in communities, including the home, classroom, school, as well as the larger world. One classroom creates a bakery. They bake breads, and run a classroom café. Another class makes musical instruments and hand puppets.

Critical thinking skills are emphasized from early on. A fifth grade class studying Greek myths switched the gender roles—Hercules became a she—and there was much discussion about the implications. There are many ways in which students are asked to examine the underlying assumptions about our culture. A parent told us that when a student brought in a Barbie doll for a model science fiction project the class got into a discussion about cultural artifacts: If Barbie were found by an advanced civilization, what conclusions would be drawn about our civilization? Students brought in other objects. A fifth grade class studying ancient Egypt and Rome had a discussion about heroes. "Malcolm X, Superman and Audrey Hepburn" were some of the names written on the board.

Ethical has two full-size gyms: the sixth-floor gym, which is large enough to be subdivided, and a lower level gym with an overhead track. The gym program stresses individual skills development, games and sportsmanship. Ethical makes use of its location next to Central Park in many ways. The park is used as a laboratory and playing field, and of course, the children get to play in the snow and mark the change of seasons.

Manhattan parents should note that while Fieldston Lower, a second ECF elementary division located in Riverdale, primarily serves families from Upper Manhattan, all sections of the Bronx, Northern New Jersey, Riverdale and Westchester, almost 15% of its students travel from Manhattan. Parents should request a copy of the *Wheel Book* from Fieldston Lower that explains its true "core" curriculum, and tour its lovely campus and outdoor play areas, if they are interested in this unique program. Following are some examples of the subjects Fieldston Lower uses in constructing the core curriculum. First graders become experts in North American bird life. Third graders enact the lives of the Northern Woodland Indians who once inhabited the school's site. Fifth graders have a medieval fair; one class built a model cathedral and played roles in the social hierarchy of the time.

Fieldston is "a big school that seems small." In good weather, the grassy quad surrounded by fieldstone buildings is full of students. But the "Senior Grass" is not to be trod upon by underclassmen/women. The Tate Library is an award-winning facility (students say it's the best of the three "hill" school libraries) with over 40,000 volumes, an on-line catalog, multiple databases, media center and classrooms. Unique to Fieldston is a state-of-the-art print shop where everything from invitations to personal notepads are printed. In the spirit of founder Felix Adler, who believed in learning by doing, Fieldston is the only school that produces its own school publications from composition to final product. There are no bells, dress is casual and students seem relaxed. Sophomores can leave school grounds during "frees" and lunch. But by first form (seventh grade), college preparation has begun in earnest.

Fieldston's course guide is clear, descriptive and informative. The curriculum is broad, with electives that reflect a diversity of interests in the student body. Requirements are similar to those of the other independent high schools: a minimum of five academic courses per semester, with more elective choices as the students progress. Students do make choices about their academic careers; ninth graders have electives in language, arts and science. By junior year students can choose electives in English, math, history, language, science, visual arts, performing arts or computer. Six year sequences are offered in French, Spanish, and Latin, beginning in seventh grade. Conversational Spanish is part of the EC and Fieldston Lower experience. Courses are offered in Modern and Ancient Greek as well. An ethics course is required each year in Forms I through IV (grades 7–12). Although not designated as "AP" Courses, advanced college preparatory courses are offered in all disciplines.

Two programs that typify Fieldston's unique approach to learning are "the summer reading book" and the "Vietnam teach-in." The summer reading book is tied into a theme, such as "global studies," "science and math," or "social justice." In the fall, a student/faculty group plans an entire day of activities related to the author's visit to the

231

school. Recent books were Dava Sobel's *Longitude*, and Elias Miguel Munoz's *Brand New Memory*, about a "female Holden Caulfield" who re-discovers her Cuban identity. On the day of Munoz's visit, students planned Cuban dancing, invited political groups to talk about Cuban politics and so on.

Students also work with faculty to plan activities and invite speakers to the Vietnam teach-in, part of the tenth grade integrated American History/English curriculum, in which students enact the roles of key players in the conflict.

Although independence is fostered in the high school, support is always available. A tenth grader said that she could talk to her advisor about anything and that students feel "the administration is on your side." Respect for individual learning styles continues at Fieldston, and the Learning Center helps students with individual learning differences. Generous grants established a Writing Center and History Writing Center where English and history teachers and peer instructors are always available. Students can also meet with teachers during free periods. Outside tutors are recommended if necessary but in the words of one student, "Most people don't hire a tutor unless it's a desperate situation." Students say that although a lot is expected of them and they work hard, homework is not oppressive. One student said she has friends who are "drowning in work" at other schools.

Elective choices in English include "Social and Political Issues in Literature," "African-American Literature," "Russian Literature" "Women and Literature" "Dramatic Literature and Theatre" and "Shakespeare." Course offerings change annually.

All seventh graders ("firsties") are required to take "Patterns of Human Behavior," an anthropology course. History survey courses in eighth through tenth grades provide a solid footing for later electives, which include: "The Middle East," "African Studies," "History and Science," "China" and "Russian Civilization."

There is a six-year unified mathematics sequence culminating in "Advanced Calculus." There are many offerings in computer science.

At Fieldston there is a continued commitment to the artistic development of the students. As at Ethical and Fieldston Lower, the arts at Fieldston are considered an essential part of the curriculum and the offerings are extensive. Seventh graders begin with a visual arts sampler. In tenth, eleventh and twelfth grades a visual arts major is available. Elective offerings include "Ceramics," "Life Drawing" (with live models), "Creating from the Keyboard," "Architecture" and "Photography." Fieldston's Graphic Communications Department, based in its print shop, offers electives and a major for grades 10–12.

Dance at Fieldston is considered a key part of the performing arts program. In addition to modern, jazz and ballet, electives include "Dance and Sports," and "Hill Schools Dance Workshop." There are numerous opportunities to perform: The dance company tours and there is an annual dance concert with student choreography.

Students who like drama can take advantage of a well-developed theatre program. There is a theatre minor or major for juniors and seniors. There are six student-directed shows every year, plus one major drama (*The Rhinoceros* one year) and a musical (*Gypsy* one year). Students can take a course in stagecraft and practice their skills in the Alex Cohen Memorial Theatre. The drama and dance groups tour elementary schools. All "firsties" (seventh graders) must study a musical instrument or sing in an ensemble. Small group and ensemble instruction is available.

In addition to arts there is a full athletic program. Fieldston has a three season interscholastic sports program for eighth graders. Ninth through twelfth graders have a full interscholastic sports schedule, including strong teams in girls' field hockey, tennis and volleyball; coed cross-country, boys' basketball and soccer. Fieldston has two large gyms, four tennis courts, a weight room and a renovated pool. There is a healthy competitive spirit. One student said, "At Fieldston team sports are for fun; at Riverdale and Horace Mann they're out for blood." That doesn't mean Fieldston doesn't play to win. In recent years, the girls volleyball team were the Independent School Athletic League champions, girls tennis was Prep League champion. The baseball team won the Ivy Prep League Championship. Basketball games always draw good crowds. During football season the school mascot, the Eagle, walks around campus. Homecoming is a major event at Fieldston. First there is a pep rally the day before big games, which besides football include soccer, volleyball and field hockey.

Student government is the PAC or Principal's Advisory Committee, a longstanding organization that meets regularly to discuss academic and social affairs. One year students initiated a program to get teachers to bring a mug from home instead of using Styrofoam cups. The money saved was donated to a charity to benefit the environment. PAC also deals with social aspects of life at Fieldston and the bolstering of school spirit. PAC organizes the annual fall barbecue and

Fieldston Awareness Days that raise community awareness of the school's mission and goals. In addition to PAC there is STS, a student-to-student counseling program. In the high school there are electives in ethics including an advanced course in peer leadership and peer mentoring.

Tolerance and respect for difference are at the heart of Fieldston, and by and large relations between different groups are harmonious. One student said, "Fieldston is a lot more politically correct than other schools; I've become a lot more aware here." Fieldston students flew yellow flags during the Gulf War, but gave Clinton a landslide victory in the '96 schoolwide election. At a recent awareness assembly on race relations, David Mura, poet and educator, spoke about understanding and embracing individual differences. Hugo Mahabir, Director of Multicultural Programs says, "The Office of Diversity Multicultural Development serves as an advisor to students and as a resource for the faculty in working with students and parents from many different backgrounds.

There are over forty clubs at Fieldston that vary from year to year, depending on the interests of the student body. An activity period is built into the school day so that students can participate in a club and perform in a school play or compete in interscholastic sports. Some clubs are the ever-popular Amnesty International, Social Justice Watch, Environmental Club, Golf, Rugby and S.U.M.E. (Students United for Multicultural Education).

Rachel Friis Stettler, Fieldston principal said, "The ECFS mission to provide a humanistic, ethical and progressive education really is present in the day-to-day life of the school. ECF attracts and nurtures people who question, think and aren't afraid to act."

Parents say that ECFS is not merely a college preparatory school, but that Fieldston prepares students to be citizens who are analytical thinkers, creative problem solvers, lifelong learners and agents of positive change in the world. Apparently the colleges agree; Fieldston students are accepted at a range of colleges and universities including the big Ivies—one recent year ten students went off to Yale.

Popular College Choices   Brown, Columbia, Connecticut College, Dartmouth, Emory, Harvard, Oberlin, Northwestern, Stanford, University of Chicago, University of Colorado (Boulder), University of Wisconsin-Madison, Vassar, Wesleyan, Yale

Publications   Yearbook: *Fieldglass* (since 1929)
Newspaper: *The Fieldston News* (since 1929)
Multicultural magazine: *Kaleidoscope*
Literary magazine: *Litmag*
Alumni paper: *The ECF Reporter*
Student community service magazine: *Community Server*
Student visual arts magazine: *Eagle Eye*
Alternative student literary magazine: *Maverick*
Student history magazine: *The Fieldston Historical Review*
Student on-line young women's magazine: *Roxine*
Faculty newsletter: *Fieldston performing Arts Newsletter*
Parent and Teacher Association newsletters
Note: Most of ECF's publications are printed at Fieldston's own printing press.

Community Service Requirement   60 school hours or 120 summer hours beginning in 9th grade; Academic community service courses are offered

Hangouts   The Quad, Student-Faculty Center, Riverdale Diner (if you have a car), the cafeteria for breakfast

The Family School

323 East 47th Street
New York, NY 10017
(212) 688-5950, FAX (212) 980-2475

The Family School West

308 West 46th Street
New York, NY 10036
(212) 582-1240

Coed
Nursery (18 mos) through 6th grade
Not accessible

Mrs. Lesley Nan Haberman, Headmistress
Mrs. Ann Baker Reed, Director of Admissions

Birthday Cutoff   Children entering nursery school must be 18 mos by September 1st
Children entering kindergarten must be 5 by September 1st

Enrollment   Total enrollment: 140
Toddler places: 24 (18 mos-3 years)
Kindergarten places: 20
Graduating class size: 8–10

Tuition Range 2001–2002 $11,000 (5 full days—Toddler Program)–$11,500 (Elementary, 6–12 yrs)
Additional payment is required for children with special needs who require additional support

Financial Aid/Scholarship   None

Endowment   None

After-School Program   Monday through Friday, 3:00–6:00 P.M., supervised homework time and a variety of recreational and creative activities for an additional payment; vacation programs are also available

Summer Program   Weekly camp program from mid-June through the end of August, 8:45 A.M.–5:45 P.M.; a variety of recreational and creative activities and academic maintenance, weekly field trips, older campers swim three times a week; if families enroll for the entire summer they receive one week free

---

Founded in 1975 by the current Headmistress Lesley Nan Haberman, The Family School East is a member of the American Montessori Society. "We call ourselves eclectic Montessori," explained the admissions director, a comfort to those who think of pure Montessori as too rigid. All of the teachers are certified Montessori teachers and traditional Montessori materials are used in the classrooms. Children are placed in heterogeneous mixed age groupings, also characteristic of the Montessori approach.

Getting in: All candidates are interviewed. Applicants to kindergarten and above are required to take the ERB.

The Family School was founded as a nursery school, added a toddler and elementary school program, and now serves children through twelve years of age. The Family School is housed in a bright, up-to-date (and meticulously clean) building adjacent to the Holy Family Church. Although the school rents space from the church there is no religious affiliation. The school has a large gym downstairs but children also play outdoors in McArthur Park next to the United Nations building. Children bring their own bag lunch and a snack is provided by the school. The Family School West serves twenty children (ages 2½ through 7) in a one room school house, the former gym of a Lutheran Church.

As its name suggests, The Family School is an inclusive, warm community. The students come from all parts of the city. Some parents commute to work in the neighborhood. Thirty-five percent of the student body is composed of children of color. The school also has a limited program for children with special needs, some of whom receive additional support services.

In a pre-primary classroom (ages three to six) each day begins with the morning circle. Children then choose materials and work either independently or in a small group. Areas of study include geography, math and practical life. Children experiment in all art media, and the school has a kiln and pottery wheel. Music and foreign language classes enrich the curriculum, and creativity is encouraged. Examples of the children's work adorn the walls of the school. In the primary school children continue learning in a practical context (for example using math manipulatives) and begin to move toward the understanding of abstract concepts. Reading is taught using several methods including the use of "Mack and Tab" readers.

Parents receive written narratives twice a year and the ERB is offered each spring. The school-parent partnership is an essential component of the Montessori experience and parent-teacher conferences are held three times a year. Parent classroom observations are mandatory.

Traditions   Grandparent's Day, holiday programs and Family Field Day in Central Park's Sheep Meadow.

Popular School Choices   Independent schools such as Riverdale, Dalton, and Browning; and various public school programs.

Friends Seminary

222 East 16th Street
New York, NY 10003-3703
(212) 979-5030, FAX 979-5034
website: www.fsnyc.k12.ny.us

Coed
Kindergarten–12th grade
Partially accessible

Richard Eldridge, Principal
Harriet Burnett, Director of Admissions

Birthday Cutoff   Children entering kindergarten must be 5 by September 1
Children entering first grade must be 6 by September 1

Enrollment   Total enrollment: 628
Kindergarten places: 40
6th grade places: 18
9th grade places: 25
Graduating class size: approximately 54

Grades   Semester system
Lower, Middle and Upper Schools: conferences and written reports
Letter grades begin in 9th grade
Departmentalization begins in 5th grade and is completed by 7th grade
Final exams begin in 7th grade

Tuition Range 2001–2002 $18,375 to $19,275, Kindergarten–12th grade
Additional fees: Building Improvement Fund, PTA dues, accident insurance, beverage plan, $883. Books and supplies are additional after 8th grade
There is an optional lunch program

Financial Aid/Scholarship   25% of students receive some form of financial aid

239

Endowment $4.5 million

Diversity   26% students of color
16 Prep for Prep students enrolled as of Fall 2000
Friends participates actively in Early Steps, Prep for Prep, The
TEAK Fellowship Program, Albert G. Oliver, and ABC (A Better
Chance) programs
Friends receives foundation grants to support diversity
CARE (Cultural Awareness Reaching Everyone) is a student-run
organization that "takes an active role in discussing and educating
the community about cultural diversity"
Director of Multicultural Affairs: liaison for both students and
parents; Multicultural Parents Committee and the Multicul-
tural Faculty Diversity Committee provide a forum for issues of
concern
Student-led "Day of Concern" (a recent topic: Race in America)
Student committee on gender issues

Homework   Begins gently in 1st grade
2nd and 3rd: 20–30 minutes per night
4th: 1/2–1 hour per night
5th and 6th: up to 1–1 1/2 hours per night
7th and 8th: up to 2–2 1/2 hours per night
9th–12th: up to 4 hours per night

After-School Program   Early Bird Program: (Lower School)
8:00 A.M. to 8:45 A.M.
Friends After Three Program: 5 days a week for Lower and
Middle School; creative and athletic activities from 3:00 P.M.–
4:30 P.M., Monday–Friday
Extended coverage available until 5:30 P.M. each day
Vacation program during school breaks
All of the above programs require an additional payment
Athletics: Middle School intramural sports, Upper School junior
varsity and varsity team sports

Summer Program   Summer Friends: A seven-week program in
June and July, open to 4–18 year olds from all over the city,
offering a variety of recreational and creative activities

Friends Seminary, the oldest continuing coeducational day school in New York City, is hardly the most traditional. Friends is distinguished by its Quaker heritage. Founded in 1786, Friends is owned by the New York Quarterly Meeting of the Religious Society of Friends. The brochure says: "Administering the school is viewed as a team effort." There is a Principal rather than a Headmaster. Friends provides a value-based program that is centered on the tenets of Quaker philosophy: the belief in each person's unique strengths and possibilities; the value of community and the individual's role within the community; decision-making by consensus; and the peaceful resolution of conflict.

Richard Eldridge, a Quaker, has been the Principal of Friends for over eleven years. Mr. Eldridge is described as "gregarious, charming, intensely focused and spiritual." One parent said: "His office is a welcoming place; he's always quoting something wise and thoughtful and knows all of the kids' names." Another parent said that at Friends "there are no walls up around anyone; my children feel free to go to the Lower School head if they are having a problem."

Academically, Friends begins gently and becomes increasingly rigorous as students progress. A former Parents-Teacher Alliance president told us: "Friends is not a socially competitive school but Friends does create competitive students."

Getting in: Parents are invited to tour Friends before making application to the school. For kindergarten and first grade, a group of six students meet with two teachers for one hour during which time each family has a twenty-minute interview. Friends is a very popular choice not only for downtown parents but also for families throughout the city, and admissions are competitive. It is the school's policy to give priority consideration to qualified children of members of Quaker Meetings. Qualified siblings and children of alumni are given priority as well. Admission, however, is not automatic; one parent told us her daughter was deferred a year even though she had an older sibling at Friends. There is a wait list.

Parents: Parents talk about the family feeling at Friends. One mother described the school as "a community of shared values. Everyone is on a first-name basis." There is a buddy system called Parent Connection to help parents get involved in the school. Parents say there are more working mothers than not. Fathers are very involved in the school; in fact, several fathers serve as class representatives and pick up their children at day's end. In response to the changing needs of two-career families, Friends provides programs before and after school and during vacations.

Socially the parents are very low-key; there is a form of reverse snobbery: "Downtowners don't flaunt," we were told. A prominent parent in the media business makes a point to park his limo down the block and walk his child into the school. "Nobody really knows who's wealthy," says one parent.

The Friends Fair is an annual spring event made possible through the efforts of hundreds of parents and students. In addition to the Friends Fair, there is an auction every other year and annual class potluck suppers. Many Friends parents remain involved long after their children have graduated; Because it is a Quaker school, raffles and games of chance are prohibited. A capital campaign was recently completed which raised money for improved technology, faculty salaries, financial aid, and a new Upper School science, math and technology building which opened in September 1998.

Friends parents feel they have a voice. Throughout the year the PTA sponsors dialogue meetings for each division of the school. Examples of topics discussed include seventh graders and their need for independence, the role of the advisor, substance abuse and conflict resolution. The PTA has organized a PTA-community service partnership in which parents and students work together in support of a specific community service project.

Program: "Quaker philosophy permeates the school and after you've been there a while you recognize it," said one parent. Service to the community is important at Friends. It begins in kindergarten and extends through grade 12. Walking through the hallways you might see tenth graders working with first graders; fifth graders helping in the library, and parents working with students of all ages in workshops to decorate bags for God's Love We Deliver. At night, a common room at Friends is used to shelter and feed the homeless. A few years ago, when some parents expressed fears about tuberculosis, alterations were made to the building to provide adequate ventilation rather than do away with the program.

Quaker Meeting is the heart and soul of the school. Meeting is a time for students and teachers to come together in silence, and if moved to do so, to share thoughts and feelings with their community. In Lower School, a few moments of silence. takes place in the classroom during the beginning of circle time. In the Middle and Upper

Schools, Meeting is held in the landmarked Meetinghouse. Middle School Meeting always begins with ten minutes of silence, followed by announcements, assemblies and so on. Upper Schoolers have silent Meeting twice a week for twenty-five minutes. Most of these Meetings focus on relevant issues and school business. The mother of a fifth grader says, "Everybody thinks that because it's a Quaker school there are hours of silence, but that's not so; Meeting is a quiet time to come together, discuss the day, and to hear announcements." A former PTA president said that "even the shy child will speak out and feel comfortable at Meeting." Parents are invited to attend Meeting whenever they can.

The Lower School, focuses on academics as well as the child's emotional and developmental needs. Friends recognizes that young children learn at their own pace and that the development of good self-esteem early on will lead to future success. Mixed-age grouping supports this thinking and is an important aspect of the Lower School program. (Note: Middle and Upper Schools are traditionally structured.) The aim of mixed-age grouping (which covers a two-year age span) is to help "students master skills at the appropriate level in their development." In the early years some students benefit from being the oldest in a class, others learn well from older peers. Placement is considered carefully at Friends. Teachers know their students well and consider a variety of factors before making placement decisions. A father told us that his children's reports were "wonderfully detailed with a huge space for comments."

Parents say the emphasis at Friends is on learning how to learn. "Students don't just memorize the date of a battle but rather what really happened at the battle," said one. "Learning is an ongoing process," said another. "My daughter's teacher said, 'Just because you turn it in doesn't mean it's over.'" Some parents whose own educations stressed rote memorization have asked, "Are they getting enough facts?" But while the students may not realize that when they are measuring and baking they are using mathematics, this integrated approach to education in the Lower School is becoming the norm in even the most traditional schools.

The Lower School classroom is a "combination of teacher-directed instruction and self-directed exploration and learning." Children spend much of their time working in groups toward a common goal (collaborative learning), and learning is hands-on whenever possible. No one approach to the teaching of reading is used because teachers consider the approach that is best for each child. Students use math manipulatives as well as workbooks, and computers are in every classroom to support the curriculum. Spanish begins in kindergarten. In social studies students begin by looking at themselves and their families, widening their perspective to include the city, the country, and the world of other cultures. Lower School children at Friends leave their classrooms for science, art, music, library, gym and multi-media workshop.

Middle School consists of grades five through eight. Middle Schoolers hang out in the courtyard, cafeteria or library, not in the hallways. The head of the Middle School, Pam Wood, is well-liked and students feel they can talk to her about almost anything. Students and parents say that the workload increases in fifth and again in seventh and ninth grades. In fifth grade departmentalization begins. Concrete work (including plenty of homework) is given "and the kids crave it," one mother said. A parent said, "The kids are more comfortable and really show progress quickly and early in the year." Math for fifth and sixth graders is grouped by homerooms with subgroups based on ability. One mother said her daughter started to slack off and wasn't keeping up with her math work. The teacher discussed the problem with the student before it became a pattern, and she got back on track without her parents having to exert pressure. Students who need enrichment can get it. One mother said her son needed more work, so creative homework, not just busywork, was given.

Beginning in fifth grade students have increasing opportunity to make choices for themselves in the areas of foreign language and performing arts. French or Spanish begins in fifth grade. In seventh grade students are required to add two years of Latin.

Literature, grammar, and good writing are emphasized in English. Eighth graders have weekly writing assignments using creative and analytical skills. Topics in social studies begin with the study of ancient civilizations in fifth grade and progress through Medieval and Renaissance history in sixth grade, including the history of civilization in Africa or the Americas. Seventh graders study the American Constitution and government, African-American history and "The Immigrant Experience." Eighth graders examine topics in anthropology including gender roles and ethnocentrism.

The Middle School science program is comprehensive, beginning with a hands-on general curriculum for grades five and six and extending to earth science and ecology in seventh grade and an introduction to biology in eighth grade. Middle Schoolers also take a human relations course that examines the physical changes and social issues of adolescence.

The visual arts program at Friends includes both two- and three-dimensional offerings as well as many performing arts electives. In addition to two art studios there is the Seegers Arts Center that houses a photography lab and art gallery. Seventh and eighth graders can take art electives. Under the direction of Jennifer Fell Hayes, an award-winning playwright, the Friends Seminary drama program features three major theatrical productions annually. Recent productions include: *The Pirates of Penzance, Into the Woods, The Adventures of Nicholas Nickleby,* and *A Midsummer Night's Dream.* In addition, drama electives are available to students in seventh through twelfth grades. Theatre is performed in both the Meetinghouse and in the new "black box" theatre.

In Middle School, each day begins with Meeting, and Quaker values continue to play a central role in school life, particularly regarding discipline. Each student from seventh through twelfth grade has an advisor who offers curricular guidance and is an advocate in matters of discipline. At Friends, one incident does not make for a bad reputation. A mother told us that when her son was in Lower School, a Middle School boy picked on him. The Middle School boy was suspended for four days, then required to work in the Lower School student's classroom. "He turned out to be a good kid," said the Lower School parent.

The Middle and Upper School music program at Friends is focused in two areas: classical and jazz. Students can also choose from a range of electives including chamber music, instrumental music and vocal jazz ensemble, wind ensemble and instrumental instruction. Students can learn an instrument in fifth grade; jazz instruction begins in seventh grade. Bob Rosen, Friends' jazz impresario, exemplifies the private school teacher who not only teaches but *does.* Mr. Rosen is a clarinetist, saxophonist, composer and conductor. He arranges for Friends students to jam with noted jazz musicians: One fundraiser brought Chuck Mangione to the school for a session. Students perform at a year end concert. Some graduates pursue jazz as a vocation.

Athletics at Friends is competitive. There are varsity and junior varsity teams in soccer, basketball, softball, baseball, volleyball and tennis as well as coed teams in squash, track/cross-country and swimming. (One seventh grade boy said he longed for football.) Friends has championship varsity boys and girls basketball teams as well as boys soccer, and track.

President Theodore Roosevelt, an alumnus, would be pleased to note the schoolwide emphasis on experiential education. The wilderness and outdoor adventure programs at Friends begin in kindergarten with apple picking and become more sophisticated in the Middle and Upper Schools. First and second graders make their own maps of their routes from home to school and go to a nature study workshop. Third and fourth graders go to Nature's Classroom in Connecticut for an outdoor education program. Middle Schoolers also travel to Nature's Classroom and learn mountain climbing and rappelling. Upper School students take backpacking trips, go sea-kayaking and master rock-climbing skills.

A large number of new students enter Friends at sixth grade. "Friends is an easy school to start," says the mother of two. "There are many new kids and there's an enormous effort to be welcoming." Current Upper School students mentor ninth graders. Ninth graders and above can leave school for lunch or relaxation in adjacent Rutherford Place (but have to sign out first).

The Upper School consists of grades nine through twelve. It is considered a rigorous program, with up to four hours of homework a night. Minimum requirements for graduation include four years of English, three years of history and math, two years of foreign language, two years of laboratory science, and twenty-seven hours of community service per year. Students must demonstrate proficiency in the use of the computer (though most students go beyond the minimum requirements). Advanced Placement courses are given in all major disciplines. If a student is interested in pursuing an AP course and if there are not enough students to form a full class, a teacher will mentor that student so he or she can sit for the AP exam. In addition, Friends has a relationship with New York University, enabling qualified juniors and seniors to take courses for high school credit.

One Upper School parent commented that the Upper School course offerings looked like a mini-college catalog. For example, English electives include "Is Hamlet Mad: Great Works in Madness," "Great Works: Conflict and Consequences," "Fiction and Ethnography" and "Fiction and Film." Choices in history include "History of Western Thought: The Quest for Certainty," "The Holocaust and

Human Behavior," "African-American History" and "International Relations: Latin America."

Friends has made a serious commitment to technology. There are two newly renovated computer labs in addition to computers in most classrooms. Network systems are in place, and the new Upper School facility houses multi-media classrooms. Students interested in media can take advantage of the outstanding Chapman Media Center which houses a screening room with editing capability.

Upper School students can participate in several international and national study programs including School Year Abroad, a semester at St. Stephen's School in Rome, and The Network of Complimentary Schools.

The Social Action Committee "informs the Upper School on issues and activities of community and global concern." Friends students volunteer to help the less privileged or donate time to Amnesty International, "Children of War" or to an environmental group. Friends students are not afraid to speak up and speak out. They are socially aware and committed to service. A father of two children at Friends told us, "The philosophy of the school prepares children to deal with the outside world. They become independent and self-assured."

The centerpiece of the Friends graduation is Quaker Meeting. One parent said that out of the silence of the Meeting "the students speak with remarkable self-possession; some of their speeches are political and some are nostalgic." There are no caps and gowns.

Popular College Choices   Brown, Cornell, Oberlin, Georgetown, Wesleyan and University of Chicago

Traditions   Quaker Meeting, nature and wilderness trips, Friends Spring Fair, Book Fair, Potluck Suppers, concerts, God's Love We Deliver bag decoration workshops, Lower and Middle School Field Days, Halloween Party, drama and musical theater

Publications   Literary magazine
Yearbook
Middle School newspaper
Upper School newspaper: *The Penn*
Photography journal

Community Service Requirement   Kindergarten–Grade 6: performed within the school

Grades 7–8: minimum of 15 hours, within the school
Grades 9–12: minimum of 27 hours, within or outside of school
Eleventh graders take a required service seminar

Hangouts   Mariella's Pizza, Joe Jr.'s Coffee Shop, Gramercy Coffee Shop, Rutherford Square Park

The Geneva School of Manhattan

Nursery School
250 East 61st Street
New York, N.Y. 10021
(212) 755-5269
Amy Buckner, Director

Grammar School
583 Park Avenue
New York, NY 10021
(212) 754-9988
FAX (212) 754-9987
e-mail: Genevanyc@aol.com
Ms. Rim An Hinckley, Director

Coed
Nursery–8th Grade
Not accessible

Uniform   Girls wear a plaid jumper or navy skirt, a white blouse, and a navy cardigan sweater with the school logo. Boys wear khaki pants, white shirt, and a navy cardigan sweater with the school logo.

Birthday Cutoff   Children entering nursery (beginners) must be 3 by November 1
Children entering kindergarten must be 5 by November 1

Enrollment   Total enrollment: 130 in 2000, increasing each year as the school grows
Beginners places: 8
Pre-K places: 6
Kindergarten places: 18

Grades   Parent conferences and progress reports six times a year. Report cards are issued three times per year. Letter grades begin in 4th grade. The Stanford Achievement Test is given each year in the spring

Tuition Range 2001–2002 $2,260 to $10,300 Nursery through 8th grade
Additional fees are approximately $200

Financial Aid/Scholarship Tuition is based on a sliding scale so as to make it affordable for families of all income levels. Tuition is further reduced for families with more than one child

Diversity Approximately 30% students of color

After-School Program None

Summer Program None

The Geneva School of Manhattan was founded by a small group of Christian parents and educators who wanted to provide a classical education based on Christian tenets. Funded by private individuals and foundations, the school opened in 1996–97 with pre-kindergarten through first grades. Each subsequent year the school hopes to add one additional grade, continuing through grade 12. The Nursery School is located in the Trinity Baptist Church building on East 61st Street, but is not affiliated with any church, and the Grammar School is located at 583 Park Avenue. A Christian-based independent school, the first in Manhattan, is likely to appeal to many parents who now home-school their children and to others who want a correlation between their faith and their children's schooling.

The founders were inspired by Dorothy Sayer's essay "The Lost Tools of Learning." The school name refers to Geneva, Switzerland, a center of the Protestant Reformation in the 1500's. "Geneva was a training ground for missionaries who went out all over Europe to spread the Gospel," says the school's Director, Ms. An.

Getting in: A personal interview and a screening test, administered by the school, are required. The school has a non-discriminatory policy but parents must sign a statement of faith and a statement of cooperation. (The school will discipline children but corporal punishment is not permitted.) The registration form asks parents to describe their children and also to "Please give a short explanation of who you understand Jesus Christ to be and what His death and resurrection means to you," as well as to "Describe briefly your relationship with Jesus Christ."

Parents: All parents are required to volunteer three hours per week at the school. Parents are also involved in planning field trips and other extracurricular activities.

Program: The Director of the School, Ms. Hinckley, taught mathematics at UNIS for six years and at various public schools before that. She explained that the school will be "teaching the truth from the Bible," including creationism, but adds "Our school doctrine is not specifically in support of the fundamentalist movement." According to the school's literature, the educational program is founded on the principles and values set forth in Scripture. The Geneva School will revive the educational style that uses the classical "trivium," a three phase model that corresponds to the different phases in child development. The Geneva School's distinctive characteristics include: 1) curriculum based upon the Bible as God's Word; 2) classics taught as enduring works of excellence; 3) rigorous academics and small classes; 4) emphasis upon languages with foreign language instruction beginning in pre-school; 5) disciplined and nurturing Christian faculty; 6) involved parents who volunteer time and talents; 7) affordable tuition based on financial need. Latin instruction begins in third grade, and all students are required to go on weekly field trips.

Grace Church School

86 Fourth Avenue
New York, NY 10003
(212) 475-5609, FAX (212) 475-5015
e-mail: zwarner@gcschool.org
website: gcschool.org

Coed
Junior Kindergarten–8th grade
Accessible

Mr. George Davison, Head
Ms. Zelda Warner, Director of Admissions

Birthday Cutoff   Children entering junior kindergarten should be 4 by September 30
Children entering kindergarten should be 5 by September 30

Enrollment   Total enrollment: 394
Junior kindergarten places: 30
Kindergarten places: 12
Graduating class size: approximately 35

Grades   Semester system
Letter grades begin in 5th grade
Departmentalization begins in 5th grade

Tuition Range 2001–2002 $16,500 to $19,350, junior kindergarten–8th grade
Additional fees: Lower School approximately $50; Upper School approximately $300
Families with more than one child enrolled receive a discount on the additional tuition

Financial Aid/Scholarship   25% of the student body receive some form of aid

Endowment $4.8 million

After-School Program   The GCS After-School Program is for Grace Church School students only; Monday–Friday until 5:30 P.M., for an additional fee; however, each child is entitled to take one class free each semester, but may sign up and pay for as many as space allows

Play groups meet every day and there is an hourly charge that is billed monthly (reductions are given to families who receive financial aid); advance registration for play group is not required

Vacation play groups are available

Summer Program   June School from the close of school until the end of June; a variety of creative and recreational activities for an additional payment

---

Grace Church was founded in 1894 as the first Choir Boarding School for Boys in New York City and celebrated its centennial year in 1994. Coeducation at Grace Church began in 1947. The school occupies nine renovated adjoining buildings. ERBs are required for admissions as well as an interview. (Kindergartners are interviewed in groups of three.) The school is traditional and follows a structured curriculum. There is a dress code and teachers are addressed formally ("Mr. Smith," "Miss Jones"). A renovation in 1993 created a new dining room (hot lunch is included in the tuition) and a greatly enlarged library with state-of-the-art computer catalog and research facilities. The computer lab was updated and relocated next to the library. The computer center, all classrooms, and the library are connected via a local network with Internet access. Further expansion in 1999 created a new arts center with a sculpture studio, gallery, and digital technology lab integrating computers with the arts. The Technology Access Project will make modem-equipped computers available to all Upper School students for home use. E-mail links the community. There is a separate playroof for the junior kindergarten and kindergarten children in addition to a gymnasium, outdoor play yard and dance studio. Park facilities, Chelsea Piers, Basketball City, and a neighborhood indoor swimming pool are used to augment the physical education program.

Grace Church School has three divisions: junior kindergarten and kindergarten; Lower School: grades one through four; Upper School: grades five through eight. A choice of French or Spanish is offered in third grade. Latin is offered in seventh and eighth grades. The arts play a vital part in the curriculum. GCS has two art studios, each with its own kiln and children gain experience in a variety of media. Students in grades seven and eight may elect a major arts course in place of a second language. Instrumental music is offered beginning in third grade. Children may sing in the school chorus or audition for the church choir, which now includes girls. Three major drama productions are staged each year. In a recent year students performed in *Through the Looking Glass, Oliver* was the spring musical and *Through a Glass Darkly* completed the season. Younger children perform at music and dance assemblies and in class plays.

There is weekly chapel and students study the Bible: The Old Testament for grades three and four, and The New Testament for grade 5, and ethics (grades six and eight). Seventh graders complete an overview of world religions. Grace Church School families observe a wide variety of faiths. Community service is required in the Upper School. In recent years Grace has become a very popular choice among downtown families. Grace Church School has a support group for parents of color. In 2000, Grace Church enrolled four students from Prep for Prep.

Graduates attend independent day schools, boarding schools and the specialized New York City high schools.

The Hewitt School

45 East 75th Street
New York, NY 10021
(212) 288-1919
website: www.hewittsch.org

All girls
Kindergarten–12th grade
Not accessible

Ms. Linda MacMurray Gibbs, Head of School
Ms. Anita S. Edwards, Director of Admissions

Uniform   Lower School: a Black Watch plaid jumper; a white blouse tights or socks and sensible, non-skid shoes
Middle School: a Black Watch plaid kilt, a white blouse, tights or socks and closed low-heeled shoes with non-skid soles. Casual options for both Lower and Middle School include uniform slacks, skirt, and a variety of uniform shirts, blouses, and sweaters. Sneakers can be worn
Upper School: a dress code requires comfortable and school-appropriate clothing. No sweatpants, jeans, shorts, T-shirts, no excessive makeup, jewelry, clogs, high-heeled platform shoes or sandals

Birthday Cutoff   Children entering kindergarten must be 5 by mid- to late October but readiness is the most important factor

Enrollment   Total enrollment: 390
Kindergarten places: 36
Average graduating class: 20-24

Grades   Semester system
Letter grades begin in 6th grade
Semester exams begin in 7th grade

Tuition Range 2001–2002 $16,694 to $18,155, kindergarten–12th grade
Additional fees: for activities, publications, trips, $278–$781. For books, $244–$637. Food service, $949, for grades 8-12 laptop purchase or lease required

255

Financial Aid/Scholarship $450,000 available

Endowment   Approximately $3 million

Diversity   4 Early Steps, 5 Prep for Prep students enrolled as of September 2000
Cultural Awareness Club

Homework   Kindergarten: none
Grade I: 15 minutes
Grade II: 30 minutes
Grade III: 45 minutes
Grade IV: 1 hour and 15 minutes
Grade V: 1½ hours
Grades VI, VII, VIII: 30–45 minutes per subject (4 or 5 subjects a night)
Grades IX, X, XI, XII: 45 minutes–1 hour per subject (4 or 5 subjects a night)

After-School Program   Hewitt Afternoon: (primarily a service for Lower School girls) 3:15 to 4:45 P.M. Monday–Friday; study, sports, music lessons, crafts, field trips; an additional payment is required
Clubs that meet after school include gymnastics club, crafts club, computer club, French club, and chess club
After-school study hall: a supervised study period Monday–Thursday 3:15–4:00 P.M., for grades V–XII

Summer Program   None

Hewitt consists of two connecting five-story townhouses on East 75th Street. The library, quiet and cozy with a fireplace and piano, also has several computers with networking and CD-ROM capabilities and a periodical room. The winding staircase and floral wallpaper lined with class pictures of girls in white dresses holding bouquets harks back to the 1920s, when the school was known as "Miss Hewitt's Classes" and educated the daughters of the city's socially prominent families. In the seventy-plus years since then, Hewitt has evolved to meet the needs of modern young women. In July 2000, Ms. Linda Gibbs became head of school, Ms. Gibbs says that Hewitt, as the smallest of the girls' schools in Manhattan, "offers an academic environment that meets the strengths and challenges of each girl, all within a safe atmosphere." Ms. Gibbs' goal for Hewitt includes long range strategic planning "to reexamine and reaffirm everything about the school and to give us clarity about the future. We've formed a steering committee and we've had a Board retreat, and we're planning a community retreat with parents and students. Out of this patterns will emerge—what drives us is what's best for the students," says Gibbs. By September 2001, the school will begin to incorporate the results of their research.

Getting in: The application fee is $50. Parents visit Hewitt with their daughter for a tour and interview. They are interviewed by the director of admissions in her office. Kindergarten and grade 1 candidates take a brief screening test before visiting classes. The director of admissions and the early childhood specialist also observe every kindergarten candidate at her own nursery school. One parent told us "Hewitt spent one and a half hours with the family and demonstrated a real appreciation of who my daughter was. Not only did they remember us but they were able to describe her whole personality." She felt the other girls' schools were much more aloof. Parents of girls who will be entering Hewitt in the fall are invited to a breakfast to meet the head of school and Lower School head. In recent years Hewitt has set record levels in kindergarten enrollment.

Another parent said, "Hewitt lacks some of the social crustiness of the other girls' schools"; Hewitt is "definitely nurturing and traditional, with a less aggressive atmosphere than some other places." There are achievement assemblies for the Lower, Middle and Upper Schools that recognize accomplishment in academics, athletics, art and community service. A parent said: "They play down competition but there are prizes and awards." One mother said her "tomboy/nonconformist child fits in just fine at Hewitt." The brochure says that Hewitt provides "an environment of understanding, trust and affection." Many parents describe Hewitt as "a very comfortable environment."

Parents: Hewitt is a multicultural community. Although most mothers and fathers work outside the home, parental involvement is encouraged. One parent describes the Hewitt atmosphere as "small, cozy and inviting; you never feel out of place. You can be there as much as you want." In addition to open Parents Association meetings, there are many social and fund-raising events throughout the year. Some highlights are the annual Book Fair and Art Show, the Spring Benefit Dinner Dance, the Father/Daughter Dinner Social for grades eight through twelve and the Hewitt Barn Dance for Lower School families. Parents may accompany their daughters to breakfast at Hewitt, from 7:45 A.M. until 8:15 A.M.; working and nonworking mothers say it's a nice way to spend some quiet time together each day. Siblings are invited and there is no additional charge.

Program: Each morning Hewitt students shake hands with the head of school. During the first week of school, Lower School students are met downstairs and the teacher escorts them to the classroom. One mother whose daughter had trouble separating said the Lower School head "saw me struggling and together we designed a strategy that worked."

The Lower School at Hewitt consists of kindergarten through fourth grade. The kindergarten is a full-day program. Girls stay until 3:00 P.M. Monday through Friday. A parent said that Hewitt girls are very busy after school; she has to book play dates at least three weeks in advance because girls are enrolled in ballet, swimming or religious classes.

Hewitt has a "spiral curriculum." Academic subjects are introduced in kindergarten and are built upon in developmentally appropriate ways in the succeeding years. Kindergartners are introduced to reading, literature, writing, math, science, social studies, music, dance, physical education and library. French is introduced in kindergarten "without pressure" twice a week through songs and oral and verbal games such as "letter of the week." There are computers in the kindergarten classrooms and computer instruction in the computer lab. Hewitt has laptops in its High School, training for teachers, and all of the classrooms are wired for LCD's. The computer labs were recently renovated with help from a $50,000 Edward Ford Foundation Grant.

Individualized attention is a hallmark of instruction at Hewitt. The teacher-student ratio at Hewitt is high. About three-quarters of the faculty hold advanced degrees. Students learn at their own pace and teachers pay careful attention to different learning styles. There is individual as well as small-group instruction in writing and reading. Kindergartners begin journal writing. One mother said her kindergartner came in reading and received one-on-one reading enrichment.

Math is taught with manipulatives like unifix cubes and games that develop a strong number sense. There's no one way to do something. "There are a lot of creative children here," the director of admissions told us. One mother told us her daughter, who has musical ability, takes private lessons at school and was encouraged to write a song that she'll sing with her class.

In addition to physical education and dance classes, kindergarten girls go to the playroof, which is equipped with tricycles, wagons and jump ropes. After-school options include ice skating, swimming, art clubs and chorus.

In the first grade classrooms are furnished with tables in clusters. By second grade there are weekly spelling tests. Parents receive anecdotal reports twice a year; letter grades begin in sixth grade. Assemblies begin with the pledge of allegiance. In special assemblies the author of a children's book might speak, or a dance or musical group might perform. One assembly featured the Yale Whiffenpoofs. A highlight of the Lower School year is the annual Hewitt Hop.

Parents say at Hewitt, which is committed to single-sex education, "there is an implicit validation of female values." One mother praised the emphasis on women in society. In each division students gain experience with leadership in the Student Council.

Middle School at Hewitt is composed of grades five through seven and occupies the 75th Street building. The girls have advisors who monitor each student's program. Departmentalization begins in sixth grade. Girls continue to study a full schedule of subjects including English, history, math, science, computer, French or Spanish (with the addition of Latin in grade 8), studio art, drama, music and gym. There is a new emphasis on math and science in the Middle and Upper Schools. Eighth grade students take algebra I or II and conduct experiments and write lab reports in eighth grade earth science. For a history assignment, a seventh grader told us students had to pick a country or state and write a research paper about a cultural aspect of it; topics chosen included African dancing and photography in China.

The Middle School has its own student council and its own literary magazine, *Enterprise*.

Overnight trips begin in Middle School. Sixth graders travel to Mystic, Connecticut and learn about a maritime village while staying on a whaling ship. Seventh graders go on a leadership training program with Project Adventure. One student who didn't want to go was given the option of writing a paper on the environment instead. There is an eighth and ninth grade trip to Sharpe Reservation. Tenth graders got to Washington, D.C.

The High School at Hewitt is composed of grades eight through twelve. Students have faculty advisors. A minimum of four academic subjects per year is required but most girls take five major subjects and one or two minors in the arts. Three lab sciences are required as are four years of English and three years of math, history and foreign language. There are six AP classes offered, significant since Hewitt is so small. In addition, the school offers "Anytime, Anywhere Learning" through an Upper School laptop computer program that gives students universal access to the Internet and other digital resources such as CD-ROMs and integrated software.

There are two dramatic productions a year, one of which is performed in conjunction with boys from other independent schools. Many students participate in the production, either as cast or crew. Recent musicals were *Pippin, Annie* and *Grease.*

There is a Field Day for Lower, Middle and Upper Schools. After interscholastic sports games, Hewitt girls are expected to give a cheer and a handshake to their opponents.

Clubs at Hewitt include: Art Club, Drama Club, Chorus, Model U.N., Cultural Awareness Club and Environmental Club. There are also junior and varsity sports teams. Students can work on the school newspaper, *The Hewitt Times,* or the art and literary magazine, *The Venturer.* Students also produce a yearbook, *Argosy.*

Senior privileges include using the front staircase the "Senior Stairs," instead of the back stairs and a four-week year end independent project with an individual faculty advisor. Eleventh and twelfth graders can leave school with parental permission.

Community service is required at Hewitt. Beginning in Lower School, there are many opportunities for students to volunteer. One Lower School class held a bake sale to benefit the Jewish Guild for the Blind. There is a Birthday Book Club—girls may donate a book to the Hewitt Library on their birthday. Middle Schoolers often work in the school in the library, cafeteria or art room. Outside of school students visit the Marymount Nursing Home, participate in "You Gotta Have Park," walk for The March of Dimes and volunteer in the St. James Church soup kitchen. Faculty advisors and student council leaders publicize and coordinate many of these activities.

Highlights of the Upper School include the spring musical, the December chorus and handbell concert and the Sports Banquet. On Founder's Day flowers are laid at the foot of Shakespeare's statue (Miss Hewitt's favorite) in Central Park. Hewitt has teams in volleyball, basketball and softball as well as a very strong gymnastics program.

Commencement exercises at Hewitt are traditional. The seniors gather onstage and the kindergarten class walks in wearing white dresses and white gloves. Each kindergarten student presents a senior with a small bouquet and then walks, hand in hand with her, down the aisle.

Popular College Choices   Brown, Duke, Skidmore, Vassar, Trinity, Georgetown, Boston University

Traditions   Parents' Association Annual Holiday Fair, Arts Festival and Book Fair; new parents' dinner, Parents Association luncheon, Father/Daughter Dinner Social, Parents' Visiting Day, Thanksgiving Concert, Holiday Concert, Lower School Square Dance, Science Fair, Hewitt Birthday Book Club, Hewitt Corner (school store), major donors cocktail party at Dr. Yurchak's apartment, class trips to Mystic, Connecticut, Model U.N. trip to Washington, D.C., Middle School musical, Upper School play, Upper School musical, Lower, Middle and Upper School Field Days, Founder's Day, Lower School Final Assembly and Concert, Sports Banquet and Upper School Achievement Assembly, senior projects, commencement, young alumnae play

Publications   Upper School newspaper: *The Hewitt Times*
Middle School literary magazine: *Enterprise*
Lower School literary magazine: *Safari*
Art and literary magazine: *The Venturer*
Photography magazine: *Perspicacity*
Yearbook: *Argosy*
School magazine: *The Hewitt Anchor*
School newsletters: *Hewitt Happenings*

Hangouts   La Viande Coffee Shop, 3 Guys Coffee Shop (on Madison Avenue)

Horace Mann School

Horace Mann Nursery Division
55 East 90th Street
New York, NY 10128
(212) 369-4600

Horace Mann Lower Division
4440 Tibbett Avenue
Riverdale, NY 10471
(718) 432-3300

Horace Mann Middle/Upper Division
231 West 246th Street
Riverdale, NY 10471
(718) 432-4000
e-mail: admissions@horacemann.org
web-site: www.horacemann.pvt.k12.ny.us

Coed
Nursery–12th grade
Accessible for Nursery Division and Middle/Upper Division
Not accessible for Lower Division

Dr. Eileen Mullady, Head of School
Dr. Lawrence Weiss, Head of Upper Division
Ms. Marian Linden, Head of Middle Division
Dr. Steven Tobolsky, Head of Lower Division
Ms. Lisa Moreira, Director of Admissions
Ms. Wendy Steinthal, Director of Admissions, Lower School
Mrs. Patricia Yuan Zuroski, Director, Nursery Division
Mrs. Lydia Hechter, Director of Admissions, Nursery Division

Birthday Cutoff   Children entering nursery 3's must be 3 by September 1
Children entering kindergarten must be 5 by September 1

Enrollment   Total enrollment nursery–12: 1,660
Total enrollment nursery division: 160
Kindergarten places: 35

Total enrollment lower division, grades kindergarten–5: 440
Total enrollment upper division, grades 6–12: 1060
Graduating class size: varies, from 150–170
The largest point of entry is at nursery level (approximately 40 places) and you must call for an application to the nursery school the first week after Labor Day
Horace Mann also has a kindergarten with one class of up to 21 children located in Riverdale, serving families from Riverdale, Westchester, the Bronx and New Jersey
The sixth grade admits 40 new students

Grades   Trimester system
Kindergarten–3: detailed anecdotal reports, conferences and checklists; check, check-plus or minus grades; weekly quizzes
Letter grades begin in 4th grade, and anecdotal reports continue
Departmentalization begins in 4th grade, is completed by 5th grade
First final exam is given in 7th grade

Tuition Range 2001–2002 $14,890 to $21,500, nursery–12th grade
Additional fees for books, transportation, lunch and trips approximately $1,300 to $2,000 in Middle and Upper Divisions

Financial Aid/Scholarship   Over 4 million is awarded annually for financial aid
There are 12 named scholarship funds in the Upper Division

Endowment   Approximately $48 million

Diversity   52 Prep for Prep students as of Fall 2000
The Union is an organization of students of color at Horace Mann
There is a parent support group

Homework   1st grade: Worksheets, always due on Fridays
2nd: 4 times a week, 10–15 minutes in the beginning of the year going up to 20 minutes, 2 worksheets per night
3rd and 4th: 30–45 minutes a night
5th: 1 and 1/2 hours a night
9th: 2–2 1/2 hours per night

263

10th–12th: 50 minutes per subject per night, approximately 3 to 4 hours; more time is required for studying for exams and long-term projects

After-School Program   For grades K–5: a variety of recreational and creative activities; an additional payment is required
Upper Division: 40–70 clubs, which vary from year to year depending on the interests of the student body
Competitive sports in the Ivy Prep League

Summer Program   Six weeks of courses for credit or review for Horace Mann students and new students; many summer camp programs available.

———

"Harvard man" is what many parents are wishing for when they enroll their four year olds at this very selective school. If you have a vision of your youngster in crimson uniform cavorting on a grassy field with the best and the brightest, then this might be the right place. (HM's colors are crimson and white.) And as at an Ivy League campus, most of the old stone buildings at Horace Mann High School are named after former headmasters and founders: Tillinghast Hall, Van Alstyne Auditorium, Pforzheimer Hall, the Loeb Library, the Pretty-man Gymnasium.

The school opened two new buildings in 1999: a new Middle School building for grades 6 through 8 and an Arts and Dining Center serving grades 6 through 12. A complete renovation of most of the other buildings will be completed in 2002. The new buildings and renovation will highlight the Middle Division programs, increase student and public spaces, focus on art and music offerings, and make the existing T1 Internet and WAN accessible from every classroom.

It is somewhat ironic that this prestigious private school is named after a man known as the father of public schools. Horace Mann actually had nothing to do with this namesake. According to HM's history *The First Hundred Years*, it was founder Nicholas Murray Butler who chose the name because "at the time it was the only household name in American education." Blessed with strong leadership through the years, HM has served as a model for both public and private schools, combining the traditional and the innovative, and has always encouraged physical hardiness as well as academic rigor. Originally coed, except for a forty-year hiatus when the campuses were separate (under Inslee "Ink" Clark), Horace Mann readmitted women in 1974. Along with Clark, Dr. Mitchell Gratwick, HM's head for seventeen years, left an indelible stamp on HM: "High standards, conservative values and innovative methods." Gratwick was a founder of the AP program and acquired the John Dorr Nature Laboratory, two strong components of the HM experience.

HM uses the building-block approach to learning: "Each step leads to the next." This philosophy is carried all the way through HM, ultimately leading to preparation for advanced college study. HM's bottom line: With superior preparation, a good measure of ability and the willingness to work like an ox, a student can achieve excellence here.

Horace Mann Nursery Division was originally established as a service for the children of alumni "who wanted to start their offspring in a Horace Mann system." It is located in a tight but tidy converted coach house on 90th Street between Madison and Park. There is no indoor gym but children use a rooftop playground or a yard for at least an hour a day and go to Asphalt Green once a week. Classrooms are colorful and well ordered—if crowded—reflecting a structured but stimulating "hands-on" curriculum. The staff psychologist is available to parents for consultation. All the head teachers have a Masters in Education.

Getting in: You must apply to the Nursery Division (HMND) when your child is two and a half years old. Getting in at the nursery level is far easier on the parents because the WPPSI-R (administered by the ERB) is not required for admission at that time. However, there is a caveat here. At the age of three there is really no way of knowing if your child will be able (or willing) to keep up with the high expectations and the work required later on. Also, potential learning differences that might be picked up by the WPPSI-R are not apparent. We know too many parents who boasted about their children getting into HM Nursery only to have to tutor them after school or (like one parent we know) over the summer. Parents may have to consider a change of school by third grade because a child is falling behind. It is not that HM weeds out children. The school is prepared to give as much support as is needed but there is a process of self-selection.

Applicants to Lower, Middle and Upper divisions come to campus for a student and parent interview. Tours are led by student "ambassadors." Applications should be filed by December 1st and must be completed by January 15th. Families who request an application are invited to Fall Open Houses. The ratio of applicants to places is about ten to one. It's easier to get into HM at sixth or ninth grade.

The relocation of the sixth grade to the Middle School campus has led to a significant change in Middle School Division admissions. At present HM enrolls approximately 40 new sixth graders and 15 or fewer seventh graders. Lisa Moreira, Director of Admissions, says the transition resulted in four applications for every place in sixth grade and more than six applications for every seventh grade opening.

The Upper Division enrolls approximately 30 new students each year in ninth grade with six applications for every place and receives 30–40 applications for 5 to 10 tenth grade places. Few openings are available at eighth and eleventh grades.

Kindergarten applicants may be observed at their nursery schools if there are many children applying from those schools, but most children are observed in a group interview at HM in the afternoon (1:30 or 3:30). "By kindergarten," one interviewer said, "it doesn't bode well if a child doesn't separate well in the interview." It is very helpful if an HM parent who really knows your child writes a letter of recommendation.

Some entering students don't know how to write their names while some come in reading. But by the end of kindergarten most kids have "cracked the code." Formal instruction begins in first grade, and reading is expected to be well under way by second grade. "The curriculum in the early years is geared to the readiness of the children," says the brochure. There is a strong emphasis on basic skills balanced with new techniques and tools. Experiential learning is stressed, and computer, chess and other learning games are introduced. There is a resource room with six computers for kindergarten. One parent praised the fact that here children "capture the enthusiasm for learning young." During the second half of the year kindergartners travel up to Riverdale to get acquainted with the elementary school campus. (We suggest that parents applying to the Nursery Division take a tour of the Elementary Division, because before you know it your child will be up in Riverdale.)

Parents: The Nursery Division is homogeneous. Parents describe it as predominantly Jewish and financially mixed. One said, "I thought the parents would be a lot hipper." There is a very active Parents Association. One mother recalls attending her first parents' meeting thoroughly underdressed. Where do many families go on weekends and vacations? "You know," said one parent, "it's the triangle: the Hamptons, Boca, Vail." But parents report that once they reach Riverdale the school community is more mixed. Communication with the parents is frequent, and there is a Parents Association newsletter. Nursery Division parents can be class representatives and they may also serve as elected members on the Horace Mann Board of Trustees.

Since the Elementary Division, located in Riverdale, is "no one's neighborhood school," communication between home and school is very important. Teachers often call and chat with parents. There are many student-teacher conferences.

Program: Horace Mann is very honest in acknowledging that this school is not for everyone. Director of Lower School Admissions Wendy Steinthal says, "There is a quick pace with lots of enrichment." Most children thrive on the stimulation—the classrooms are buzzing with activity and the students are clearly engaged. The PA president said that the school "breeds independence." At the beginning of third grade a letter is sent to parents urging them not to help their children with their homework, and parents must sign it. Parents may only suggest, "Try this or that." Wendy Steinthal stresses that Horace Mann is supportive and committed to each child. "Yes, there is a lot to do but the children meet the challenge," she says. "This is a school for children who really like to learn." There is a real emphasis on teaching study skills and on learning how to be a student. One parent summed up the issue of competitiveness at HM astutely: "It's not that the school or the kids are necessarily so competitive; it's the high-powered parents behind them." The same can be said for all the top tier schools in New York City.

The Elementary Division has large open areas, although there are no "open classrooms." Some of these large areas are shared by four classes, with cubbies in the center. Some classes have two sections, one for reading lab or language arts, one for math. Formal reading instruction begins in first grade with an eclectic approach. There are three reading specialists and a communication skills specialist. Emphasis is placed on the writing process. HM children are tested for reading each year and there is a full reading lab.

HM is known for having strong math students. The elementary school hired an additional math teacher for sixth grade pre-algebra. There are many classroom projects: The computer program begins in kindergarten. Elementary students have computer lab (Macintosh) at least once a week for forty-five minutes. Beginning in fourth grade, they learn word processing and keyboarding; in fifth grade, graphics and programming. By fifth grade nearly 90 percent of the students use a computer at home.

The new Middle Division facility prompted a re-evaluation of the Middle School curriculum. There is increased emphasis on inter-disciplinary works and team teaching at the sixth, seventh, and eight grade levels. Students have more choices to make and more account-ability, including the introduction of "free periods." Lower School PA president Pam Stuchin says: "It's wonderful for the sixth graders to experience the independence and increased responsibility that comes with the Middle School environment. Until my older daughter started seventh grade I didn't realize how much they crave that sense of freedom."

There is an Artist-of-the-Month Program and three art teachers on staff. The Art Enrichment Program is an enhancement to the Lower School curriculum. Using a variety of media (painting, collage, papier-mâché, ceramics, metal tooling and felt appliqué) students create two and three dimensional forms to go with a topic being studied in English, reading, social studies or science. Students from first grade through fifth work to create individual as well as large group projects. The completed work is often used as a learning tool or teaching aid in the classroom.

Foreign language study begins in first grade. First through third graders take *both* French and Spanish. In fourth grade students choose French or Spanish for the remainder of the Lower School. In seventh grade students can elect Latin, German, Spanish, French, or Japanese.

Parents of active children will be glad to know that there is time for physical exercise: In first through fourth grades gym meets five times a week in a huge gymnasium. Fifth graders have gym four times a week. Students use a playground and the AstroTurf field year-round, and can use the tennis courts and pool at the upper division.

Special trips: Fifth graders take a three-day trip to Washington, D.C.; all second, third, fourth and fifth graders spend time at the John Dorr Nature Lab.

Programs are held at the John Dorr Nature Lab for incoming sixth and incoming seventh, eighth, ninth, and tenth graders for orien-tation and exploration, which includes the Searchers program, an adapted Outward Bound program.

The Upper Division: Now the group is larger and more diverse (26 percent are children of color), "large enough to be happy as they grow and change." In general "students respect the school" and enjoy the freedom of an open campus. There are no bells, and teachers are addressed formally. In 1995, Dr. Eileen Mullady became the first woman to head the school. Her background is in higher education (Columbia and Princeton). Parents say she has "cleaned house" and has successfully run a capital campaign. One of Dr. Mullady's realized goals was to "build an exemplary Middle School." She notes that while HMHS is known to be hard and rigorous it is also "a school that celebrates intellectualism; a joyful, adventurous place."

In preparation for the challenge of the upper grades, students who need review attend the six-week summer session. Seventh and eighth graders also take mandatory study skills courses. The foundations course in seventh grade is a unique program combining English, history and anthropology described as "an explanation of the human experience." Readings include *Inherit the Wind*, *Things Fall Apart* and *Ishi: Last of His Tribe*. Students gain experience in creative and critical writing. Eighth graders celebrate "Pi Day" (on 3/14 of course) and build solar houses which are tested for temperature and heat retention on the football field on a cold day.

Historically HM has been strong in English and history, and now HM's science labs are state of the art. Four out of ten faculty members hold Ph.D.'s and the chemistry department has three research-quality lab instruments. The science library and resource room has six microcomputers and is often open for independent study. Science teachers are very accessible to students with an interest in advanced study.

The course catalog says that most of the eighth grade courses are equivalent to ninth grade courses at many high schools. And even the introductory courses move along at quite a clip. One alumnus said, "It was like going to college before college." In keeping with Dr. Gratwick's legacy, HM was a pilot school for the AP program, and HMHS offers more AP courses than any other school, including "AP Psychology," "AP Latin: Epic Poetry" and "AP Economics." The math department offers calculus AP, AB and BC, including calculus with computers. English courses stress the classics but there are interesting electives in South African literature, Women's literature and an interdisciplinary course: "Explorations in English and Biology." Other opportunities for interdisciplinary study are available to students through IIRS (Independent Interdisciplinary Research Seminar). Internships and tutorials can also be arranged.

One Horace Mann (class of 1990) and Cornell (class of 1994) alumna says, "Academically there's lots of freedom and choices but there are no gut courses at HM, no course can be blown off." The average grade is a B-, which, one student boasts, "would be a B+ anywhere else." One HMHS student says, "Some people work hard for grades, and some people work harder for excellent grades." "It's as hard to get an F as it is to get an A" is also heard. Testing is so frequent (quizzes every week, exams every other), "you always know how you're doing." What is not listed in the catalog is the advanced level of maturity and independence required of students at HMHS, qualities already ingrained in students who came up through the HM system. The pressure is real, but one student said, "It's mainly self-inflicted." Yet another student told us that "teachers go to extremes to make the homework challenging." All homework requires a lot of time and thought, and one student said that he might blow off homework in one subject to study for an exam in another but if he missed two nights of homework assignments, he would fall behind.

Some students thrive under pressure and rise to the challenge of the competitive atmosphere, like the young woman (a HM "lifer" who has been at HM for twelve years) who takes three AP courses, does four hours of homework a night and still manages to watch *Buffy*. The minimum amount of homework is three to four hours each night, more on weekends. "This school makes you hungry," a student told us. "You get used to working hard and getting what you want, and you take that with you." One private school advisor tells families who are considering a most demanding school like Horace Mann to consider their family lifestyles. Some students will be able to accompany the family on weekend ski trips and still get their work done (one student trains for competitive ski racing). Others will be hitting the books in the chalet.

Contrary to popular belief, students at HM do support one another. There is a peer leadership training program and a student tutorial program, and most evenings HM students spend lots of time on the phone or on-line discussing homework or exams.

Does this leave time for extracurricular activities? One student put it this way, "If you want to be in a play or a sport and you don't mind sacrificing that time, then you do your work when you get home." Still, extracurricular activities are encouraged even for kids who aren't excelling academically. Lisa Moreia says, "Because the academics are so challenging, it's even more important for students to pursue their other interests. We want every student to experience successes, to explore abilities in and out of the classroom."

The community service requirement also contributes to personal

270

growth. One alumna told us that HM helped her find a job as a counselor at a summer camp for homeless children and she then returned for four consecutive summers and found it an invaluable experience.

HM students are far from one-dimensional math nerds, as evidenced by the variety and number of their extracurricular activities. Every year there is a huge musical, and three smaller plays are put on annually. HM produces more than a dozen publications. Students can choose from up to seventy clubs in any given year. Popular ones include The Union (formerly the Joint Minority Coalition), which is open to everyone, political clubs (there is a Young Republicans of HM Club), the East Wind, West Wind Asian Club, Glee Club, Model U.N., Junior Statesman Club (debating) and a Shakespeare Club. The Glee Club and Chamber Chorus are very popular; they have made their own CD and traveled to Europe and the Middle East.

Students do have a voice in setting policy affecting student life at HM through the governing council, comprised of twenty-four students and fifteen faculty members who are elected annually. There is an annual tenth grade health survey (anonymous), and students are required to take health courses. In 1997 the Governing Council passed the "Teacher and Course Evaluation Bill." The Council spent three meetings debating the document, which called for written evaluations by the students twice a year. The bill compelled the school faculty and administration to pass a similar resolution, making teacher and course evaluations a reality.

They say that Harvard is tough to get into, but easy to stay in; HM is tough to get into and tougher to remain in, but there is no question that the child who stays the course at HM will receive a superior, accelerated education. One alumna told us, "Horace Mann's great strength is it instills good work habits and is superior in college placement: HM goes above and beyond to get you into one of the colleges of your choice." It's prep for success. If your child makes it through, maybe you'll get to the Harvard-Yale tailgate picnic after all.

Popular College Choices University of Pennsylvania, Cornell, Yale/Columbia, Brown/University of Wisconsin, Harvard

Traditions Gilbert and Sullivan production in the Lower School once a year, the Buzzell basketball game (vs. Riverdale), Senior Absurdity Day, Holocaust Remembrance Assembly and Martin Luther King Assembly, Native American Day, East Wind–West Wind Dinner (Asia Night), Lower School Family Picnic

Publications   Yearbook: *The Mannikin*
Newspapers: *The Lower School View, The Record* and *The Journal*
Literary magazine: *Manuscript*
Prose literature: *Legal Fiction*
Science magazine: *Spectrum*
Math magazine: *Mantissa*
Business journal: *Businessman*
Journal of opinion: *Outlook*
Multicultural paper: *The Drum*
Photography: *Insight*
Music: *The Riff*
Alumni publication: *Alumni Bulletin*
Student Opinion Journal: *The Horace Mann Review*

Community Service Requirement   80 hours in grades 9–12; special activities in grades 7–8
Student Voluntary Service Organization

Hangouts   Riverdale diner, the library or cafeteria, The BBQ or the field outside on nice days

La Scuola D'Italia G. Marconi

12 East 96th Street
New York, NY 10128
(212) 369-3290, FAX (212) 369-1164
e-mail: LaScuolaNY@prodigy.net
website: www.LaScuolaItalia.org

Coed
Pre-kindergarten–12th grade
Not accessible

Ms. Bianca Maria Padolecchia Goodrich, Head of School
Ms. Pia Pedicini, Vice Principal
Ms. Augusta Fleischer, Middle School Coordinator
Ms. Marisa Laroca Piccioli, High School Coordinator

Birthday Cutoff   Children entering at the nursery level must be 3 and toilet-trained by December 31
Children entering kindergarten must be 5 by December 31
Children entering first grade must be 6 by December 31

Enrollment   Total enrollment: 190
Pre-Kindergarten 3/4's places: 24
Kindergarten places: 20
Graduating class 2001: 7–10

Tuition Range 2001–2002 $10,500 to $12,250, pre-kindergarten–12th grade
Additional fees: for application, registration and activities supplemental fees are approximately $850 for all grades

After-School Program   For children in grades Pre-K through 5, from September through May; Monday–Thursday; 3:15 P.M. until 5:30 P.M.; for an additional charge activities include: English and Italian homework, Italian Language, Arts & Crafts, Singing, Creative Movement and Computer

———

La Scuola D'Italia G. Marconi, of New York was founded in 1977 by the Italian Ministry of Foreign Affairs and is dedicated to Guglielmo Marconi, the inventor of the wireless. Due to the increasing interest of Italian and American families, the school has grown into a unique bilingual educational institution that reflects the best features of both Italian and American instruction. The bilingual curriculum is rooted in the European classical tradition. La Scuola is now housed in a historic building, once a private mansion, on East 96th Street.

This year, La Scuola's Middle School (grades six through eight) opened a new facility at 406 East 67th Street New York, NY 10021, and introduced a new, challenging curriculum. The new program, with English as the language of instruction, allows students to acquire strong language skills along with a classic academic curriculum.

Students must become fluent in at least two languages: Bilingual instruction in English and Italian begins in pre-kindergarten. There is a four-year requirement in Latin for the ninth through twelfth grades and in French for the seventh through ninth grades. High School students graduate after passing the end-of-the-course State Exam, with the equivalent of the International Baccalaureate. Students must bring their own lunches.

La Scuola is legally recognized by the Italian Ministry of Education and chartered by the Regents of the University of the State of New York as a private, independent American school.

Graduates attend European universities and major American colleges.

Little Red School House and Elisabeth Irwin High School

Lower and Middle Divisions
196 Bleecker Street
New York, NY 10012
FAX (212) 677-9159
website: www.lrei.org

Upper Division
40 Charlton Street
New York, NY 10014
(212) 477-5316 (main number), FAX (212) 675-3595

Coed
Pre-kindergarten–12th grade
Not accessible

Mr. Andrew McLaren, Director
Ms. Sally Tannen, Director of Admissions
Ms. Kai-Anasa George, Director of High School Admissions,

Birthday Cutoff   Children entering pre-kindergarten must be 4 by October 31
Children entering kindergarten must be 5 by October 31

Enrollment   Total enrollment: 440
Pre-kindergarten places: 24
Kindergarten places: 25
Graduating class size: approximately 25–30

Grades   Semester system in Middle School: Trimester "mod" plan in High School
Letter grades begin in 5th grade
Departmentalization begin in Middle School

Tuition Range 2001–2002 $16,230 to $18,700, Pre-K–12th grade
Additional fees for lunch, trips, books and student activities are approximately $1,500

Financial Aid/Scholarship   36% of the student body receives some form of aid

275

Endowment $400,000

After-School Program   All programs are for LREI students as well as for students outside the community

The Early Bird Program: for 4–13 year olds, 7:30 A.M. to 8:30 A.M. The general after-school program is divided into three age groups: four-year olds–1st graders, 2nd–4th graders, and the Middle School group. The program runs from 3–6P.M., Monday through Friday, and includes a structured variety of creative and recreational activities.

The Enrichment Program also runs from 3–6 P.M. Monday through Friday, includes weekly classes such as French, Mandarin Chinese, karate, dance, theater, tennis, super sports, chess and parent/child yoga

The Instrumental Program includes private instruction in such instruments as flute, saxophone, piano, guitar and drums

Summer Camp Program   Open to children from other schools, the traditional Day Camp is offered for age 3.5 through 14. The camp includes age-appropriate activities including arts & crafts, drama, recreational sports, swimming and field trips. Also offered are specialty camps in Super Sports, Musical Theater and Mandarin Chinese Language and Culture. Camps run from mid-June through July. An additional payment is required.

———

Little Red School House and Elisabeth Irwin High School (LREI) was founded in 1921 by Elisabeth Irwin. Working closely with John Dewey and Eleanor Roosevelt, Ms. Irwin set up a "model school" within New York City's public school system with an emphasis on experiential (or active) learning. She eventually moved the program out of the public schools. Ms. Irwin selected students she thought reflected the diversity of New York City and aimed for a school with an exceptionally involved parent body. Today, faculty, parents and students all have very active multicultural committees.

In the early 1930s Ms. Irwin moved the school to Bleecker Street and Sixth Avenue, where it has grown by acquiring adjacent houses and, most recently, by building a major addition in 1999. A second site was acquired on Charlton Street when the high school grades were added in 1941. The new facilities include a cafeteria, a new library and technology center, and five Middle School classrooms, including a skylit art studio. In the summer of 2000, the High School completed extensive renovations, which include a library, a performing arts center, a media lab, new classrooms and a new lobby.

Getting in: The ERB is required for admission to grades four through twelve. All applicants and their families tour the school and are interviewed. The school is composed of three divisions. Lower School: four year olds through fourth grade; Middle School: fifth through eighth grades; High School: ninth through twelfth. Hot lunch is available for an additional fee. Formal foreign language instruction begins in the fours with Spanish; in sixth grade students may choose between beginning French or continuing Spanish.

Parents: LREI parents are active in the school. The PA sponsors a Book Fair, a Spring Fair, a Literary Evening, and a silent auction at a gallery in Chelsea. The parent body includes many notable area artists.

Program: Little Red and Elisabeth Irwin recently celebrated its seventy-fifth anniversary and maintains a progressive approach which nurtures both intellectual rigor and a genuine joy of learning. The school retains its original emphasis on experiential and collaborative learning, and a commitment to diversity—both in the student population and curriculum. During the 1960s the "Red" in the school-name supposedly implied sympathy for the leftist viewpoints. Today, Director McLaren says, "We are still an activist school, with many students impassioned about human rights, but as an institution our concern is with critical thinking."

True to its mission as a model school, LREI provides an atmosphere in which innovative teaching thrives. The faculty create exciting curricula which can then be replicated in other schools. We were particularly impressed by a fifth grade science/history project designed to introduce students to the problems of interpreting archeological artifacts. Three teams of students design clay artifacts that represent different aspects of ancient civilization and bury them in a dig box in the school's backyard. They dig up each other's artifacts, analyze them in the lab and write up an interpretation of each piece. The project culminates in the creation of a "physical museum" in the classroom as well as a computer museum where students can "click" on a fragment and see a picture of the whole artifact and text explaining its meaning. The project integrates art, science, history, English, computer and math; through their active participation, students are stimulated to think in new ways.

At LREI the classes are small and the student teacher ratio is seven to one. Classes are structured but informal; everyone is on a first name basis. Formal reading instruction begins in first grade. A student's progress is constantly being assessed, and teachers are able to address each child's progress in kindergarten and first grade by working in very small groups. There is always a reading teacher along with the classroom teacher in every Lower School classroom during reading time. "There are rigorous academic expectations while allowing for plenty of creative expression," says McLaren. Community service is a requirement beginning in the Middle School. LREI enrolled eight Prep for Prep students in 2000.

Parents say that LREI has always been in the forefront of innovative education. "Elisabeth Irwin has taught my son to solve problems and think through issues. Yet at the same time it has encouraged him to take risks regardless of the outcome," said a parent. Essentially it provides a very comfortable learning environment with a solid academic foundation: "The day is tightly structured without being constraining; one subject flows into the next"; "The Gestalt at a school has to be right for learning and at Little Red, it is." A teacher at LREI told us "Their first priority is to really love and care about the kids . . . they feel it is their responsibility to find a way so that each child can grow and be challenged."

The High School and Middle School each perform one musical and one drama production every year. Drama in the Lower School is usually something that grows out of the classroom curriculum. At LREI the classroom meeting is a long-standing tradition, as is the assembly program. Guest speakers address a range of topics. Student representatives organize and run Middle and High School assemblies. Every class in the school is paired with a buddy class in another division. They meet informally during the year to read together, as well as for special days, such as Poem in Your Pocket Day, Founders Day and Field Day.

The Thanksgiving Assembly is a tradition that reflects the sense of community at LREI. The room is decorated with a beautiful display of autumn cornucopia and corn stalks. The children and teachers sit in chairs and on the floor and there is a big basket in the middle. Representatives from each class get up and read a poem and put something they've made—cornbread, for example—into the Thanksgiving basket (the gifts are donated to the needy.) One of the faculty talks about the origin of the Thanksgiving tradition and they sing a Native American song. "It was not a spectacle for the parents, it had real meaning and was very moving," said a participant.

At LREI another important tradition is the overnight trip. Every class from second grade through High School goes on an overnight trip related to the curriculum. For example, third grade goes to the New Jersey Conservation Center, as part of their study of Native American life; the seventh grade goes to Colonial Williamsburg for a week as part of their study of Colonial America; the high school freshman and sophomores go on an environmental trip.

Juniors and seniors can take courses at NYU; recently students have taken courses in Italy in the time of Dante, Russian Literature, Anthropology and an Introduction to Philosophy. The academic year is divided into trimesters during which students focus on three major subjects rather than the traditional five or six. At the end of each trimester there are exhibitions of student work. These range from traditional research papers and reports to performance pieces and film. Students can make their own documentaries using the new expanded media center LREI has a no-cut policy for plays and musicals.

Lower School students have physical education three times a week in a large gym. Younger children play on the school's rooftop playground. Older students use the Houston Street playground down the block for recess. Competitive sports begin in Middle School. Fifth and sixth graders have intramural sports and seventh and eighth graders compete against other schools. The High School offers track and field, volleyball, soccer, basketball and softball. The PE program for high school students includes rock climbing, yoga, dance, tennis, swimming and personal training.

Popular College Choices: Bard, Barnard, Brown, NYU, University of Pennsylvania, Vassar, Wesleyan and Williams

Traditions   Weekly Assembly Program, Buddy classes, Division and class trips, Book Fair, Halloween Fair, Spring Fair, Arts Auction Literary Evening, Poetry Slam, Poem is Your Pocket Day, Founders Day, Lower, Middle and Upper School Chorus

Publications   Yearbook: *Expression*
Literary Magazine: *i.e.*
Newspaper: *The School Times*
Lower School yearbook: *Really Red*
LREI newsletter (three times a year)
Monthly: *Monthly Mailings*

279

Community Service   Community service is a requirement in all
three divisions of the school. Lower School students hold food
and clothing drives to help support families in need. Middle and
high students work in local soup kitchens, clean up the neighborhood and participate in such events as the AIDS Walk. LREI is
also the headquarters of the city wide Urban Citizen Project,
which involves students in issues of urban life and governance

Hangouts   Student lounge, Pizza Box, In the Black Coffee Shop

Loyola School

980 Park Avenue
New York, NY 10028
(212) 288-3522
website: www.loyola-nyc

Coed
9th–12th grade
Not accessible

Rev. Joseph J. Papaj, S.J., President and Headmaster
Mr. Joseph Yung, Director of Admissions

Uniform   Dress code consists of blue blazer with Loyola patch for all students. Boys: collared shirt, tie, slacks. Girls: collared blouse, skirt or slacks. No jeans, T-shirts or sneakers

Birthday Cutoff   None

Enrollment   Total enrollment: approximately 200
Graduating class size: approximately 50

Grades   Semester system
Numerical grades for exams and report cards; letter grades for progress reports

Tuition   2001–2002 $14,900

Financial Aid/Scholarship   Approximately $400,000
Approximately 36% of the student body receives some form of financial assistance

Endowment $5.4 million

Diversity   As one student said: "Loyola has a very diverse group of students from different walks of life. When the student body comes together a very special atmosphere is created."

Homework   Approximately 2½–3 hours per night

After-School Program Extracurricular activities and clubs meet after school and during a mid-day period set aside for this purpose. Varsity and Junior varsity teams compete in the Independent School Athletic League, the Girls Independent School Athletic League, and the Independent Baseball Association

Summer Program None

Loyola School was founded in 1900 by Jesuits at the request of parents who wanted a Catholic alternative to non-sectarian prep schools. At that time the school was "up in the country" but featured the most up-to-date classrooms in the city. It became co-ed in 1973. Loyola School is the only independent coed Jesuit high school in the New York tri-state area. Loyola combines Jesuit traditions with a strong college preparatory program. The school's motto, *Ex Fide Fortis*, means "From Faith, Strength." The school is governed by a lay board of trustees and has been named a School of Excellence by the U.S. Department of Education.

The school is housed in an imposing stone building at Eighty-third Street and Park Avenue. In September 1996, Loyola completed a half-million dollar renovation of the fourth floor. This expansion allowed the school to enlarge its science and computer labs. The school's technology coordinator is Mr. Jeffrey Alpi. In September 2000 a 2.8 million dollar renovation of the cafeteria, student life office and locker rooms was completed. The gym is now air-conditioned.

Since 1995, Father Joseph Papaj, S.J., (pronounced "PAPeye"), has been President and Headmaster of the school. Father Papaj has served as Director of Campus Ministry at St. Joseph's University, had served on Loyola's board and was principal of two other Jesuit high schools.

Getting in: Applicants and their families are invited to an Open House in the fall. Applicants are evaluated on the basis of their academic and personal qualifications. Admissions requirements include: a transcript from the current school, a personal interview, two letters of recommendation, and Loyola's entrance exam, which is similar to the ISEE. In addition, the tour applicants are encouraged to spend a day visiting classes.

Parents: A "New Parents" evening is held in the fall of the freshman year, an opportunity for parents to socialize and to familiarize themselves with their child's daily life. Parent-teacher conferences are held four times a year and either a written report or a report card is sent home every six weeks. There is an active Parents Association and the Headmaster distributes a newsletter to parents regularly.

Program: There is a warm and friendly family atmosphere at Loyola. As one student said: "At Loyola, they care about us as students and as teenagers getting through today's world." Every student has a faculty mentor who assists with student's academic, spiritual and extracurricular options. Assistant Headmaster for Academics, Sister Nora Cronin, has been a role model and inspiration to the young women at Loyola for over twenty years. Many of her pupils have gone on to successful careers in the sciences. One Loyola alumna is a recent graduate of West Point, another was named a Rhodes Scholar.

Loyola's goals are to promote religious, intellectual, cultural, social and physical growth in every student as well as a concern for social justice. "Jesuits are known for being very independent," we were told. While the majority of students are Roman Catholic, a wide variety of faiths are represented. According to the school, Loyola's philosophy is: "Strong faith must be founded on a solid understanding which extends to theology classes, where knowledge rather than belief is stressed." The curriculum in religious studies is complemented with a program of retreats, and each morning, before classes begin, optional Mass is available in the chapel.

The core curriculum consists of four years of theology, English and physical education; three years of history, math and foreign language; two years of science, one year of speech, composition skills, art history, computer, health and music history. Writing skills are stressed; freshmen are required to take seven periods a week in English and composition skills.

Students may take elective courses in art history, art studio, computer science, writing fiction, poetry, discrete mathematics, Latin, modern drama, modern American fiction, film study, chorus, ensemble, modern British and American poetry, philosophy in literature, global perspectives, political science and economics. French, Spanish, Italian and Latin are offered. Advanced placement courses are offered in American history, European history, biology, physics, calculus, computer science, English, French and Spanish. Advanced Italian is offered in conjunction with Fordham University as a college credit course.

Loyola students excel in speech and debating, and there is a trophy case filled with the forensic and debate clubs' winnings. Loyola usually places first in the small school division for State Championships. The school competes successfully in many local, regional and national competitions. In addition to Speech, Loyola also has a Model Congress.

There is a large art studio and students work in many media including drawing, pastels, prints, watercolors, and oil painting. Students' musical activities include solo, ensemble instrumental and choral performances. "The Loyola Players" produce two professional level drama productions each year, and a major musical every other year. Recent productions: *All In The Timing* and *Bus Stop*.

The elected student government is an integral part of school life at Loyola. Representatives help plan school dances as well as address student's issues. The volunteer service program, whose motto reflects the Jesuit motto, "Men and Women for Others," provides opportunities for students to help others.

During Spring Break, fifteen to twenty seniors and some faculty spend two weeks traveling through Italy from Milan to Rome, with Easter at the Vatican. The school also sponsors three overnight ski trips a year. Loyola also offers a spring vacation trip to another country, open to all students. One year the trip was to France, another year it was to Austria and Germany.

The athletic teams at Loyola are competitive. For boys, sports teams include junior and varsity soccer, basketball and baseball. Girls teams include volleyball, basketball, softball and co-ed varsity track and cross country. In a recent year the girls were finalists in the GISAL volleyball championship. The girls varsity softball team was season champions in GISAL. In recent years the boys' varsity basketball, soccer and baseball teams won championships. A professional quality gym, paddle tennis courts, and a fully equipped fitness room are also available to students.

The school has a cafeteria that serves a hot lunch daily. Beginning in ninth grade with parents' permission, students may leave for lunch.

Popular College Choices   Amherst, Brown, Boston College, Columbia, Georgetown, Holy Cross, Loyola College, New York University, Princeton, Wesleyan, Williams

Traditions   Freshman/Senior Night, Junior Talent Night, Family Day, Fall/Spring Drama Productions, Christmas Concert, Awards

Convocation, Sports Night, Sophomore/Junior Semi-Formal, Senior Prom, Senior Trip to Italy

Publications   Newspaper: *Blazer*
Literary Magazine: *Knight*
Yearbook

Community Service Requirement   There is a four year Christian service requirement. Choices include: annual school-wide service projects at Thanksgiving, Christmas and during Lent, which provide food, clothing, toys and monetary donations. Students also tutor underprivileged children, visit shut-ins, prepare and deliver meals to an SRO and to the homeless, work in metropolitan area hospitals, and help senior citizens. In addition to community service, students also volunteer in the weekend homeless shelter at St. Ignatius Loyola Church.

Hangouts   The Commons, Ray Bono Pizzeria, the steps of the Metropolitan Museum of Art, Loyola Cafe and Senior Section

Lycée Français de New York

The French Baccalaureate School

Pre–N through 5th grade
7–9 East 72nd Street and
12 East 73rd Street
New York, NY 10021

6th through 9th grades
Admissions and Administrative Offices
3 East 95th Street
New York, NY 10128-0795

10th through 12th grades and Baccalaureate Prep.
60 East 93rd Street
New York, NY 10128-0795

(212) 369-1400, Admissions x 3111, FAX (212) 423-1275
(for all three locations)
website: www.LFNY.org

Coed
Nursery–12th grade
Not accessible

Mrs. Ghislane Hudson, Head
Mr. Jacques Donadieu, Director of French Studies
Mrs. Carol Chaitkin, Director of English Studies
Ms. Haifa Bautista, Admissions and Director, Early Childhood
Programs
Elise Maman, Admissions at all levels

Uniform: Classical navy Lycée blazer, skirt for girls, trousers for boys; white shirt

Birthday Cutoff   Children entering at the pre-nursery level must be 3 by September, at the nursery level they must be 4 by September 30 Children entering kindergarten must be 5 by September 30

Enrollment   Total enrollment: 1025
Pre-nursery places: 30
Nursery places: 53
Kindergarten places: 70
Graduating class size: approximately 55–60

Tuition Range 2001–2002 $10,500 to $15,750, 3's–12th grade
Additional fees of under $1,000

After-School Program   After-school program for nursery and kindergarten only; an additional payment is required

Summer Program   École Buissoniere ECP and Elementary

———

Founded in 1936 by a group of French and American individuals, the Lycée Français de New York offers a classical Franco-European education as well as an English/American Social Studies program. Fifty-four nationalities are represented in the student body. In December 2000, the school announced its plan to build a seven-story schoolhouse that will serve 1,000 students. Lycée has sold its existing buildings, a collection of architecturally beautiful townhouses with grand staircases and marble fireplaces, and will use the proceeds to fund the new facility on York Avenue between Seventy-fifth and Seventy-sixth Streets. The same firm that was hired to plan the Clinton Library will design the new facility which will have central offices, a cafeteria, a gym, and many new classrooms and labs, scheduled to open in the fall of 2002.

The tone of the school is formal and there is a uniform requirement.

Getting In: Applicants to nursery through fifth grade are admitted on the basis of interviews and school records. Applicants to the secondary school (sixth grade through *terminale*—thirteenth year) must take an entrance examination unless they are transferring from an accredited French School (in France or elsewhere). The school is accredited by the French Ministry of National Education and by NYSAIS. No knowledge of the French language is required for nursery through kindergarten. Applicants to grades two and above should have a working knowledge of the French language. Bilingual instruction is given in nursery and kindergarten. By first grade classes are taught only in French except for English, American literature and history, and other foreign languages. Beginning in ninth grade, in addition to French and English, a third foreign language is required; choices include German, Spanish and Italian. An introduction to Latin and Greek is required in eighth grade, further instruction is elective. Because of an accelerated curriculum, a high school diploma may be awarded to students after *premiere*—twelfth grade. Most students continue to the end of *terminale* and take the French Baccalaureate.

Graduates attend a variety of American or European colleges and universities or take preparatory classes for the "Grandes Écoles" in France.

Manhattan Country School

7 East 96th Street
New York, NY 10128
(212) 348-0952, FAX (212) 348-1621
website: www.mcs.pvt.K12.ny.us
e-mail: mcs@mcs.pvt.K12.ny.us

Coed
Pre-Kindergarten–8th grade
Not accessible
Dr. Michèle Solá, Director
Ms. Elizabeth Jarvis, Director of Admissions

Uniform   None

Birthday Cutoff   Children entering the 4/5's must be 4 by October 31

Enrollment   Total enrollment: 190–195
4/5's places: 18
Graduating class 2000: 22

Grades   Detailed anecdotal reports
Three parent conferences required per year
No letter or number grades in the Lower School (through 4th grade); Effort is graded in the Upper School
Departmentalization begins in 5th grade and is completed by 8th grade

Tuition Range 2001–2002 $15,000 to $19,000, 4/5's–8th grade
All parents pay according to family income on a sliding scale. The maximum compares to full tuition at other schools
Fees are included in the tuition
Parents can pay tuition on a monthly basis
There is a 25% deposit required when contracts are signed

Financial Aid/Scholarship   Approximately 65% of the student body receive some financial aid

Diversity   50% students of color

Endowment $8 million

After-School Program   A variety of creative, academic, and recreational activities. MCS After-School Program meets Mondays–Thursdays from 3:00 P.M. until 5:30 P.M. for 4 year olds to 8th graders, an additional payment is required

Homework   Nursery and K—None
1st grade: Once a week, 30 minutes
2nd: 30 minutes, 3 x a week
3rd and 4th: 45 minutes, 4–5 x a week
5th and 6th: 1–1½ hrs per night
7th and 8th: 2–3 hrs per night

Summer Program   Three-week summer farm camp program in the Catskills; for 20 children age 9 and up; open to students from other schools; an additional payment is required

---

In 1966, Manhattan Country School was founded by Augustus and Martha Trowbridge, on Manhattan's Upper East Side, in an elegant private landmark building designed by Ogden Codman. Manhattan Country School's origins are deeply rooted in the social and ideological principles of the Civil Rights Movement. Its commitment to equality, social justice and cultural diversity are at the center of its curriculum. MCS has achieved what many independent schools with far greater endowments and financial aid claim is their goal: a truly diverse school. Fifty percent of the student body and faculty are people of color. There is a unique tuition/scholarship program at MCS. The school is a recipient of a private family foundation grant to develop a gender-equity curriculum. In 1997, "Gus" Trowbridge, director and founder of MCS, retired. Michèle Solá, formerly Assistant Director, is now Director.

Getting in: All parents applying to MCS should visit the school as a first step in the admissions process. From mid-September until mid-May, tours are held during the school day. Parents of children applying to Pre-K through first grade should attend a tour before January. In the fall, an evening Open-House is held at the school. Parents who have requested admissions materials prior to October will automatically receive an invitation.

For applicants from pre-kindergarten through first grade, MCS does not require the ERB test. However, if the test is administered MCS should receive a copy of the test results. Children are observed and asked to play games, draw or do a puzzle at the group interviews. For applicants for second grade and above, ERB test results are required, as well as the applicant's school report and an interview. "Most importantly, we're looking for a good match, families that are comfortable with a diverse community." says Michèle Solá, Director of MCS.

Parents: Parents at MCS, as well as parents of alumni, are active fund-raisers for the school. They help organize many events throughout the school year. The parents of each class are responsible for one event, a total of ten in any given year. These include: Farm Festival, Grandparents' Day, Kwanzaa Festival, Spring Benefit, Dr. Martin Luther King, Jr. Commemorative Walk, and Farm Outing Day. There are many opportunities for parents to come together with the faculty and administration, to discuss common issues relating to education and child development. Parents Association Meetings are well attended and committees meet regularly.

Parents are an integral part of the social studies curriculum. The 4/5's class take "home visits"; the 7/8's study their families in depth for one semester; the sixth grade invites parents and other relatives to share their histories as part of their study of the Civil Rights Movement. Teachers at MCS welcome the opportunity for parents to share stories and talents and accompany students on class trips. Parent-teacher conferences are held three times a year, and parents may meet more often if there's a need.

Program: The Lower School at MCS is composed of six mixed-age groupings from 4/5's through 9/10's. The Lower School groups span two overlapping age levels. These mixed-age groupings offer flexible academic and social placements for children and enable the school to meet the developmental needs of each child. Within this framework, a grade level for each student is designated by the school. The average class is eighteen, but many classes are taught in smaller groups of eight to ten students. Each of the four youngest classes has a head teacher and an assistant, as well as student teachers, in most classrooms throughout the school. One parent told us, "To me the most important characteristic of MCS is the deep respect shown to students and their individuality. In this school community, students learn to value themselves along with their peers. The artificial barriers that schools routinely set regarding the teaching experts and the learners are less visible in the MCS environment. Everyone is learning and everyone is teaching."

The core curriculum at MCS is its social studies program. It allows the school to apply its multicultural perspectives and fosters positive social values. In the Lower School, social studies is integrated into all areas of the classroom through graphs, geography and mapping, creative writing, literature, drama and art. In the Upper School, social studies and history follow a chronological organization. Students refine research skills, and learn how to write formal research papers, as well as point-of-view essays.

Formal reading instruction begins in the 5/6's class. In small groups, (approximately half the class), students have reading and writing times. MCS takes into account that children learn to read in a variety of ways, and the teachers use many materials, including basal readers, structured phonics materials and literature. For students who need reinforcement, a reading specialist works in the classroom with small groups of students. If additional support is needed, a student will work with the specialist in another room. If a tutor is recommended, the school will work together with the student's tutor to help meet the student's needs.

The school considers Spanish to be an essential component to the multicultural experience at MCS. Beginning with the four-year-olds, Spanish is taught at every level in mixed-age groupings. Signs throughout the school are written in Spanish. The Lower School Spanish program is culture-based and integrated into the classrooms. The Upper School Spanish program is textbook based and prepares students for the New York State Proficiency Exam in Spanish.

The Upper School at MCS is composed of grades five through eight. Departmentalization begins in fifth grade. Fifth and sixth graders study English, social studies and math with their group teacher. Specialists teach Spanish, science, art, music, shop and physical education. In seventh and eighth grades, students are divided into two mixed-age homerooms, and each student is assigned a faculty advisor. Classes for seventh and eighth grades are fully departmentalized.

The math program follows four fundamental themes: making sense of data, patterns and predictions, numbers and number sense, and geometry and spatial sense. In the Lower School, math is integrated into the children's daily activities and manipulative materials are used. Upper School students follow a common text.

MCS has taken a hands-on approach for the science curriculum.

Teachers and science consultants make use of Central Park as a nature laboratory. Students learn to use the scientific techniques necessary for accurate observation, problem-solving and recording. Classrooms have work areas for experimentation, science displays, and science libraries. A goal of the science program is to instill a critical understanding of the ethical questions surrounding scientific issues.

Technology: In 1996 MCS was chosen as one of only two NYC private schools to work in collaboration with Teachers College's Institute of Learning Technology's Eiffel Project. As part of the project, MCS has been wired for Internet access via a T1 line and classrooms are networked. Beginning in the second grade, students have computer and Internet access available in their classrooms. Fifth through eighth graders must complete a four-year computer literacy course and older children are offered electives in computer graphics and design. An after-school computer class is offered to the 4/5's through fifth grades.

Computer use is directly related to the curriculum. For example, the seven and eight year olds host their own website on Mammal Study; the eight and nine year olds communicate via e-mail with the Zuni nation in New Mexico; shop students use AutoCAD to design woodworking projects, and the seventh graders produce a literary magazine, *Lit Mag.*, using desktop publishing.

Art, music and drama enhance the curriculum. Art is required of all students through sixth grade; seventh and eighth graders must meet a combination requirement in the arts, with additional electives available in each subject.

All students have weekly library classes. The library hosts presentations by visiting authors, such as Jamaica Kincaid, Milton Meltzer, Brian Pinkney and Vera B. Williams. It is also where class plays and family story-telling gatherings are held.

Children in the 4/5's through 7/8's have daily outdoor activities at a nearby playground or in the meadow at Central Park. There are structured group activities with a physical education teacher once a week either in the school's music room or in the park. The 8/9's through eighth grade have outdoor time in Central Park three times a week and a structured physical education class twice a week at the Boys Harbor Gym, located on Fifth Avenue at 104th Street. There are elective classes in track, basketball and tennis for older students.

MCS owns a small working farm, located on 177 acres in the Catskill Mountains in Roxbury, New York. Students with their teachers, begin going to the farm in the spring of their 7/8's year. By fifth grade, they have three week-long trips a year. The farm acquaints students with a self-reliant way of life. "One of my favorite times was at the farm. My farm education gave me an appreciation for a completely different lifestyle, as well as teaching me various things like milking cows, tapping trees, creating textiles," says an alumna. The farm program leads to six graduation requirements: to milk a cow; to plan and cook an evening meal for the entire class and to bake bread or another yeast dough product without adult assistance; to identify birds, plants, animals and their tracks, to describe the life cycle of one animal; to produce an original textile from fleece to a finished garment, artifact or material; and to participate in a "town meeting" on an environmental issue. A recent graduate told us, "Looking back at my years at MCS, I realize that I loved everything about it. At the time I remember feeling that the school was so small and undeveloped. However, MCS had everything I needed. The diverse community and the close relationships with my teachers were experiences that I would not have gotten anywhere else."

Graduates: About half go on to the specialized public high schools; half go on to the independent schools including Riverdale, Fieldston, Friends, Dalton, Calhoun, Trevor Day

Marymount School of New York

1026 Fifth Avenue
New York, NY 10028
(212) 744-4486, FAX (212) 744-0163
website: www.marymount.K12.ny.us

All girls
(boys in nursery and pre-kindergarten)
Nursery–12th grade
Accessible

Sister Kathleen Fagan, Headmistress
Ms. Concepcion R. Alvar, Director of Admissions

Uniform   Lower School—Fall/Spring: blue cord jumper, white short-sleeved blouse, navy blue blazer. Winter: navy blue jumper, white or red turtleneck, navy blue sweater or blazer
Middle School—Fall/Spring: blue cord skirt, white short-sleeved shirt, navy blue sweater, navy blue blazer. Winter: plaid or gray skirt, white turtleneck, navy blue or green sweater or blazer
Upper School—Fall/Spring: blue cord skirt, white short-sleeved, navy blue sweater, navy blue blazer. Winter: plaid or gray skirt, white turtleneck, navy blue, green, white or yellow sweater or blazer

Birthday Cutoff   Children entering at the nursery level should be 3 years old by August 31
Children entering kindergarten should be 5 by August 31st

Enrollment   Total enrollment: 472
Nursery places: 15
Kindergarten places: 20–25
Graduating class sizes: approximately 45

Grades   Semester system
Letter grades begin in class V. Grades are distributed each quarter, report cards given out in January and June at parent-teacher-student conferences 2x a year
Departmentalization begins in class IV

Tuition Range 2001–2002 $11,600 to $19,600, Nursery–12th grade
Additional fees for books and activities approximately $700

Financial Aid/Scholarship   Available to those who qualify
Approximately 27% of students receive some aid

Endowment   N/A

Diversity   Approximately 25% students of color
3 Prep for Prep students enrolled as of Fall 2000
Cultural Awareness Club, Diversity Committee, Jazz Festival, Harambee Night, International Week, Senior Class trip to the U.S. Holocaust Memorial Museum, Native American Exchange Program; Japan Exchange Program; China 2000 Program

After-School Program   Marymount's after-school program for K–III requires an additional payment
After-School Activities Program: for grades kindergarten through Class III, Monday–Thursday until 6:00 P.M., Fridays until 5:00 P.M.; a variety of creative and recreational activities
The Instrumental Music Program offers private lessons
Middle School offers sports and clubs 3 days a week until 4:30 P.M.
Supervised Study Program, Monday–Thursday until 6:00 P.M. for Lower and Middle School

Summer Program   Marymount Summer Program: coed, ages 3–8, open to students from other schools; mid-June through July; a variety of creative and recreational activities; *Drama Camp:* a six-week coed program for ages 8–14; mid-June through July; acting, improvisation, and set design; the program culminates in the production of a full-scale musical; *Science/Technology Camp:* 6 weeks, coed, ages 8–14, exploration in laboratories, field trips; team sports and swimming are part of all of these programs

---

The Marymount School of New York was founded in 1926 as part of an international network of schools directed by the Religious of the Sacred Heart of Mary. The founder, Mother Butler, believed that women should be leaders in society and that, "the world never needed women's intelligence and sympathy more than it does today." The school became independently incorporated in 1969. Sister Kathleen Fagan, a graduate of the school, has been headmistress since 1976. She previously taught at Marymount schools in London and New York.

The Marymount School is housed in three adjoining Beaux Arts mansions on Fifth Avenue, part of the Metropolitan Museum of Art landmark district. The breathtaking ballroom on an upper floor serves as an auditorium, lunchroom and gymnastics/movement room. The Middle School will be housed at 2 East 82nd Street, a six story turn-of-the-century townhouse, currently undergoing renovations. Sixty-five percent of the student body is Catholic and thirty-two different nationalities are represented. The director of admissions told us: "Spiritual values, community service and liturgy are the moral thread that binds the school." Chapel service, held once a week, may be conducted by students of any faith. Students attend Mass at least four times a year. Students can participate in an exchange program with other Marymount Schools in Los Angeles, London, Paris or Rome.

Getting in: Parents are invited to attend a fall Open House. After applying, parents meet with the director of admissions and tour the school. Older children may accompany their parents on the tour. On a separate date, applicants are interviewed individually at the school. Beginning in kindergarten testing at the ERB is required for admission. The school says it "thoroughly considers the unique qualities of each applicant including academic ability, special interests, talents and personalities."

Parents: The parent body includes business people, artists, academicians, engineers, doctors, lawyers, researchers, technocrats and government employees. Parents are an active and integral part of the school. They visit classes, set up exhibits, volunteer to read to children in the library, accompany classes on field trips, etc. Activities sponsored by the Parents Association include parent meetings, spring benefit, Christmas Fair, Book Fairs, and others that strengthen school-family ties. Parents and alumnae give career seminars and offer their places of work for senior internships.

Program: The Lower School is composed of nursery through third grade. Each morning students are greeted in the lobby by the division head. Each Lower School classroom has a head teacher and an assistant. The program is structured and traditional, but aims to be creative and dynamic. Organized learning centers are equipped with hands-on, interactive materials that encourage experimentation and collaboration. Students are grouped according to skill levels in reading and math. French begins in Class IV. Science and technology education begins at the nursery level in the state of the art science and technology laboratories. The children are taught by specialists in art, music, science, foreign language, computers and physical education. There is a reading and learning specialist on staff.

Marymount has a unique relationship with the Metropolitan Museum of Art, ranking first among all city schools in the use of the museum as a learning resource. Other city resources that the school uses include the United Nations, Ellis Island, the Stock Exchange, the Central Park Zoo, the Staten Island Observatory and various galleries and museums as classroom extensions.

Each Lower School student has a big sister in the Middle or Upper School. This bond is strengthened throughout the year by trips, special events and collaborative projects.

The Middle School consists of grades four through seven. According to the brochure, in the Middle School "Each student is encouraged to develop and pursue areas of interest, to think honestly and critically about the world around her and to acquire a sense of social responsibility in school, at home and in her community." The integrated core curriculum gradually increases in the degree of departmentalization at each grade level. Latin is introduced at grade 5. Readings and written composition are incorporated into the study of French. Students begin the study of Shakespeare in sixth grade. They also begin a leadership training program in seventh grade to prepare them to be peer counselors to the other Middle School students. Research and study skills with a focus on time management and organization are emphasized. Speech, debate and drama are incorporated into the program and students participate in weekly assemblies, chapel services and an annual drama production.

Marymount School integrates technology into the curriculum creatively, and appropriately. Technology provides multiple tools for gathering data, sharing information and completing assignments. It features three wireless science labs with ibooks that connect to probing peripherals, and web based coursework. All Class IX students create e-businesses in collaboration with students from Marymount Schools in LA, Rome, London and Paris.

Beginning in nursery school, Lower School students learn in the general science laboratory with its child-size tables and stools.

Upper School students take three years of laboratory science and 95% elect a fourth year of science. AP courses are offered in chemistry, biology, statistics, calculus AB and BC, English, French, Latin, Spanish, American History, Art and Art History.

The Upper School consists of grades eight through twelve. Students continue to study French or Latin or they may choose to study Spanish. Some students opt to study two languages. Graphing calculators, computers, and other technological tools are used frequently in math, science and computer courses. The ninth grade Integrated Humanities Program links interdisciplinary themes in English, history, art history, religious studies, and studio art. Students visit the Metropolitan Museum of Art at least once a week. In the second semester, seniors attend weekly seminars hosted by alumnae who share their career and life experiences. In May, seniors begin a five-week internship program, sponsored by alumnae and parents, during which they are exposed to a wide range of careers. The student-interns return to school periodically to report on their experiences in a group setting. Seniors also participate in an ethics class. The Director of College Counseling, provides academic advice and helps prepare students and parents for college.

All Marymount students are encouraged to participate in a variety of extracurricular activities and they can select from a wide range of sports and clubs. Fourteen team sports are offered, including swimming, field hockey, tennis and fencing. The school's basketball team is the AAIS League champion and had also won the NYSAISAA State Championship in 1995. In addition to varsity sports there are junior varsity and seventh and eighth grade intramural teams.

At weekly assemblies, students make presentations and gather to hear various speakers address the school community. The alumnae sponsored Lisanti Speaker Series has brought in well-known speakers such as activist Gloria Steinem, 1996 Inaugural Poet Miller Williams, Nobel Prize winner Dr. Rosalyn Yalow, the technology guru Esther Dyson, Dean of the White House Press Corps Helen Thomas and many more.

Each year students from classes nine through twelve spend time at retreats. Ninth grade students travel to Frost Valley to bond as a class, sophomores focus on community service, juniors on leadership and seniors on ethical values/transition into colleges and careers. All students participate in community and school service. Students in tenth grade are required to contribute forty hours of volunteer service at hospitals, schools or agencies in New York City as part of their Social Justice class. Lower and Middle School students visit senior citizens and participate in holiday food drives. Students volunteer as student ambassadors, office assistants and peer tutors.

Federal Judge Katharine Sweeney Hayden, Class of 1959, described her experience at Marymount: "We were always encouraged to express ourselves! We read and read and learned to absorb, synthesize and digest large amounts of material. As a lawyer and judge, I draw upon the benefits of my Marymount training every day."

Popular College Choices   Columbia, Yale, Harvard, University of Virginia, New York University, Boston College, Duke, Tufts, University of Pennsylvania, Vassar, Georgetown, Holy Cross, Wellesley

Traditions   Founder's Day, Father-Daughter Square Dance, Vespers, the Christmas Pageant, Lessons and Carols, Family Ice-Skating Party, Family/Friends Day, Grandparents Day, the Book Fair, New Parents Reception, Field Days, Upper School retreats, Family Picnics, Science Fair, Athletic Awards Evening, Spring Benefit, Junior Ring Day, Alumnae Reunion, 100 Nights Dinner, Mother/Daugther Book Club, Sports Clinic

Publications   Student Newspaper: *The Joritan*
Student Literary Magazine: *The Muse*
Yearbook: *The Marifia*

Community Service   Community Service is required of all students. Opportunities include participating in New York Cares Day and the Achilles Club; visiting the elderly at Kateri Residence; and sponsoring food and toy drives for the families of New York's Incarcerated Mothers Program. Community service activities are coordinated through Campus Ministry, one of the largest student clubs at the school

Hangouts   Amity Coffee Shop, Metropolitan Museum of Art steps, Marymount teahouse

Metropolitan Montessori School

325 West 85th Street
New York, NY 10024
(212) 579-5525, FAX (212) 579-5526

Coed
Pre-kindergarten through 6th grade
Accessible

Ms. Mary Gaines, Head of School
Ms. Margi Doherty, Admissions Director

Birthday Cutoff Children entering Pre-kindergarten must be 2.9 years old by September 1st

Enrollment Total enrollment: 200
Pre-K and Kindergarten places: 30
Kindergarten places only: as available
Graduating 6th grade class size: 15

Tuition Range 2001–2002 $12,500 (primary half-day) through $16,200 (upper elementary)
For new students only, the school requires a one-time fee of $1,500 paid upon enrollment

Financial Aid/Scholarship Limited aid available
33 students receive some form of aid
10% of the annual budget of $2.5 million goes to financial aid

Endowment $1 million reserve fund
A capital campaign was begun in 1996 to replenish this fund which had been used for the renovation of the new building

Homework 1st grade: 20 minutes
2nd: 30–45 minutes
3rd: 1 hour
4–6th: 1½–2 hours

After-School Program Primary half day program for 3 and 4 year olds, 12 noon–3:00 P.M.: 9–12 P.M. or 1–3 P.M., program optional for those enrolled in morning half day

Elementary program for 1st–6th grade: hours 9–3 P.M.

Clubhouse: hours 3–6 P.M.

Creative Arts Program: a variety of creative, recreational and academic activities, Monday–Friday, 3:00–4:30 P.M.

Early morning drop off program (8:00–9:00 A.M.)

An additional payment is required for all programs

Summer Program Metropolitan Montessori School Summer Camp is open to 2.9 to 6 year old children. There are two 3 week sessions available in the months of June and July

---

Metropolitan Montessori School, formerly St. Michael's Montessori, was founded in 1964 and took its name from its previous location in St. Michael's Church on West 95th Street. In August of 1996 this popular nursery and elementary school moved 14 blocks south into a stately red brick building in the heart of the gentrified West Side. The new building, an extensively renovated 1865 carriage house which once belonged to William Randolph Hearst, provided the growing school with an additional 5,000 square feet of space. Characteristic of this nurturing school, when digging the foundation for the new building they took great care to preserve two one hundred year old London plane trees at the building site.

Getting in: After submitting an application, parents are invited to tour the school. Tours are given twice a week in the mornings. There is a question and answer period after the tour. Children are invited back with their parents for a small group visit with a primary teacher to "see if they are developmentally ready to start." ERB testing is required for applicants to first through third grades. Students of color constitute approximately 20% of the school.

Program: The brochure states that "While educational method and classroom materials are firmly rooted in the philosophy of Dr. Maria Montessori, the school addresses the unique issues and concerns of today's children." Parents are pleased with the way the school imparts the academic groundwork necessary for later learning.

Mixed-age groups of children remain with the same teacher for three years. Children in grades 1 through 6 keep journals for all subjects and continue working in them as they move up through the school producing a visible record of their academic progress. Grammar is taught through the use of symbols; it looks difficult but most children have achieved mastery by third grade. Attention is paid to individual development within a group setting and students are ability-grouped for every subject. For instance, a first grader might be reading at a fourth grade level, a sixth grader might be doing seventh grade level math.

Children leave their classrooms for music, art, French (or Spanish), library and physical education. The new lending library's computers are networked throughout the school. Quizzes and tests begin in fourth grade and students receive letter grades in all subjects. A checklist and narratives are sent home once a year and there are two parent/teacher conferences.

Community service is an important component of a Metropolitan Montessori education. An integrated program allows students to visit a local home for the elderly who are also invited for a holiday lunch prepared and hosted by the children. One year students prepared Easter baskets of toiletries which were delivered to AIDS patients at St. Luke's Hospital.

Metropolitan Montessori has its own literary journal and yearbook. There are numerous special events at the school, including a yearly spelling bee for grades one through six. Fourth through sixth graders put on a theatrical production; one year it was *Wind in the Willows*, another year it was *Macbeth*. There is an annual Sports Day at John Jay College gymnasium, a day of family bowling at Leisure Lanes, the March auction fundraiser, and a welcome picnic each September for the entire school.

Graduates: The majority of Metropolitan Montessori graduates attend various independent schools. At least fifteen graduates of the school currently attend Stuyvesant High School.

The Modern School

870 Riverside Drive
New York, NY 10032
(212) 568-0010

Coed
1st–6th grade
Not accessible

Mrs. Sandra Carter, Director/Director of Admissions

Uniform   White blouse or shirt, grey skirt, jumper or slacks. Sixth graders may wear a light blue top.

Birthday Cutoff   Children entering 1st grade must be 5.6 years old by September 1st

Enrollment   Total enrollment: 75
1st grade places: 15
Graduating class size: variable, approximately 11–23

Tuition Range 2001-2002 $3,870–$4,185, 1st to 6th grade
Tuition can be paid in 10 monthly installments
Registration fee is $50

Financial Aid/Scholarship   Limited amount available
15% of the student body receives some form of aid

Endowment   None

After-School Program   Children can arrive as early as 8:00 A.M. Daily after-school program: homework and study skills supervision as well as creative and recreational activities from 3:00-5:45 P.M. for an additional payment of approximately $40 per week

Summer Program   Summer Day Camp and tutorial program for an additional payment. The camp is not a part of the school's program; it is privately operated

---

The Modern School might seem like an oxymoronic title for one of the oldest black independent schools in New York City and the nation, but the school's mission—to provide an alternative to dismal inner-city public schools—is just as relevant today as it was in 1934, the year The Modern School was founded. In the succeeding sixty years multicultural scholarship and diversity programs such as Early Steps and Prep for Prep have been instituted to help prepare and to place children of color in other independent schools. But the school is still essential and the choice of many families. In 1999 The Modern School moved to its present location on Riverside Drive in a common space of an apartment building. Viacom paid for the renovation of this small, but adequate facility. "They brought in the works," says Marilyn Mance, Modern's financial supervisor. "Viacom even bought lunch for the entire school community. They adopted the school." The charismatic founder, Mildred Johnson, is still actively involved in the school. The school's brochure states that Mrs. Johnson's composer-father J. Rosamond Johnson, and her author-diplomat uncle, James Weldon Johnson, were important architects of the movement known as the Harlem Renaissance. Mrs. Johnson's numerous awards for service include a Martin Luther King Jr. Lifetime Achievement Award and a 1984 citation from Mayor Edward Koch for distinguished service to the children of the city.

Getting in: Applicants for first grade are tested in-house. Second through sixth graders must submit the results of the Metropolitan Achievement Test.

Program: Despite its progressive origins, The Modern School's methods are described by Mrs. Carter as "traditional and structured." In the classroom desks are organized into rows. The teachers seem young and committed, the students are attentive and eager to learn. Portraits of black heroes (drawn by a former teacher) are displayed throughout the school. A new library has books on Black history, the Classics and other popular childrens literature that are integrated into the program. Columbia University donated computers to The Modern School's computer lab. In third grade and up there is a computer in each room. All students bring their own lunch. Hot lunch is served to nursery school students.

Special events at The Modern School include: fifth and sixth grade plays in February, the annual International Festival; two Book Fairs and the Science Fair.

Graduates attend many of the District 4 alternative programs as well as various independent schools.

The Nightingale-Bamford School

20 East 92nd Street
New York, NY 10128
(212) 289-5020 (main number), Admissions: (212) 933-6515
FAX (212) 876-1045
website: www.nightingale.org
e-mail: ceverett@nightingale.org
info@nightingale.org
All girls
Kindergarten–12th grade
Accessible

Ms. Dorothy A. Hutcheson, Head of School
Ms. Carole J. Everett, Director of Admissions

Uniform Lower School: navy or houndstooth jumper with white collared shirt

Middle School and Upper School: navy skirt, gray or light blue lightweight kilt, white blouse or turtleneck, navy knee socks or navy or white tights

Upper School: navy, light blue or gray skirt, solid-color collared shirt, solid-color ankle or knee socks or tights. Middle and Upper School: navy corduroy pants, Thanksgiving to Spring Break. Seniors can be out of uniform on Fridays and after Spring Break

No boots, clogs, or sandals

Birthday Cutoff "No strict birthday cutoff" but most girls are 5 by the start of school

Enrollment Total enrollment: 550
Kindergarten places: 40–42
Graduating class 2000: 46

Grades Semester system, K–IV detailed narrative reports and checklists. Comments continue through upper grades
Letter grades begin in 5th grade
Departmentalization begins in 5th grade
First final exam in 7th grade

Tuition Range 2001–2002 $19,000 to $20,300, kindergarten–12th grade

Additional fees: for trips, lunch, books, supplies, Parents Association dues and yearbook approximately $950

Financial Aid/Scholarship   22% of students receive some form of aid
$1,306,780 was budgeted for financial aid in 1999–2000
Average grant per student is $14,195

Endowment $30 million
$54,545 per student

Diversity   22% students of color, 30 Prep for Prep students enrolled as of fall 2000, 5 ABC; C.A.F.E.: Cultural Awareness For Everyone (school multicultural club that meets biweekly) sponsors assemblies, dinners, evenings
Parents of C.A.F.E. (meets once a month) for potluck supper and discussion
Nightingale students participate in the Interschool Multicultural Coalition which meets monthly
S.E.E.D. (Seeking Educational Equity, Diversity) seminars for faculty and administrators

Homework   Lower School families are expected to read aloud with their children from kindergarten on, a half hour a night reading or being read to by the child.
Kindergarten: none
1st and 2nd: 1/2 hour
3rd and 4th: 45 minutes
5th and 6th: 1 1/2–2 hours with built-in study hall during the school day
7th and 8th: 2 1/2 hours
9th–12th: approximately 45 minutes per subject a night (with one homework-free subject per night) Weekly assignments are given to encourage long-term planning

After-School Program   Hobbyhorse, co-ed, a variety of recreational and creative activities for kindergarten–Class 4 until 6 P.M. Boys from Allen-Stevenson and St. Bernard's Schools also participate. 12–15 courses are offered including gymnastics, drama, dance, chess, fencing, tennis, swimming, cooking, magic, knitting, photography, computer; an additional payment is required.
Junior varsity and varsity sports for Middle and Upper School girls, NBS participates in interscholastic athletic competition and

307

also the 12-team Athletic Association of Independent Schools. The NBS gymnasium is usually open every Saturday for "pick-up" games and practices and Nightingale girls can participate in Saturday sports at St. Bernard's School.

Some special interest clubs, Glee Club, drama and dance rehearsals, literary magazine and newspaper also meet after school. There is also music instruction available.

Summer Program   Sunny Days Program: coed, a June program for children ages 5–12 from 8:30 A.M. to 3:00 P.M.; trips, arts and crafts, swimming, computer, cooking and so on; open to children from the community; an additional payment is required

———

The Nightingale-Bamford School began with classes held by Miss Nightingale in 1906. In 1919 Miss Nightingale was joined by Maya Stevens Bamford and together they founded The Nightingale-Bamford School in 1920. In 1989 the school began a $15 million renovation and expansion, completed in 1991. The school now has central air-conditioning, state-of-the-art science labs and a hi-tech theatre/auditorium, a photo lab, three computer labs and a new cafeteria. "Formal, but not rigid, for very bright girls who know where they stand; not overly competitive," is the way one mother describes the school.

Traditional in the early years, Nightingale offers more choices later on. There is a conscious attempt to avoid gender stereotyping, while still instilling the social graces. They've struck a nice balance—keeping the best of the old while incorporating the new. "Academic rigor with a soul," says one parent.

Only the sixth head in the history of the school, Dorothy Hutcheson was preceded by the formidable Mrs. Edward McMenamin, who reigned for twenty-one years. "Ms. Hutcheson, now the senior head amongst the girls' schools, can be warm, accessible and fun and also strict and firm. She listens to and also takes action for the students," a senior said. Ms. Hutcheson knows each student by name and often greets them and shakes their hand as they enter the blue doors in the morning. A ninth grader told us, "Ms. Hutcheson cares and is very open to new ideas and suggestions. It's good to be able to tell her the way we feel." A full-time working mother, Ms. Hutcheson has already made her refreshing presence known in other ways too. She accepted the Student Government's proposal to add pants to the dress code (after allowing female faculty members to wear pants). She re-established the Senior Independent Study project which allows qualified seniors to drop some of their required courses and pursue in-depth a topic of their choosing. There is great emphasis on integrating technology into the classroom. One parent remarked after her tour, "At Nightingale there was a sign that said 'Have you checked your e-mail today?'" Nightingale's time to gather by division, a time to reflect, to make announcements, and to discuss issues of moral and ethical concern, was formerly known as "Prayers." By renaming it "Morning Meeting," which more accurately describes it, Ms. Hutcheson has shown that she is not afraid to break with tradition.

Getting in: One parent described NBS's application process as "warm and welcoming." Parents can arrange for a tour before applying. When the application is received, parents are given an appointment for a tour and an interview with a member of the admissions staff. On another date kindergarten applicants will have a group interview with Lower School teachers while their parents meet with Ms. Hutcheson and Mrs. Blanche Mansfield, the head of the Lower School. Middle and Upper School girls take their tours with student tour guides. (Significant points of entry in addtion to kindergarten are seventh and ninth grades.) Individual interviews with the division heads are required. Girls do placement work during their visit. If admitted, girls and parents are invited to re-visit and spend time in the school. There are welcome parties for all new students and parents in the spring and early fall. A great deal of care is given to having families make a smooth transition to Nightingale. Preference is given to siblings and legacies, but they are not automatically accepted, and an active wait list is maintained after admissions decisions have been made. No letters of recommendation are required or desired as part of the process, and admissions at Nightingale reacts negatively to any political or social pressure or influence. Admission is based on the right academic match, not the correct social connections, they say. Nightingale has made a major commitment to diversity and there are more girls from different racial, ethnic and socio-economic backgrounds than in the past.

A mother who eventually chose NBS said that she "couldn't sit up straight enough at some of the other schools," and while she noticed "a lot of scarves on the parents at other girls' schools," she was impressed by "the sensible shoes" she saw at NBS.

Is there a typical student? It depends on whom you ask. According to one parent, "She has blond straight hair, uses little or no makeup and carries an L. L. Bean bookbag." Yet another parent told us the typical student is "earnest, engaging, vibrant and aware," refer-ring to an Upper School student she felt exemplified NBS qualities. A tenth grader said "We are smart, involved in the life of the school and have learned to speak with confidence." Obviously!

A parent told us that NBS delivers "a ton of nurturing." She felt her daughter walked the line between "funny and fresh." Since it sometimes seems that outgoing girls receive the most attention, it was refreshing to see that Nightingale awards the Molly Hemmerdinger Scholarship Fund, in memory of Molly Hemmerdinger, "for support of a shy student with hidden potential." An NBS mother with two daughters at the school said she feels the school "is making little Eleanor Roosevelts out of the girls: self reliant, inner-directed and well versed." A father said, "They learn to be independent, to do for themselves." He also believes there is a hidden agenda, to teach the girls the social graces. He also said he thought "Nightingale makes feminists of the fathers."

Parents: The parent body is diverse and varies from class to class. "There are lots of mixed [religion] marriages," said one parent. Jewish and Christian holidays are observed. "When you give at Nightingale, you receive," said one parent. "It's good to be an involved parent and make yourself known." One father who admits he always shaves before attending a school event or dropping off his daughter, yet describes himself as "one of the youngest and loosest" parents there, said he enjoys serving on "Daddy Patrol" (safety patrol) and walking his daughter to school with other Nightingale fathers and daughters.

A mother remarked, "As a parent of color in the school, I wanted to be vigilant, vocal and visible. Nightingale has welcomed me and my daughter fully and made us feel comfortable and I've loved the C.A.F.E. dinners and volunteering for various committees."

The Parents Association plays an integral role in the life of the Nightingale community by providing communication among parents, staff, administration and faculty and by supporting the school. Many parents volunteer their time and talents for school activities and events such as Grandparents' Day, Father-Daughter breakfast, pro-grams on parenting, Safety Patrol and the Book Fair. Other ways that parents are involved include speaking to classes and assemblies, asking friends with special areas of expertise to share them at school, inviting students to visit them on the job, singing at an all-School concert, per-forming in or helping with costumes and make-up for an all-School play, chaperoning class trips, volunteering in the library and cooking or baking for class get-togethers. In addition, the Parents Association sponsors the fair, a "Fathers Who Cook" dinner, and other major fundraising events to benefit the scholarship fund. There are other outings, including family picnics and skating parties. Courses are also offered for parents in the evening. One of the most beloved English teachers, Christine Schutt, who has just had her book of short stories, *Nightwork*, published by Knopf, has a parent reading/discussion group. Various faculty members will also teach classes in computers.

The Parents Association meets monthly to discuss issues of general interest; meetings are scheduled at convenient times for working parents, there is childcare provided and meetings are well attended. Mothers are listed by their first names with their husbands' names in parenthesis. Nightingale's Speaker Series is one of the best in the city. The series is sponsored by the Parents Association and seeks to address issues concerning girls' intellectual, social, and emotional development. Recent participants include Joan Jacobs Blumberg, author of *The Body Project*; JoAnne Deak, a specialist on "cliques" and girls' social development and author of *How Girls Thrive* (a NAIS publication, see *infra* page 483); and Catherine Steiner Adair, author of *How to Counter the Culture: the Challenge of Raising Healthy Girls*. The public is invited to attend these lectures, an example of the N-B sense of community extending beyond the schoolhouse. Parents also publish a very helpful monthly newsletter, *The Nighthawk*, which includes calendars, updates on what is going on throughout the School, and thoughts from Dorothy Hutcheson, the Head.

"Socially the school is low-key," said a parent. The kindergarten new parents' dinner is usually potluck. The fundraising functions are "a lot of fun," said another. Class coffees to discuss parent concerns at each grade level are held at the school throughout the year. A parent who summers in the Hamptons told us that there is an annual August picnic there for about seventy-five NBS families hosted by a member of the NBS board.

Program: A great deal of care and intelligent planning went into the physical renovation and updated curriculum at Nightingale, taking into account the latest research into how girls learn. Carol Gilligan, author of *In a Different Voice*, which examines the differences in girls' and boys' approaches to life and learning, was invited to speak to the Nightingale parents. Based upon some of this research, furniture in the math teaching rooms was changed. Even the rooftop playground is completely modernized with an emphasis on play that strengthens the

311

upper body, an area where girls are traditionally weak. Math and science are taught by hands-on methods. Girls use math manipulatives and play math games such as chip trading. Extra math periods have been added at the Lower School level to permit special attention to spatial relations, another area where girls tend to need reinforcement.

According to the brochure, in the Lower School homeroom teachers in each grade teach reading, English, math, history, and geography, and all of them incorporate use of computers. Other Lower School faculty, specialists in their fields, teach science, music, art, library and physical education. Collaborative learning, an interdisciplinary approach and other innovative educational techniques are used in the Lower School. "Girls at Nightingale are not allowed to talk their way through understanding. When they study machines, they create an invention; they build castles in conjunction with the Class III study of the Middle Ages. This helps them with their spatial relationships and understanding of three dimensions." We saw a group of first grade girls on the floor doing a lesson with the Cuisenaire rods. Differences among teachers are also respected. Each classroom is set up differently, a few with desks in rows, most with desks in groups, depending on the teacher's preference.

Kindergarten at Nightingale is described as "nurturing," and we would add "busy." Each kindergarten girl is paired with a senior "big sister" who shows her to her room. There are four full-time teachers with master's degrees. Basic number concepts and reading readiness are stressed. The structured reading program emphasizes phonics, but is eclectic, employing a Whole Language approach as needed. Girls keep journals, and practice their D'Nealian handwriting. They study communities, cultures, traditions and occupations and endangered animals. Kindergartners use the computer in their classroom as well as in the computer lab. Art and music are integrated into the curriculum. Girls go out for library (cozy and carpeted) and cooking (a recipe each week for each letter of the alphabet). There are museum trips and visits to other local points of interest, as well as talks by parents. Independence is valued, cooperation not competition encouraged—all things to all parents!

The Lower School curriculum is integrated where possible. Kindergartners studying communities make clay houses; second graders studying Native Americans make kachina dolls, clay animals and learn techniques of weaving. Third graders studying the Middle Ages make unicorns, swords, stained-glass windows and prepare a medieval feast; fourth graders studying colonial America examine early American crafts including quilting, and make traditional toys like dried apple-head dolls with currant eyes and cotton hair.

We noticed that the Lower School science lab houses a live snake and rabbit. In a lovely example of how the Lower School science curriculum is integrated, fourth graders studying skeletons in science also study the use of gesture in dance and art. Fifth graders construct papier-mâché whales in coordination with a unit on marine life in science.

Classes I through IV learn to read using an eclectic approach which stresses phonics but also employs elements of Whole Language and other programs. "Whatever will break the code," one teacher told us. Girls are expected to read every night. There is "daily practice in oral and written communication." A parent told us that her third grader has reading and writing homework every night. We saw work with corrected spelling hanging up on the walls; attention is paid to grammar and vocabulary too. By Class IV girls are writing book reports and short essays. Public speaking is reinforced through recitation in class, at assemblies and dramatic productions and on Class III's traditional Famous Women's Day. Older girls are required to take a public speaking course in Class XI.

History and geography in the Lower School "draw upon materials from the Boston Children's Museum, which provides authentic artifacts and activities." The curriculum guide says, "An interdisciplinary approach incorporates trips, projects, novels and discussions of current events." For instance: in Class III girls create a persona and deliver a "famous woman monologue" while dressed in costume; Class IV girls create a Plasticine terrain model to learn about features of landscape. Projects are researched in the state-of-the-art computerized library and on the Internet.

The school gathers together twice a week, once for Morning Meeting and once for assembly. Assembly is for discussion of current events or curriculum issues (environmental, cultural, political), with student participation.

In a music program, girls sing folk songs and songs from different cultures in various languages. They start with Orff instruments and the Kodaly system of sight-singing. They are introduced to opera and perform their own opera in Class IV. Girls learn to play the recorder in the Lower School. Music appreciation classes are offered at many levels. Each class presents musical performances integrated with other studies. Instrumental instruction after school is available.

There is always academic support available at NBS. In the Lower

School, tutoring in-house is a way of fulfilling the students' community service requirement, and a learning specialist is assigned to the Lower School. After school, "labs" in math, languages and science are available four days a week with Nightingale faculty for girls who would like enrichment or extra help. In class, if there are two teachers, one will offer individual help. A third grader told us there is an "I did it" board in her classroom to mark achievements large and small. A parent said, "They feel it's really important for every child to have one special thing to be an expert at." Exams preceded by one week of review begin in seventh grade. "Some girls fall apart and some sail through," a parent said.

In the Upper School there are built-in study halls during the school day and after-school lab time when teachers are available for extra help. While many describe Nightingale as rigorous, no parent or student described it as a sweatshop either.

The Lower School library was located on part of the Upper School floor to facilitate interaction between divisions. "Younger girls see what is ahead of them and the Upper School girls are reminded of where they came from," said an administrator. The girls consider it a real rite of passage to change from their Lower School tunics to the skirts and blouses of Middle and Upper School. Few girls seem to object to the dress code, saying that it removes competition in clothing. Girls do accessorize with jewelry and hair items.

Middle School at NBS is composed of Classes V through VIII. The Middle School homeroom teacher is the anchor. She says hello and goodbye each day and follows each girl's progress offering guidance along the way. The academic program includes English, history, math, science, Latin (beginning in Class VI), a choice of French or Spanish (beginning in Class V), visual arts, music, physical education, ethics and health. A parent said "They are building study skills all the way through." There is a new Middle School advisory program.

An extensive offering of extracurricular activities begins in Middle School. Choices include: Arioso, a select chorus for Class VIII; the Middle School newspaper, *Bytes from the Bird*; the Middle School literary magazine, *Out of Uniform*; dance club, recycling, student government and drama. There is an annual Gilbert and Sullivan production and a musical performed with boys from Allen-Stevenson. Class VIII performs a Shakespeare play. Team sports begin and there is a no-cut policy.

Part of the Middle School art program is the photography

requirement for fifth through eighth graders. The photo lab has fourteen processing stations. The high quality of the photography program is evident from the results published in the *Philomel*, the Upper School literary magazine, some of the best photography we've seen in terms of selection, subject matter and quality of the printing. For five out of the past six years, *Philomel* won the Gold Crown, the highest award given by the Columbia University Scholastic Press Association for excellence in writing and production. The ceramics studio is open to fifth through twelfth graders.

The Upper School at NBS consists of Classes IX through XII. Tenth through twelfth graders have the privilege of being able to sign in and out of school during the day at the front desk, a privilege that can be revoked. The Nightingale school jacket cannot be purchased until tenth grade, and the entire class must raise enough money for every member of the class to purchase one.

Peer group counseling, in which a group of eight or nine freshmen meet with two seniors to talk about topical issues, such as dating or eating disorders, is a feature. Students pick their own faculty advisors in the Upper School, and interaction among the grades is encouraged.

Most seventh through ninth graders carry six courses per semester. NBS's commitment to math and science is evident in the four-year Upper School math requirement (algebra starts in eighth grade); two years of lab science are required. (Ninety percent of the girls take three or more lab science courses.) Eighteen credits are required for graduation, but most students complete more.

Grades are compared but not posted. The average grade is a C, one student said. Many teachers seem to go at the pace of the smartest students. Teachers notify students of forthcoming tests on a "test board" so that a balance can be maintained in students' workloads and schedules. Ninth grade is a big jump in difficulty from eighth grade, we were told. A new interdisciplinary unit in Class IX on Humanism continues the collaborative learning of earlier years. English, history, science, Latin, French, Spanish, art, music and drama teachers team-teach this unit.

"The Diversity and Richness of World Literature" is explored in tenth grade with a focus on the classics. There is a single semester requirement of public speaking. Eleventh and twelfth grade English electives include "Exiles: The Lost Generation in Paris" and "The New Woman in Shaw and Ibsen." After a solid grounding in modern history and non-Western history, eleventh and twelfth graders can take electives that include "Social Movements in the Twentieth Century," which examines reform movements, and "The Advent of Feminism, Black History and Civil Rights." Students can take advanced study in English, languages, history, math and science. A parent told us: "The girls are intelligent about current events; they have common sense. There are articles in the school newspaper about how much the students know about government, for example."

The science department offers a course in Applied Chemistry, "ChemCom" ("Chemistry in the Community") as well as Environmental Science and Marine Biology and Genetics. The new science labs (separate biology, physics and chemistry labs) are state of the art, complete with an air vent for working with hazardous fumes, emergency eyewash and shower, and a laser disc player. NBS has three computer labs with both IBMs and Macs. Josh Feder, Director of Technology at N-B, facilitates the seamless integration of technology into the curriculum. "At Nightingale our goal is to have every teacher in every subject be fully capable of using technology to augment the best methods of instruction." Feder, author of *Teaching With the Web*, designs and conducts workshops on multimedia, the Internet, and Website design for teachers at N-B as well as other independent schools. The school is fully networked and all Middle and Upper School students have e-mail addresses.

NBS students can enroll in Interschool courses, design an independent course of study, or take courses at Barnard, Columbia or other New York universities with school approval. There are some intriguing opportunities for travel and study abroad: The Japan trip and the Latin study trip to Italy are offered over spring vacation. For those who want to spend a semester or full year abroad Nightingale has sister schools in Australia, France, Switzerland and Spain. Two juniors and a faculty member visit St. Paul's Girls School in London. For those who love the outdoors there is The Mountain School option, a Maine coast semester, and the Island School.

Socially, one student noted, there was a definite "in" group, and because the school is so small, it can be quite obvious. But a ninth grader said she had made "friendships that will last for life" at NBS and the "family-like environment makes learning more bearable and enjoyable." On the subject of single-sex education, one ninth grader told us, "You won't get distracted by a guy you like, it's easier to focus on schoolwork. On the other hand, it can be very hard to feel comfortable around boys because you don't get to spend much time with them." There are ample opportunities, however, for coed experiences through Interschool activities. At a recent open house an eleventh grader commented: "I came to NBS from a downtown coed school in ninth grade and I thought I'd really miss boys. Instead, I feel liberated. I don't have to worry about distractions during classes and I've kept my old friends who are boys and made new ones through interschool activities."

Community service is a requirement and in the Upper School thirty hours in school and thirty hours outside of school are mandatory. The Nielsen Service Prize "endows an award to a student who makes a genuine commitment and important contribution in the area of social service." A student said, "Community service is stressed." NBS girls are very concerned about their community and participate in park cleanups, Special Olympics and AIDS walks and tutor at a nearby public school or volunteer at hospitals. In-house service includes library work, assisting the school nurse, stuffing envelopes, tutoring, helping in art studios or the science labs.

Popular clubs in the Upper School include C.A.F.E: Cultural Awareness for Everyone, and the Gender Issues group. Other choices include the Drama, Dance and Glee Clubs, Interschool plays and musicals, student government, yearbook, newspaper, literary magazine, Model U.N, Photo and Film Clubs, Debate Club and Environmental Club. The Glee Club had toured Italy where, among other events, they sang for the Pope, and in a recent year went to London. Students can work on stage crew or perform in the Interschool drama or musical. There is an Interschool drama production as well as an Upper School musical in alternate years. A recent production was *Bye, Bye Birdie*, with Conrad played by a Collegiate student. Faculty, staff and parents join the students in producing the Upper School musical. Those who have an interest in the visual arts can take a full year of studio art: design, painting, photography, video, ceramics, or sculpture.

The new gym has bolstered school spirit in the area of athletics. Teamwork is stressed. The Nightingale Nighthawks field strong teams in soccer, basketball, tennis, gymnastics, badminton and swimming.

During "Senior Weeks" girls take courses in everyday living including: "How to Manage Your Money," "How to Change a Tire," "Date Rape on Campus" and "Let's Experience New York's Cultural Life" with trips to the opera, ballet, Philharmonic or a play.

Seniors at NBS have the use of a senior lounge (all others hang out on the sunny back terrace), and can ride the school's elevators. There is an Honors and Awards Assembly the day before graduation: Achievements in academic areas are rewarded as well as effort and improvement.

Director of Admissions, Carole Everett, describes NBS girls as "wholesome" and well-prepared for life after NBS.

Nightingale alumnae feel a strong connection to the school. "During a recent visit last spring I was pleased by the friendliness, the familiarity of the uniforms, and the sense that Nightingale is still a superior learning environment and a safe haven in a frenetic city," said an alumna. According to a mother, "Nightingale is a traditional community where people really care about each other, the girls are well mannered and well behaved . . . there are high expectations and they measure up from day one."

Popular College Choices   Harvard, Brown, Cornell, Vassar, Wesleyan, Yale, Dartmouth, University of Pennsylvania

Traditions   All-School Fair (proceeds support the Scholarship Fund), Big Sisters/Little Sisters, singing holiday songs before winter break; the Daisy Ceremony for Class IV; Honors Assembly; Athletic Awards dinner; Class VII Gilbert and Sullivan production; Class VIII Shakespeare play with Allen-Stevenson; Festival of the Written Word assembly; Famous Women's Day; Field Day; Cum Laude and other weekly assemblies with a mix of prominent speakers and student-led discussions; Winter Concert; Homecoming, an annual soccer and volleyball game against Brearley on a Saturday in the fall; C.A.F.E. (Cultural Awareness for Everyone) dinners for students and their parents each year; The Father/Daughter breakfast; Grandparents Day; Book Fair

Publications   Middle School newspaper: *Bytes From the Bird*
Upper School newspaper: *Spectator*
Middle School literary magazine: *Out of Uniform*
Upper School literary magazine: *Philomel*
French Journal
Alumnae magazine
Yearbook
Monthly parents newsletter: *Nighthawk*

Community Service Requirement   30 hours in school, 30 hours of service in the community; a 9th grade social service project with Class IX at Collegiate

Hangouts   The Upper School terrace, Jackson Hole Burger Restaurant, Ciao Bella, Yura's, Timothy's, senior lounge, Student Center

The Packer Collegiate Institute

170 Joralemon Street
Brooklyn, New York, NY 11201
(718) 875-6644, FAX (718) 875-1363
website:www.packer.edu

Coed
Nursery–12th grade
Not accessible

Mr. Geoffrey Pierson, Head of School
Ms. Valorie Iason, Director of Admissions,
Preschool and Lower School
Mr. Matthew Nespole, Director of Admissions,
Middle and Upper School

Birthday Cutoff   Children entering at kindergarten must turn 5 in
December
Children entering first grade must be 6 by August 31

Enrollment   Total enrollment: approximately 875
Kindergarten places: 25
First grade places: 10
Ninth grade places; 25
Graduating class size: approximately 55

Grades   Semester system:
K–4, detailed anecdotal reports and checklists
Letter grades begin in 5th grade; in addition, detailed anecdotal
reports are sent twice a year

Tuition Range 2001–2002 $8,380 to $17,620, Nursery–12th grade
Additional fees: under $300 for books (5th–12th grades only)

Financial Aid   30% of students receive some form of tuition
assistance

Endowment $11 million

Diversity   25% children of color
Packer Collegiate has a Diversity Committee

Homework   Kindergarten and 1st grade: none
2nd grade: formal homework begins
3rd and 4th grades: 1 hour, each school night
5th and 6th grades: 1–2 hours
7th and 8th grades: 2–3 hours
9th–12th grades: 3–4 hours

After-School Program   Packer Plus is open to Packer Collegiate students only in kindergarten through 8th grade; a variety of creative and recreational activities from 3:15 P.M. until 6:00 P.M.; for an additional charge
Packer Plus Courses are offered on a trimester basis and meet from 3:30–4:30 P.M. for eight weeks. Vacation Packer Plus Playgroups are available during Winter Break, Spring Break and between the close of school and the beginning of the summer day camp.
Extracurricular clubs and activities
Junior varsity and varsity athletic competition

Summer Program   Summer Camp: open to children from other schools; mid-June through the end of July; an additional payment is required

Founded in 1845 as the Brooklyn Female Academy, and endowed by Harriet Packer, The Packer Collegiate Institute is the oldest independent school in Brooklyn and was the first to offer higher education to young women. It became coed in the early seventies. Packer's architecturally unique landmark building boasts fully equipped science and two computer labs, two libraries, a student lounge, two theatres, music, art and dance studios and two full-court gymnasiums in addition to an elegant chapel with a 1906 Austin organ and nine Tiffany stained-glass windows. Chapel attendance is required once a week at which social, political, environmental and ethical issues are discussed. Packer also has an outdoor play area known as "The Garden." The style of the school is informal and there is no dress code. Hot lunch is available for grades three through twelve only.

Packer's diverse student body represents the five boroughs of

New York City and the outlying metropolitan areas. Approximately 55% of Packer's Upper School students live in Brooklyn and 40% live in Manhattan. In 2000, Packer enrolled seventeen students from Prep for Prep. Parents say a distinct feeling of community exists among children of all ages and backgrounds and the faculty.

Getting In: Open houses are offered throughout the fall so prospective parents can tour the facilities and talk with students, faculty and administration. For Pre-kindergarten through fourth grade applicants, Packer requires a completed application and fee with school and teacher evaluations when appropriate. Pre-school candidates, ages 3, 4 and 5, meet individually and in small groups. Applicants to kindergarten and first grade are interviewed and evaluated at the school to assess their aptitude and learning style. Candidates for grades 2 through 4 are interviewed at the school and tested at the ERB. Applicants for grades 2 through 4 also spend a day visiting a Packer class. Applicants to grades 5 through 12 have a personal interview and must submit previous school records, two teacher evaluations and results of the ISEE or the SSAT. There is a sibling and legacy policy for qualified candidates, but admission is not automatic. The main points of entry to the school are in kindergarten and ninth grades.

Program: The Lower School at Packer emphasizes an interactive, individualized, developmentally appropriate approach. The junior first grade program is a transition program for children who will turn six in the fall of the year. The transition program is like a kindergarten program in the fall semester and evolves into a beginning first grade program soon after the children return from winter break. The following year children move to first grade. Reading is taught using eclectic methods. "We use a wealth of materials to accommodate the variety of learning styles so characteristic of young children."

The Middle School at Packer begins in fifth grade. Students have one extended core class in English and history and another in mathematics and science. Computer, music, dance, theatre, chorus, gym and health round out the curriculum. All fifth graders must take a course called Frameworks which reinforces good study habits and skills such as note-taking, test-taking, research and so on. In sixth grade, some students, upon recommendation by their teacher, continue in Frameworks II, with the expectation that they will begin foreign language in seventh grade. All other sixth graders begin study of a foreign language in French, Latin, or Spanish.

In seventh and eighth grades, the program is fully departmentalized. There are competitive sports teams and a variety of extracurricular activities from which to choose. Throughout Middle School homeroom teachers and advisors stay in close contact with both students and their families.

Each Middle and Upper School student has an advisor who is a teacher in the school. The Peer Support program involves juniors and seniors who are selected to attend a leadership training seminar preparing them to meet with freshmen in small groups throughout the year to discuss their transition to high school.

In the Upper School, the freshman year is built around a study of major literary works. A collaborative program that involves faculty from the English, History, and Arts departments integrates the study of ancient civilizations through the Middle Ages. Freshmen also take a rigorous year of conceptual physics, foreign language and mathematics. The interdisciplinary approach continues in the sophomore year as students study "The American Experience" from historical, literary and artistic perspectives. Chemistry, foreign language and mathematics complete the academic program. Students in their junior and senior years have many electives from which to choose, including AP courses in 15 areas. A junior year English course, biology, and Modern European History are requirements. Packer has an outstanding Science Research course where students work with mentors from across the country. The average class size in the High School is fifteen; the student-teacher ratio is 7 to 1 and the advisee to advisor ratio is 10 to 1.

Graduation requirements include four years of English and physical education; three years each of foreign language, mathematics, history, and sciences; two years of electives; two years of arts; one year of Health; and 45 hours of school and community service. Older students can participate in independent study, Senior Emphasis Program, Maine Coast Semester, High Mountain Institute, or a Cultural Exchange Program. Most seniors also use the second semester to work on a senior thesis.

Offerings in the arts are broad and include visual arts, photography, computer graphics, modern dance, orchestra, brass, choir, woodwind ensemble, jazz band and women's ensemble.

Clubs and organizations available to students include Amnesty International; Brothers and Sisters; Chorus (the Packer Chorus has been on two European Tours during the past four years.); Debate; Mock Trial; Model Congress; Multicultural Student Association; Drama Club, SAFE (feminist club); Packer Civil Liberties Union and the Social Action Committee; Student Government; and various school publications. There are numerous athletic teams in Middle and

Upper School, including a Middle School coed soccer team, judo and fencing, girls' volleyball, gymnastics, basketball, and softball, and boys' soccer, basketball, baseball and volleyball.

Popular college choices   Brown, Harvard, Yale, Cornell, Wesleyan, University of Pennsylvania, Dartmouth, Columbia, Emory

Publications Art and literary publication: *Packer Current Items*
Yearbook: *The Pelican*
Newspaper: *The Prism*

Community Service Requirement   45 hours in the Upper School (9th-12th), tenth grade service project at a day care center, senior center, or soup kitchen

Hangout   Upper School Student Center, McDonald's around the corner

Poly Prep Country Day School

Coed
Nursery—12th Grade
Not accessible
website: www.polyprep.org

Poly Prep Lower School
50 Prospect Park West
Brooklyn, NY 11215
(718) 768-1103
(Nursery–4th Grade)
Maureen Walsh Heffernan, Head

Poly Prep Country Day School
9216 Seventh Avenue
Brooklyn, NY 11228
(718) 836-9800
website: www.Polyprep.Brooklyn.ny.us
(5th–12th Grade)
David B. Harmon, Headmaster
Lori W. Redell, Director of Admissions
Pat Montero, Director of Lower School Admissions

Birthday Cutoff   Children entering nursery school must be 2.3 years old by September 1st;
Children entering kindergarten must be 5 years old by September 1st

Enrollment   Total enrollment: 800
Nursery–4th grade: 140
Nursery places: 45
K–4th grade places: 10
5th grade places: 35–40
7th grade places: 30
9th grade places: 35–45
Graduating class 2000: Approximately 110
39 Prep for Prep students enrolled as of Fall 2000

Tuition Range 2001–2002 $9,200–$19,900, ½ day Nursery–12th grade
Additional fees: for lunch and graduation for grades 5th–12th approximately $820
No additional fees for grade N–4th

Transportation for students from Manhattan, Staten Island, Brooklyn and Queens is provided at no extra charge.

After-School Program Arts Program Monday–Thursday for N–4th grades, an additional payment is required; for grades 5th–12th, extracurricular activities and clubs, Varsity and Junior Varsity athletic competition.

Summer Program For grades N–4th, Day Camp and Drama Camp; For grades 5th–12th, Day Camp, Performing Arts Camp, Sports Camp and Computer Camp; from the end of June until the beginning of August; open to students from other schools; an additional payment is required

---

Founded in 1854, as part of the Country Day School Movement, Poly Prep has been located on a twenty-five acre campus in the Dyker Heights area of Brooklyn since 1917. The campus has a new science building, playing fields, a theatre, swimming pool, tennis courts, squash courts and a new fitness center and a dance center. ERB testing or the SSAT is required for admissions. The school is becoming increasingly popular and admissions are competitive.

The school's motto, *Virtus Vitrix Fortunae,* or "Hard Work Conquers the Vagaries of Fortune" is as relevant now as it ever was. It's one of our favorite school mottos. Poly Prep is diverse—children of color represent approximately 29 percent of the student body. In spring 1995, Poly Prep took over the Woodward Park School, in Park Slope, Brooklyn adding a lower division that will feed students into Poly Prep's Middle School. The Poly Prep Lower School is located in an historic 12,000 square foot mansion overlooking Brooklyn's Prospect Park. The Lower School emphasizes hands-on learning, and the use of manipulative materials across the curriculum. Transportation to the school from Staten Island, Brooklyn and parts of Manhattan and Queens is provided at no extra charge. Approximately 20 percent of students in grades five through twelve come from Manhattan and approximately 18 percent come from Staten Island. There is a dress code. Hot lunch is provided.

Popular college choices Wesleyan, NYU, Columbia, Amherst, University of Pennsylvania, Boston College, Johns Hopkins, SUNY-Binghamton, Wesleyan, Yale

Professional Children's School

132 West 60th Street
New York, NY 10023
(212) 582-3116, x135 Admissions answer line,
x112 Admission Director
www.pcs-nyc.org

Coed
4th–12th grade
Not accessible

Dr. James Dawson, Head of School
Sherrie Hinkle, Director of Admissions

Birthday Cutoff   None; applications are accepted at various times during the year

Enrollment   Total enrollment: 180
4th grade places: 10
Graduating class size: variable, from 35–60

Tuition Range 2001–2002 $17,500, 4th grade—12th grade
Additional fees for books and supplies total approximately $500

After-School Program   Extracurricular activity groups are formed if there is enough interest in the student body

Summer Program   None

———

Professional Children's School was founded in 1914 as an academic program for children appearing in vaudeville or on the Broadway stage. Today, Professional Children's School is the only fully accredited independent school providing a college preparatory curriculum for children actively involved in the performing and visual arts as well as competitive sports. (It is to be distinguished from LaGuardia High School for the Performing Arts, one of the New York City specialized public high schools, depicted in the movie *Fame*.)

Applicants must have a serious interest in the arts/sports and academic ability—no auditions are required for acceptance. A transcript, personal interview and standardized testing complete the application process. About 40 percent of the student body receives partial financial aid.

Students follow a regular school day but the periods are slightly shorter so that students can schedule professional engagements during school hours.

A Guided Study Program is available for students whose professional commitments keep them away from the classroom for an extended period.

Approximately 70% of Professional Children's School graduates attend college on a full or part-time basis; another 15% go on to college after completing professional commitments. The rest pursue their careers and may enroll in college at a later time.

Rabbi Arthur Schneier Park East Day School

164 East 68th Street
New York, NY 10021
Tel (212) 737-6900
FAX (212) 570-6348

Coed
2's–8th grade
Accessible

Rabbi Arthur Schneier, Dean
Rabbi Yehoshua Kamensky, Dean of Administration
Mrs. Marilyn Meltzer, Principal of English Studies
Mrs. Sarah Platovsky, Principal of Hebrew Studies
Mrs. Harriet Ingber, Early Childhood Director
Mrs. Toby Einsidler, Administrator

Birthday Cutoff   Children entering at the nursery level must be 2 by August 31
Children entering kindergarten must be 5 by December 31

Enrollment   Total enrollment: 300
2's places: 35
Kindergarten places: 10
Graduating class size: approximately 12

Tuition Range 2001–2002 $5,900 to $12,400, 2's (two half days)—8th grade, additional fees. $300 for 2's to $1,800 for 8th grade
There is a discount for synagogue members
There is a discount for families with two or more children enrolled in kindergarten—8th grade

After-School Program   For Park East students only; a variety of creative and recreational activities Monday–Thursday from 3:30 P.M. to 4:30 P.M., 1:30 to 3:00 P.M. on Fridays; an additional payment is required

---

The Park East Day School was founded by Rabbi Arthur Schneier as a nursery school and merged with East Side Hebrew Institute in

1979, adding an elementary division. Park East Day School is affiliated with Congregation Zichron Ephraim and the adjoining Park East Synagogue (founded in 1890).

Park East's eight-story school building includes classrooms, a science laboratory, computer center, art studio, library, music room, auditorium, cafeteria, gym and outdoor playground. The program combines Jewish traditional religious values with a demanding secular curriculum.

Getting In: Students come from diverse Jewish backgrounds. ERB testing is required for admission to kindergarten and above. Admissions decisions are based on observation of the children, an interview with the parents and ERB test results.

Program: There are two teachers in each kindergarten classroom. The program is geared to the individual child's readiness and includes beginning reading and personal writing. A hot kosher lunch is served beginning in kindergarten. Kindergarten students eat lunch with their teachers in their classrooms. First through eighth grades eat together in the school cafeteria.

There is a dress code beginning in first grade. Class size from first grade through eighth grade averages 15 students. Beginning in first grade students take a dual curriculum, with half the day devoted to secular studies and half of the day devoted to Hebrew/Judaic studies. Formal Hebrew instruction begins in this year. Students are introduced to Hebrew grammar and vocabulary, Jewish culture, Torah, prayer and holidays. Both boys and girls participate equally in prayers. Thematic studies (Holocaust, immigration and the history of modern Israel) are integrated throughout. The curriculum is supplemented by trips to museums, Jewish theatre productions, and the study of Jewish authors. There is weekly instruction taught by specialists in science, computer, library, art, chess, gym and music.

Students who show proficiency in math receive enrichment several times a week. Park East students have the opportunity to participate in city, state and national math and chess competitions throughout the year. Students with a special interest or proficiency in English are enriched with in-depth assignments. Beginning in third grade students can attend a weekly book discussion club moderated by one of the teachers. There is a learning center staffed by a specialist for students who need strengthening in Hebrew, reading and mathematics.

The artist-in-residence program exposes students to various facets of the arts. Guests have included a classical pianist, songwriter, radio announcer, actor, stamp collector, opera singer, cellist and designer.

Literary Week, in November each year, is a school-wide celebration of books. Lecturers have included publishers, book designers, authors and illustrators.

A spirit of community is reinforced through various school assemblies such as the Biography Fair for grades 3 through 5, the first grade Siddur play, the second grade Chumash play and the Science, Math and Technology Fair presented by students in grades 1 through 8.

Extracurricular activities include: Chess, science, computer, painting, museum club, basketball, creative writing, cooking, costume design, team sports, softball and mathematics.

Graduates   attend a variety of NYC private and specialized public high schools. Recent choices include Ramaz, Dalton, Columbia Grammar and Prep, UNIS, Solomon Schecter High School, Yeshiva of Flatbush, Elisabeth Irwin High School, Bronx Science, Stuyvesant, LaGuardia School for the Performing Arts, and Frisch High School.

Traditions   Annual Purim Carnival, Chanukah party, Literary Week, Sukkoth dinner celebration, participation in the Salute to Israel Day Parade, Student Art Exhibit

Community Service Requirement   Park East students are encouraged to participate in a wide-range of community service activities such as visiting nursing homes, helping to support synagogues on the Lower East Side, organizing coat drives, collecting Passover foods for Project Dorot, and entertaining the elderly during holidays

Ramaz

Lower School
125 East 85th Street
New York, NY 10028
(212) 774-8010

The Rabbi Haskel Lookstein Middle School
114 East 85th Street
New York, NY 10028

The Rabbi Joseph H. Lookstein Upper School
60 East 78th Street
New York, NY 10021
(212) 517-5955
website: www.ramaz.org

Coed
Nursery–12th Grade
Accessible

Rabbi Haskel Lookstein, Principal
Mrs. Daniele Gorlin Lassner, Director of Admissions

Birthday Cutoff   Children entering at the nursery level must be 3 by August 31
Children entering kindergarten must be 5 by August 31

Enrollment   Total enrollment: 1082
3's places: 30
Kindergarten places: 25
9th grade places: 60
Graduating class size: approximately 100–110

Tuition Range 2001–2002 $13,300 to $17,125, nursery 3's–12th grade
Ramaz has a scholarship and special needs fund: nursery, $1,500; K–12, $2,500
Additional fees: for registration, lunch, student activities and overnight trips approximately $1,000

After-School Program   Lower School: a variety of creative and recreational activities until 5:00 P.M.; an additional payment is required

Upper School: a variety of creative and recreational activities until 6:00 P.M.; there is no additional charge

Summer Program   None

––––––––

Ramaz is an Orthodox Jewish day school founded in 1937 by the late Rabbi Joseph H. Lookstein. The initials (in Hebrew) of the rabbi's name make up the acronym that is the school's name. Ramaz is committed to modern or centrist Orthodox Judaism. Applicant families may also be "conservative and committed" but all families keep kosher homes. The school just added a fully renovated top-of-the-line Middle School on East 85th Street to its facilities. Formal Hebrew language instruction begins in first grade. Half of the school day is devoted to Judaic studies and half the day is devoted to the general studies curriculum. Although all classes are coed, the sexes are separated during morning and afternoon prayers. Ramaz has a dress code and a kosher hot lunch is served.

Popular College Choices   Barnard College, Columbia University, Harvard University, New York University, University of Pennsylvania, Yale, and Yeshiva and Stern Colleges of Yeshiva University

Regis High School

55 East 84th Street
New York, NY 10028
(212) 288-1100, FAX (212) 794-1221
website: regis-nyc.org

All boys
9th–12th grade
Not accessible

Rev. Vincent Biagi, S.J., Principal
Mr. Eric P. DiMichele, Director of Admissions

Birthday Cutoff   None

Enrollment   Total enrollment: 522
9th grade places: 135
Graduating class 2000: 128

Tuition   None: all students receive tuition-free scholarships and pay
only laboratory and activity fees

After-School Program   A variety of extracurricular activities until
5:30 P.M.
Varsity sports competition in the Catholic High School Athletic
Association

Summer Program   None

———

Regis High School was founded in 1914 by the Society of Jesus as
a tuition-free school for Catholic boys. Regis High School is sustained
through the original bequest of a generous parishioner of the Church
of St. Ignatius Loyola as well as contributions from alumni.

Regis High School is highly selective. Only baptized Catholic
eighth grade boys may apply. Regis does not accept transfers. The
admissions process is rigorous: Applicants must score in the ninetieth
percentile and above on standardized tests and have an outstanding
elementary school record. In addition, students must sit for the Regis
scholarship examination. Semifinalists are interviewed by faculty and

alumni, and approximately half of this group is selected for admission to Regis. Financial need is one factor in the admissions process.

Regis offers a traditional liberal arts curriculum. The pace is accelerated, and the work load and expectations are most demanding. Four years of theology are required as well as participation in community service projects, liturgies and religious retreats. Catholic holidays are observed.

The average combined SAT score for the Class of 2000 was 1379.

Popular College Choices   Harvard, Columbia, Cornell, Fordham, Georgetown, Yale, New York University, Johns Hopkins, Williams, Princeton, Holy Cross

The Riverdale Country School

Upper School or Hill Campus
5250 Fieldston Road
(at West 253rd Street)
Riverdale, NY 10471-2999
(718) 549-8810, FAX (718) 519-2795
e-mail:@riverdale.edu
website:www.riverdale.edu

Lower School or River Campus,
Spaulding Lane (between Independence and Palisades
Avenues)
Riverdale, NY 10471
main number (718) 549-7780, FAX (718) 432-4793
admissions (718) 432-4782 FAX (718) 432-4794

Coed
Pre-kindergarten–12th grade
Not accessible

Dr. John R. Johnson, Headmaster
Mr. Kent Kildahl, Head of the Upper School
Mr. Sandy Shaller, Head of the Lower School
Ms. Ridie Lazar, Director of Admissions
Mr. Dan DiVirgilio, Director of Lower School Admissions

Uniform   Lower School: casual and neat, turtleneck, shirts with collars, no logos, no white T-shirts
Upper School: appropriate attire

Birthday Cutoff   Children entering pre-kindergarten must be 4 by September 1
Kindergarten: children entering kindergarten must be 5 by September 1

Enrollment   Total enrollment: 1040
Lower School: 420
Upper School: 620
Kindergarten places: 54
Graduating class 1998: 114

Grades   Semester system

Kindergarten–5th: detailed anecdotal reports and checklists

Letter grades begin in 6th grade

7th–12th: grades with comments twice a year; grades alone twice a year

Modified departmentalization in 4th–6th grade

Full departmentalization by 7th grade

First midterms and finals begin in 7th grade

Tuition Range 2001–2002 $19,200 to $22,500, pre-kindergarten–12th grade

Riverdale has a monthly payment option and a quarterly payment option running from June to March

Extended repayment plan (educational loan)

Tuition refund plan (insurance)

Busing from Manhattan is approximately $2,000 for Lower School students, approximately $1,000 for Upper School students

Financial Aid/Scholarship   20% of students receive some form of tuition assistance

$2.8 million available

Endowment   Approximately $22 million

Diversity   20% children of color

9 Prep for Prep students enrolled as of fall 2000

Lower School parents of color meeting held three times a year

Lower School multicultural literature program at all grade levels

The Upper School has a diversity coordinator who works with the entire student body and faculty on issues of diversity and multiculturalism

Homework   1st: 15 minutes, Monday through Thursday

2nd and 3rd: 30–40 minutes, Monday through Thursday

4th: 45 minutes–1 hour, Monday through Thursday

5th and 6th: 1–2 hours a night

7th and 8th: 2–2½ hours a night

9th–12th: average of 3½ hours per night; more for those taking many APs

Assume 40 minutes per subject per night

In addition, parents of young children are encouraged to read to them for at least 20 minutes each night from the Lower School recommended reading list

After-School Program   Riverclub: For grades Pre-k through 6th; 3:30–5:00pm; a variety of creative and recreational activities for an additional payment; transportation home is available
Grades 7–8: intramural and interscholastic sports
Grades 9–12: interscholastic sports, theatrical productions

Summer Program   The Summerbridge Program: a privately funded 6-week-long program (established in 1992) that prepares 90 talented Middle School students from the inner city for competitive high schools; it is tuition-free and taught by Riverdale High School students as well as college students under the guidance of two directors and several other teachers.
Summer camp: 7 weeks, for ages 6–11; sports, nature and creative activities; for an additional payment

---

After coming upon an intoxicated schoolboy in the street in New York City, Riverdale Country School's founder, Frank Hackett, decided to found a school in the countryside, far from the degrading influences of city life and offering abundant opportunity to play in the open air. Hackett coined the term "independent school" to distinguish his school from the "hoity-toity private schools." From the outset, Hackett had a vision of a "world school" with an "international curriculum."[*]

Today RCS offers a strong community with a diverse population. The curriculum is grounded in liberal arts basics. Parents say academic expectations are high and many types of students can find success here, but they must be committed to doing the work that is expected of them. Moreover, gaining admission to RCS has become increasingly competitive. "It happened because we're making it better by maintaining our curriculum standards and staying committed to them. We have a really good academic program and a C.A.R.E. (Children Aware of Riverdale Ethics) package and we've worked hard on our physical plant and that attracts people. We're a school that never sleeps," says Sandy Shaller, Head of RCS's Lower School.

The Lower School consists of grades pre-kindergarten through

[*] *The Quickened Spirit*, by Allen Hackett (The Riverdale Country School, New York City, 1957), p. 51.

sixth. At RCS's Lower School "There really is no typical student. Sixty per cent of our students come from Manhattan. The others come from The Bronx, Westchester or Northern New Jersey." One parental concern is that a car is necessary if you send your child here. Not true. Parents can easily find a ride to Riverdale for Parents' Night, two conferences, one music program, three parenting evenings and one play (in each grade), the Academic Fair, Book Fair and the carnival.

Getting in: Respect and consideration for the individual is a hallmark of RCS, beginning with the admissions process. RCS is one of very few schools to grant each Lower School applicant a one-on-one interview with either the Director of Admissions or one of his assistants. Continued interest in the Lower School by an ever-increasing number of qualified applicants has made it more difficult than ever to be accepted at RCS. Children who are shy in a group of strangers have nothing to fear here. "We don't have a mold that children must fit into," says a member of the admissions staff. The mother of a girl who transferred from a single-sex school said, "My child has never been negatively typecast here."

Cake, cookies and hot coffee greet you on the morning of your tour. Leave the Chanel suit at home, and it will not count against you if your husband cannot make it to Riverdale for the tour. Please don't brag about *your* many accomplishments; RCS is not scrutinizing the parents.

Admission to the Upper School is also very competitive. The RCS Upper School admissions staff are personable and friendly and offer students and parents a one-on-one interview with either Ridie Lazar, Director of Admissions, or one of her associates. "Careful attention is paid to making sure that RCS is the right personal and academic fit for each applicant," says Ms. Woodward. Once admissions decisions have been made, RCS maintains a small selective wait list.

Riverdale's pre-kindergarten program, at the River Campus, is helpful for parents of children with borderline birthdays and parents who know from the start that they want to send their children to Riverdale.

Parents: There isn't a typical student, nor is there a typical parent at RCS. All types can feel comfortable here. The class cocktail party might be held in an apartment on Park Avenue or on Riverside Drive. "There are as many Gucci loafers as there are Birkenstocks," one parent said after attending several school functions. Parent involvement is welcomed and parents can volunteer to go on class trips, work in the library or help teach computer. Communication between teachers and parents is just a phone call away, and one parent said her children's backpacks are always full of correspondence from Riverdale. One mother said, "A note came home the first day homework wasn't done." The school's bus service says they will drop off homework at your door "every day if necessary" if your child misses school (Lower School only).

Program: The Upper, or Hill Campus, serves grades seven through twelve, and the Lower School, or River Campus, serves prekindergarten through six. At the Lower School learning is more experiential; the Upper School is more traditional and structured.

Each morning as the younger children arrive at the River Campus, Sandy Shaller, head of the Lower School, is there to greet them. He knows every child (and nearly every parent) by name, and is involved in almost every aspect of the Lower School. Parents say, "Mr. Shaller *is* the Lower School." Almost all prospective parents have a chance to ask Mr. Shaller questions about RCS, either when they tour or certainly after acceptance. Mr. Shaller and Ms. Terri Hassid (assistant head of the Lower School) each teach a class a day. At the 1998 Spring Carnival, with booths operated by each class relating to the theme "Broadway Theatrical Productions," Mr. Shaller roamed the campus as The Phantom of the Opera, "complete with mask, black costume, hat and cape," said one parent.

An architecturally eclectic group of buildings make up the River Campus. The latest addition is a brand-new three-story, twelve-classroom building with a 6,000-square foot gymnasium (designed by an alumna whose sons and daughter attend RCS). The Perkins Building houses an auditorium, library, classrooms, administrative offices and science resource room. The Junior Building contains admissions, the cafeteria, a computer complex and music classrooms. The Senior Building (Arts Building) houses two art studios, special music classes and support services. In addition, there are four newly resurfaced tennis courts, a soccer/football field, an environmental education area, patios and a well-designed play area. The River Campus is large enough to accommodate all these facilities in one place, and intimate enough to feel like a community. Children have the freedom to jump rope, build a snowman, enjoy the playground or throw a football at recess, depending on the season. Students are not allowed to wander around the River Campus alone; they are always well supervised, particularly at busing time.

Like a traditional elementary school, RCS has recess (formal recess ends after third grade), and four gym periods per week. "It's an intense day and at recess there is an explosion of energy. This is a country campus and we use it," says Ms. Hassid. Each grade puts on a music and drama performance and there are weekly assemblies where folk songs are occasionally sung. Pre-kindergarten and kindergarten at Riverdale stress readiness and provide individualized attention. Classes in pre-kindergarten through first grade all have a head teacher and an assistant teacher. There is traditional circle time, along with job charts and journal writing with invented spelling. Since the school is in a country setting, much attention is paid to the study of nature and environmental issues. For example, every Lower School student gets three seed pots and plants them in the wetlands area and will have a hands-on opportunity to work on the grounds. Pre-kindergarten and kindergarten children have garden plots where they plant flowers and vegetables as part of the Spring science program. Nearly every kindergarten and first grade class has a pet: guinea pigs, turtles or fish. Math instruction is hands-on in the early years. One kindergarten mother came in to make pizza for a math project that included grating the cheese and measuring the circumference of the pizza (she brought her own homemade sauce).

By first grade formal academics are introduced and the teachers have serious expectations. For those who need strengthening there is the Small Group Reading Program. By first grade there are daily homework assignments four times a week. The Lower School administers the CTP III (a standardized test that measures academic skills and compares the test scores to other independent schools' test scores).

In second grade there is one teacher, and reading and math skills continue to develop and expand. Foreign language is introduced in third grade; those who need strengthening in language arts take "Fundamentals of Writing," in sixth grade. Writing is stressed in all subject areas, and creative expression is encouraged. The Lower School has its own publication called the *Rivulet*. In sixth grade, students pick topics and learn how to research and write term papers. The first final exam is given in sixth grade.

Many class trips are scheduled, including a train trip for kindergartners up the Hudson for a picnic lunch. Third graders tap maple trees and collect and process the syrup. The science resource room is a popular place filled with natural treasures such as materials, nests, leaves, bark and fish as well as all types of equipment for conducting hands-on experiments.

RCS students may breathe fresh air each day but the resources of

Manhattan are not neglected. For example, sixth graders are introduced to independent research through "The Concrete Garden" project. They pick any building in New York City and write an in-depth report on it. Modified departmentalization begins in fourth grade but is not complete until seventh.

Computer study at Riverdale is strong. The school has recently installed a fiber optic cable that connects all of the buildings and allows the RCS community to gain access to the Internet in all of the classrooms. The usage of the Internet is curriculum driven and is primarily for educational purposes. An "Acceptable Use Policy for Technology and Computer Networks" is sent to all Riverdale families to inform parents of possible issues concerning the use of this technology. For parents who aren't as computer savvy as their children, RCS provides parents with on-line (Internet) and off-line (books, videos, etc.) materials, a Parents Association course on computers and technology, and a list of books that offer guidance to new users. Almost all members of the administration, teachers and Upper School students have e-mail addresses. Lower School students do not presently have e-mail accounts, but e-mail can be sent through their teachers. A publicly viewable list of e-mail names at RCS is in the works. General queries can be sent to webmaster@riverdale.edu, admin@riverlake.edu or postmaster@riverdale.edu.

There is a beautiful new computer lab and several mini-labs on both campuses. In addition, there is an updated computer room with twenty laptops and twenty IMACs for fourth through sixth grade students. RCS also has a Computer Coordinator (at the Lower School), a Director of Technology (at the Upper School), and a support staff of at least four trained professionals who run the computer science department and provide information on the use of computers. "Technology is a powerful tool. At Riverdale our curriculum drives technology, not the reverse," says Mr. Shaller in describing the Lower School's integration of computers and academics. From kindergarten through second grade, parent volunteers (who are trained) work with students on games and problem solving. In third grade formal instruction starts, in fourth grade LOGO is introduced. Fifth grade students collected science data and set up a data base to coordinate, record and graph information. For students in grades seven through twelve RCS offers four computer science courses—Introduction to Technology is a required course for all seventh and tenth graders—including two AP courses and Programming in C/C++. "The computer and the Internet are helpful tools, but they should be used sparingly. Children have a great deal of exploration to do away from the illuminated screen," says Mr. Shaller.

Although RCS is a coed school, there is concern about gender issues. In a recent year, the parents were invited to attend a Gender Issues Forum where the latest theories about gender and intellectual development were discussed. Mr. Shaller says RCS is sensitized to gender issues (and at least one kindergarten parent has seen him roll up his sleeves and invite girls into the block corner).

When asked what values are stressed at RCS, many parents and students said "teamwork," both on and off the field. One student described Riverdale as "a healthy environment that promotes community feeling." In 1989 the RCS Lower School Student Council created C.A.R.E. (Children Aware of Riverdale Ethics), a program that emphasizes problem-solving strategies, respect for differences and consideration for the feelings of others. The official C.A.R.E. song was written by the Lower School drama specialist, January Akselrad, and it evokes the spirit of the program in an entertaining way. This sense of consideration and caring extends to the larger community as well. Recently, Lower School students held a walk-a-thon that benefited the Children's Blood Foundation. Another year, Lower School students held a penny drive for Juvenile Diabetes.

There is positive interaction between the grades at Riverdale. Friendships between children in different grades begin on the bus ride to school, and also through various planned activities. Fifth graders prepare the Holiday Feast with pre-kindergartners, second and fifth graders work together on a butterfly project, and second graders and kindergartners work together sewing an alphabet with each pair of children working together on a letter square. Sixth graders interact with younger children during lunch or recess. This community of students extends all the way up to the alumni. One student said, "The alumni are not just donors, they are people you know because you've worked and connected with them." Every three years, former Riverdalians return to conduct workshops and talk to the students about their professions.

The Upper School consists of grades seventh through twelfth; the two largest points of entry are seventh and ninth. The Upper School is structured but not rigid. Bells mark the end of class periods. There are many required courses, but by eleventh and twelfth grades over sixty electives are available, including: "Masterpieces of Western Literature," "Philosophy," "World Religion in History and Literature," "African-American Literature," "Native American Literature," and

"Race and Class in New York City." Math is "ability grouped" in the Upper School: Students with aptitude in this area move at an accelerated pace and those who need more reinforcement get it. There are twenty four AP courses, and there are honors as well as regular sections. No class ranking is made. The curriculum is challenging and rigorous, however, students are supportive of each other and there is no cut-throat competition. "It doesn't matter what anybody else gets as long as you did your best" is the message. And one student talked about "growth in grades": As the work got harder, her grades improved.

In October 1997, Riverdale underwent a NYSAIS (New York State Association of Independent Schools) evaluation. RCS was reaccreditated, and in its official report the NYSAIS Visiting Committee stated that many aspects of the school impressed them. "The vitality of RCS's academic program; outstanding, dynamic, creative teaching; diversity; and the balance of academics, arts, activities, and athletics. Students are friendly and confident and display a strong sense of community. Riverdale students are outstanding examples of civility, which is a reflection of the care offered by the faculty and staff," states the NYSAIS report.

It's very difficult to fall through the cracks at RCS because there is a strong support network of people and programs. Advisors (for groups of ten or twelve) meet regularly. There is easy access to faculty, whose schedules are posted and who stay for the entire long day even if they finish early.

Seniors are required to take a year-long interdisciplinary course called I.L.S. or Integrated Liberal Studies. Introduced into the curriculum in 1980, I.L.S. surveys the cultural history of the West from the perspectives of four disciplines: literature, philosophy, the history of science and the history of music and art. The course culminates in a final oral examination.

Students help students in several ways. Eleventh and twelfth graders are selected, as an honor, and trained to act as peer counselors to seventh graders, dealing with academic and social issues under the Peer Advisory Leadership (PAL) program.

RCS welcomed Dr. John R. Johnson as the school's new Headmaster in 1997. Dr. Johnson previously served as the President of The Mary Institute and St. Louis Country Day School in St. Louis, Missouri where he is credited with orchestrating the merger of the two single sex schools. He also taught classes in European History, including AP European History during his twelve years at the school. Dr.

Johnson was also the Director of Studies at the Harvard School in Los Angeles where he was responsible for the school's academic program. In addition, he has served as Director, UCLA Summer Sessions at UCLA (Los Angeles.) He is a warm and supportive leader and he attends almost every school event. Recently, he attended the Annual Fund committee's end-of-the-year bowling event held at Chelsea Piers where he fostered a feeling of support and appreciation among the attendees. When asked what Dr. Johnson's vision for Riverdale includes, he says "Riverdale has a balanced approach to education. It is a school that values first-rate training across the board, in academics, the arts and athletics. We attend to the whole child. Our faculty really knows their students and their concern extends beyond the classroom."

RCS has recently acquired approximately seven acres and several buildings that were formerly part of the Manhattan College campus. The property is adjacent to the Upper School campus and plans are well underway for its use. So far, plans include: the renovation of the existing gymnasium, swimming pool, locker room and physical fitness facilities, the complete renovation and slight expansion of the three hundred seat theater, an expansion of the center for the arts, ten to twelve classroom renovations, a new full-sized playing field, expansion of the existing practice field and four new tennis courts.

Mr. Satish Joshi, head of Visual Art, has been inspiring students for many years. Graduating seniors leave farewell messages to him painted on the walls of the art room: "Satish, you know me. That in itself is a great thing. I ❤ you." and "Thanks for the best homeroom ever." Riverdale's art and literary magazine *Impressions* recently won the award of the National Council of Teachers of English, the highest award for excellence in student literary magazines.

Seniors have their own lounge, complete with posters and comfortable couches, and can use the newly landscaped courtyard. Backpacks are dropped casually in the halls. Seniors can leave the campus for lunch and free periods. (These are privileges, not rights, and can be revoked for bad behavior.) Each year a Senior Leadership Conference is held at Frost Valley at which seniors explore their own leadership style; teachers conduct workshops on writing college essays and coping with senior-year stress. Class officers are elected at Frost Valley and seniors get a sense of solidarity as a class. The weekend launches them in their role as leaders of the Upper School. The student government has three representatives from each grade.

The junior class is pushing for more privileges: RCS juniors can't leave campus until April of junior year. (At Horace Mann and Fieldston students can leave in ninth grade.) But one student maintained that having to stick around campus contributes to the feeling of community. Each year the senior class parents give a gift to the school.

Though sequestered from many of the ills of urban life, RCS students are concerned about the wider world. At the recent One World Day, students chose to focus on AIDS awareness. Upper School students spent the day in workshops and special events in the classrooms: They made an AIDS quilt, put on skits and dramatizations and listened to doctors who clarified medical aspects of AIDS and who advised students how to protect themselves.

Frank Hackett's "spirit of internationalism" is translated into respect for differences between people. Relationships between groups at RCS are good. A tenth grader told us: "It's not too cliquey; everyone knows what they like to do and no one gets in anyone else's way." In athletics, "Everyone works together on the field."

There are over thirty-eight clubs, and new ones are added each year. They include the successful Mock Trial Club, S.C.C. (Students of Color Committee), Film Club, Environmental Club, Amnesty International, Model Congress and Community Service. An activity period for clubs is scheduled during the school day, so that students can find time to engage in extracurricular interests.

School spirit at RCS is manifested through athletic competition in the Ivy Prep League. Riverdale has a newly renovated athletic center that was completed in the Fall of 1998. The athletic center houses an Olympic-size pool, where many trophies are on display. There are sixteen junior varsity and varsity sports teams including a swim team and a strong fencing team. Riverdale's football team achieved sports fame in the sixties when Frank Bertino coached Riverdale to seventeen undefeated seasons. Horace Mann alumni wince when they remember how future pro player Calvin Hill led RCS to a winning streak of fifty-one games. Today, the annual "Buzzell" basketball game in February against arch-rival Horace Mann draws a crowd of over one thousand people. The game was named for a Horace Mann student who died and the proceeds are donated to charity. In 1990, Riverdale made a politically correct decision to change the name of the school mascot and team name from The Indians to The Falcons.

A Riverdale junior who plans to be a litigator describes RCS as "a healthy, fun environment that promotes community feeling. If you work hard and apply yourself, you'll really succeed and help is always there if you need it."

Popular College Choices   Brown, University of Pennsylvania, University of Michigan, Harvard, Duke, Yale, Macalester, Wesleyan. Although RCS students apply and gain admission to the top Ivy League colleges, they select a variety of colleges, which is consistent with RCS's emphasis on perceiving students as individuals, rather than types

Traditions   Grandparents' Day, Spring Carnival, Winter and Spring Concerts, Book Fair, Academic Fair, Parents' Association Dinner/ Dance and Auction, Buzzell games, Talent Show, Children Helping Children (charity outreach program), C.A.R.E. program (Children Aware of Riverdale Ethics), Homecoming Day, Career Day, One World Day, Shakespeare Recitation Contest, Policy Reading Competition, Friends of the Arts evening, Sixth and Twelfth Grade Graduation Ceremonies, Reunion and Winter Gathering for Alumni

Publications   Lower School publications: *The Rivulet*
The Flying Falcon
Upper School newspaper: *The Riverdale Review* (since 1916)
Literary magazine: *Impressions* (1997 National Council of Teachers of English Award)
Alumni magazine: *Quad*
Yearbook: *The Riverdalian*
Photography journal: *Exposures*

Community Service Requirement   14 hours on the River Campus for grade 6
20 hours for grades 7 and 8
72 hours for grades 9–12

Hangouts   Dino's Pizza, Riverdale Diner, Bagel Corner, RCS cafeteria (with a view of trees and fields) and library

Rodeph Sholom School

Nursery Division
7 West 83rd Street
New York, NY 10024
(212) 362-8800

Lower Elementary Division
Grades Pre-Kindergarten–1st
10 West 84th Street
New York, NY 10024
(212) 362-8769

Upper Elementary Division
Grades 2–6
168 West 79th Street
New York, NY 10024
(212) 362-0037

Middle School
Grades 6–8
168 West 79th Street
New York, NY 10024
(212) 362-0037
(opens 2002–2003)

Coed
Nursery–8th grade
Accessible at 7 West 83rd Street and 168 West 79th Street
Not accessible at 10 West 84th Street

Mr. Irwin Shlachter, Headmaster
Mrs. Alice Barzilay, Director of Admissions and Placement

Birthday Cutoff   Children entering kindergarten must be 5 by September 5
Children entering at the nursery level must be 2.6 by September

Enrollment   Total enrollment: 560
Nursery enrollment: 140
Elementary enrollment: 420
Average graduating class size: 30–35

Tuition Range 2001–2002 $7,400 to $19,500, nursery 2 1/2's–6th grade
Temple membership is included
Additional fees: materials and insurance are under $650
Lunch fee grades 2–6 $800
There is a tuition reduction of $500 per sibling for each enrolled child beyond the first
Financial aid available

After-School Program   for Nursery through 6th graders; weekdays until 5:00 P.M.; a variety of creative, recreational and educational activities for an additional charge

Summer Program   Rodeph Sholom Summer Camp from late June through mid-August; an additional payment is required

Founded in 1958 as a nursery school; the elementary level was added in 1970. The Rodeph Sholom Day School is a Reform Jewish day school affiliated with the reform synagogue, Congregation Rodeph Sholom. It is the only Reform Jewish day school in New York City. The nursery division is housed in the temple building on West 83rd Street. Pre-kindergarten through first grade are housed in a modern building on West 84th Street, connected via a courtyard to the 83rd Street building. Second through fifth grades (upper elementary divisions) meet in fully renovated brownstones on West 78th and 79th Streets which house three gyms, three libraries (two are fully computerized and linked to the Internet), two computer labs, science labs, art studios and a cafeteria. The school added a Middle School in 2000.

Getting In: Parents should call in the fall for an application and to reserve a place in a group tour. ERB testing results, a school report, and a group interview with the child are required for admission to kindergarten and above. "We are looking for students who can meet the demands of our challenging and enriched academic environment," the admissions director told us. Students come from a variety of backgrounds; most live in Manhattan but some come from Riverdale and Westchester.

Parents: It's an eclectic mix of executives, artists, academics, physicians and so on. A parent who has been at the school for several years points out that as the school has expanded, the parent body has evolved from a fuzzy West Side school to a school with more polish and considerably more money: "Formerly the parents were psychologists, painters, a social worker—your basic West Side shleppers. Now they're media executives, managing directors, executive editors; people who golf." One parent said, "We have kept our child in Rodeph Sholom from nursery through sixth grade because it provides top-notch academic preparation without the personal competitiveness we see at many other schools. It's a warm community and the administration welcomes parental involvement. The sports and visual arts programs are great and the kids place into the top private high schools."

An active PTA organizes several annual fund-raisers including the book fair (open to the neighborhood), and the Spring Auction held at an art gallery downtown. The PTA also sponsors dialogue meetings throughout the year; recent topics include: computers, Jewish studies, and neighborhood safety. The PTA frequently purchases blocks of tickets to sporting events and Broadway shows.

Program: The Rodeph Sholom School provides a combination of rigorous academics and a supportive environment. The school believes "the higher you place the bar, the higher the children will reach." Although there are three divisions (nursery, lower elementary, and upper elementary) there is interaction between older and younger students. For example, first graders read to nursery students, sixth graders perform Shakespeare for fourth graders, and the entire school visits the Science Week exhibit created by the fifth grade.

The lower elementary division is comprised of pre-kindergarten through first grade. All classrooms have a computer and are filled with children's artwork creative writing, poems and graphs. Younger children play outdoors in the courtyard daily. Judaic studies is woven into the curriculum and each Shabbat (Friday) a different child's parent/guest is invited to participate with the class.

The school's approach to teaching is a balance of traditional/instructional and discovery-based methods. Literary instruction begins in Pre-K. By first grade students write, edit and publish their books. Math, handwriting, writer's workshop, Hebrew and Jewish studies are taught in the classroom. Students leave their classrooms for special instruction in science, computer, library, art, music and physical education. Rodeph Sholem School uses the "Everyday Math" program developed at the University of Chicago (see "Chicago Math" in *Glossary*), supplemented with practice of computational skills.

Computers are used in all classrooms at RS. The technology curriculum includes: keyboarding, graphics, spreadsheets, database management, telecommunications, Internet, e-mail and desktop publishing.

The science curriculum focuses on problem solving skills. Fifth graders study the weather. They run their own weather station, plot the readings, compare the metro forecast to the RS forecast and announce their weather watch results to the school.

The integrated curriculum is driven by social studies. Pre-kindergartners focus on "Me and My Family." Kindergartners study citizenship and their community. In first grade, the social studies curriculum expands to "The Neighborhood and the Market." First graders learn how fruit is grown, transported and sold; they take field trips to various neighborhood and open-air Greenmarkets in the city; they create their own market in the school lobby and sell produce to students, faculty, and parents; and they donate their profits to a charity of their choice. Second graders study New York City. Third graders study Native Americans; fourth graders examine early Colonial America, which continues in fifth grade with the study of American history from the Revolutionary war up to the Civil War. Sixth graders analyze ancient civilization and medieval studies.

The Jewish Studies curriculum includes music, art, dance and theatre projects in the Hebrew language, Shabbat, teaching of the Torah portion, holidays and festivals, charitable deeds, Israel, and Jewish history, life and traditions. Beginning in first grade, Hebrew is taught using a combination of phonics and whole language techniques, including reading, writing, conversation and music. Fourth graders write and perform a short play in Hebrew.

Music is taught by two full-time instructors utilizing Orff instruments, Dalcroze Eurhythmy for movement and Kodaly Training for singing. Beginning in third grade, students study opera, including *The Magic Flute*, *Carmen* and *The Marriage of Figaro*. Fourth through sixth graders have the opportunity to participate in instrumental lessons, band, string or flute ensembles and to give concerts/recitals.

As you walk the halls you notice that art is an important part of the Rodeph experience. The school has two fully equipped art studios. Two full-time art instructors help the classroom teachers integrate art projects into the regular curriculum. Students use the resources of nearby museums, including the Metropolitan, Natural History and Children's Museums. A Native-American artist-in-residence works with the third graders.

Students have physical education four times a week in three modern gymnasiums. There are three full-time coaches on staff. After-school athletic offerings include: soccer, basketball, baseball, and track in partnership with the Westside JCC.

Activities that take place during the school day include: Literature Club, Science Club, Pet Club, school newspaper, school store, orchestra, band, and choir. The "Future Problem Solvers" team has been reigning State Champions for the past eleven years.

The school has a partnership with Family Academy in Harlem to promote tolerance and awareness. Classes in kindergarten through fifth grade meet with classes from Family Academy throughout the year to work on projects together. Recently the first grade classes created a ten-foot mural that traveled between the two schools.

Parents say that Rodeph Sholom provides a well-rounded education. One father told us, "They do a great job of combining Jewish identity with a solid academic grounding. It's a first rate education without any pretensions, the kids work hard because the school makes it fun."

Popular on-going school choices   Riverdale, Horace Mann, Columbia Prep, Spence, Fieldston, Dalton, Hunter High School, Trevor Day

Traditions   Jewish Holiday Celebrations (Purim Carnival, lunch in the Sukkah, Passover Seders, etc.), Science Week, Native American Art Show, PTA Book Fair, Model Cities, Teva Environmental trip

Publications: *The Rodeph Sholom Sun*
The Rodeph Sholom PTA Newsletter
Newsletter
Graduation Yearbook

The Rudolf Steiner School

Lower School
15 East 79th Street
New York, NY 10021
(212) 535-2130

Upper School
15 East 78th Street
New York, NY 10021
(212) 879-1101 (main number)
(212) 327-1457 (admissions), FAX (212) 744-4497
website: www.steiner.edu

Coed
Nursery–12th grade
Not accessible

Ms. Sabine Kelly, College Chair
Ms. Barbara Shields, Director of Admissions, N–3
Ms. Jennifer Holman, Director of Admissions, 4–12
Ms. Irene Mantel, School Administrator

Birthday Cutoff   September 1

Enrollment   Total enrollment: 300
2's places: 18 (mother & child program)
3's places: 23
4's and 5's places: 6–10, only if there has been attrition
1998 graduating class: approximately 20

Grades   Semester system
Letter grades begin in 7th grade
Departmentalization begins in 7th grade

Tuition Range 2001–2002 $11,750 to $18,000, nursery 2's–12th
grade
Additional fees under $200
Lunch is included through 2nd grade and is optional thereafter
for a payment of $800 per year; Organic produce and milk and
vegetarian alternatives served daily

Financial Aid/Scholarship   A fair portion of the student body
receive some form of aid

Endowment $1 million

After-School Program   Grades 1–5, Monday–Friday, 3–4:30/5:00
A variety of activities for an additional payment, availability
depends on enrollment

Summer Program   A 2-week June Days Camp is offered for chil-
dren in preschool through grade 3 for an additional charge
A 3-week June Music Program is offered for children in grades 4
through 8 for an additional charge
Both summer programs are open to students from outside the
Rudolf Steiner community

The Rudolf Steiner School in New York City (established 1928)
is part of an international community of schools (160 in the U.S., 700
worldwide) that integrate intellectual and artistic development. Rudolf
Steiner (1861–1925), was an Austrian scientist, philosopher, artist and
educator. The school is housed in a beautiful Stanford White mansion
just off Fifth Avenue; a sweeping marble staircase graces the foyer. At
the heart of the Waldorf philosophy is the belief that education is an
artistic process. There is a holistic approach to learning. "Innovative
teaching methods work to develop clarity in thought, balance in
feeling, and conscience and initiative in action." Steiner provides an
education that balances individual development with a sense of social
responsibility. There is even an emphasis on the "spiritual" side of
children's growth—not religious, but focused on developing imagination, compassion, and ethical principles.

Getting In: "The Rudolf Steiner School isn't looking for any one
type of child," we were told. In fact, the WPPSI-R (ERB testing) is
not required for admission to the Lower School, but ISEE scores
are required in grades six and above, along with two years of recent
class records. The school's philosophy dictates that they teach to a
broad spectrum of styles and abilities within each class and students
come from varied economic and cultural backgrounds. Because of
increased interest in Waldorf education and the competitive private
school admissions climate, Rudolf Steiner maintains a wait list for
admission.

Parents should call in early September for dates of Fall open houses and to receive an admissions packet. Parents may tour the school without applying but must reserve space in advance. Children applying for pre-school, kindergarten, and first grade are interviewed in small groups. Students applying to second grade and up might be interviewed in a small group or individually. A parent interview is scheduled separately.

Parents: Parents are very involved in the life of the school and the Waldorf method depends on a certain level of parent support. An eclectic group of parents—business types and artists—animates the lobby at drop-off and pick-up times. Parents run the annual Fall Fair, worth attending if you're interested in the school, as it showcases Waldorf education. The Parent Association has two co-presidents, and there is a six-member Parent Council elected by the parent body, which meets monthly. There are evening parent study groups, and parent education forums throughout the year.

Program: the Waldorf method is based on the belief that children pass through three basic stages of cognitive development, and the curriculum is designed to engage the abilities of the growing child at each of these stages. In preschool this is accomplished through creative guided play; in elementary school through the imaginative and artistic presentation of material by the class teacher; and in high school through challenging the student's awakening capacity for independent thought. What's different about the Waldorf method is not so much the content—there is an in-depth curriculum—as in how and when they are taught. Parents say once you see it in action you will "fall in love with the school."

The preschool is a gem for those who like natural materials and loathe plastic primary colored toys. It has a timeless feeling: there are wooden blocks and toys; shells and stones; colorful cloths and soft dolls. The children model beeswax (a favorite Waldorf material), paint with watercolors, bake bread and make soup every week. They also play in Central Park every day, weather permitting, and end every morning with a story.

Don't think is not academic—there's lots of learning going on: songs, stories and nursery rhymes expose children to the world of words; watching marionette shows and participating in dramatic play strengthen the power of memory and the imagination. Counting games and rhythmic activities build a foundation for arithmetic and number skills, and so on.

Beginning in first grade, reading and math are taught with the aim of developing each child's pictorial imagination. Foreign languages—Spanish and German—are introduced. Each morning includes a "main lesson block" in one subject area, which is studied in-depth for approximately four weeks. Instead of textbooks, all students write and illustrate their own "main lesson books." (These are beautiful and impressive.) "The curriculum is designed as a unity and its subjects are introduced and developed in a sequence that mirrors the inner development of the growing child." Academic subjects such as English, math and foreign languages are scheduled for several weekly periods. Afternoons are reserved for additional academic work and for drama/movement, gym, music, or crafts.

In accordance with the Waldorf method, teachers stay with their class for several grades; a teacher might stay with her students from first all the way though eighth grade! Needless to say, students develop lasting relationships with their teachers. One parent said, "The Waldorf teachers are intellectual as well as artistic and they have amazing respect for the children."

The high school academic program prepares students for college. At this point new students join those who have come up from the elementary school. Individual attention and guidance are hallmarks of the high school. Each class has its own faculty advisor who coordinates class activities, monitors the students' academic and personal progress, and serves as a liaison between the school and home. Students say that the social life is lively and warm.

Popular College Choices Boston University, Bard College, Brandeis University, Bryn Mawr, Columbia University, Mount Holyoke College, NYU, Oberlin, University of Chicago, The School of Visual Arts, Skidmore, Sarah Lawrence College, Princeton University, Wellesley, West Point Military Academy

Traditions: Annual Fall Fair and Spring Auction, all-school seasonal and holiday festivals, concerts, annual book fair, grandparents and special friends day, 5th grade Olympics, class plays grades 1–12, 6th grade farm trip, 7th grade outward bound trip, 8th and 12th grade class trip of their choice, end of the year class picnics, alumni reunions

Publications:
Monthly bulletin for the entire school community
Upper School literary magazine   *The Key*

Student newspaper   *15 East*
Biannual alumni newsletter
Student yearbook

Community Service: 20 hours per year for students grades 8
through 11, 12th grade has an internship of their choice

Hangout: The Nectar Coffee Shop, Viand, Central Park

Saint Ann's School

129 Pierrepont Street
Brooklyn Heights, NY 11201
(718) 522-1660
e-mail: admin@saintanns.K12.ny.us
website: www.saintanns.k12.ny.us

Coed
3's–12th grade
Not accessible

Mr. Stanley Bosworth, Headmaster
Ms. Linda Kaufman, Assistant Headmaster
Ms. Mary Russotti, Director of Admission

Uniform   None

Birthday Cutoff   None specified; readiness is stressed

Enrollment   Total enrollment: 1,050
Preschool total: 56
Kindergarten places: 30
9th grade places: 5–10
Graduating class: approximately 75

Grades   Semester system
No letter grades are given throughout the school; standardized tests are given each year, and the results in Middle School and High School are reported to parents
Departmentalization begins in 4th grade

Tuition Range 2001–2002 $16,000 to $18,600, Lower School (kindergarten–3rd grade) to 12th grade
No additional fees
A tuition refund plan is available
Private bus service (for an additional fee) is available from Manhattan; also accessible by subway or car

Financial Aid/Scholarship   15% of the student body receive some form of aid

358

Endowment $1.3 million

Diversity   17% children of color
25 Prep for Prep students enrolled as of Fall 2000

Homework   1st and 2nd grades: none
3rd and 4th: 1 hour
5th and 6th: 1½ hours
7th and 8th: 2 hours
9th–12th: 3–4 hours
°The guideline is 20 minutes per class, but there is usually more

After-School Program   Open to current or new Saint Ann's students only
Kindergarten through 6th grade: 3:00 to 5:30 P.M. (6 P.M. if necessary)
Creative activities, computer, games, sports, study, art, theatre and so on; an additional payment is required

Summer Program   Open to current or new Saint Ann's students (preschool through 6th grade); Six-week program that begins at the end of classes and continues through the end of July, offering creative activities, sports and field trips
Three-week gymnastics program for grades 3–8
Soccer Program for grades 3–6

———

Saint Ann's School was founded with seventy children in 1965 under the aegis of St. Ann's Episcopal Church. The rector of the church envisioned a school for gifted children, "with uniforms and a healthy dose of religion." Founding Headmaster Stanley Bosworth (known to all simply as Stanley), a former French teacher at the progressive (now-defunct) Walden School, was only thirty-five years old when he came to Saint Ann's. He came with his own vision: "It was my vow all those years ago that this particular school would somehow provide 10 percent of our nation's poets." It was Stanley's vision that prevailed.

In 1981, Saint Ann's was chartered by the New York State Board of Regents; in 1982 Saint Ann's was formally disaffiliated from the church. The sixties are long gone but Stanley's idealism has not dimmed; he still says that "no student should approach us without stars in his or her eyes." Saint Ann's is a school where gym is called "Recreational Arts," where there are no grades, no class rankings and no rigid curriculum. Saint Ann's has produced award-winning playwrights as well as a Westinghouse Scholar. A parent said, "The unconventional tone of the school gives these kids a shared bond and a respect for the unconventional in life . . . these kids are not afraid to break the mold."

Saint Ann's is a progressive, arty school for very bright children. "It's what Dalton used to be," parents say. Located in Brooklyn Heights, now thoroughly gentrified, the school attracts many local families. Approximately one-quarter of the students come from Manhattan. Several years ago, the school renovated the basement of the main building and added a gym, a lecture room and an art gallery, plus five additional classrooms. More recently, the two-story dining room was redesigned to create two balcony rooms (which are used both as additional dining space and as classrooms). The entire area also doubles as a performing space.

Getting In: The brochure states: "We admit the talented." Saint Ann's students must be self-motivated and have the ability and maturity necessary to handle freedom and rigorous academic requirements. They use a "holistic approach" when it comes to admissions. Director of Admissions Mary Russotti says, "Our admissions process is an eclectic one that considers both achievement and glimmers of special talent." Candidate profiles are cross-checked with ERB scores where appropriate. In addition to testing and interviewing the applicant, the admissions director will observe a child in his or her nursery school on occasion. Parents of applicants to the lower grades are interviewed with special concern for receptivity to the values of humanism and the arts. The admissions director provides parents with an opportunity to offer insights and/or additional information about their child that might help in making a decision. The appropriate division head also interviews Middle and High school applicants. Parents say that there is little of the "admissions anxiety" found at the Manhattan schools because "kids at Saint Ann's don't get their sense of self-worth from outshining others; there is very little glitter or glitz." Another parent said, "The atmosphere was informal and friendly." Saint Ann's maintains a wait list but there is not much movement on it.

Saint Ann's is not a member of ISAAGNY (Independent Schools Admissions Association of Greater New York) but does adhere to the same admissions notification and parent-reply dates as the other independent schools. The school's midwinter break is scheduled in February, a week before that of the public schools. Spring break is scheduled to coincide with Easter and Passover.

The typical Saint Ann's student is "bright, arty, concerned for others and confident." Is there a self-consciousness about being gifted? A parent says, "It has the effect of creating among the children a sense of community and specialness that overrides all other differences including ethnic background, family income and gender."

Although admittedly it is more of an accomplishment to make an award-winning scholar out of a mediocre student, Saint Ann's is nonetheless remarkably good at encouraging bright children to fully realize their potential. A mother told us, "All of my children's special talents—repeat, *all* of them—were nurtured, developed and tested in the very loving laboratory of Saint Ann's." One parent told us that her son's first grade teacher recognized that he had a talent for art. "She was so enthusiastic and encouraging that it brought out more than his ability to draw and paint—it also developed his interest in art history and a strong sense of himself." He is now in college majoring in a different subject but he is on the staff of the humor magazine, and art will be his lifelong avocation.

Aside from the excitement of teaching exceptionally able students, teachers say Saint Ann's is a great place to work because of the freedom and flexibility: "Teachers get to teach exactly what they want to teach; there is no rigid curriculum." In the Lower School most teachers have a special talent or interest; they are painters or writers, for example, "and the administration encourages these interests." A significant portion of the student body is made up of the children of faculty. The Middle and High School teachers are selected not because they have a master's in education but because they have expertise in a creative area: Stanley's original vision was to have actors, painters and musicians as teachers. There is a "master teacher" and the student is his "apprentice": The drama teachers are playwrights and actors, the English teachers are writers and so on. Many of the teachers are young and "There is an enormous energy, excitement and commitment." Eleven percent of the faculty are Saint Ann's alumni. Another of Stanley's tenets is that "art and literacy serve the scientist as well as the artist." However, a former teacher confided that Stanley's attempts to have poets teach science have not always been successful.

Parents: With respect to the parent body, one parent said she never felt that her bank account, background or lifestyle made a difference at Saint Ann's: "If I didn't fit in, I never noticed." Many fathers, such as those who work as full-time writers or illustrators or songwriters, are able to bring their children to and from school. One parent said, "Saint Ann's isn't interested in the parents; when you drop off your child, he becomes Saint Ann's child." Consequently, the Parents Association is not particularly strong. The same people have been running the Parents Association for several years. Parent events include Parents Night at school, cocktail parties, dance concerts, two Middle School and High School productions each year, voice recitals and instrumental concerts. Saint Ann's students act as hosts. There is a welcoming party for new parents at the school. Because the alumni body is so young (the first alumna graduated from Saint Ann's in 1970), alumni fund-raising was started only recently. Saint Ann's alumni keep in touch: The *Saint Ann's Times* reports on news of over four hundred alumni.

Program: Lower School at Saint Ann's is composed of grades kindergarten through third. Separation is handled gently. Parents say: "They are unbelievably sensitive." A parent can stay in the classroom if necessary. Kindergartners come for a playtime in the spring and begin with half/class half/day for the first two days of school in the fall. The head of the Lower School, Gabrielle Howard, is outstanding; she has been at Saint Ann's since 1973, initially as a teacher. Cathy Fuerst is the head of the Preschool. She has served as a Lower School master teacher for eleven years, as an assistant to the Director of Development, and as Coordinator of the Lower School after-school program.

Classes are identified by teachers' names. In a kindergarten class of twenty children there is a master teacher and an assistant. Students in the Lower School address teachers by their first names.

The brochure says, "Reading is central." Writing, math, science, art, music and dance round out the rest of the Lower School schedule. Reading is taught with eclectic methods—"any way the child needs"— including phonics. By the end of first grade about 95 percent of the children are reading. A former Lower School teacher told us that "many first graders are reading Beverly Cleary or Roald Dahl, but some are still on *Mack and Tap*. But by the end of the first year most are on a second grade reading level." A parent told us that one short-coming at Saint Ann's is if a student needs remedial help his parents must pay extra for it. "Parents must be aware of any learning difficulties their child is having," she said. There is no learning specialist on staff at Saint Ann's; however, several trained specialists are permitted to use the school premises for private instruction.

Parents say, "You have to get the daily and weekly information from your child but the school will let you know if your child isn't working up to his potential." The anecdotal reports are extensive. And the ERB and standardized tests are given during the year as objective measurements of aptitude and achievement. According to the brochure, these tests are used to see if students are at the proper level or need to be moved along.

Although the student body is a narrowly selected group of very bright children, the academic atmosphere at Saint Ann's is not one of cutthroat competition. "It's very nurturing and informal; kids are allowed to be who they are." For instance, parents say, a first grader can take a sixth grade math class and not feel out of place. (In fact, a first grader once did take sixth grade math; a teacher accompanied him to the class and stayed with him.) And of course there is no competition for grades because there aren't any. (On longer research papers students might receive a "good" or a "check", in addition to extensive comments.)

In the Preschool and Lower School, students leave their classrooms for "specials" in art, music and recreational arts. Kindergartners also leave the classroom for dance. Beginning in second grade, students leave their homeroom class for math and computer, and in third grade for science. Third grade is the last year of the classroom-based program; there are still blocks in the classroom. Formal instruction in computer begins in third grade. Third graders learn to type, use Hypercard, and even some programming. One Lower School group studying Greek mythology wrote an epic poem seventy pages long. Lower Schoolers produce one play or musical each year.

Middle School at Saint Ann's is equivalent to grades four through eight. Bells ring between classes in the Middle and High Schools. It is up to the teacher whether or not students use their first or last names. Full departmentalization begins in the first year of Middle School (fourth grade), which requires a lot of maturity. Says a former Lower School teacher, "There's a lot of choice for a ten year old." Each fourth grader also has a locker with a lock.

The brochure says that "subject achievement and aptitude define placement, particularly in math and language groups. The makeup of English and history classes is largely determined by age." Sixth graders learn the structure of language. Formal language instruction begins in the seventh grade, and students can choose from Latin, Greek, French, Spanish, Chinese and Japanese. Science is part of the curriculum each year. Middle Schoolers take five years of science, and health issues are part of the eighth grade biology course.

One parent said, "My fourth grader is learning what I learned in college. In our conversations she talks about Greek and Norse myths and Latin."

The arts are considered academic subjects at Saint Ann's. The Middle School has its own literary magazine. Nancy Fales Garrett's playwriting course is so good that nearly every year a play by a Saint Ann's student is accepted for production by the Playwright's Horizons Festival's annual off-Broadway run in the fall.

Middle Schoolers perform in mixed-age plays and musicals; recent productions include *The Skin of Our Teeth* and *The Enchanted*. A parent told us that when her son was in fifth grade, his drama teacher, an off-Broadway director (the kind that Saint Ann's delights in hiring), sparked his interest in performing and he eventually was selected as a member of a well-known theatre troupe.

Athletics are popular at Saint Ann's. There is girls varsity softball and soccer; varsity and junior varsity basketball and volleyball. Boys play varsity and junior varsity baseball, soccer and basketball. Coed teams include fencing, track and field. In the Middle School there is interscholastic competition in girls' volleyball, softball, basketball, and soccer; boys' baseball, basketball, and soccer; coed track. There are gymnastics teams for Middle and Upper School girls. Classes are offered in team sports such as basketball, soccer, volleyball, softball and also in badminton, exercise and fitness, fencing, floor hockey, karate, weight training and yoga. There is plenty of school spirit exhibited at basketball games. Saint Ann's has several gymnasiums and uses nearby parks for playing fields.

Students cannot leave school for lunch until the second half of eighth grade. Milk and fruit are provided free of charge; lunch is available for an additional fee.

The high school at Saint Ann's is composed of grades nine through twelve. There is a tremendous amount of freedom and choice in the high school at Saint Ann's so students must be self-motivated.

The teachers in the high school—all "masters" in their disciplines—"love what they do and they communicate it to the students." The brochure describes the high school curriculum as "adventurous." Saint Ann's is progressive but the school is not embroiled in the multicultural debate rocking the public schools. Parents say the school stresses "Latin, writing, reading, theatre and playwriting." Stanley says the school has "a commitment to Western civilization" and respect for the Western canon. (In this way it's not so different from a "traditional" school like Trinity.)

We observed an English class discussing Nabokov's *Lolita*. Some of the students had their feet up on their desks, others were sprawled or supine yet the conversation was electric. In a classroom nearby, a young attractive Spanish teacher gave her student a high five for a correct answer. The history class down the hall was studying the recent elections in Russia. History classes often have seminars on current events. A parent had praise for many teachers and for one standout, Victor Marchioro, who teaches "The Bible as Literature", described as "an unbelievably rigorous and unforgettable class." Also singled out for praise were Ruth Chapman, an art history/English teacher, and Angelo Belfatto an art teacher elected graduation speaker by the class of 2000. "It's worth insisting that your child take one of his classes just to read the evaluations he writes—you will not believe anyone could be so articulate about your child," said a parent.

Extracurricular activities keep Saint Ann's open seven days a week. Over the weekend the school may be used for play rehearsals, sports and yearbook meetings. There is a playwriting class for High School students and one for Middle School students and a playwriting festival each spring. Students can work on photography or literary magazines.

Students with a scientific bent can participate in the science research program in addition to the broad range of science courses offered. And several each year are selected for the Science Honors Program at Columbia University, and junior and senior math teams compete in the New York Interscholastic Math League.

High School students travel and work abroad. Visits to museums in New York City and foreign capitols, cathedrals in Europe, inaugurations in Washington, D.C., and model congresses at universities in the northeast corridor complement in-class curricula.

A parent of two Saint Ann's students told us: "My son had four years that were so spectacular in every way that college was a bit of a letdown." Saint Ann's students are encouraged to strive for awards and honors (Saint Ann's produces numerous National Merit Scholarship Finalists and AP scholars), and these accomplishments are conspicuously listed in the *Saint Ann's Times* each year. In addition, Saint Ann's students outshine their peers at other independent schools in the Johns Hopkins Center for Academically Talented Youth Competition. (The CTY talent search is based on achievement on the PSAT and the SAT.)

Technology: The Director of Computers and Technology supplies an overview of the present and future role of computers at Saint

Ann's, maintains the schoolwide network, coordinates computing activities among the various departments, and runs the Computer Resource Center located in the Main building—a fully-equipped lab where teachers can bring classes to use programs such as A.D.A.M. for science, Civilization for history, and Geometers Sketchpad for math. A lab manager offers a wide range of courses for faculty so that teachers can keep up with their students' expertise. "We've attempted to make computers available and useful to all of our students and staff, from the third grade to the twelfth, and from the Headmaster to the kitchen staff." Thus the Saint Ann's population is largely computer-literate.

The main library is fully computerized with Internet access. The school has a T1 high speed connection to the Internet in place and all students and staff have e-mail addresses and can create their own web pages if they wish.

Two newly renovated science labs are wired for network access. In addition to networked computers, the science labs have ten PowerBook computers and data acquisition instruments that enable students to conduct experiments and collect data in real time. The students then analyze the data on the spot as part of the lab.

The math department makes much use of computers as well. Students have published math papers on the school website. The Middle School Problem Solving class visits the Resource Center on a regular basis to obtain new problems and share solutions on the MATHCOUNTS website.

Ever aware of the arts, Saint Ann's has a multimedia computer lab in one of the music rooms, and the High School film classes make use of digital editing software.

Saint Ann's students apply to and are accepted at a broad spectrum of colleges including the top Ivy League universities. Oberlin, a small liberal arts college in Ohio, is popular. A parent said, "Stanley and his team devote enormous energy to getting the students into the best schools—that means the best school for the child, not necessarily the parent."

Graduation is held in the Church of Saint Ann and the Holy Trinity. Caps and gowns are not worn but "Pomp and Circumstance" is played. According to tradition, the president of the board of trustees speaks as well as a member of the faculty. There are four student presentations that can be in any medium.

Popular College Choices   Yale, Princeton, Brown, Oberlin, Amherst, University of Chicago

Traditions Fun Run, Founders' Day, Senior Cruise, Grandparents Day

Publications Middle School literary magazine
High school literary magazine
Photography or art magazine
Publications on a variety of subjects including: art, humor, nonfiction
Development office publication: *Saint Ann's Times*

Community Service Requirement None

Hangout On the steps in front of school

St. Bernard's School

4 East 98th Street
New York, NY 10029
(212) 289-2878, FAX (212) 410-6628
website: www.stbernards.org

All boys
K–8th/9th grade
Not accessible

Mr. Stuart H. Johnson, III, Headmaster
Elizabeth B. Ketner, Co-Director of Admissions
Anne S. Nordeman, Co-Director of Admissions

Uniform   Kindergarten: St. Bernard's shirts, khaki pants, Grades I–III: Monday–Thursday: navy blazers must be worn to and from school, St. Bernard's shirt or turtleneck, khaki-colored trousers or shorts, belt must be worn if pants have belt loops;
Grades IV–IX: Monday–Thursday: navy blazers to and from school, polo or turtleneck or oxford shirts tucked in, khaki pants or shorts with belts; all clothing must fit; no jeans, no T-shirts with logos, no sneakers except at gym
Fridays: blazers, ties and oxford shirts required, all day (except K)

Enrollment   Total enrollment: 381
K places: approximately 40–43
Half of the 2001 graduates will attend city day schools, half will attend boarding schools

Grades   Kindergarten: checklist and written reports
Grades I–III: detailed anecdotal reports, no checklists or rankings, no grades given in sports or art
Grades IV–IX: letter grades accompanied by detailed written reports
Departmentalization begins in grade V
Grade VII: first final
Grade VIII: first midterm

Tuition Range 2001–2002 $18,000 to $18,500, Kindergarten–9th grade
Additional fees: for lunch, books, supplies, physical education and trips total approximately $2,000
Tuition reimbursement and accident insurance plans are available

Financial Aid/Scholarship   16% of the student body received some form of aid in 2000

Endowment   N/A; reputed to be large

Diversity   Children of color represent 10% of the student body
8 Prep for Prep students enrolled as of fall 2000

Homework   Grade I: 10 pages of reading out loud to parent every two to three nights plus 1–2 pages of a workbook every other night, approximately 20 minutes
Grade II: spelling tests once a week; reading: 1 chapter every 2–3 days, approximately 20–30 minutes
Grade III: written compositions and journals, some math, approximately 30–40 minutes
Grades IV and V: compositions begun at home and math every night, approximately 1 hour; prep (study hall) begins 3:30–4:30 P.M.; most 4th and 5th graders use this time to complete some of their homework, but prep is not mandatory until Grade VI
Grade VI: 1½–2 hours; prep is mandatory
Grade VII–IX: 2–3 hours

After-School Program   St. Bernard's boys can participate in the Nightingale-Bamford Hobbyhorse after-school program, Monday–Thursday 3:15–5:00 P.M. or 6:00 P.M.; offered are crafts, sports, computer, ice skating, photography, chess, science; at moderate cost; financial aid is available
Afterschool sports at St. B's are available for K–4
Grades III–IX participate in intramural games including soccer, basketball, baseball, softball, lacrosse
Varsity and junior varsity Red & White teams in all sports
St. Bernard's is a member of the Manhattan Private Middle School League
Lessons in ice hockey are offered for an additional fee
Saturday Sports Club in the St. Bernard's gym: open to children

from other schools; Saturdays from 9:00 A.M. to 3:00 P.M.; $50 a day; supervised coed activities

Summer Program   Summer sports camp, June 15 through July 31st.

———

Although the school emblem shows a St. Bernard dog, St. Bernard's School was named after the rue St. Bernard, a street in Belgium. It is pronounced with the accent on the first syllable. Founded by an Englishman in 1904, St. Bernard's has always had an affinity for English traditions. It unselfconsciously calls its alumni Old Boys, and many of the devoted faculty still hail from Great Britain. But St. Bernard's is a kinder and gentler place than its British counterparts. Parents say there is a family feeling here. As Mrs. Forster, former co-director of admissions, says: "There is a crispness of attitude, with fun." A parent said "There's enough leeway so that the boys can be boyish."

Stuart Johnson, a Yale man, was thirty-two when he was appointed to his post as headmaster. He succeeded Englishman Amos Booth. Mr. Johnson is described as "unpretentious, caring, witty and a bright and stylish writer" and it is said that he "writes wonderful messages in bulletins and follows the traditions set forth by the other heads." "He goes out of his way to know everyone," said a parent. "He even came to a lacrosse game in Greenvale!" Manners are very important; Mr. Johnson shakes each boy's hand each morning. Mr. Johnson listens to all complaints and dispenses "punishments without tears." In addition to his administrative duties, Mr. Johnson teaches European history and directs the annual Shakespeare play. He knows all the boys by name and invites alumni to his apartment around Christmastime.

Getting in: Parents are advised to call for an application and brochure in September or October of the year before the child will enter kindergarten. St. Bernard's does not require any application fee. There is no birthday cutoff because they try to judge each boy on his own merits. Readiness is what is important. Boys in this year's kindergarten have birthdays spanning the entire year, including some younger boys with summer birthdays.

After the application is received by the school, they will call you to arrange a parent tour as well as a separate time for your child's interview. The tour is usually for two families at a time. Don't be afraid to ask questions, but you should be familiar with the catalog so that you can ask meaningful ones. "Really, we love parents to ask us *any* questions about the school and their child," say the co-directors of admissions. Leave plenty of time for the tour because it is very thorough. You are not rushed if you wish to linger in a classroom. After the tour, each set of parents meets privately with Mr. Johnson, for anywhere from ten to twenty minutes (longer if necessary). A parent at St. Bernard's recalls that she took her time on the tour: "I loved that we had the opportunity to tour the school and meet with the headmaster before we decided to apply."

The co-directors visit as many nursery schools as possible to see the boys in their current setting. All boys have a thirty minute interview at St. Bernard's. You are told not to prepare your son for the individual interview. It is a formal evaluation but the boys usually enjoy themselves (thirty minutes of undivided attention!) while their nervous parents sit and wait. Reading material is provided for those parents who are able to concentrate. There is a strong sibling and legacy policy. There is not a typical St. Bernard's boy although they look remarkably similar walking up Madison Avenue in their blue blazers.

Parents: A lot of Old Boys send their sons to St. Bernard's. Parents say the parent body is composed in part of "families with good values, 'Eleanor Roosevelt' types—women who work, even though they don't have to." One parent described the typical St. B parent as "an old New York family, with oil paintings of their ancestors on the walls and well-worn furniture." Certainly the tone of the parent body is "understated." Those who have means do not flaunt it. Although the ethos is WASP, families of all faiths are comfortable here.

Many parents who are prominent editors, writers or journalists send their sons to St. B's because of the school's emphasis on literacy. The beautifully written brochure says one of the basic premises at St. B's is "a regard for the beauty and power of English—in reading, writing, speaking, listening."

Class cocktail parties are held in the fall or winter and everyone gets a turn to host. The event can be casual or catered; the Parents Association reimburses parents for their expenses. The Parents Association sponsors events such as the Book Fair, a School Fair and a Raffle. On Parents' Night mothers and fathers gather in the gym and then go to the classrooms where they are joined by the teachers. There is a special visiting day for grandparents in the spring.

In the words of one alumnus, "In the old days St. Bernard's was a hatchery for the progeny of millionaires." The scions of some of New York's old families still attend. (St. Bernard's is rumored to have one of the largest endowments among city independent schools.)

371

Program: Traditions are an integral part of life at St. Bernard's, and parents say the boys—and Old Boys—look forward to many of them. Every morning St. Bernard's boys shake hands with the headmaster and then with their teachers. Every afternoon they say good-bye to their teachers with another handshake. Each day begins with an assembly in the gym. There are Tuesday-morning Bible stories told by Rosemary Lea whose Bible stories were published in 1995. A school-wide assembly is held on Fridays. At assembly a hymn is sung, announcements are made and there is a program. After Christmas each grade I boy receives a hymn book with his name on it and the date that he received it, and he keeps it for the whole time he is at St. B's. Parents talk about the family feeling at assemblies, to which they are invited several times a year. Each boy gains experience in public speaking beginning in grade I. Each boy recites a poem or performs in a play at assembly. Topics at assembly range widely. There might be a group of Old Boys reminiscing about life at St. Bernard's in the fifties or a performance of music of the Middle Ages by the Interschool Orchestra. A particularly witty assembly used the theme Lingo Limbo to personify elements of bad writing. The Oxy Morons, the Euphemism Unit, Club Cliché and the Grammar Goons painlessly pointed out the pitfalls of poor writing.

There is a tradition at St. Bernard's involving a stuffed alligator given to the neatest class. At Friday assemblies the alligator is presented by one class to another with some original poetry or a song.

On your tour you will see desks arranged in traditional rows with the teacher at the front of the class speaking to the students. You might hear a student reciting a poem, or a nine year old reciting his multiplication tables, but don't be misled; although there is plenty of structure, there is flexibility and creativity within each classroom. Boys may stand upon their chairs, work on the floor in groups, sit in a circle and read aloud. "The combination of bright kids and unusual teachers makes St. Bernard's unique. The real beauty of St. Bernard's is its teachers," says Mr. Johnson. There is little turnover in staff at St. B, there are some eccentrics and there's a big age range. One parent described her sons' teachers as "warm, kind and intellectual." Another parent said, "Some teachers are rough and tough, but adored. Some teachers give the boys nicknames." Another parent said: "There are kids whose fathers had the same teachers, they are all well remembered, some revered, for generations." From fifth grade up all home-room teachers are men.

A major expansion of the building is complete. The renovations include: a state-of-the-art gymnasium, science wing with new labs, a teaching theatre, two kindergarten classrooms with separate play-deck, and a carpentry room.

Junior School at St. B's is grades K–III. Parents told us that reading is expected to be under way by Christmas of first grade. Grade I boys are divided into two reading groups with much fluidity between them. Boys must read aloud to their parents ten pages every two to three nights. "From the first day of school boys get into the homework habit," says one parent. Homework is never unreasonable, but there is a certain amount expected every night.

There are two reading specialists and one math specialist on the staff of the special learning department. There is concern for the individual child. One mother told us her son needed a little extra help in math in first grade, and a St. B teacher who happened to be in the same summer community offered to work with him over the summer free of charge, so that he wouldn't have trouble with second grade math.

One mother spoke about the progress her son made in grade I: "It's a caring environment and they keep a close watch. My son is shy but they've helped him to socialize. Also, at first he couldn't write and now he writes pages; he also wasn't a team sports player and now he participates fully."

A typical grade I schedule: The day begins with an assembly in the gym and goes on to art, gym, library, science, sums, spelling, phonics, reading, math, recess, lunch, physical education, work-time/crafts and dismissal. The curriculum is well rounded, parents say, and there is time for physical activity every day, either on the outdoor play deck or in the fields of Central Park just a block away. There is a computer in every classroom, in addition to a large new computer lab with PC's. The science labs for grades I through IX are very well equipped.

Third graders do a lot of written work. They study Greek mythology "and are very devoted to it," a parent said. Awards for best and most-improved handwriting are given in each class.

Music begins in first grade. We toured around Christmastime and strains of "O Come All Ye Faithful" were floating through the halls. Tryouts for the St. Bernard's singing group begin in fourth grade and most boys make it. Rehearsals are held twice a week before school. At performances, boys wear special ties and trousers. One recent year they sang at Carnegie Hall, and they have also appeared at Alice Tully Hall, the youngest musical group to perform.

Art is hands on, with an academic approach. One Christmas, boys made ornaments for the Florence Nightingale Nursing Home.

The Middle School is grades IV through VI. Fourth graders have a meeting before the school year begins to discuss the transition to Middle School.

Fifth graders always sponsor the Science Fair, a midwinter event in which experiments are demonstrated. There is a fifth and sixth grade environmental group that organizes an Earth Day program and raises money for environmental causes.

Every homeroom performs at an Assembly; one recent year a fifth grade class did the story of Prometheus. A parent described the play as "pure entertainment" with St. Bernard's characteristic wit and English humor." The boy who played Hercules was the skinniest boy in the class, but he came out swaggering, with his sleeves rolled up. "The boys really loved performing!"

From time immemorial every fifth grader has written a ten-page research report on an animal, and, says a parent, "Every alumnus remembers his animal." They also do a unit on Native Alaskans in the winter and Native Americans in the spring. Latin begins in sixth grade.

The Garrett McClung Prize is a special award given in grade V for achievement. Six prizes are given out at the end of grade VI.

The Upper School consists of grades VII through IX. Special events during these years include the annual eighth grade Shakespeare production, directed by the headmaster. The play varies from year to year (in recent years it has been *The Tempest* and *The Taming of the Shrew*), and St. Bernard's boys play all roles. Another sixth grade tradition is a visit to Civil War battlefields in Virginia. There is an eighth grade debating society, an Upper School public speaking contest, and a Model Congress elective.

In grade VII *To Kill a Mockingbird* is read and in grade IX, Solzhenitzyn's *One Day in the Life of Ivan Denisovich*. Parents say the boys are very well prepared for the ongoing schools because of St. B's emphasis on reading and writing.

The student council is composed of elected members from grades IV through IX. The council meets each trimester and each class elects its own president, vice president and secretary. The entire council meets with the headmaster. Recent issues have included the usual plaints: calls for better food, more recess, less homework, more holidays.

Clubs include the Computer Club, the Photography Club and the St. Bernard's Singers. St. Bernard's boys can participate in Nightingale-Bamford's Hobbyhorse after-school program too. Ninth graders are permitted to go out for lunch.

The entire school benefits from the handsomely renovated Jenkins Library, in which an oil painting of the stern-faced founder overlooks the stacks. There are shelves of O.E.D.'s and study carrels for the older boys as well as CD-ROMs and other research tools. A separate section of the library is reserved for the younger boys so that they do not disturb the concentration of the older boys.

Intramural sports competition begins in grade III. Ninety percent of boys from grade V through grade IX play on at least one team each year. There are varsity and junior varsity Red and White teams in all sports. St. Bernard's teams excel in soccer, lacrosse, and baseball. Ice hockey is offered in addition to the traditional sports.

Values are stressed throughout St. Bernard's and there is a code of conduct. In addition, one parent said, "High value is placed on both grades and awards." There are essay and composition prizes and a public speaking prize. At the final assembly numerous awards and prizes are given out; one of the highest awards is the Payne Whitney Honor Cup.

Consistent with the belief that "a good heart is finally more valuable than a well-stocked, well-trained head," community service at St. B's starts at the top with the headmaster, who is on the board of the Yorkville Common Pantry. Food drives are held at Thanksgiving, Christmas and Passover/Easter. Boys in grades I through II can work with the Clown Care Unit of the Big Apple Circus by writing poems or making gifts that the clowns take to children in area hospitals. In addition, each class does a project or community service work. Older boys visit the elderly at the Florence Nightingale Nursing Home or decorate the cafeteria or other common areas of the home for the holidays; the St. B's singing group performs or just visits informally. Other community service opportunities include the Environmental Club and recycling program, and bake sales for charities. There is usually a student-led response to a major disaster: For hurricane and earthquake victims, a well-decorated jar for contributions will be placed in the lobby and a check sent to a relief fund. There is a public school tutoring project in East Harlem at a school located at 115th Street and Second Avenue.

St. Bernard's imparts a palpable enthusiasm for learning, and the techniques for mastering any subject. An alumnus told us that the only times he wasn't at the top of his class were at St. Bernard's and The Harvard Business School. One parent said what surprised her the most about St. Bernard's was its warmth: St. Bernard's is not just for Anglophiles.

About half of the graduates go to boarding school and the rest transfer to independent day schools in the area, after either eighth or ninth grade.

Traditions   St. Bernard's book of school songs, Friday assemblies, eighth grade Shakespeare play, eighth grade trip (one week), fifth grade animal report, Alligator Award for neatness, Science Fair, Book Fair, Sports Day, Parents' Evening, Father's Dinner, Father/Son Soccer Game, The Caslon Spelling Bowl, Author's Night, Junior Old Boys' Lunch, Old Boys' Dinner, Grandparents' Visiting Day, Spring Concert, Middle School Music Festival

Publications   Yearbook: *The Keg*
Literary magazine: *The Budget*
Parents' Association Publication: *St. Bernard's Gazette*
Alumni Bulletin: *St. Bernard's School*

Community Service Requirement   No specific requirement but each boy must perform community service in a number of ways available through various programs within the school. There are also many opportunities to serve the local community: Yorkville Common Pantry, the Florence Nightingale Nursing Home, the Clown Care Unit at various hospitals

Hangouts   Richie's Deli on Madison, the Italian ices man outside school

Saint David's School

12 East 89th Street
New York, NY 10128
(212) 369-0058, FAX (212) 289-2796
website: www.saintdavidschool.org

All boys
Pre-Kindergarten–8th grade
Accessible (3 elevators)

Dr. Donald T. Maiocco, Headmaster
Ms. Janet Sughrue, Director of Admissions
Ms. Julie Sykes, Director of Admissions

Uniform   Grades pre-kindergarten through Kindergarten: collared or turtleneck shirts only, no jacket required, sneakers are allowed Grades 1–8: tie and jacket (jacket can be any color); Bermuda shorts allowed in September and May, no sneakers

Birthday Cutoff   Children entering Kindergarten must be 5 by September 1
Children entering 1st grade must be 6 by September 1st

Enrollment   Total enrollment: 365
Pre-kindergarten places: 16
Kindergarten places for incoming children: 20
Graduating class size: approximately 35

Grades   Trimester system
Pre-kindergarten through 3rd grade: detailed anecdotal reports and conferences
Letter grades begin in 4th grade
Departmentalization begins in 4th grade
First final exam is given in 7th grade

Tuition Range 2001–2002 $14,000 to $20,675, pre-kindergarten–8th grade
The cost for lunch, books, and athletics is included in the tuition
There is a 8-month tuition payment plan available to parents
A 10 percent discount is given on the tuition of the second child of parents with three or more children in the school; there is a

discount of 25 percent for the third child and 50 percent for the fourth and additional children

Financial Aid/Scholarship   10% of the student body received some form of financial aid in 1999–2000

Endowment   N/A

Diversity   7% children of color
6 Prep for Prep students enrolled as of fall 2000

Homework   1st: 15–20 minutes
2nd: 1/2 hour
3rd: 1 hour
4th and 5th: 1 1/2 hours
6th: 1 1/2–2 hours
7th and 8th: 2–2 1/2 hours

After-School Program   The Saint David's after-school program is open to Saint David's boys only; an additional payment is required Grades 1 through 8: Monday–Thursday, 4:30–5:30 P.M.; various activities including sports, art, cooking, computer, woodworking, pottery, rocketry and chess

Summer Program   The June Program for kindergarten boys during the last two weeks of June; an additional payment is required
June Summer Sports program (9:00 A.M.–3:30 P.M.) for grades 1–8, two weeks in June: a variety of sports, games, activities and field trips; an additional payment is required
March sports program for grades 1–8 either first or second week of spring vacation

---

Although Saint David's School, founded in 1951, is relatively young, it is interesting to note that the school has more traditions than most of the long-established East side boys' schools founded at the turn of the century. The school building, originally three private homes designed by Delano and Aldrich in 1919, retains much of the beauty, warmth and architectural detail of the period. Saint David's is a Catholic school for boys but the Saint David's community is inclusive; almost half of the boys practice other religions, and the catalog states that St. David's "is a family school in every sense of the word." Parents say St. David's "offers a balance of academics, arts and athletics with a spiritual component." St. David's is known for an emphasis on literature, languages, history and art "bolstered by practical anatomy, mathematics and a growing computer science department."

Saint David's was founded by lay Catholics and, according to the mission statement, Saint David's remains grounded in the traditions of that faith. Saint David's students are taught "to respect and learn from all religious traditions, to prize diversity and to develop the spiritual and ethical values necessary for successful moral decision making." One parent described St. David's as a place where "the school and teachers work to develop boys who will be able to think critically about what life presents them with, and they do that by providing the boys with a foundation of ethical and moral instruction." One parent who is not Catholic and who recently relocated to New York City with her family from another country said she chose this school for her son because, considering the language and cultural differences, she felt Saint David's would provide "a challenging but nurturing academic environment with less pressure than at some other schools." Another parent said she chose Saint David's for "its heart, soul and mind."

Getting in: Applications should be filed by early Fall. After the application is filed (there is a $45 fee), tour and interview dates are scheduled. Individual tours of the school are given by the directors of admission. Applicants for grades kindergarten through third have a one-on-one interview with a teacher. Applicants for grades four through eight spend a day in a classroom. The directors of admissions say that a diverse group of boys is chosen from a variety of nursery schools; approximately fifteen schools are represented in a class of thirty-six. Admissions at Saint David's is not stressful, and parents are made to feel comfortable about the process.

Parents: The parent body at Saint David's is described by a parent: "There is wealth and there are some limos but parents are far from ostentatious." Parents do dress well, and many wear suits to school events. An annual dinner dance is held in early March. A recent event consisted of a very successful dinner and auction. Parents mingle more informally at the frequent cocktail parties, teas, morning coffees, a theater benefit, and family skating at Wollman Rink.

Program: Saint David's has had remarkably few heads of school in its history; David Hume was headmaster for thirty-plus years. In July 1992, Dr. Donald Maiocco became the school's fourth headmaster. Parents describe Maiocco as "academically oriented and well travelled." (The original Normandy war maps we saw on the walls are courtesy of a former headmaster.) Dr. Maiocco greets the boys in front of the school almost daily, and parents say he is very accessible and returns calls promptly. When parents were concerned about their seventh graders hanging out at Jackson Hole (a hamburger restaurant), Dr. Maiocco established a setting in which parents could discuss these issues—like a fireside chat with coffee. Dr. Maiocco is the guiding force in the school's "rededication to the humanities." One of the first things he did was to change the names of the homerooms from A and B to Pi and Theta. The new school alma mater is sung to a Mozart melody. Dr. Maiocco teaches "Humanities VIII." According to the catalog, "Saint David's is deeply committed to exploration of the civilizations that most shaped our own: Democratic Greece and Republican Rome." Latin is required in the fifth grade and becomes an elective in seventh and eighth grades.

Dr. Maiocco has written that Saint David's mission is "to provide the finest education available within the best traditions of the church." Religious instruction at Saint David's is based on an inclusive, not exclusive, Catholicism. Requirements include: morning chapel, religion classes, mass (four times a year, third grade and up, held at the Church of St. Thomas More) and the celebration of Christian holidays. Preparation for First Communion is optional. Religion classes are ungraded, and holidays of other faiths are also examined during the course of the year. The catalog states that "students of all faiths are encouraged to draw from their religious traditions for class discussions and assignments."

The chapel is the former library and contains a fireplace and servant's bell in addition to pews. First and second graders attend chapel once a week for Bible stories. Third through eighth graders begin each day with chapel, at which hymns are sung and faculty members relate a personal story that reflects a particular moral or ethical lesson. These "chapel talks" can be humorous, serious, spiritual or merely enlightening, and range from an account of a close call with bears on a hiking trip to an explanation of the Book of Kells, an English teacher's description of the significance of the Jewish holidays to him or a well-loved member of the kitchen staff singing spirituals.

Saint David's calendar lists eight fêtes de l'écoles or celebration days. Each day is marked by a special program. There is a celebration for the founding of the city of Rome, and on every March 1, Saint David's Day, members of the school community bite a leek to symbolize their becoming a son or daughter of Saint David's (in the year of his introduction Dr. Maiocco did his part).

Lower School is composed of pre-kindergarten through third grade. There is one pre-kindergarten class of approximately sixteen students and three kindergarten classes (of eighteen students each.) The brochure states, "In the early years the school seeks a balance between work and play." A parent told us about a wonderful celebration in the Lower School for "Cinco de Mayo," a Mexican feast day: "They had a piñata, food and clothing from Mexico." One second grade project focused on how each boy could do his part to help save the earth. One year, the family of one of the second grade boys had lived in Japan and helped the class celebrate Children's Day with a Japanese Tea Ceremony.

In the Lower School basic skills are emphasized. Homework is introduced in first grade. Formal reading instruction also begins in this year with special small group instruction. Manipulatives are used for math instruction. Math is tracked or grouped by ability starting in first grade. Fourth graders begin learning how to write a research paper. There is a computer in every classroom.

Drama, music and art are integrated into the academic curriculum. Lower School boys choose a famous painting to study. Parents look forward to the yearly first grade Christmas play. Students go outside their homerooms for instruction in pottery, woodworking, music, science and gym. Project Charlie, an anti-drug program, is taught in second and fourth grades. Sixth graders take a full health course called D.A.S.H. (drugs, alcohol, sex and health).

Lower School boys have a break midmorning for recess in the little gym, or they may go to the play yard. They change for sports in the afternoon. From kindergarten up, boys eat in the downstairs Lower School dining room. Lunch is served family style, and, said one mother, the boys are expected to eat what is on their plates. Parents praise Lower School Head Jane Warwick: "She knows each boy as an individual—his strengths and his weaknesses."

Sports at Saint David's begins with intramural competition in third grade. From grade 5 on there is All-Star Team competition with other schools, but a hallmark of the sports program at Saint David's is that all fifth and sixth grade boys get a chance to play at the varsity level; there are no team cuts at this age. The school's athletic facilities have recently been expanded to include a new 16,000 square foot sports center located at 215 East 94th Street. The athletic director says, "a lot of attention is paid to skill development, and the coaching staff is strong," which enables the Saint David's boys to compete with the best of them. The Red Team has fielded championship basketball and soccer teams. On Friday afternoons some faculty and boys sometimes go to the park for informal sports, or play pickup basketball in the gym. There are seasonal parent/faculty games and an alumni soccer match. The Player of the Week program recognizes outstanding performance in a game, enthusiasm or sportsmanship.

Another incentive for boys in the Lower School is the Saint David's armband, which is awarded at a monthly assembly to boys who did something special. The armband has been awarded for "recognition of academic excellence," for "neatness" or for "simply smiling." One parent said her son got it for mastering the "bird's nest" in gymnastics.

There is no Middle School at Saint David's: Grades four through eight are considered part of the Upper School. Letter grades begin in fourth grade. Boys begin lab science in fourth grade. Math continues to be grouped according to ability.

Latin, introduced in fifth grade, continues through eighth grade. In sixth grade boys can choose between French and Spanish. Fourth through sixth graders are taught the science of geography and they have a "map of the month" to study. April has been designated "Science Month" at Saint David's. Guest lecturers talk about the sonar systems in dolphins, the cardio-vascular system and advances in heart surgery and the impact of El Nino.

Drama continues to be incorporated into the curriculum. For example, Tom McLellan's fifth grade class stages a mock Revolutionary War battle, the Battle of Macgowan's Pass, in Central Park. Boys also take a field trip to Old Bethpage, Long Island. Class plays usually tie in with the history or English curriculum; past productions have included *Casey at the Bat, Philoctetes* and *The Pirates of Penzance.*

There are many opportunities for boys to practice public speaking: Sixth graders recite original poetry and eighth graders deliver research reports on art to students and teachers and sometimes give the chapel talks.

Opportunities for musical performance include handbell choir, recorder, Glee Club, Interschool orchestra, philharmonic and two ensemble performances with Brearley each year.

There is interaction between the grades in which students act as teachers. Eighth graders talked to third graders about Greek coins they had made; a fifth grade class addressed fourth graders about aspects of Native American cultures.

Visiting Day provides students an opportunity to interact with girls at the single-sex schools. They pick an activity such as library or music and go to a girls' school for the library or music hour in the fall. In the spring, they reciprocate and host the girls. Exchanges are matched by grade and age.

Boys in the Upper School are assigned many long-term projects in order to develop their time-management skills. Seventh and eighth graders have trimester exams. In addition to Dr. Maiocco's humanities course there is an eighth grade course in comparative anatomy. The eighth grade "Humanities" course, which is taught by the headmaster, is a "survey of architecture, music and literature of three distinct eras: ancient Greece, Europe during the Renaissance and the United States during WWII. The course includes fundamental Greek and culmi-nates in a trip to Italy before the spring break. Eighth grade boys study Renaissance art and architecture in Rome, Siena and Florence.

Although there is a definite emphasis on the classics, Dr. Maiocco states that "Saint David's has increased its efforts to include in its cur-riculum the achievements of women and of members of a wide range of ethnic groups . . . what we strive for is contextual understanding." Observance of Martin Luther King Day at Saint David's is not just a holiday but an opportunity for discussion of Dr. King's contributions across many subject areas. For instance, a discussion of the poetry of Langston Hughes might serve as a springboard for discussion of "Dr. King's impact on the moral consciousness of the American people and the world." Similarly, a study of Gandhi's influence on Dr. King's "I Have a Dream" speech is part of an Upper School study of the American civil rights movement.

Art is not an elective in the Upper School. Seventh and eighth grade boys receive letter grades in art, with the emphasis on attitude and effort, not talent. Some boys objected, some boys thought it would encourage them to take the arts more seriously.

Saint David's is proud of its honors math program for grades seven and eight. Students participate in the annual Math Bowl.

Outdoor education takes place on the week long annual seventh grade Cape Cod trip in October, during which boys are led on explo-rations by instructors from the Cape Cod Museum of Natural History. The sixth grade boys visit Mystic, Connecticut for two overnights to study the history and culture of an old whaling village.

Extracurricular activities in the Upper School include working on the school literary magazine *(The Canticle)* or the yearbook and playing on sports teams. The student council president (grades five through eight) is elected and he then selects his cabinet.

The Saint David's Social Action Committee participates in many community service projects, such as contributions to charity boxes, the Annual Thanksgiving Drive, Christmas gifts to the Graham-Windham home, and a sixth grade remote-control model car rally fund-raiser. Seventh graders make weekly visits to the Florence Nightingale Nursing Home. The soda machine profits go to a charity.

At the end of their eight-plus years at Saint David's, the school magazine asserts that the boys will have "painted grapes and dissected frogs, studied Greek and conversed with computers." Graduation takes place at the Church of St. Thomas More in a nonreligious ceremony (boys wear ties and jackets). Awards are given in athletics, music, art and academic areas. The ceremony is followed by a reception with hors d'oeuvres and cocktails on the terrace at Saint David's. Afterwards, many families get together for dinner. Saint David's graduates attend a variety of day and boarding schools.

Traditions   Morning chapel talks, class plays, Math Bowl, History Bowl, weekly poetry recitation in Lower School, St. David's armbands, Player of the Week, fêtes de l'écoles, all-school Christmas concert, Gala Spring Art Show, clothing and book sales, seventh grade Greek play, Upper School Science Fair, Annual Dinner/Dance and Auction, faculty-father athletic contests, annual alumni soccer match, alumni Christmas party, Eighth grade Art History lectures with Nightingale-Bamford School

Publications   *Saint David's Magazine*
Literary magazine: *The Canticle*
Lower School literary magazine
Yearbook

Community Service Requirement   7th grade nursing home visits are required; class projects; Upper School Social Action Committee coordinates community service activities

Hangout   Jackson Hole (hamburger restaurant)

St. Hilda's & St. Hugh's School

619 West 114th Street
New York, NY 10025
Tel (212) 932-1980
website: www.StHildas.org

Coed
Toddlers–8th grade
Accessible

Ms. Virginia Connor, Head of School
Ms. Roxandra Antoniadis, Director of Admissions

Birthday Cutoff   September 1

Enrollment   Total enrollment: 300
Toddler program places: 20
Nursery places: 30
Kindergarten places: 34
Graduating class 2000: approximately 20

Tuition Range 2001–2002: $16,750 to $18,400, 2's–8th grade
Additional fees: for materials and activities are approximately $550
An optional hot lunch program for 3rd through 8th graders for $900
Hot lunch required, 3's through 2nd grade

After-School Program   St. Hilda's & St. Hugh's After-School Program is open to children from other schools; a variety of creative and recreational activities; 3:00 P.M.–6:30 P.M.; an additional payment is required
Vacation camps in September, December, March, June for an additional charge

Summer Program   Summer camp is open to children from other schools; there is an additional charge; a variety of recreational and creative activities
First session: mid-June–July 4
Second session: July
Third session: end of August–second week of September

St. Hilda's & St. Hugh's is a coed Episcopal day school founded in 1950 by the Reverend Mother Ruth of the Community of the Holy Spirit, an Episcopal religious order for women. The faculty is entirely a lay faculty. The curriculum at St. Hilda's & St. Hugh's is traditional and integrated. There is a uniform requirement in grades one through eight, and teachers are addressed formally as "Mr. Smith," "Miss Jones." Although chapel attendance in first through eighth grades is required, the student body is diverse. French or Spanish is required from nursery on, Latin is required in seventh and eighth grades. The music and art program includes an English Brass Band and a theater arts program. Parents praise the warm, cohesive community.

St. Hilda's & St. Hugh's Schools graduates attend a variety of secondary schools including the New York City specialized high schools (Stuyvesant and Bronx Science), and independent day and boarding schools including Horace Mann, Trinity, Nightingale-Bamford, Spence, St. Ann's, Riverdale, Friends, Sacred Heart and Marymount.

St. Luke's School

487 Hudson Street
New York, NY 10014
(212) 924-5960
website: www.Admin@StLukeSchool.org

Coed
Junior kindergarten–8th grade
Not accessible

Ms. Ann Mellow, Head
Ms. Susan Parker, Director of Admissions

Birthday Cutoff   Children entering junior kindergarten must be 4 by October 1
Children entering kindergarten must be 5 by October 1

Enrollment   Total enrollment: 202
Junior kindergarten places: 16
Kindergarten places: between 5 and 10
Graduating class 2000: 21
3 Prep for Prep students enrolled as of Fall 2000
7 Early Steps students enrolled as of Fall 2000

Grades   The Lower School is on a semester system (grades junior kindergarten–4)
The Upper School is on a trimester system (grades 5–8)
Letter grades begin in 5th grade
Departmentalization begins in 5th grade

Tuition Range 2001–2002 $16,710 to $17,540, junior kindergarten–8th grade
Additional fees: $460 (junior kindergarten through grade 4), $645 (5th and 6th), $660 (7th and 8th)

Financial Aid/Scholarship   20% of the student body receive some form of aid

Endowment $275,000

After-School Program   St. Luke's After-School Program: Monday–Friday, from dismissal time until 5:45 P.M.; a variety of creative and recreational activities; an additional fee is required

----

St. Luke's School was founded in 1945 and retains its affiliation with the Episcopal Church. The program is ecumenical but there is mandatory chapel from one to three times a week at the Church of St. Luke's in the Fields, a landmark building dating from 1822, rebuilt in 1985, and 15 percent of students take communion. ERBs are required for admission to junior kindergarten and kindergarten. Most classrooms in this West Village school face the tree-lined campus, affording good light and little street noise. The classrooms are spacious and bright. The school has a library, and media center, gymnasium, art studio, small theater, music, computer and foreign language rooms, a science lab, and a large dining room. There are three outdoor play areas, and students use school facilities and local sports fields for junior varsity and varsity sports. St. Luke's has no formal dress code—the only requirement is that students be clean and neat. Hot lunch is not provided; students bring their own.

The curriculum is highly structured but a variety of educational approaches are used. Interdisciplinary teaching is strong. St. Luke's is divided into two divisions: junior kindergarten through fourth grade; fifth through eighth grades. Students select either French or Spanish in sixth grade. There is a very active Parents Association. The school works with Early Steps and Prep for Prep.

Popular High School Choices   The Nightingale-Bamford School, Packer Collegiate Institute, Polytechnic Preparatory School, Riverdale Country School, Collegiate, Trinity School, Berkeley-Carroll, Loyola, the Dalton School, and Friends Seminary.

The Solomon Schechter School of Manhattan

at Park Avenue Synagogue
50 East 87th Street
New York, N.Y. 10128
(212) 427-9500
website: www.sshsny.org

Solomon Schechter High School of New York
1 West 91st Street
New York, NY 10024
(212) 877-7747

Coed
Kindergarten–12th grade
Wheelchair accessible

Dr. Steven C. Lorch, Head of School, Elementary and Middle School
Rabbi Judd Kruger Levingston, Principal, High School
Barbara Gerstel, Director of Admissions and Financial Aid
Sondra Weiss, Early Childhood Director, Admissions Contact

Uniform   Boys: navy or gray slacks, blue shirt, navy sweater with crest
Girls: navy jumper or skirt or slacks, white blouse, navy sweater with crest

Birthday Cutoff   No strict cutoff; developmental readiness is the main consideration

Enrollment as of June, 2001   (K–4): 112
(9–12) 97
Kindergarten places 36
9th grade places 36

Grades   Detailed anecdotal reports
Letter grades in the High School

Tuition Range   2001–2002 Kindergarten–12th grade: K–5 $17,000; 9–12 $15,000 (Tuition is based upon a sliding scale depending on parents' ability to pay)

Endowment N/A

Financial Aid/Scholarship 25%

Diversity 8% students of color

After-School Program Available subject to interest

Summer Program None

———

The Solomon Schechter School of Manhattan opened its doors in 1996 with a kindergarten and continues to grow, adding a new grade each year; the lower school will eventually have eight grades and the upper school will extend to twelfth grade. The school is currently housed at two sites: kindergarten and first grade are located at the Park Avenue Synagogue at 87th Street and Madison Avenue, while the upper grades located at 1 West 91st Street. The Solomon Schechter School is one of a network of over 70 Solomon Schechter schools throughout the United States and Canada, the first of which was established in 1951. Among these sister schools is the Solomon Schechter High School of New York, with which the school collaborates on a number of joint community initiatives. The two schools are separate entities, though there have been discussions from time to time about possible future affiliation.

The Solomon Schechter School of Manhattan was conceived in 1994 as an initiative of the United Synagogue of Conservative Judaism and the rabbis of the nine Conservative synagogues in Manhattan. During its formative period, a group of dedicated parents and community leaders came together to develop the school's mission and character. Elie Wiesel serves as Honorary Chairman of the Board of Trustees, Dr. Samuel Klagsbrun as Chairman of the Education Committee. Dr. Klagsbrun says that at the school "children learn to participate fully in modern society and contribute to our general culture while feeling completely at home in the Jewish world." The aim was to "establish a Jewish day school . . . where students will be given a rich understanding of their Jewish heritage, a fluent command of the Hebrew language, and a passion for Jewish learning. The goal is to nurture culturally aware, compassionate, and socially responsible individuals who will constitute the future leadership of the American Jewish Community."

In 1999, the High School was established, located on Central Park West; it plans to serve 140 students in grades nine through twelve.

Getting in: Parents are welcome to visit the school and meet with admissions staff members prior to applying. In addition, an open house is held in the fall at which time prospective parents can meet with the faculty and with parents of children already enrolled in the school. After an application has been filed, the child visits the school for an individual interview. The results of ERB or any other standardized testing should also be forwarded to The Solomon Schechter School. Finally, the parents come in to meet with the Head of School, Dr. Lorch. To fulfill the family education requirement parents in the school must participate in a series of classes in Jewish life and texts but they are not required to know Hebrew.

Parents: One parent described the social mix as "An eclectic group who are down-to-earth and 'heimish,'" diverse geographically and religiously (although all the children are Jewish). Parents help out in the office, go on field trips and volunteer in the classroom. The PA sponsors brunches, and an annual kosher food tasting evening and Education Night. All parents are members of the PA and invited to attend meetings.

Program: The Head of the Elementary and Middle School, Dr. Steven Lorch, who has degrees from Harvard and Columbia, has previously been the head of three other Jewish schools in North America, Australia and in Israel. According to Dr. Lorch, there are two language objectives for the kindergarten year: 1) that every child will read and write in English by the end of the year; and 2) every child will become proficient in Hebrew. "To achieve these objectives the classroom has to truly be an enriched bilingual environment."

The classroom teachers are bilingual (English/Hebrew) and work with the Early Childhood Director to design the curriculum. The classroom emphasizes experiential or active learning. There are early childhood materials, including blocks, as well as computers in the classroom. The classes often break into smaller groups for math activities, block building, computers, and so on.

A main feature of the program is an interdisciplinary (or thematic) approach to learning. Topics of study are chosen by the students on the basis of their interests and each topic is then investigated from a variety of perspectives: social studies, Jewish tradition, the arts, science, literature, mathematics, writing: all contribute to a rich and textured understanding of the topic at hand.

Reading is taught by combining elements of both Whole Language and phonics. Children use manipulative materials when learning math and sciences. Children are instructed by specialists in music and physical education twice a week. There is daily physical exercise, either on the outdoor playroof or in nearby Central Park.

Children are introduced to Jewish life through the Jewish Studies curriculum and Hebrew is taught using the natural method of language study. Religion plays a central role in the life of the school. Prayer, activities related to holidays, the observance of dietary laws and acts of kindness (charity) are stressed. Girls are offered full egalitarian privileges and participation.

Jewish issues and religious thought play a central role in the life of the school. Students study math, science, history, English, Bible, rabbinical thought, Hebrew and French or Spanish. Extracurricular courses and activities include the Bridges to Brotherhood, Blacks and Jews in Dialogue, Investment Club, City Lights (which brings students to special *High Five!* Performances), Solomon Society (student government), choir, drama, studio art, theater production arts, newspaper, yearbook, web design, festival and daily prayer planning committees. There are interscholastic sports programs offered in cross-country, soccer, volleyball, basketball and softball. Most of the school's Jewish rituals and holiday celebrations are entirely planned and carried out by the students in consultation with the school's rabbi.

The school has a junior exchange year program with a high school in Jerusalem. Annual community service activities include tutoring children from the public school next door and helping in soup kitchens.

Popular College Choices: Brandeis, Columbia, Hampshire, Oberlin, Princeton, Smith, University of Arizona, University of Chicago, University of Pennsylvania, Washington University and Wellesley

Traditions: Monday and Thursday prayer in the Chapel (parents are welcome), Friday friendship circles, *Kabbalat Shabbat*, Family Holiday Programs for Sukkot, Chanukah, Purim, Pesach, and Yom Ha'atzmaut, First Grade Siddur ceremony on TuBish'vat, Grandparents and Special Friends Day "exhibitions" (class-wide celebrations at the end of a unit of study).

Publications: Weekly newsletter: *Daf Kesher*
Yearbook

The Spence School

22 East 91st Street
New York, NY 10128-0657
(212) 289-5940, FAX (212) 289-6025
website: www.spenceschool.org

All girls
Kindergarten–12th grade
Accessible

Ms. Arlene J. Gibson, Head of School
Ms. Alice Shedlin, Director of Admissions

Uniform Grades kindergarten–5: plaid jumper and white shirt, solid-color stockings, tights, socks
Grades 6–8: navy blue skirt, navy blue pants and white shirt
Grades 9–12: solid gray skirt or gray slacks, any shirt that has sleeves and covers midriff; no leg warmers, leggings or long underwear, low-heeled shoes only
Uniform is not required on Fridays
After fall trimester, seniors may petition to cease wearing their uniforms
Before the start of school uniform fittings are held at Spence
Gym outfits are given to the girls free of charge

Birthday Cutoff Girls entering kindergarten must be 5 by August 31

Enrollment Total enrollment: 587
Kindergarten places: approximately 45
9th grade places: 10–12
Graduating class 2000: 41

Grades Semester system in Lower School
Trimester system in Middle/Upper Schools
Grades kindergarten–5: checklist (skill acquired, developing skill, needs support, exhibits strength marked improvement)
Grades 6–8: letter grades begin in 7th grade, detailed anecdotal reports plus a checklist
Grades 9–12: letter grades and detailed checklist

Departmentalization begins in 6th grade
First final exam in 6th grade

Tuition Range 2001–2002 $18,750 to $19,845, kindergarten–12th
grade
Additional fees: for lunch, books, supplies, Parents' Association
dues and miscellaneous supplies approximately $1,257 to $1,807

Financial Aid/Scholarship Approximately 14% of the entire stu-
dent body receive some form of tuition assistance, 26% in the
Upper School
Financial aid accounts for 10% of the operating budget

Endowment $47.2 million (as of June 2000)

Diversity 21% students of color; 26% in the Upper School
15 Prep for Prep students enrolled as of fall 2000
5 ABC (A Better Chance) students
2 TEAK students
11 Early Steps students
Cultural Awareness Club
The Afro-Latino Alliance
Jewish Culture Club
Asia Society
Spence Women's Action Network (SWAN)

Homework Kindergarten: none
1st and 2nd: approximately 10–20 minutes
3rd and 4th: 30–45 minutes
5th: 1 hour–1½ hours, plus reading assignments
6th: 20–30 minutes per subject per night plus reading assignments
7th–8th: approximately 2½–3 hrs
9th–12th: approximately 3–4 hrs

After-School Program Second Act After-School Program: coed,
open to students from other schools; a variety of creative and
enrichment activities for an additional charge; Monday–Thursday
from 3:00–6:00 P.M., Friday from 2:00 to 4:30 P.M.
Middle School: interscholastic sports program
Upper School: varsity teams
Some club meetings and choir, drama and dance rehearsals for

grades 6–12 are held after school; choruses rehearse during school periods except for select choir and glee club

Summer Program   Second Act June Program: a two-week program in June with a different theme each year; open to students from other schools; there is an additional charge
Jumpstart: a two-week voluntary program for new students grades 9–12

———

The Spence School, founded in 1892 as Miss Spence's School for Girls, is housed in an elegant red brick building on East 91st Street and offers a well-rounded, rigorous academic program, strong in performing arts, the sciences, visual arts and foreign language studies. Spence artfully combines the traditional and innovative; it was one of the first independent schools to use the computer in the lower grades, and multicultural perspectives add excitement and relevance to the traditional core of studies.

"Relevance" is a key concept at Spence. Spence's mission, "to inspire students to meet the ethical and intellectual challenges of life," is summed up in the school motto: "Non Scholae Sed Vitae Discimus: Not For School But For Life We Learn." Spence is committed to a diverse, academically talented student body. One parent said, "It's very fast paced; you need to have a child who can handle that."

In 1998, Head of School Mrs. Edes Gilbert retired; she was the last of a generation of Grand Dames who governed the prestigious Manhattan girls' school over the past twenty years. Arlene Joy Gibson was selected to lead Spence into the twenty-first century. Educated at Bryn Mawr College, Ms. Gibson's area of study is Latin America; she was a Fulbright Scholar in Political Science at the University of the Republic, Montevideo, Uruguay. An advocate of single sex education, Gibson was formerly headmistress of a girls' school in Summit, New Jersey, and she was founding President of the National Coalition of Girls' Schools. "What attracted me to Spence," Gibson told us, "was the relationship between the students and the faculty. The atmosphere, which I observed in the classrooms, was positively electric. Students were asking such intelligent and insightful questions that they stretched the thinking of the entire class, while teachers challenged students to probe ever deeper into the material. Everywhere, there was the excitement that comes from learning. Even in the youngest grades of the school, Spence truly forms a community of scholars."

Recently, Spence successfully completed a ten-year NYSAIS evaluation for reaccredidation. "The Spence traditions of rigor and inquiry, as well as its concern for meeting the challenges of diversity and the demands of a rapidly changing world are strong themes. The celebration and promotion of the role of women are inextricably entwined with all aspects of the life of the school," wrote the Visiting Committee in its report about Spence.

In August 1999, the Board of Trustees purchased a landmark building at 56 East 93rd Street, just two blocks from the school's main building. By September 2002, Spence anticipates that the newly renovated state-of-the-art facility that is to be the new home for the Lower School (grades kindergarten through 4th) will be open. There will be more homerooms and the kindergarten spaces will be larger. Computer and science labs will be designed to serve the needs of Lower School girls. At 91st Street, the expansion of Middle and Upper School facilities will include a Library Media Center and additional science labs. There will also be more meeting and conference spaces for students and teachers and a new gym.

Getting in: Spence is one of the few very selective schools where parents can have an individual tour and interview before they even apply. In recent years, transferring in after kindergarten has been very difficult. Admissions personnel told us, "No letters of recommendation and no photos please." What are they looking for? "We are offering a place to a girl who will take full advantage of everything a Spence education has to offer." One parent was very impressed by the Upper School student who led her tour: "She was so open, obviously not scripted, and she answered all our questions, which indicated to me that Spence is proud of what it does, and the girls are not afraid to talk about it." Parents are given a card with the name of the young woman who led their tour so that they can contact her through the admissions office if they have any additional questions. Once the application is made, parents applying for kindergarten are given an appointment for their daughter's interview. In the Lower School, this takes place with a small group of other girls at the school. In the Upper and Middle Schools, the appointment is individual. Spence has a wait list.

One mother told us that there is no typical Spence girl: "What distinguishes Spence from the other girls' schools is that there is no norm here. The girls are individuals and all are enthusiastic about learning."

Parents: A parent described the parent body at Spence as dominated by two groups: "Those with well-worn, polished shoes (old money), and those with brand-new $450 Ferragamos (new money)." There is a growing contingent of media types. Another parent described the parent body as "some families who don't live on their salaries—attorneys, investment bankers, independent entrepreneurs." But the Upper School is more diverse. Many prominent Jewish families feel comfortable at Spence; we were told that "Ascension through the ranks of Spence's Parents Association requires a certain amount of social skill and savvy." Held at the Millennium Hotel, "Celebrating Excellence," the 2000 PA Benefit featured a panel discussion with moderator Katie Couric and panelists including Cokie Roberts and Stanley Crouch. Class cocktail parties or suppers are held at Spence. The Spring Event for new parents is a reception in the dining room at which fifth grade girls serve as hostesses.

Program: The Lower School curriculum is integrated where possible; drama and art are often incorporated. The girls spend lots of time in the big block area in the kindergarten classroom. Each kindergarten class has two teachers, and the class frequently breaks into small groups. Reading readiness begins in kindergarten using both Whole Language and phonics. There is a resource center for students who need support. A parent said, "Teachers reinforce learning through writing, speaking, observation, drawing." Classes write and illustrate their own books.

In kindergarten, students learn about world cultures (China, Korea, Puerto Rico, the Amazon) through through the lens of the family unit. Kindergartners do units on various countries for which they make passports and cameras, and as the teacher reads from a book about a country, a student says "click" and later draws a picture of the mental image she had "taken." The girls bring in items from other countries and create their own museum in a corner of the room.

In kindergarten parents are invited to spend a morning with their daughters sometime during the year to share a special talent or interest with the class. They also come in for Parents' Visiting Day. In one kindergarten class a parent came to talk about his trip to China. If parents have any questions, teachers are always available.

Computer classes are part of the curriculum in all division of the school. Alumni from the late seventies remember an emphasis on computer even then. In grades kindergarten through fifth, LOGO, a computer graphics language, is taught. Keyboarding and word processing are taught in fourth. The Lower School has its own computer lab with Macintosh computers. There is a fully equipped Lower School science lab and two science teachers whose sole responsibility is to work with kindergartners through fifth graders. One computer science course is required in the Upper School and several advanced courses are offered, including "AP Computer Science."

In addition to academic subjects, first graders take courses in art, music, and physical education. Art, dance and drama teachers are working professionals. In the spacious art room we saw highly individualized stick puppets and masks. Throughout the social studies curriculum, the brochure states, there is a "special emphasis on the role of women in history and focus on the rich diversity of cultures," and social studies is coordinated with language arts, music and art. For example, a parent told us about a unit on East Africa during which the girls "built African huts, lived in them, did homework in them." Second graders read biographies and write book reports about "someone who made a difference." Eleanor Roosevelt, Florence Nightingale and Ann Sullivan are particularly popular because the unit includes coming to school in period costumes.

Second graders are also introduced to chess with each devoting a semester to learning the intricacies of the game. The Spence Second Act Chess Team was the first all-girls chess team to compete in the NYC Scholastic Chess Championship.

One year, for an integrated second grade unit on baseball, a parent told us, "For English they read the biography of Jackie Robinson, for art they studied baseball murals and created their own, in history they examined integration and baseball and in gym, they learned the essence of the game—they played it!"

Third graders participate in an immigrant project; they study a person or family from another country. They also study the history of New York and take many field trips to places such as Philipsburg Manor, Ellis Island, The Museum of the City of New York and the Natural History Museum.

"Simulations" enrich the fourth and fifth grade social studies curriculum. Art is incorporated into these simulations as well as research and writing skills. Fourth graders play the Economics Game, an activity in which the girls apply their mathematical knowledge to real world experiences. Each week the girls are paid a salary of $7.50. From that salary they must pay certain fixed expenses such as rent, food and taxes. Their variable expenses also include charitable donations and health expenses. To supplement their income, the girls write business plans, consult with the Better Business Bureau (their teacher) and set up their own businesses. Eventually the girls are able to invest in the stock market, just like Mom and Dad. As part of the fifth grade United States history unit, students imagine that they are colonists trying to survive in the New World. In the spring they take a "simulated" covered-wagon trip across the Western United States and construct detailed models of their wagon train.

Foreign language begins in third grade, with a choice between French and Spanish. One parent said games and songs are used to teach language in the early years. An optional second language can be elected in seventh grade.

Health education starts early and covers a variety of topics from nutrition to body image and anatomy to peer and family relationships. As part of the social and emotional learning curriculum, the fifth grade participates in the prepare/personal safety program. More important, parents say that self-confidence, self-esteem and leadership are constantly reinforced in the girls: "They are always supporting the girls in their choices and decisions," "The girls are self-confident from beginning to end."

Drama, dance and music are part of the curriculum in each grade. The head of the Lower School told us, "Everyone should see herself as a dancer, researcher, geographer; there is always a place for each student to excel." Kindergartners perform at the Holiday Pageant in December. Fourth graders perform a ballet. Lower School chorus begins in third grade. The sixth grade chorus, a Middle School chorus and Glee Club are open to all. The Select Choir (which travels abroad) and three chamber ensembles in the Upper School are open by audition. There is an instrumental music program for grades one through twelve, and private lessons at Spence are in great demand.

The dance program is extensive: folk, jazz, ballet, in addition to physical education classes. One second grade mother said of her daughter's dance performance: "They were in unison doing these routines; we were all stunned." The Middle and Upper School dance company performs at Symphony Space each year.

All girls gain experience with public speaking. One parent said her daughter, who is normally reluctant to perform on stage, got up in front of the Lower School to read her own poem: "She never would have had the confidence if she hadn't been at Spence." The other girls were supportive. "There was no competitiveness. All the girls' poems were great."

To mark the transition from Lower School, Middle Schoolers (sixth through eighth grades) have their own floor at Spence, and their own uniform. The head of the Middle School told us "there is a real esprit de corps in Middle School; it has its own identity." Middle

Schoolers have their own student council. The sixth grade is fully departmentalized and in the seventh grade letter grades begin.

Art continues to be integrated into the curriculum. The sixth grade class studies a unit on Egypt. The girls learned the names of the gods and pharoahs and all of their attributes and contributions and learned about Egyptian culture and religious beflefs. In math they studied the geometry of the pyramids. In art they made their own hieroglyphics. The Egyptian unit culminated with a visit to the Metropolitan Museum of Art to see the permanent exhibit on pyramids, the Sphinx, dynasties and relevant artifacts.

Eighth graders read *Jane Eyre*, *Romeo and Juliet* and a selection of poetry and American short stories. In history both Western and non-Western cultures are explored, and students hone their research methods. Seventh graders study the Middle Ages and the history of Africa and Islam.

The Middle School fields teams in basketball, softball, soccer, volleyball, track and field and swimming. These teams participate in interscholastic competition.

Middle Schoolers participate in community service projects through the Community Service Club for grades six through twelve and volunteer in the Lower School. Middle Schoolers perform in the annual eighth grade play with boys from neighborhood schools. Annual dances for seventh and eighth graders provide other opportunities to socialize with the opposite sex.

Contact among grades is important to Spence girls. Middle and Upper School students attend Wednesday morning assemblies together as well as their own assemblies. The Middle School has its own assembly on Tuesday mornings, the Upper School on Mondays. Mixing of grades occurs in the lunchroom: Upper School students eat all together according to their schedule, not by grade. The head of school and teachers eat with the girls. In Middle School, during Secret Sisters Week, Middle School girls from different grades are assigned to give small gifts to each other. Field Day offers students on mixed teams a chance to work together with girls from other grades.

If you go straight through Spence from kindergarten to twelfth you are known as a "survivor." Attrition typically occurs after eighth grade when some girls go to boarding schools or, occasionally, to a coed day school. According to a survivor, "The work builds up in eighth and ninth grades and then increases again in tenth and eleventh, but if you're good at budgeting your time you don't notice."

The Upper School at Spence consists of grades nine through twelve. The Upper School is academically rigorous. Students who enter at ninth grade are required to ease their transition by attending the summer Jumpstart Program, an orientation program that is free of charge. Girls with a problem subject can go to the Resource Center. "If necessary," says a student, "teachers will even look over your notes with you." Classes are kept small, about twelve to fifteen students. The average course load is five to six full credit courses. In addition to the usual core subjects, computer science, performing arts, speech and health are Upper School requirements, as are four years of foreign language or three of one language and two of another. Six APs are offered, including foreign language, studio art, calculus, biology and physics. Students are required to take two years of lab science; most choose to take another advanced-level science course. In 1993–1994 the science labs were completely updated. Each of the science labs now has a computer with CD-ROM.

Students say that a friendly teacher-student relationship at Spence makes their school unique. One reason for this is that teachers in the Middle and Upper Schools must teach a range of grades and as a result get to know the girls as they mature. Teachers also act as advisors to their students both as homeroom teachers and as faculty advisors to student-led clubs.

According to the brochure, in English a "special emphasis is placed on a cross-cultural study of literature so that students are exposed to a range of material outside the Western tradition that enriches their understanding of other cultures." An elective course in world literature is required. Senior Seminar and/or independent study are also available.

Clara Spence, visionary educator and founder of The Spence School, believed in a broad curriculum to meet the interests of the students. Today, many courses at Spence are developed based upon student interest or faculty initiative. Reflecting increased student interest the history elective program in the Upper School includes "Conflicts in the Middle East," "Latin America: From Conquest to Independence," as well as Indian History and Japanese History. In a thoughtful course called "African-American Literature," students are introduced to the writings of the men and women who shaped contemporary black American culture: DuBois, Hurston, King, Baldwin, Malcolm X and others.

Students with proficiency in the arts can take advanced course work in studio art, photography and the performing arts.

401

Spence has wonderful opportunities for foreign language study abroad including "Adventures in Real Communication," open to tenth through twelfth graders, who can take a one- or two-month program in France, Spain or Latin America. There is the School Year Abroad option for eleventh and twelfth graders, the Swiss Semester in Zermatt for tenth graders, the San Patricio Exchange in Madrid for tenth or eleventh graders and for ninth graders, a one- or two-month spring program in Evreux, France. For those who prefer an experience closer to home, participation in the Maine Coast Semester in Chewonki, Maine, study at the Mountain School in Vermont in association with Milton Academy or the Island School Program in the Caribbean are offered.

An eleventh grader told us that after school most girls either do homework, participate in school clubs or go out with their boyfriends, who pick them up at school. "Athletics are popular, chorus is fabulous and so is the choral master. Attendance at dance concerts and Glee Club events is good," she said.

Ninth and tenth graders have privileges; they can leave school if they have parental permission. Eleventh and twelfth graders can simply sign out. Ninth and tenth graders share "the Pit," a lounge area contiguous with the ninth and tenth grade lockers. Juniors and seniors each have their own lounge (visitors are not given a tour through it). Senior privileges include not wearing their uniform in spring of senior year, coming in late Thursdays and Fridays (if they don't have a class) and being allowed to use the elevators. "You'd think they'd never used an elevator before. They stop at every floor," says one parent.

There is an Upper School student council. One student council event is Color or Theme Days: Themes are picked such as Western Day or Come As You Are Day and the faculty dress up too. The Upper School student council is currently grappling with weightier issues such as considering graduation requirements, discussing the school uniform and establishing an honor code.

There are numerous opportunities for faculty-led and student-led extracurricular participation at Spence. Faculty-led activities include dramatic productions, dance company, athletic teams and chorus, while student-led activities include drama club, Amnesty International, French club and Spanish club. Because of the size and unique nature of its community, many students have the opportunity to assume a leadership position in a club or activity by the time they graduate.

Commencement is held at the Church of the Heavenly Rest.

Awards are given out at the Athletic Awards Banquet for athletic achievement and sportsmanship. The White Blazer Award is given to a student who is well respected in the athletic community, demonstrating determination, sportsmanship, cooperation, dedication and leadership. At Final Assembly external academic awards, such as National Merit Scholarships, are announced, but graduates no longer have the traditional Spence prizes for special academic achievements bestowed upon them. It is thought this will discourage excessive competition, according to the school. But one junior told us, "They didn't acknowledge the good work that everybody did."

When asked what embodies the spirit of Spence, Head of School Arlene Gibson replied: "The joy that is noticeable in the halls of the school." The NYSAIS committee added, "It's the emphasis the school places on academic rigor, self-discovery, the pleasures of risk taking and the realization of the potential of every child."

Popular College Choices   Yale, Cornell, Princeton, Harvard, University of Pennsylvania, Wesleyan, Brown, Duke, Oberlin, Tufts, Vassar, Amherst, Columbia

Traditions   Opening Assembly, Lower School Halloween party, Lower School New Parents' Dinner, Lower School Field Day, grade five sleepover and breakfast, spring drama, eighth grade play, eighth grade trip, skating party, Middle School Sing-Off Competition, Middle School picnic, Saturday movies (winter), Lower School holiday program, Father/Daughter Evening, Mother/Daughter Tea, third and fourth grade foreign language breakfasts, Grandparents' and Special Friends Day, Secret Sisters Week, Dance Concert at Symphony Space, Middle and Upper School Concert at Church of St. Thomas More, Book Fair, clothing sale, Choral group, Spence Boutique, student council 91st Street Fair, grade ten Interschool trip to Frost Valley.

Publications   Newspaper: *Spence Voice*
Literary arts magazine: *Fingerprints*
Yearbook: *Threshold*
Newsletter on current political issues: *Spark*

Community Service Requirement   No specific number of hours: in grades 6–12 the board of the Community Service Club is made up of two elected representatives from each of the grades, along with an elected student head; weekly meetings are held to plan a variety of fund-raising and volunteer activities such as tutoring projects in local public schools, food and clothing drives, visits to the elderly or homebound, work in soup kitchens or daycare organizations. The service club plans an annual Community Service Fair

Hangouts   Jackson Hole (hamburger restaurant around the corner on Madison), junior lounge, senior lounge

The Studio Elementary School

124A West 95th Street
New York, NY 10025
(212) 678-2416

Coed
Nursery (22 mos)–6th grade
Not accessible

Ms. Janet C. Rotter, Head of School
Ms. Barbara Kolenda, Director of Admissions

Birthday Cutoff   none

Enrollment   Total enrollment: approximately 100
Nursery places (2's and nearly 2's): 10
3's and nearly 3's places: 12
Early childhood: 16
Kindergarten and up: 5 to 6 places in K, as available in upper grades

Tuition Range 2001–2002
All day program, 5 days a week (8 A.M.–6 P.M.) 9/1–7/31: $16,225
2's and nearly 2's: 2 mornings $3660
3's and nearly 3's: 3 mornings $6100
Early childhood: 5 mornings $8,925, 5 full days: $13,230
K–6th grade: 5 days kindergarten through 6th grade $13,230–13,545
All fees are included

Financial Aid/Scholarship   10% of the student body receives some form of aid
Approximately $75,000 budgeted annually

Endowment   None

After-School Program   Extended day program until 5:50 P.M.; a variety of creative and recreational activities for an additional payment

Summer Program   Summer Camp from mid-June through the end
of July; a variety of creative and recreational activities for an additional payment

———

The Studio Elementary School was founded in 1971 by Robert
and Dolores Welber as a "one room schoolhouse" in Greenwich Village. Three years later Janet Rotter, a graduate of Bank Street,
came to Studio as an assistant teacher. She is currently Head of the
School, as she has been for the past sixteen years. The Welbers retain their affiliation as honorary members of the board of trustees.
In addition, Mr. Welber continues to teach Music and Movement
classes.

In 1977 the school moved to a building on the Upper West Side
which is leased from the adjoining synagogue. (The school has no religious affiliation.) In addition to several bright classrooms, the school
has a well-equipped kitchen, a sunny yard, a library, and a large
common room which also serves as the cafeteria and a toddler gym.
The Studio Elementary School has always emphasized a sound traditional curriculum combined with a developmental approach paying
attention to each child's social and emotional growth. The school has a
neighborhood feeling and parent involvement is welcome.

Getting in: Parents can attend an open house/tour before
applying. Applicants and their parents meet with the head of the
school. Children over age 5 also visit a classroom. ERB testing is
requested for applicants age 8 and above.

Program: One of the founding principles of the Studio Elementary School is that children of all ages can learn from each other; the
school still uses cross-age and cross-grade grouping. There is a teacher
and an assistant in each classroom through second grade. Class groupings are reshuffled each year.

"The school's emphasis is on learning how to think and create and
not just fulfilling requirements," says Ms. Rotter. "Students learn that
there is not just one way to get to the solution of a problem. Thinking,
and the interaction between student and teacher, is the point." The
school provides a lot of unstructured materials so children are free to
experiment. Children can work independently within a group setting,
focusing on the concepts and skills that will help them move on to the
next level of development.

Attention is paid to the emotional life of the students. A parent
told us, "The teacher is very aware of my child's attitude towards her

work. They work with her on the development of self-discipline, organization and self-evaluation in addition to teaching the curriculum."

A unique aspect of the Studio school curriculum is the Kitchen Science class. Each day a hot lunch is prepared by a team of students (ages three and up) and served to the entire school. Cooking combines skill work in math (measuring), reading and writing (recipes and menus), science (mixing different things together) and social studies (a group studying colonial America will prepare a lunch representative of that period).

The block room is used by all groups through the six and seven-year-olds. After "walking and exploring" the neighborhood, younger children will recreate what they saw in blocks. For physical education, younger children go to the play yard every day, older children (five and up) go to Central Park.

Reading is taught using eclectic methods including Whole Language, sight words, basal readers, and phonics. Children are also read to every day. We noticed a cozy carpeted platform with cushions for independent reading in the hallway between nursery classrooms. In math students might have a group lesson, then work independently on problem solving and skills.

Homework begins at age six (an assignment time is built into the school day) when they begin to introduce the requirements of the outside world. Parent/teacher conferences are held three times a year. Grading begins in the middle elementary classes.

Graduates Attend various independent schools including: Saint Ann's School, Ethical Culture/Fieldston, Friends, Trevor Day and Trinity, as well as various public school programs (including the Computer Schools and the Delta Honors Program at M.S. 54).

The Town School

540 East 76th Street
New York, NY 10021
(212) 288-4383
website: www.townschool.org

Coed
Nursery–8th grade
Accessible

Ms. Joyce Gregory Evans, Head of School
Ms. Natasha Sahadi, Director of Admissions

Uniform   None for nursery and kindergarten divisions
Lower and Upper School girls: plaid kilt or navy jumper or navy
and tan skirt; solid-colored collared or turtleneck shirt; girls may
wear solid navy, gray or tan pants except on Fridays; sweaters,
socks, leggings and tights may be worn in the colors of the plaid
Lower and Upper School boys: solid navy, gray or tan pants; solid-
colored, collared or turtleneck shirt in the colors of the plaid
Friday is dress-up day for assembly: Girls wear skirts, boys wear
navy jacket, white or blue shirt and tie
The first Tuesday of each month is a non-uniform day: Denim and
sweat clothes may be worn

Birthday Cutoff   Children entering nursery school must be 3 by
September 1
Children entering kindergarten must be 5 by September 1

Enrollment   Total enrollment: 385
Nursery places: approximately 18
Kindergarten places: approximately 26
8th grade graduating class: approximately 36

Grades   Trimester system
Letter and effort grades are given in the Upper School beginning
with the second trimester of 5th grade
Departmentalization begins in 5th grade

Tuition Range 2001–2002 $11,000 to $20,800, nursery–8th

Tuition includes lunch, trips; Parents Association dues are $30 annually.

A tuition refund plan, extended payment plan and accident plan are available

Financial Aid/Scholarship   Approximately 14% of the student body receive some form of financial aid

Endowment $16 million

Diversity   11 Prep for Prep students enrolled as of Fall 2000

Diversity Curriculum Guide developed by Town School faculty

Diversity Committee: a school-sponsored committee comprising parents, teachers and administrators, for the purpose of sharing multicultural interests, concerns and suggestions; monthly meetings are posted on school calendar; the committee includes members from the Parents Association

Homework   Because of the long school day, homework in the early years is kept to a minimum:

Kindergarten: occasionally

1st grade—HomeLinks twice a week

2nd: beginning in the second half of the year, about 15 minutes

3rd and 4th: 45 minutes–1 hour

4th, 5th and 6th: 1 hour–1½ hours

7th 8th: 2–3 hours

After-School Program   The Town School After-School Programs are Postscript and Clubhouse

Junior Postscript Program: for pre-K and kindergarten students, Monday through Thursday, 2:45–4:00 P.M., Friday, 12:30–1:30 P.M., a variety of creative and recreational activities; a fee is required

Postscript Program: for grades 1–6, Monday through Thursday 3:45–5:00 P.M., Friday, 1:00–2:30 P.M., with extended day option until 6:00 P.M.; activities include: fencing, basketball, computer, photography, woodworking, gymnastics, arts and crafts, CATS tennis, theatre; a fee is required

Clubhouse Program: a multi-aged option with rotating choices daily, beginning at 12:00 until 6:00 P.M.

Intramural sports program

Interscholastic athletic competition for grades 5–8

Summer Program   Summersault program for ages 3–9, open to children from the community, an additional payment is required

---

The Town School is a coed elementary school that ends with eighth grade. It overlooks the East River on quiet East 76th Street, opposite John Jay Park. The Town School emphasizes warmth and is sensitive to the developmental needs of young children. A traditional core of academic skills is taught using an innovative curriculum. The 1936 school brochure description of Town was accurate then and now: "Progressive but not radical . . . its object is to create an environment in which the child may develop the best that is in him and give him a thorough understanding of every subject he studies." Expectations are high but this is not a pressure-cooker environment. Because of the focus on the elementary grades, parents say there is an intimacy that provides an opportunity for leadership and the development of self-confidence. Students leave Town well prepared and well rounded.

Founded in 1913 by Miss Hazel Hyde and originally known as "Miss Hyde's School," The Town School acquired its present name in 1936 during the era of the town car and town house. The school motto roughly translates as "Be joyful in the pursuit of knowledge." Former head of school Fred Calder describes the committed faculty and administrators at Town School as "a group of people who [still] believe that the education of young children begins and ends with warmth, humor and good sense." Miss Hyde was known for attracting exceptional faculty who were very involved in running the school. To this day, the teachers at The Town School retain their influence through the "corporation" (once known as "the members"), who advise the head of school.

As of July 1993, Joyce Gregory Evans became the head of school. As head of an elementary school in California, Evans was successful in diversifying the school population, parent education, fund-raising, administration and curriculum development. Evans' view of the challenges in education for the twenty-first century indicate that The Town School will be staying the course upon which it has already embarked: "Education used to be seen as filling students with a body of knowledge. Now we recognize that the process of learning is at the core. Critical thinking, problem solving, gaining access to information and learning cooperatively are all vital ingredients of a superior education." Parents agree that there has always been an emphasis on the process of learning at Town rather than the rote accumulation of facts. Parents say, "Children learn how to think, and they learn that it's OK to be wrong or to fail."

In 1985 The Town School sold air rights to Glick Development Affiliates for $7 million. Some of this windfall went toward a capital improvement and maintenance fund, some toward the school's sizeable endowment and a portion went into renovation and addition of facilities, including two new science labs for Lower and Upper School students, a new darkroom and a computer room. Town students have use of their own auditorium, as well as a full-size gym. The school is uncluttered, clean and carpeted (no echoing hallways here). It's easy to see why children are comfortable here.

Getting in: There are no essay questions on the application. Parents may tour the school before they apply for their child. Our tour guide was very knowledgeable and didn't mind answering numerous questions. At a later date, parents bring their kindergarten applicant in for a small group interview while the parents meet with the director of admissions.

Parents: The parent body at Town is relatively low-key. Says one parent, "These aren't all parents who went to private schools themselves." The Parents Association was founded in 1951. There is a monthly newsletter to inform parents about activities and meetings. Curriculum evenings and parent education seminars keep parents apprised of what's going on in the world of education and at Town (a recent panel discussed gender issues in elementary education). Head of School Evans realizes that "parents [today] particularly need to discuss the challenges they face with their children." Activities for Town families include the Welcome Back Picnic in the Fall in Central Park, Science Night, the Book Fair and the Spring Benefit. One mother described the events she attended: "Everyone came, there were nice feelings, nothing was hyped up, just a wonderful, warm environment."

Programs: Kindergartners have a fairly long day, from 8:15 A.M. until 2:30 P.M. Monday through Thursday and until noon on Fridays. First through eighth graders eat hot lunch at school; pre-kindergartners and kindergartners have to bring their own lunches. There are two kindergarten classrooms, each with two teachers. (All of the nursery and kindergarten division head teachers have a master's in Early Childhood Education.) In addition to the teachers, there are three language arts specialists and two school psychologists. The kindergarten rooms are situated at opposite ends of a short carpeted hallway where, during activity time, children from each class can play and socialize. Each kindergarten classroom has a block area, wood shop, listening corner, two computers, lots of pets and their own bathroom and kitchen. The children were busily working in small groups, some with clay or wood, some painting.

The Town School has traditionally celebrated the arts, and art is integrated into the curriculum at every level. Grades one through four visit the Lower School art studio once a week. We saw bas-relief self-portraits and still lifes in the style of Matisse. There is a kiln for firing clay. Students frequently visit museums, and visiting artists come in to share their art, music, or drama expertise.

The music and dance curriculum begins in nursery when both are taught simultaneously. First and second graders learn the Orff method. Third graders learn to play the recorder. Private instrumental instruction is available both before and after school. Students who love to perform have the opportunity, and can work on costumes, scenery and stage managing as well. Children can perform at assemblies, and there are two full-scale musicals a year. The fourth grade musical typically has more than one lead: There were four Charlies for "Charlie and the Chocolate Factory" one year. There is an Upper School chorus and band. A highlight of the year is the annual eighth grade musical.

Unique to The Town School is the community based curriculum, used in kindergarten and developed by Town School teachers. It is a curriculum revolving around a year long study of how the neighborhood community mirrors the school community. It integrates language arts, science, math and the arts into a comprehensive educational program using field trips as the central core to build skills in observing, collecting and recording information.

The language arts program is literature based and by first grade students are writing in response journals daily. Invented spelling is used, but spelling skills are taught in second grade. First graders move out of the classroom for science in the Lower School science lab, library, gym, dance, music, art and Spanish.

Students from kindergarten through second grade have computers in their classrooms. By third grade students use the computer lab (which is equipped with PC's where they learn keyboarding skills and word processing. Students learn to use software related to the language arts, math and social studies. By fifth grade students take a trimester of math in the computer lab, writing workshop, and Internet research in science, social studies and foreign language.

Fourth graders study their own family unit, write letters to relatives, study their own country (countries) of origin and use this as a basis to learn about other immigrating groups. A book-publishing party is held in the spring. A multicultural curriculum is in place. We were impressed by a project in the first grade that examined the Cinderella myth from the perspective of different cultures, including Chinese and Egyptian. Assemblies often feature multicultural performers. Irish step dancers performed at one assembly and invited the students to come onstage and participate.

In math, using the University of Chicago Math Program, children learn to reason logically, see mathematical patterns and relationships, and understand the presence of math in everyday life. Manipulatives, math games and literature are woven into the curriculum to develop abstract mathematical thinking while reinforcing computational concepts. The Lower School science lab features scaled-down versions of the familiar black tables and stools; the curriculum stresses the process of inquiry. For instance, second graders studying the Northeast woodlands create a nature mural; each child researches a forest animal to add to the mural. Fifth graders studying oceanography use *The Voyage of the Mimi*, a computer companion program. There are numerous trips to reinforce laboratory learning: Third and fourth grade students travel to a working farm; fifth and sixth graders go to Nature's Classroom, an environmental center in northwestern Connecticut. Seventh and eighth graders go to Blairstown, New Jersey, for an Outward Bound-type program.

Parents say that The Town School really "honors individual learning styles." Educators recognize that some children function better with lots of background noise and others appreciate a more quiet setting. (Outside the second grade classroom there is an inviting bench with pillows, perfect for quiet reading, and there are other nooks and crannies for small group activities.) Throughout the Lower School there is no tracking; collaborative units are used instead. Students might have a group lesson and then divide into smaller groups.

There is also recognition that children learn at different rates. Our tour guide told us: "They journey from first through fourth grades at their own rate, but by fourth grade they are all at the same place." The learning specialists at Town move into the classrooms, avoiding the stigma to certain children of being "pulled out" for remedial help. One parent with three children in the school said her children are having different experiences, "as if it were three different schools."

Students use the full-size gym, one of four playroofs or John Jay Park playground, a wonderful resource right across the street. From kindergarten through fourth grade coed cooperative games and skills are stressed. In fifth grade, intramural competition begins. There is a full-size gym, and Upper Schoolers have two double periods a week for sports at Randall's Island. They have a very fine basketball program. In the Upper School the athletically inclined can participate in a variety of single-sex interscholastic sports. Parents say Town is a great place for girls who are interested in sports.

The Upper School at Town is composed of fifth through eighth grades. As in the Lower School, desks in the upper grades are grouped for collaborative learning. But fifth grade is an important transition year with new responsibilities and expectations. The fifth grade day is fully departmentalized and fifth graders begin to receive letter grades in the second trimester of the year. French is introduced in fifth grade; Latin instruction begins in seventh grade. Support is provided: A special study skills course is built into the fifth grade curriculum to help students acclimate to the Upper School. Fifth through eighth graders take a "Lifeskills" program taught by a team including the school nurse that covers AIDS, drugs and alcohol education.

The social studies curriculum in the Upper School compares different cultures during the same time period or with the same theme. Fifth grade studies ancient Egypt, Greece and China; sixth grade studies Medieval Europe and Japan. Seventh grade focuses on The Age of Discovery and Exploration and Pre-colonial America. The eighth grade studies the colonization of America through the Constitutional Convention.

Readings in English focus on the classics and are often related to the social studies curriculum within a spiral curriculum. Science continues to be experiential. The science lab is networked with the computer lab. Collaborative science projects require tremendous research and culminate in a science fair. Town School graduates place well in advanced science and math in the ongoing schools. Each year a number of students are accepted at Stuyvesant High School (one of the specialized New York City public high schools.)

Students have the opportunity to perform in class plays and in musicals. Fifth graders have an intensive trimester of art, music and dramatic arts. The eighth grade performs in a play as a graduation year culminating activity. Upper School students can work on the literary magazine, yearbook or newspaper. Student photographers help provide photographs for the yearbook.

Town students have the opportunity to assume positions of leadership. The student senate is an elected body with co-presidents, co-vice president and class representatives. The senate plans assemblies and organizes social events and community service activities. The Town School has a relationship with Yorkville Common Pantry, and food and clothing drives are often organized on its behalf. There is an in-house recycling program. Town also has a sister school, P.S. 36.

Eighth grade is an important and exciting year at The Town School. The eighth grade musical is the culmination of years of musical training and performance. At graduation the William Lee Younger, Jr. Educational Award is given to "the student who flourished at Town [and] developed into an individual of fine character and dedication to excellence."

Discussion about ninth grade placement begins early in the year when recent Town graduates return to talk about their high schools. All eighth graders take a "Decisions" course and learn to recognize and articulate their own particular talents, strengths and interests. They discuss interviewing and essay writing.

A parent who has sent two children to Town (one is now at Trinity, the other attends an Ivy League college) says, "They care for each child as an individual and work with them until the children find something good in themselves. Kids admire kids with different strengths, and they cheer for each other. Although expectations for academic achievement are high, they care equally about the emotional and social development of each child." A parent says, "My child is known and understood as a whole person." Most Town School graduates choose to go on to the coed day schools. (We ran into Town grads at Trinity—the graduation speaker—and at Dalton—the Student Senate President.) A number also go to the specialized public high schools each year. The close-knit feeling at Town persists after graduation. Parents say: "There is a strong feeling of community. Students go back to school to visit their teachers."

Popular Secondary School Choices   Dalton, Trinity, Horace Mann, Riverdale, Brearley, Spence, Nightingale-Bamford, Columbia Grammar and Prep and Stuyvesant

Traditions   Fall Welcome Back Picnic, Book Fair, parent-faculty musical, Spring Benefit, parent education seminars, class trips for grades 3–8, 4th grade musical, annual 8th grade musical, alumni reunions

Publications   Alumni News: *Currents*
Annual report
Yearbook
Newspaper
The Town School Family News (monthly)
Literary magazine
The Cry of the Wolf Eighth grade short story collection

Community Service Requirement   Community service begins in the nursery program. Every class has a buddy class in another division; student senate organizes community service projects, often in conjunction with the Yorkville Common Pantry; during winter trimester, 5th–8th graders participate in a community service period once a week, going to a nearby soup kitchen and serving lunch to the homeless and so on; 8th graders also work with second grade students at P.S. 36 every Friday after school.

Hangouts   Bagels & Co., John Jay Park, Little Robin's Pizza Parlor (on Friday afternoons)

Trevor Day School

Lower School
Early Childhood Division
(Nursery–Kindergarten)
11 East 89th Street
Elementary School
(1st–5th grade)
4 East 90th Street
New York, NY 10128
Tel (212) 426-3355
FAX (212) 410-6507
e-mail: LSAdmissions@trevornet.org

Upper School
(6th–12th Grade)
1 West 88th Street
New York, NY 10024
Tel (212) 426-3380 Admissions
FAX (212) 873-8520
e-mail: USAdmissions@trevornet.org
website: www.trevor.org

Coed
Nursery–12th grade
Accessible (Both Campuses)

Dr. John H. Dexter, Headmaster
Ms. Deborah Ashe, Director of Admissions, Lower School
Ms. Marcia Roesch, Director of Admissions, Upper School

Uniform   Published dress code that emphasizes safety

Birthday Cutoff   September 1

Enrollment   Total enrollment: 750
   Nursery places: 28
   Kindergarten places: 56
   Graduating class size: approx. 50

Grades   Semester system/trimester system in high school
   Extensive written reports twice a year, plus family conferences for

417

Pre-K through 12
Letter grades begin in 9th grade
Full departmentalization by 5th grade
First final exam in 6th grade

Tuition Range 2001–2002 $13,725 to $22,725, Nursery–12th grade
No additional fees.
Families purchase laptops in 5th and 9th grades

Financial Aid/Scholarship   Approximately 27% of the students receive some form of financial aid, totaling $1.85 million
Average award is $14,000
Percentage of financial award extends to the Afterschool program and to laptop purchase

Endowment $5 million

Diversity   Approximately 17.5 percent students of color
7 Prep for Prep students enrolled as of fall 2000
Students come from Early Steps, Albert G. Oliver Scholarship Program, A Better Chance and TEAK

Homework   Kindergarten–1st: parent/child reading for 30 minutes
2nd: 45 minutes (reading, math, spelling)
3rd: 1 hour
4th: 1½ hours
5th and 6th: 1½–2 hours
6th–8th: 2–2½ hours
9th–12th: Up to 4 hours
(An additional 30 minutes of reading is expected each night for all grades)

After-School Program   Available for Pre-K through 12th grade for an additional fee, includes recreational activities and athletics with numerous team sports offered in the Upper School.

Summer Program   All programs require an additional payment
June sports program (ages 4–11), Trevor Day Students only
Summer Day Camp: for 3–5 year olds; 5 weeks, 9 A.M.–3:00 P.M.
Trevor Day Students have priority in enrollment

Trevor Day School, previously known as "The Day School," was founded as a nursery school in 1930 under the aegis of the Church of the Heavenly Rest. In 1971, The Day School, having grown into a primary school, became independent of the church. The rector of the church continues to serve ex-officio on the board of trustees but Trevor Day School has no religious affiliation or instruction.

In 1991 Trevor Day School expanded further by purchasing the old Walden-Lincoln school building on West 88th Street and creating a high school division (grades nine through twelve). In 1992, the school connected its Early Childhood Division located on East 89th Street to its East 90th Street Elementary Division. Today, Trevor Day School is divided into the Lower School and the Upper School. The Lower School has two divisions: Early Childhood through kindergarten and grades one through five. The Upper School, located at 1 West 88th Street, is comprised of the Middle School (grades six through eight) and the High School (grades nine through twelve).

According to a spokesperson, the School recently changed its name from "The Day School" to "Trevor Day School" because the former name sounded too "generic." The school took the last name of long-standing board member, Paul Trevor, who had made many significant contributions to the school.

Trevor Day School offers an eclectic blend of the old and the new. There is an elegant marble staircase in the limestone lobby of the East Side building suggesting that this is a staid traditional school, but don't be misled. Trevor Day School has incorporated many innovative features into a curriculum that stresses active learning: common rooms, Miniterms, family conferences and a policy of no letter grades until ninth grade. Although these can be considered elements of progressive education, Head of School John "Jack" Dexter says, "We do not categorize ourselves as progressive. We pay attention to a traditional curriculum but actively engage students in their own learning with investigation, discovery, discussion and evaluation."

Dexter has a definite philosophy about education and the development of young children. A parent told us: "Dexter is warm, articulate, with a great sense of humor. He's relaxed and in tune with the kids; it's hard to talk about Trevor Day School without mentioning him." At the Upper School open house Dexter described Trevor Day School as a learning community, "a community that values diversity, in which each person is a natural resource." The school's mission statement emphasizes cooperation and collaboration rather than competition as a motivational device.

Getting in: Trevor Day School offers information evenings and tours in the Fall that parents may attend before they apply. Do call and ask for these dates. Once they have applied, parents come to the school twice, once for a parent tour and once with their child. Children applying for kindergarten are met in the lobby of the 89th Street building and go upstairs to work at a table with age-appropriate materials, followed by a snack and free play. One parent who said that she barely survived the admissions process in general, commented that "Trevor was wonderful at handling the shy, quiet child, both through admissions and in the classroom."

On a separate date parents are taken on a tour of the school and then meet with a member of the admissions staff for about twenty minutes. Parent representatives and admissions staff lead the tour groups and they are very informative as well as candid. Nursery applicants are not separated from their parents, but are engaged by a teacher while the parents talk to a member of the admissions staff. Recommendations are optional.

Parents: Parents describe the parent body at Trevor Day as a "mixed but cohesive group of East Siders, West Siders, Jews, WASPs and families of color. But the parents, along with the students, teachers and administrators, all share a strong enthusiasm for the school." All parents are automatically members of the Parents Association, which sponsors community-building activities, such as the two-week-long program "Everybody Reads at Trevor Day School," and runs several fund-raising events including the very popular Auction and Fall Festival.

Program: Trevor Day School is composed of four divisions, Early Childhood, Elementary, Middle and High Schools. The Early Childhood Division consists of Nursery, Pre-kindergarten and kindergarten. The kindergarten day at Trevor Day School is long, from 8:40 to 3:00 P.M., Monday through Thursday, and until 2:00 on Friday. There are four kindergarten classes, each with twelve to fifteen children, a head teacher and an assistant teacher. Parents say that Day School students have the benefit of two teachers in all Early Childhood classes. Our guide told us that "the homeroom is an extension of the home." The smallish square classrooms are neat, well-equipped, clean and carpeted and each has its own bathroom and a locker for each child. Students visit the library weekly in half groups, where parent volunteers read to children and help them select books. Foreign languages

(French and Spanish) are introduced in Nursery. Pre-Kindergartners and kindergartners visit the well-equipped art and music studios twice a week in half groups; they participate in physical education and roof time (on the padded playroof), daily, in half groups and as a class, and there are specialists in physical education, foreign language music and art. Lower Schoolers go to a well-equipped art room staffed by a full-time teacher and an assistant. Their expressive and very individual work is permanently displayed throughout the 89th Street building a part of a school-wide Art Show.

Parents say kindergarten at Trevor Day School is "academic" but nurturing and "takes into account the varying rates of development of the children." Along with traditional skills the children gain a sense of security. "The development of self-esteem is important," say parents. "They know each child is cut from a different cloth." The curriculum is structured but not too much so. In Pre-kindergarten and kindergarten the classes split into half groups for traditional academics, including reading and math Pre-kindergartners and Kindergartners begin working with math manipulatives and math games, using big books, practicing letter sounds, writing in their journals using approximate spelling and handwriting skills.

We observed a group of focused children sitting in chairs in a row learning letter sounds, but parents say, "There is very little recitation or rote learning, it's not learn or else—it's learn at your own pace." Dexter says, "Kids should always be working on things they don't know. We want children to make conclusions rather than just remember the answers."

The Elementary Division consists of grades one through five. Hot lunch is offered starting in grade 1. Classroom life in this division is informal but the day is structured. The school believes that children should feel free to make mistakes: "We'd rather have a child take chances, do something daring." In order to free children from the constraints of working for grades, there are no letter or number grades until ninth grade. Students in nursery through eighth grade receive narrative reports, with extensive checklists, sometimes as long as three to four typed pages, and also receive regular feedback from teachers. Family or cooperative conferences starting in Pre-kindergarten and continuing through the High School are a feature unique to Trevor Day School. Students participate in the family conference whose goal is to reinforce the idea that the students share the responsibility for their own education. Teachers and parents remain in close contact throughout the year.

There are three homerooms in the first and second grades with two teachers in each class of about eighteen children. There are several computers in each first grade classroom. But by third grade students are divided into four small homerooms with about twelve students and one teacher, adjacent to a common room. The common room at Trevor Day School is considered the nucleus of the learning community—a place where students can do homework, use the computers, play chess or learn independently with the guidance of faculty. Time-management and a cooperative teacher-student relationship are two themes central to the school's philosophy. Homework assignments begin in second grade. Assignments are usually posted by the teacher. Students can complete some of their homework in school during common room time, which is part of their daily schedule.

Parents say there is more social interaction with the entire grade during the early years because groups are mixed, not tracked. One parent said of a new student, "He was so happy at Trevor Day School that he wanted to spend weekends there!"

Classroom life in this division is informal but the day is structured. Reading and math groups might be as small as four to eight children. Third grade uses literature and word processing as part of the writing experience while the children continue to practice their handwriting in workbooks. During math we saw some of the class using Cuisenaire rods, some doing math with numbers on a blackboard and some sitting or lying on the floor working with manipulatives or math games. The students in all three groups were actively engaged. The Investigation Colloquium Method is used to teach science, emphasizing "child-directed exploration and interpretation." First graders study snails; second graders, life cycles (which includes plants and mealworms); third graders, environmental science; fourth and fifth grade students use a newly renovated science lab and work collaboratively.

The computer program at Trevor Day School begins in the nursery school in the classrooms; beginning in third grade students concentrate on word processing, data-base use in the common rooms and some desktop publishing. All of the classrooms have computers and second, and third grades have their own computer labs. Fourth grade has a mobile laptop lab and wireless classrooms while fifth grade students have their own laptops. In the fall of 1996, Trevor Day School became the first private school in Manhattan to join the Microsoft/Anytime Anywhere Learning program. All students in grades five through twelve use laptops for inquiry and learning. (Families purchased them outright; there is a payment plan.) Students are generally enthusiastic about the project although carrying the laptops, which weigh five pounds, along with heavy textbooks in their backpacks has resulted in additional business for local chiropractors! The goal of this program is for the computer to become a "transparent" tool, like paper and pencil. "I use the laptop in every class," said a seventh grader. "In English to write essays and take notes on classroom reading, in history, foreign language and science to take notes and do homework, in math for writing assignments and graphing."

Social studies topics begin with community and interdependency, and students learn early on an awareness and respect for difference. Topics broaden from a study of family history to units on immigration and ethnic diversity in New York City and the history of Manhattan Island. The third grade studies Native American populations. Fourth graders begin a two-year sequence in American history.

Music and movement are an integral part of the curriculum. Study begins with the Orff, Kodaly and Dalcroze methods and students start learning to play recorders in third grade. A video called "Growing Musicians" is available to view on the school's website.

Grades four and five are partially departmentalized. The homeroom teacher, who is also a subject teacher, serves as advisor to approximately twelve children. Students make use of a central common room with glass-fronted classrooms on the perimeter. There are three common room periods a week as well as a daily quiet reading period.

The "Miniterm" is first introduced in grades four and five. This is a three-week period during which academic electives occupy the morning while afternoons are reserved for classes that take students beyond the traditional subjects. Sometimes, Miniterm is devoted to an original musical, a production that relates to "the lives and experiences of the students, using material taken from various literary sources as well as the students' own work." Music and dance from other cultures are often incorporated. Throughout the year there are opportunities for students to gain confidence in public speaking and to participate in plays. A parent said, "Nobody is ever excluded. Everyone is in the plays, and no one is made to feel inferior."

Fourth and fifth graders have an extended day once a week for physical education at Randalls Island.

After five years of studying both French and Spanish each year, fourth graders now choose to specialize in one language for the next two years.

Parents praise the art program, which stresses each child's individual expression, as well as the attainment of skills. According to the head of the Lower School art department, "Children need to be who they are. If one is an artist, he is given a lot of credit for becoming an artist." From an early age, Trevor Day School students learn to use and maintain a variety of art materials from a central supply area. By fourth grade they are working on projects in various media, including drawing, painting, collage, 3-D paper, ceramics and printmaking. Starting in Middle School, students can do film and computer animation, and graphics and photography in the school darkroom.

The Middle School is composed of grades six through eight. The Middle School common room is the center of student and teacher activity. The homeroom/advisor system changes somewhat in the Middle School. Eight to nine students share an advisor and meet together at the start of each day. The advisor actively supports each student's intellectual and social growth, acting as an advocate and academic counselor as well as the primary contact for both family and and school. In addition, each student meets individually each week with an academic advisor. There are still no grades in the Middle School (until ninth grade) but students do self-assessment and continue, when they meet individually with their advisor each week, to receive feedback in the form of "accountability reports." These reflect not only the content and quality of the student's weekly course work, but also the student's emerging understanding as well as critical thinking skills.

The Middle School has its own three-week-long Miniterm, during which students take academic electives in the morning and rehearse for a gala musical in the afternoon, take short courses and participate in special arts offerings. Students are involved in all aspects of putting on this full-scale production. Miniterm reinforces community spirit at Trevor Day School, with everyone working toward a common goal in different capacities. Health education is introduced during Miniterm, which includes an AIDS curriculum.

The teaching of English in the Middle School is literature based. Students write, edit and produce finished drafts. Much time is spent on the mechanics of grammar and vocabulary building. Group discussion and collaborative learning activities dominate the classroom experience. In sixth grade students are assigned "considerable homework in reading and writing." Seventh graders focus on essay writing, critical thinking and oral expression. Eighth graders engage in "formal literary analysis of classic adult literature" while continuing to improve their essay-writing skills.

Foreign language study continues in sixth grade with either French or Spanish.

The Middle School history curriculum begins with geography in sixth grade which lays the foundation for World History in seventh and eighth grades.

Science in the Middle School utilizes a laboratory format. Emphasis is on the scientific method. By the end of eighth grade, all students have covered the basics of biology, physical science and chemistry.

In mathematics, critical thinking, problem solving and competency are stressed. Eighth graders take "Algebra I" or a course to reinforce their pre-algebra skills.

Participation in the arts is not optional at Trevor Day School. All sixth graders take a rotational Arts Workshop series, sampling the arts available to seventh and eighth graders. Electives include "Video Workshop", "Designing for Illustration" and "Photography."

Middle Schoolers may select from vocal or instrumental electives in music. There is a Middle School chorus. Students interested in dance can participate in Choreolab, which meets after school and puts on an annual student dance concert.

Community service is a vital part of the Middle School. There are numerous food, toy and clothing drives and UNICEF collections. Seventh and eighth graders may volunteer to serve either in the Trevor Day School Community, or outside of school.

Middle Schoolers spend a week with their grade as part of the outdoor education program. Grade levels focus on themes such as cooperation, collaboration and leadership.

Physical education is required three times a week. After school there is a range of intramural and interscholastic sports. Parents say that no child is ever cut from a team. If you show up and participate, then you are considered a member of the team. But a participant in the physical education programs says, "We deemphasize competition in gym until 3:00 P.M. and then we don't like to lose." Trevor Day School also has a championship gymnastics team for grades six through twelve. Between 35 and 40 percent of the Middle and High School students participate in afterschool sports programs.

The High School is composed of grades nine through twelve. The High School building has a working theatre, music rooms, a dance studio, a full-size basketball court, darkrooms, ceramics studio and an audiovisual studio. The High School library has 15,000 volumes, a microfiche and is computerized. Trevor Day School anticipates having a new science floor for September 2001. The High School added the student-faculty center (common room) a space where students and staff can meet and work in a relaxed and informal setting, and which continues to function as the nucleus of the school.

Twenty-two credits are required for graduation. This includes three math, three science, three language, four English, three history and nine trimesters of the Arts. Students complete the three-year science requirement in an innovative science program that offers a coordinated course of biology, chemistry and physics each year for three years. At the end of three years, students have completed the equivalent of a year in each of the three subjects. Advanced courses in computer science, foreign language, English, history, mathematics and the sciences are offered. Letter grades are introduced in ninth grade and are sent home twice a year with written reports. All high school students are required to complete eighty hours of community service over their four years.

Highlights from the English curriculum include: "Electives in Asian Literature," "European Drama," "The Romantic Imagination, Shakespeare's History Plays," "Dostoyevsky and Conrad," "Traditions of Comedy and Tragedy," "The Harlem Renaissance and the Playwright Poet." Some history electives include: "Philosophy and Social Issues of the Twentieth Century through American Film."

Ethical Foundations, which includes Health Education, is a part of the science curriculum for ninth and tenth graders.

Trevor Day School students participate in their graduation, putting on a performance with a song or a tribute. The strong sense of community at Trevor Day School persists after graduation. A parent of two alumnae says, "There's a warmth among the children, a camaraderie that continues even though some go on to different schools. They're still friends."

Cynthia E. Bing, former president of the Board of Trustees, describes the school's unique approach: "There is an adult presence that is not obtrusive. Students are encouraged to take the initiative but there are plenty of adults around to help them make [wise] decisions." Parents and alumni say that the emphasis on independent learning and time management pays off in college.

Popular College Choices   Bard, Boston University, Brandeis, Brown, Connecticut College, Cornell, Mount Holyoke, NYU, Tufts, Tulane, Washington University, Vassar and Wesleyan

Traditions   Fall auction/dinner, head of school's fund-raising party, clothing sale, class parties, Fall Festival, parent workshops, Parent

Partners, Friday assemblies, potluck dinners, High School Conference Day, miniterm musical productions, Music Conservatory student recitals, family/faculty concerts, Choreolab dance production

Publications   Yearbook and newspaper
    Magazine: *Trevor*
    Student literary magazine: *The Flame*
    Grades 4 and 5 desktop publication: *The Friday Story*
    Foreign language newsletters

Community Service Requirement   80 hours—20 hours per year in high school

Hangout   McDonald's on 91st and Columbus
    Common Room and Center (open to 5:30)

Trinity School

139 West 91st Street
New York, NY 10024
(212) 873-1650
website: Trinity.nyc.ny.us

Coed
Kindergarten–12th grade
Not accessible

Mr. Henry C. Moses, Headmaster
Ms. June Hilton, Director of Admissions K–6
Ms. Patricia Robbins, Director of Admissions 7–12

Uniform   Lower School: For boys, Trinity polo-style shirt or turtle-neck, chinos or corduroy pants, walking shorts may be worn in warm weather, no jeans or gym shorts. Sweater or navy blazer, no sweatshirts. Tied shoes or sneakers
For girls, white uniform blouse, white or navy turtleneck, long or short sleeve Trinity polo-style shirt. Light blue cord or glen plaid uniform jumper. Tan or navy pants, Bermuda shorts may be worn in the warm weather, no jeans or gym shorts. Sweaters or navy blazer, no sweatshirts. Shoes or sneakers, appropriate legwear.
Dress code in Middle School (grades 5 through 8): no jeans, short skirts or shorts permitted; skirts or slacks and neat collared shirts are preferred; hats cannot be worn in class
Dress code in Upper School (grades 9 through 12): jeans and sneakers may be worn; clothing must be neat, clean and socially appropriate

Birthday Cutoff   Children entering kindergarten must be 5 by September 1

Enrollment   Total school enrollment: 986
Kindergarten places: approximately 60
Graduating class size: approximately 100

Grades   Semester system
Kindergarten–5: detailed anecdotal reports and checklists
Departmentalization begins in 5th grade

Letter grades begin in 6th grade
First final exam is offered in 7th grade

Tuition Range 2001–2002 $19,900 to $20,810, kindergarten–12th grade
Additional fees: approximately $1,525 for lunch, student deposit account
$300 for graduation expenses and senior retreat

Financial Aid/Scholarship   Approximately $2.3 million available
17% of the student body receives financial assistance

Endowment   Approximately $20 million

Diversity   52 Prep for Prep students enrolled as of fall 2000 (The Prep for Prep program was originally housed at Trinity School); 6 Albert G. Oliver Scholars; 10 Early Steps students
Trinity School has a Cultural Diversity Club, Asian Cultural Appreciation Club, Hispanic Affairs Club and a Middle East Club

Homework   Kindergarten: None
1st grade: minimal, beginning in second half of 1st grade
2nd: 15–20 minutes (some homework given Monday is due on Friday); nightly silent reading
3rd: 30–45 minutes (spelling quizzes and tests)
4th: 45 minutes–1 hour
5th and 6th: 1–2 hours
7th and 8th: 2–3 hours
9th–12th: 40 minutes per subject, approximately 3–4 hours

After-School Program   K–6: After-school program for an additional fee, a variety of creative and recreational activities
Some clubs meet after school
Intramural sports for 7th and 8th graders
Interscholastic sports in the Ivy Preparatory League (boys) and the Independent School Athletic Association (girls)

Summer Program   June Program
Trinity Day Camp: a variety of creative and recreational activities, including swimming; Trinity students have priority in enrollment and there is usually a wait list; an additional payment is required

Trinity School was founded in 1709 as the first public charity school in New York City. While Collegiate claims to be the oldest school, Trinity claims to be the oldest *continually operated* school in Manhattan, as it remained open throughout the British occupation of New York City during the Revolutionary War. Trinity was a coed school until the mid-nineteenth century, when the city withdrew its support from charity schools. According to the school's brochure, Trinity then reincorporated as a private boys' school, eventually moving uptown alongside the town houses of the well-to-do on Manhattan's Upper West Side. At this time Trinity modeled itself on the English public (private) schools like Harrow, Eton, Westminster and Winchester. Trinity was a single-sex traditional school until the sixties. One alumnus said that "the Kennedy days marked the fall of the 'preppie' era at Trinity." Beginning with the Upper School in the seventies, Trinity School again became coed, and by the late eighties was coed throughout. Trinity is a traditional school with "West Side" style; this is the key to the school's growing popularity. Many dualities are present in Trinity: highly selective admissions but generous financial aid, a diverse student body, with an emphasis on classical education, all bound by a respect for Trinity's traditions and a Protestant ethos.

Headmaster Henry C. Moses, former dean of freshmen at Harvard, replaced Christopher Berrisford in 1991. Parents say Moses, who gives speeches at chapel and has been seen in school plays, is approachable and cares about the students. He teaches the Upper School course: "Literature of Fact."

The headmaster and trustees are committed to diversity at Trinity. Trinity's annual report recently boasted that Trinity had enrolled a "truly diverse" kindergarten: "Our goal is a school population that reflects our city's, and we have taken a major step in that direction this year." The Parents Association has its own Diversity Committee to support this commitment, and meetings have been held with parents to discuss their concerns and also to encourage them to help with recruitment of children from diverse backgrounds.

Despite the name Trinity, compulsory weekly chapel and the presence of an Episcopalian chaplain, Trinity School strives to be inclusive; the school has recently become popular with Jewish families. Scheduled holidays include Rosh Hashonah, Yom Kippur, Christmas, Passover and Good Friday. There is the traditional all-school Christmas chapel with a candlelit procession, a holiday fair and a Lower School Christmas program, and also a Chanukah Chapel. Beginning in first grade all Lower School students attend chapel once a week and often sing as a group in chapel. The program is interfaith, and one parent said the religious component is not as prominent as the ethical and moral aspects. For example, on Valentine's Day her child's class read their own work aloud, and one child read a story about being friends forever. Chapel speakers in the Upper School might include a senior faculty member or a protester from Tiananmen Square. In the brochure, Headmaster Henry C. Moses says, "I hope the chapel will always be a place of quiet reflection for all." All students take introductory religion courses in fifth and sixth grade. Eleventh and twelfth graders can choose among seven electives, including "Morals and Ethics" and "Religion and Literature," to fulfill their one-semester religion requirement.

Getting in: There are three open houses in the fall. Parents of kindergarten applicants are advised to send in their completed application along with the $50 application fee as soon as possible to be granted an interview at the school. A wait list for interviews has been maintained in recent years. Kindergarten tours and interviews are on separate days. Children do not tour. In our opinion, the gentle-mannered Director of Admissions, June Hilton is the best part of Trinity's admissions process. The child goes upstairs with the tester while you go into Ms. Hilton's office for a conversation. Your child will join you in half an hour so ask your important questions quickly. Your four-year-old may have questions of his/her own (most likely "Can we go home now?") but this is to be expected. The fact that the school asks your child to sit on the couch while the adults are speaking suggests that they are looking for the mature child. Don't send your child to Trinity to be coddled. A parent said, "Trinity is a tough, no-nonsense school, but they really care about the kids."

Trinity requests a recent photograph of your child, so have some good wallet-size pictures made. Do not cancel your interview appointment with Trinity unless your child really is ill. The demand for kindergarten places is high; you might not get another appointment time. According to one nursery school director, "They like to see both parents." Once admissions decisions have been made, Trinity has an active wait list, and there is a strong sibling policy.

Although occasionally places are available in grades two through six and eight, ten and eleven, the main entry points after kindergarten are grades seven and nine. Each family is interviewed individually and has a student guide for the tour of the Upper School. Interviews begin in late September and end in mid-February. There are three receptions in the fall that include tours of the facilities, and throughout the process there are opportunities to meet and talk with faculty members. After a candidate has been accepted, he or she visits classes.

Parents: The style at Trinity is traditional but not formal. "It's a very relaxed atmosphere for a traditional school," a parent told us. There is no typical parent. This is definitely not a celebrity school although there are more than a few. There is a multicultural mix along with a fair share of East and West Side powerhouses. Many East Side parents said the one thing they would change is that they would move Trinity to the East Side of Manhattan. One parent said the school is financially mixed. There is money, but "by and large it's low-key." School dinners are held in the Trinity cafeteria. Parents Association meetings are scheduled so that all parents can attend, and there are meetings between the Parents Association and the trustees. Parents of entering kindergarten students attend a May reception.

Separation is handled gently. The kindergarten schedule is staggered in the beginning, and parents walk children up the stairs to their classroom. After a few weeks parents say goodbye at the bottom of the steps and the students go up by themselves. They shake hands with the teacher at the end of the day. Lower School Principal Rosemary Milliman greets the children in the morning. Parents say Milliman is always asking parents for input on how to improve the school. Lower School parents are kept informed about school and classroom events by the LS newsletter, "The Tuesday Newsday."

Program: There are three kindergartens with two teachers each, approximately twenty students in each class. The children go out of their classrooms for music, gym, swimming (on the premises) and art. There is swimming, gym or turf time daily and a new play area for kindergartners with age appropriate equipment. In first grade the three kindergartens split into four smaller classes with approximately fifteen children in each; each class has a head teacher and an assistant. Parents say that this is a great advantage academically: "Students receive a lot of individual attention—they are really focused on developing important reading and math skills early." The approach to teaching reading is eclectic, with a recent emphasis on the Whole Language approach. June Hilton says, "We use many approaches to accommodate different learning styles." The Writing Workshop includes creative writing and reading stories aloud. Trinity seeks to instill a love for reading with programs such as D.E.A.R. (Drop Everything and Read). Kindergartners deliver their own "Sunny Day Newspaper" weekly. The marvelous Lower School library at Trinity is inhabited by larger-than-life stuffed figures from children's classics: Clifford the Big Red Dog and some of Maurice Sendak's "wild things."

By second grade, expectations are greater. One parent told us she was afraid to go out and leave her second grader with the babysitter because he wouldn't be able to do his homework. New material is never introduced in homework assignments. Reading and math groups are formed according to ability. Foreign language (French or Spanish) is introduced in the Lower School. Formal computer instruction in the computer lab begins in second grade. Kindergartners and first graders are taught in their classrooms. At many points in the Lower School the curriculum is integrated. For example, second graders study Native Americans of the Eastern Woodlands in social studies, and in music they present a festival of Native American song, story and dance for parents.

There is support for different learning styles, and a staff of specialists works with the homeroom teachers. At Special Services Night parents meet the team of specialists who provide remedial instruction. As in many independent schools, some tutoring is initiated by the parents. At Trinity a breakfast was held with the school psychologist and parents to discuss academic pressure but a consensus was not reached. We were told "Some parents think there is too much pressure and some think there is too little, depending on how their child is doing." While academic achievement is appreciated in the Lower School, one parent said, "You don't have to be brilliant to be happy at Trinity. There is a spectrum of intelligence." One mother whose daughter is struggling with the academics, but bubbling with enthusiasm for Trinity nonetheless, was told by her child, "I'm really learning a lot this year!"

One of the highlights of the applicant tour is the Lower School science room, which looks like a Woods Hole laboratory with aquatic life tanks around the room and charts, specimens and waders hanging on the walls. Howard Warren, Lower School science head, oversees a hands-on science program. Warren received a Governor's Environmental Study Citation for his memorable beach cleanup with third graders (who do a unit on the environment). Warren takes the fourth graders wading into Jamaica Bay to collect specimens, which they bring back and put into the tanks, study and release at the end of the school year.

Music is an area of strength at Trinity. Twice weekly, beginning in kindergarten, students use the Orff, Kodaly and Dalcroze methods to learn rhythm and singing skills. Every class performs music, ranging from psalms sung in chapel to rap songs about the fifty states. The Adventures in Strings Program gives fourth graders the option of studying violin or cello and continues through fifth and sixth grades. There is a Lower School and Middle School orchestra.

Trinity recently reorganized and consolidated the lower Middle (grades five and six) and upper Middle Schools (grades seven and eight) into one Middle School serving grades five through eight. The Middle School is housed in its own bright, newly renovated wing and features a Middle School technology resource center. The school now has two full size gymnasiums. Departmentalization begins in Middle School. Modern language instruction, begun in the Lower School, continues in grades five through eight. Latin instruction begins in grade 6. Students who need reinforcement take a study skills course in which they meet with a learning specialist in small groups. Middle Schoolers participate in the Pythagorean Contest. In athletics, Middle Schoolers choose between coed kickball and football on the Astro Turf and Sports Club (interscholastic or intramural sports competition). Required swimming classes continue through eighth grade. There are informal "chalk talks" born out of the Project Charlie anti-drug program in Middle School.

The Upper School at Trinity is composed of the ninth through twelfth grades. After the architectural grandeur of the Lower School, Trinity's Upper School (Hawley Wing) with its cinderblock walls and bustling corridors has the feeling of a suburban public school. There are no bells in the Upper School. The Upper School library has Proquest and Newsbank, and students can work in carrels or on computers. Computers are networked throughout the school.

Approximately forty new students enter at the ninth grade. Trinity is a popular high school choice for students at the single-sex schools who want a city coed day school.

To ease the transition into high school and integration of new students into the class, ninth graders take an orientation trip to Frost Valley in the Catskills, with senior leaders and faculty, and continue to meet once a week during the school year with their Frost Valley groups.

Contact between students in the three divisions occurs formally at all-school events several times a year. Currently, twice a week, ten to fifteen seniors eat lunch with kindergarten students, other seniors help fourth graders put on plays about Greek myths, several juniors and seniors work with Lower School students on math enrichment, and Upper and Middle School students meet in programs like Kids Helping Kids to discuss social issues.

The graduation requirements at Trinity are similar to those at the other rigorous high schools. Students take a minimum of five or six academic courses in grade nine. In grades ten through twelve, they must take a minimum of four, but almost all students take more. Seniors may choose from a variety of electives, including "Cultural Diversity in America," Modern Poetry," and "Literature about Growing Up." We did not see any interdisciplinary courses listed in the course guide. English is required but seniors choose from seven different options each semester. About seventy percent of the seniors are enrolled in advanced science.

Some classrooms are set up in traditional rows or seminar style with oak lectern desks, but in English, history, modern languages and religion, the desks are arranged in a circle or the tables in a rectangle to promote discussion.

Trinity maintains its traditional emphasis on the classics, the study of Latin and Greek. The school's course guide asserts that the classics are "a rigorous and significant part of the curriculum." "The best Latin program in the country," says one student. The study of DWAMS (Dead White Ancient Males) really comes alive at Trinity. Advanced reading in elegiac poetry and Ovid's *The Art of Love*, a provocative and satirical portrait of love in ancient Rome, is offered. Advanced students can participate in The Virgil Academy, in which students read a book of the *Aeneid* in tutorial and later take part in public examination by teachers from other schools and colleges. In addition to Latin and Greek, students can continue study in French or Spanish. The English department requires Upper School students to read five books over the summer. Ninth graders begin the year with a six-week Writing Workshop to perfect their essay-writing skills. Recent eleventh and twelfth grade English electives have included "Existentialism: The Search for Meaning," "What's Going on in Poetry Right Now," "How to Tell a War Story," and "Four African Authors: Race and Related Matters."

After a solid grounding in modern European and American history, seniors can choose from the following electives (these vary from year to year): "Prejudice in America" (women and nonwhite ethnic minorities), "The Postwar World, 1945–1965" and "U.S. History, 1965–1984," and Economics.

In keeping with the commitment to diversity at Trinity there has been much discussion about the need to incorporate more views of nonwhite ethnic minorities and women into the Upper School curriculum. At the first alumni panel (with faculty), part of a Faculty Professional Day, the theme was "Perspectives in Multiculturalism and Education." Five recent Trinity graduates talked about the need to broaden the curriculum with more diverse viewpoints, and one student said that although they visited many cultural sites in New York City including, of course, the Metropolitan Museum, "We should have taken trips to the Schomburg Center along with the Guggenheim Museum."

Honors courses exist only in mathematics and modern languages. Although not all advanced courses follow the AP curriculum, AP Prep courses are offered to prepare students for the exam. Science requirements are biology plus one year of another laboratory science. Science electives include "Psychology," "Marine Biology," "Astronomy" and advanced courses in biology, chemistry and physics. The computer science department offers courses in word processing, Web Programming and AP Computer Science.

High school students can do advanced independent work in addition to the required four academic subjects. Advanced work is graded pass/fail and doesn't count as a credit toward graduation. Seniors, however, may enroll in an independent study in a specific discipline such as German literature, chemistry or studio art, but they must also take four other courses. Seniors receive a letter grade for their independent study program.

The arts and theatre programs at Trinity are extensive. Theatre at Trinity is exciting. Every year there is a major musical production and a Cabaret. We saw a rehearsal for *Fiddler on the Roof* in the chapel; another year it was *Carousel*. The Theater IV play production course allows students to direct any one-act play of their choice. These spring productions are very well attended.

Adjoining visual arts and ceramics studios are large and bright. Students make good use of New York City's museums. Students can take beginning through advanced photography for credit. There is room for individual initiative in the arts at Trinity. In fall of 1991 a small group of students with a keen interest in films and filmmaking organized the first New York National High School Film Festival and received 215 entries from across the country. Prizes were awarded. The Festival has become an exciting annual event.

When they're not studying, students can relax in the Swamp (a seating area off the main lobby) or in the Food Zone (another side of the lobby). There is no student lounge as such. There is a no-smoking zone around the school. Students can leave campus as early as the second half of freshman year.

Three representatives from each grade serve in the student senate (serving grades nine through twelve). The Senate recently voted to install a Snapple or soda-vending machine but this was not permitted. Homecoming, run by the student senate, takes place at a boys' varsity basketball game in the winter. At other times during the year the senate gives out hot chocolate.

There are numerous clubs. The most popular, we were told, is the "Free Tibet" club, with over 200 members.

There is no community service requirement, but most Trinity students participate in at least one community service activity. Often an entire grade will do a project together, for instance, clean an area of Riverside Park or give a variety show to make money for hurricane victims. The Student Volunteer Service Organization (SVSO), born in the sixties, continues to coordinate a range of student volunteer activities, such as Santa's helpers, the Thanksgiving program for senior citizens, You Gotta Have Park and the March of Dimes Walkathon.

In recent years, AIDS has been important issue on campus and there were numerous discussions at Trinity among parents and students about AIDS. "Although abstinence is preferred," said one mother, "we have to be realistic."

The athletic program at Trinity is wide ranging and strong. Some teams begin two-hour morning practice sessions at 6:00 A.M. Games are held after school and some are well attended. Soccer, lacrosse and swimming are a few of Trinity's best teams, but students say "this is definitely not a rah-rah school."

At graduation, awards are bestowed upon Trinity seniors, in recognition of excellence in nearly every area. The three students with the highest grade point averages in each grade receive the Hawley Prizes. On Prize Day in May, all academic departments announce the students in grades nine through twelve, who are recipients of endowed prizes, including four prizes that have been given annually since 1890—the Eaton Prize for Classics, the Alumni Prize in English, the Rector's Prize in Religion, and the Eaton Prize for Senior Mathematics. At a formal induction ceremony in the spring, students with outstanding academic records are elected to the Cum Laude Society, the high school equivalent of Phi Beta Kappa. There are some students who compete for these prizes, but the *real* source of competition, one alumnus told us, is college placement.

Graduation exercises, complete with academic gown, are held in a church at 96th and Central Park West. A Baccalaureate service, planned by the seniors, is held the night before graduation at Trinity Church, the original site of the school, near Wall Street. By tradition, the graduation speaker is the parent of a senior.

Popular College Choices   Yale, Harvard, Brown, Princeton, University of Pennsylvania, Cornell, Wesleyan, Stanford

Traditions   Holiday Fair, Spring Auction and Dinner, Virgil Academy, Reunion Weekend, Cabaret, Theater IV productions, senior Halloween Costume contest, Multicultural Fair

Publications   Yearbook: *The Bruner*
Literary magazine: *Columbus*
Newspaper: *Trinity Times*
Photography journal: *Malinconico*
Trinity School magazine: *Trinity Per Saecula* (Trinity through the Ages)

Hangouts   The Swamp (a small seating area in the rear of the Upper School lobby), the Food Zone (seating in the lobby where students can eat), the McDonald's at 91st and Columbus

United Nations International School

24–50 Franklin D. Roosevelt Drive
New York, NY 10010
(212) 684-7400
website: www.unis.org
e-mail: admissions@unis.org

Coed
Kindergarten–12th grade
Accessible

Dr. Kenneth Wrye, Director
Ms. Barbara Daelman, Director of Admissions

Birthday Cutoff   Children entering kindergarten must be 5 by December 31

Enrollment   Total enrollment: 1,502
Kindergarten places: 85
Graduating class size: 95–105

Grades   Semester system
Number grades begin in 7th grade
Full departmentalization by 7th grade

Tuition Range 2001–2002 $14,145 to $16,305, kindergarten–12th grade
Additional fees total approximately $400

Financial Aid/Scholarship   13% of the student body receive some form of financial aid, $700,000 available

Endowment   Approximately $17.5 million

Diversity   Students at UNIS come from over 100 countries.

After-School Program   Open to UNIS students only
A variety of creative and recreational activities from 3:00 P.M. until 6:00 P.M.; an additional payment is required
Varsity and junior varsity teams

Summer Program The six-week UNIS summer program is open to children from UNIS as well as from the community, nursery through 12th grade; a variety of creative and recreational activities as well as English as a Second Language are offered; an additional payment is required

---

UNIS is housed in a modern, spacious building overlooking the East River. A large garden forms the tranquil core of the edifice. For younger students the school has a fully equipped, multi-level playground. UNIS was founded in 1947 by a group of United Nations parents to provide their children with an international curriculum and to inspire in its students the spirit and ideals of the UN. Today, UNIS is open to all New York City families. Students at UNIS represent over one hundred countries; the faculty represents over fifty different nationalities.

UNIS is organized into three schools: The Junior School is for kindergarten through fourth grade students, the Middle School is composed of fifth through eighth grade, and the High School (tutorial house) is for ninth through twelfth grade students. Each school has its principal and staff, who insure a smooth transition from school to school. After eleven years as Director, Dr. Blaney retired in 1998. Dr. Kenneth Wrye replaced him. Dr. Wrye is a U.S. citizen and was formerly head of the Copenhagen International School.

Getting in: UNIS offers Spring and Fall tours (led by current parents) for prospective applicants; students in fifth grade and above are welcome to accompany their parents on the tour. Once an application has been filed, the school will contact parents to set up an interview date and parents can tour at this time. Children applying to kindergarten through fourth grade are observed in an informal play group of four or five. While the children are playing, their parents meet as a group (approximately twenty parents) for a Q. and A. session with the school principal and admissions staff. All English speaking students are required to submit results of ERB testing. Teacher recommendations are strongly recommended; personal recommendations are welcome but not required. The school is sensitive to applicants from other cultures and countries and they are familiar with all of the different national systems. UNIS has its own in-house assessment specialist who can test children (for placement purposes) who don't speak fluent English. Each year one or two places in each grade are held open for children of incoming U.N. diplomats. Forty-four per cent of parents are affiliated with the U.N.

Program: The curriculum is designed to provide for direct inter-action by the children with the world around them. The children are encouraged to think for themselves, while working cooperatively in small groups. Academics are stressed in an integrated International Baccalaureate Primary Years Program that includes, music, art, French, Spanish, science and computer science taught by specialists. Cre-ativity is encouraged.

UNIS recognizes that the Middle School years are critical ones for social, emotional and intellectual growth. The curriculum builds upon the basics learned in previous years, adding new subjects and addi-tional language options. The IB middle years program is the focus of the curriculum. In English, Middle School students read world poetry and explore works of literature from many countries and cultures. UNIS places high value on the teaching of foreign languages. French is offered from grade 1. Nine languages are taught by native speak-ers and there are beginning, intermediate and advanced classes avail-able. English as a Second Language is a separate course. At seventh grade level, electives, in addition to the regular curriculum, are offered in drama, art, computer, music and modern languages. Students are required to choose one of these electives for a two year period.

The curriculum of the "Tutorial House" (High School) balances electives and required subjects. In grade 10 students can pursue a spe-cial talent or interest, whether it be math, science, languages, writing, the humanities, music or art. The program culminates in the Interna-tional Baccalaureate Diploma Program (IB), study for which takes place during the last two years of high school. The vast majority of UNIS students take the full IB program. Students with high grades can sometimes receive up to one year of advanced standing at American universities. Eighty-five percent of graduates choose to attend colleges in North America.

UNIS has an articulated computer studies program. Technology is integrated into classroom instruction in many different subject areas. We saw computers in all of the classrooms and there are four computer labs. The school is networked, connecting all classrooms and bridging both campuses. The school is connected to the Internet through a T1 line.

There are numerous opportunities for leadership throughout the school. Students can be elected to Student Council as early as grade two. Members of the Student Councils of all three schools meet peri-odically with their principal and with the director to discuss issues of concern.

441

The UNIS athletic program includes twenty-six varsity and junior varsity teams.

The annual UNIS/UN conference is an exciting annual event. This conference is held in the UN's General Assembly Hall and requires months of planning and research by UNIS students and students from the more than fifty participating schools from around the world.

Popular College Choices Brown, Columbia, Cornell, Harvard, MIT, Parsons School of Design, University of Michigan, NYU, Tufts, Vassar, Yale, McGill, London School of Economics

Traditions United Nations Day, Winter and Spring Concerts, UNIS/UN Conference, Theater Workshop, English Writing Weekend at Bard College, Theory of Knowledge Weekend, Science Weekend, Math Weekend, Senior Trip, Sports Carnival, Sports Banquet, International Book and Craft Festival, World Outreach to Needy People.

Publications Yearbook
Upper School Newspaper: *UNIS Verse*
Student Council Newsletter
Junior School Newsletter
3 Literary Magazines

Community Service Requirement An important aspect of student life is community service, either in-house or at an approved public service agency in the metropolitan area.

Village Community School

272 West Tenth Street
New York, NY 10014
(212) 691-5146

Coed
5/6's (kindergarten)–8th grade
Not accessible

Ms. Eve Kleger, Director
Ms. Jennifer Trano, Director of Admissions

Birthday Cutoff   Children entering kindergarten must be 5 by December 31

Enrollment   Total enrollment: 310
5/6 (kindergarten) places: 35 to 40
Graduating class size: 32–34
7 Prep for Prep students enrolled as of September 2000

Grades   Semester system in the Upper School
Lower and Upper Schools: detailed anecdotal reports and conferences twice a year
Full departmentalization begins in 6th Grade

Tuition Range 2001–2002   Approximately $15,000 to $16,000, 5/6's–12/13's
Additional fees: for books, approximately $400

Financial Aid/Scholarship   25% of the student body receive partial financial aid

Endowment   The school has recently begun to build its endowment.

After-School Program   After School at VCS: for children ages 5 and above; open to children from other schools; Monday–Friday 3:15 P.M. to 4:45 P.M.; activities include sports, arts and crafts, music, theatre and dance; an additional payment is required
A play group is available until 5:30 P.M.

Summer Program VCS has a summer camp from mid-June through July open to students from other schools; an additional payment is required

———

Village Community School was founded in 1970. VCS's building, with its high ceilings and wide stairwells, was originally a public school one hundred years ago. VCS is governed by an elected Council which is composed of parents, faculty and administrators. Recent capital improvements include a new sky-lit library, two science centers, and an elevator. There is a full-sized air-conditioned gym on the premises in addition to two outdoor play spaces. No ERB testing is required for kindergarten admissions (it is required for second grade and above). There are two divisions: The Lower School is composed of ages five through ten. The Upper School is composed of grades six through eight. VCS has interage (flexible) class groupings until sixth grade. There is no uniform. VCS does not have a cafeteria and students must bring their own lunches.

VCS has a friendly, relaxed atmosphere but the curriculum is highly structured. Students address their teachers (as well as the director) by their first names. Parents say that in the Lower School VCS is very nurturing; in the middle years the expectations are more demanding. Foreign language is introduced in sixth grade; in seventh grade students choose either French or Spanish. In 2000, VCS admitted four Prep for Prep students.

Most VCS graduates attend a variety of city high schools including the specialized public schools, NYC independent schools and boarding schools.

York Preparatory School

40 West 68th Street
New York, NY 10023
(212) 362-0400
www.yorkprep.org

Coed
Grades 6–12
Accessible (elevator)

Mr. Ronald P. Stewart, Headmaster
Mr. Chris Durnford, Dean
Ms. Stephanie Klein, Associate Director of Admissions

Uniform   None, there is a dress code

Birthday Cutoff   None

Enrollment   Total enrollment: 300
6th grade places: 9–14
Average graduating class size: 45

Grades   Semester system
Numerical grades begin in 6th grade
Departmentalization begins in 6th grade and is complete by 7th grade

Tuition Range 2001–2002 $20,400 to $20,900, 6th–12th grades
Additional fees: for books, activities, trips, graduation and Parents' Association dues are approximately $1,400

Financial Aid/Scholarship   Approximately 33% of the school receive some form of aid
$500,000 in financial aid was distributed in 1999–2000

Endowment   None

After-School Program   Varsity and junior varsity team competition in the Interschool League
An active intramural program
Academic clubs meet after school

445

All teachers remain after school for extra-help classes

Extracurricular activities include: horseback riding, golf, computer animation, jewelry making, tennis, drama, literary magazine and newspaper, "mock trial" team, swimming and astronomy

Summer Program   An academic enrichment program is offered from mid-June–July for an additional charge; open to students from other schools

––––––––

York Prep was founded in 1969 by its present Headmaster Ronald Stewart. In 1997 the school moved from its former location on East 85th Street into its current home on the Upper West Side, a handsome seven-story granite building formerly occupied by the Hebrew Union College. After completing a "boiler to roof" renovation, the school, crisply painted in yellow and blue, reflects the can-do optimism exuded by the Oxford-educated headmaster, and his wife, Jayme Stewart, who has been Director of College Guidance since the school's inception.

York Prep is a proprietary (for-profit) school, owned and operated by the headmaster. The school is run like a high class Mom and Pop organization: The Stewarts oversee every aspect of the school which operates free of the politics of a board of trustees. Liv Tyler and Kelly Klein are two of the school's glamorous grads; so is James de la Vega, a graffiti artist (recently profiled in *The New York Times*), who grew up in El Barrio, studied art at Cornell and now teaches at his alma mater, "occasionally taking his students on a tour of Harlem street art."

When you enter the school, a regulation sized basketball court serves as the backdrop to the reception desk. A uniformed security guard stands nearby, who on closer inspection turns out to be an effigy. York Prep values both athletics and a sense of humor, both of great advantage when managing adolescents, as the Stewarts, who have three grown children, know well. Participation in athletics and other extracurricular activities is encouraged here; a component of the school's philosophy is "putting children in situations of success." A parent told us: "It's a very nurturing school, the teachers are great; it's the perfect alternative to one of the real high-powered schools; an excellent private school education."

The schoolhouse has two modern science laboratories, a library/media center (with beautiful Shaker-style windows), computer room, performance and art studios, and a sprung hardwood floor gymnasium with weight and locker room facilities. The classrooms are light and airy, carpeted and climate controlled. The classrooms are wired with a T-1 line and students and staff have e-mail addresses. In addition, all classrooms are linked to the school's in-house television station, WYRK, over which daily announcements are read.

Getting In: Open houses for parents are offered regularly by the Headmaster. Upon request, parents can tour the school individually with the Associate Director of Admissions, before filing an application. Applicants and their parents have an interview meeting and the applicant is invited to spend a day visiting the school. York Prep admits Prep for Prep students.

Program: Stewart believes that a student must be offered a real opportunity for success, and that is a major factor in student motivation. York Prep's curriculum provides a strong foundation in the traditional core subjects of a liberal arts education. For a small school, it offers an impressive range of courses with electives in most fields for qualified students and a growing number of AP courses in History, Math and foreign languages. Beginning in seventh grade each subject area is divided into at least three tracks (homogeneous ability groups). These tracks are fluid; students whose skills improve will move into the next track enabling students to experience success while always being challenged to work beyond their "comfort level." Each student's program is constantly evaluated for proper placement within the tracking system to ensure the right balance of challenge and support is maintained in all subject areas.

"York Prep's system of academic support has helped many students who've been 'over-faced' [at other schools] rediscover the thrill of learning," says Stewart. For gifted students, York Prep provides the challenge of its top track courses leading to AP courses. In addition to the tracking system and individual assistance given to students, the school uses a study skills and learning strategies program of its own design that is taught in every grade and every subject.

The school has always provided academic support and accommodation for students with different learning styles and educational needs. The *Jump Start* program is an individualized and intensive program that works to strengthen reading comprehension and writing skills. This program also imparts organizational and study skills. It was created to help students develop independence not only with day-to-day tasks but also with respect to long range goals. There is an additional fee for the *Jump Start* program. York Prep also offers an ESL program with daily English-language instruction and tutorial assistance.

Seniors and advanced eleventh graders who qualify may either take courses at Columbia, New York University, or Hunter College, or independent study and advanced placement courses.

Communication between parents and the school is frequent. "The teachers and staff have their fingers on everything that's going on; if my son was having a problem I could ask the principal to 'keep an eye on him today' and they will," said one parent.

Teachers take full advantage of the school's Lincoln Center location in addition to visiting museums, theaters and the Wall Street area.

A wide range of sports is offered at York and the full trophy cases are proof of their success. York Prep competes in the Independent School Leagues, the Private Schools Athletic Association and the Manhattan Independent Schools tennis and golf leagues. Students can choose from competitive or non-competitive basketball, softball, soccer, swimming, track, tennis, cross-country track, aerobics, gymnastic, golf and weight training. Horseback riding at the Claremont Stables is a feature of York Prep's extra-curricular program, as are ski weekends and trips to Europe and Washington, D.C. The range of clubs and activities changes each year according to student interest.

York Prep students volunteer their time at more than 150 non-profit organizations, including the American Red Cross, the ASPCA, the Legal Aid Society, and so on. Some students surpass the required hours of the Community Service Program.

Stewart says "Each child needs a feeling that he can do something well—whether it's athletics or origami. (Regarding origami, Stewart told us, 'One student got into Stanford because of it'). "We tell them 'you pick it, we'll support you.' " This philosophy is carried all the way through to graduation. York Prep is very successful at college placement thanks to the expertise of Jayme Stewart, author of *How to Get Into the College of Your Choice* (William Morrow & Co., 1991). Ms. Stewart encourages students to make realistic choices. Her thoroughness and tenacity as a student advocate pay off because more than 85% are accepted at their first choice school.

Popular College Choices   Barnard, Bowdoin, Brown, Colgate, Boston University, Cooper Union, Juilliard, George Washington, University of Michigan, Cornell, Penn

Publications   Literary Magazine: *Genesis*
Yearbook: *The Legend*
Newspaper

Community Service Requirement   100 hours

ADDITIONAL SCHOOLS

Beekman School
(Grades 9–12)
220 East 55th Street
New York, NY 10022
(212) 755-6666
web site: beekmanschool.org
Total enrollment: 80

Beth Jacob Parochial School
(Orthodox Jewish, Grades
  Kindergarten–8)
142 Broome Street
New York, NY 10002
(212) 473-4500
Total enrollment: 120

Frederick Douglass Academy
(Grades 6–12)
2581 Adam Clayton Powell
  Boulevard
New York, NY 10039
(212) 491-4107
Total enrollment: approximately
  1000

King's Academy
(Grades Nursery–12)
2341 Third Avenue
New York, NY 10035
(212) 348-7380
Total enrollment: approximately
  300

Lyceum Kennedy
(French Bilingual, Grades Pre-
  kindergarten–12)
225 East 43rd Street
New York, NY 10017
(212) 681-1877
Total enrollment: 175

**Manhattan Christian
  Academy**
(Grades Pre-kindergarten–8)
401 West 205th Street
New York, NY 10040
(212) 567-5521
Total enrollment: 365

Manhattan Day School
(Grades Nursery–8)
310 West 75th Street
New York, NY 10023
(212) 376-6800
Total enrollment: 380

Mestivta Timereth Jerusalem
(Orthodox Jewish, Grades
  Kindergarten–12)
145 East Broadway
New York, NY 10002
(212) 964-2830
Total enrollment: approximately
  150

**Montessori School of New
  York, Inc.**
(Nursery 2 year-olds–14 year-
  olds)
347 East 55th Street
New York, NY 10022
(212) 223-4630
Total enrollment approximately
  100

Northeastern Academy
(Grades 9–12)
532 West 215th Street
New York, NY 10034
(212) 569-4800
Total enrollment: approximately
  170

Robert Louis Stevenson School
(Serves children with learning
disabilities and attention
deficit disorders,
Grades 7–12)
24 West 74th Street
New York, NY 10023
(212) 787–6400
Total enrollment: 58

Saint Spyridon Greek Parochial School
(Greek Orthodox, Grades
Pre-kindergarten–8)
120 Wadsworth Avenue
New York, NY 10033
(212) 795-6870
Total enrollment: 82

Saint Thomas Choir School
(Boarding for boys only,
Grades 4–8)
202 West 58th Street
New York, NY 10019
(212) 247-3311
Total enrollment: 41

The More Learning Center
(Director, Cassandra Lewis
teaches out of her apartment.
Grades Nursery 3s–6)
614 West 157th Street
Apartment 2C
New York, NY 10032
(212) 491-5674
Total enrollment: 10 all day
students, 5 after school only

Yeshiva Rabbi S.R. Hirsch
(Orthodox Jewish, Grades
Nursery–12)
91 Bennett Avenue
New York, NY 10033
(212) 568-6200
Total enrollment: approximately
500

Yeshiva University High School for Boys
(Orthodox Jewish, Grades 9–12)
2540 Amsterdam Avenue
New York, NY 10033
(212) 960-5345
Total enrollment: 322

RESOURCES FOR CHILDREN WITH LEARNING DISABILITIES

When parents are first told that their child has been diagnosed with a learning disability they are heartbroken. They feel as if they've done something wrong that might have caused or contributed to their child's disability. Then they start shaking the family tree for any relatives who might have had a learning problem—was it your brother, grandmother, aunt or cousin who had so much trouble in school? Parents start to think that their child is the only one struggling and then they worry about the erosion of their child's self-esteem.

Learning disabilities are diagnosed in children with a wide range of IQ's; very bright children can have LD's that aren't diagnosed until later in their schooling because they came up with ingenious strategies to compensate for their deficiency! Skilled educators will usually see red flags early on, in pre-kindergarten or earlier. Most primary schools have early intervention specialists on staff, including speech therapists. Keep in mind that individual schools have different timetables for developmental skills, like reading, and with a wide age range within classrooms, children will be at different points of development until third grade when everyone should be caught up.

If you are concerned about a "developmental lag" at any point, don't be afraid to ask the teacher if she thinks you should have your child evaluated; if her answer isn't satisfactory, go to the division head or guidance counselor with your concerns. If you're still not sure why your child isn't doing grade level work the first order of business is to get a psycho-educational evaluation to determine exactly what the problem is and what you can do about it. The Parents League and the organizations listed below can refer you to a qualified tester. Word of mouth is also a good way to find one. The best bet is to find a tester who is also neuro-psychologist. The test is long and is usually given in two-hour segments, morning and afternoon, over a couple of days. Reports are detailed and sophisticated.

The best grades for testing children are: first grade (an important year for acquiring learning skills), fourth grade (skills are consolidated and more independent learning is expected); seventh grade (so you can better assess high school options), tenth grade (because now is the time to make a high school switch.) Medication is sometimes prescribed for children with related attention disorders to help them focus, settle down, and do their work.

Re-evaluate and re-test every three to four years. Your child's school should be apprised of any testing you do outside, and provided with the results so they can best work with your child. Remember this is a partnership! Alice Goldman, who runs parent workshops and seminars on learning disabilities for The Parents League, offers a comforting thought, "If a child is completely evaluated and a learning disability has been identified, there is often a sense of relief and it is much easier to set a course of remediation." Once the right type of intervention and programming are in place, learning should be enjoyable again.

Schools for children with learning disabilities are small in size and highly structured. Classes in a therapeutic setting vary in size from six to twelve students per class with an assistant as well as additional sessions with various specialists who work with students one-on-one. Often, these schools will have mixed-age groupings of students because many learning disabled children learn at different rates that don't correlate with their ages. These programs really work and are worth all the time and money that you will invest. Many children who attend a specialized school are mainstreamed back into a regular educational environment, often the goal of some of these schools. Students who stay in their present schools may require extensive and costly tutoring after school. Don't expect your child's private school to provide all the services he'll need, but most schools will provide study skills programs and extended time for tests and exams. Keep your chin up and take heart, many children with learning disabilities have gone on to wonderful colleges, (including the Ivy League) and have successful careers.

Here are some of the schools in the New York City area that educate children with learning disabilities, and/or psychological, social, behavioral or emotional issues. With the exception of the Parkside School, most of the schools listed below are very similar. The Parents League can provide a complete listing of schools for children with developmental and learning disabilities. There are many success stories out there and here are some of their alma maters:

The Churchill School
310 East 30th Street
New York, NY 10016
(212) 683-3105

Coed
Ages: 5–14 years (Kindergarten–9th grade)
Total enrollment: 235

The Churchill School serves children who have emotional and social issues, primary dyslexia or heavy attention deficit disorder with hyperactivity (ADHD). Beginning in September 2001, Churchill will be located in a beautifully renovated facility at 301 East 29th Street, at the corner of Second Avenue. A high school program is currently being phased in starting this year with completion scheduled for 2003. Churchill's objective is to eventually remediate students so that they can function well in mainstream academic environments.

The Gateway School of New York
236 Second Avenue (between 14th and 15th Streets)
New York, NY 10003
(212) 777-5966

Coed
Ages: 5–12 years
Total enrollment: 62
When Gateway was founded in 1965, it was one of the first schools in New York City to work exclusively with children who had learning disabilities. The aim of The Gateway School is to remediate and mainstream children who have moderate to severe learning disabilities.

The Gillen Brewer School
1190 Park Avenue
New York, NY 10128
(212 831-3667

Coed
Ages: 3–8 years
Total enrollment: 48

The Gillen Brewer School started as an early childhood program and evaluation site, and now extends up through second grade. Parents are very pleased with the school. The program serves children who have a wide variety of learning issues and developmental delays.

The Mary McDowell Center for Learning
20 Bergen Street
Brooklyn, NY 11201
(718) 625-3939

Coed
Ages: 5–11/12 years
Total enrollment: 104

The Mary McDowell Center for Learning educates children with developmental delays and learning disabilities. A good resource for families who live in Brooklyn.

The Parkside School
48 West 74th Street
New York, NY 10023
(212) 721-8888

Coed
Ages: 5–10 years
Total enrollment: 80

The Parkside School's program serves children who have language based communication problems. For example, children who have a hard time finding the right words and/or have speech delays. These difficulties are beyond emotional issues, but can lead to complicated problems like tantrums, anxiety and acting up because affected children can't verbalize what they need to say. This very supportive program offers a highly structured, multisensory curriculum that inspires children and makes learning fun.

Stephen Gaynor School
22 West 74th Street
New York, NY 10023
(212) 787-7070

Coed
Ages: 5–13 years
Total enrollment: 118

The oldest school in New York City, (founded in 1962) for children who have dyslexia, ADD, visual spatial and/or non-verbal learning disabilities. Stephen Gaynor is highly respected in the community and does an excellent job of mainstreaming children who have a wide spectrum of special needs.

Children's Day Treatment Center and West End Day School
255 West 71st Street
New York, NY 10023
(212) 873-5708

Coed
Ages: 5–12/13 years
Total enrollment: 40

This school helps children with a wide range of special needs. The staff works closely with each family to ameliorate the problems that affect their lives. There's a social work component incorporated into the program that has been very successful in helping many families.

Windward School
Windward Avenue
White Plains, NY 10605
(914) 949-6968

Coed
Grades: 1st–12th

Windward is a popular school in Westchester with a solid language based program for children with learning disabilities and high IQs. The school has children with specific processing issues, ADHD and other learning related problems. Windward's staff is extremely skilled at remediating children and then mainstreaming them.

Winston Preparatory School
4 West 76th Street
New York, NY 10023
(212) 496-8400

Coed
Grades: 6th–12th
Total enrollment: 130

Winston prep offers a junior and senior high school program for students who have ADD, ADHD, dyslexia and various other learning disabilities. The goal of Winston's rigorous program is to send the majority of its students on to college. There is considerable effort invested in the preparation of students for college level work. Teachers are trained in the Orton-Gillingham method, and are knowledgeable about how to teach children with severe dyslexia. The school offers very small classes and one-to-one instruction; teachers are even assigned as home tutors. Many of the faculty members are from England.

The Learning Resource Center at Columbia Grammar and Preparatory School
5 West 93rd Street
New York, NY 10025
(212) 749-6200

Coed
Grades: Pre-kindergarten–12th

This is *not* a school for severely learning-disabled children. The program is designed for high achieving students who need extra support. Columbia Grammar's Learning Resource Center is well established, organized and structured. According to the school they "will provide some degree of professional skills remediation on a temporary basis." Ten well-trained professionals staff the Learning Center, and enrollment is limited to only forty students school-wide (The school has about 700 students.) There is an additional cost for any student in the Learning Center of approximately $15,000 per year. (*Supra* page 184.)

The Quest Program at The Dwight and the Anglo-American International Schools
291 Central Park West
New York, NY 10024
(212) 724-2146 ext. 1

Coed
Grades: Kindergarten through 12th

Dwight/Anglo is also not a school for children with learning disabilities. However the school has a small program (approximately fifteen percent of the student body is enrolled) for students who have minor learning difficulties and need extra support in the classroom. The Quest Program is set up so students do not have to go to a tutor every day and can still participate in a full college preparatory curriculum. The Quest Program resembles in a way the Parisian system with lots of mnemonics, repetitive learning and drills. The program is flexible enough so that students who need help in one subject area can get it, without compromising their schedules, it also serves students with a range of abilities. Parents are kept apprised of their children's test results in speech, reading and hearing. The additional fee for the program is approximately $15,000 per year, (*Supra* page 218.)

A complete listing of educational resources in the New York City area for children with learning disabilities can be obtained from:

The National Center for Learning Disabilities, 381 Park Avenue South, Suite 1401, New York, NY 10016, (212) 545-7510 Website: www.LD.org
NCLD is a voluntary, not-for-profit organization founded in 1977 by Carrie Rozelle. NCLD operates a national information and referral service and is the nation's only central, computerized resource clearinghouse committed solely to the issues of LD.

The Learning Disabilities Association of New York City Telephone Referral Service: Weekdays from 9 A.M. to 5 P.M., (212) 645-6730
This nonprofit organization is an affiliate of the Learning Disabilities Association of America. Trained counselors will explain how to recognize symptoms, and offer referrals to community based agencies in the New York City area. The Learning Disabilities Association also provides printed material and conducts workshops.

Other resources for information about LDs:

The New York Branch of the Orton Dyslexia Society, 71 West 23rd Street, Suite 514, New York, NY 10010, (212) 691-1930
This is the New York branch of the national nonprofit Orton Dyslexia Society, which uses a multisensory approach for teaching children with dyslexia. They offer a free telephone referral service to parents looking for information on testing, schools, trained remediators, psychologists and other professionals. The Orton Dyslexia Society also sponsors an annual three-day conference on a topic of interest to parents, a conference for teenagers and parent support groups. A yearly membership is available.

The Parents League of New York, Inc., 115 East 82nd Street, New York, NY 10028, (212) 737-7385
The Parents League sponsors a workshop and provides information and referrals about learning disabilities to member parents. Mrs. Alice Goldman, an adviser with the Parents League, is particularly knowledgeable about which schools specialize in which type of LD.

Resources for Children with Special Needs, 200 Park Avenue South, Suite 816, New York, NY 10003, (212) 677-4650
Resources for Children is a nonprofit information, referral, advocacy,

training and support center for programs and services for children (from birth to age twenty-one) with learning, developmental, emotional or physical disabilities. Resources for Children publishes a family support guide listing camps and summer programs for children with special needs.

The Churchill Center, 310East 30th Street, New York, N.Y. 10016, Tel: (212) 683-3105, Fax: (212) 683-3220
An outreach center for services and programs for children and adolescents with attention and/or learning problems.

Advocates for Children of New York, Inc., 151 West 30th Street, 5th floor, New York, NY 10001, (212) 947-9779 Fax (212) 947-9790
Advocates for Children works to protect and extend the rights of children with learning and/or developmental disabilities in public schools.

National Information Center for Children and Youth with Disabilities, P.O. Box 1492, Washington, D.C. 20013-1492, (1-800) 695-0285

The A.D.D. Resource Center, Inc., 215 West 75th Street, New York, N.Y. 10023, Tel: (212) 721-0049, or (212) 724-9699 Fax: (212) 724-4519
Seminars, courses, workshops and services for parents and children.

PUBLIC SCHOOL OPTIONS

Many parents agonize over the choice of public or private school education for their children. If sending their children to private school would be a tremendous financial burden on families already stretched to their limits, we feel it is very important not to add additional pressures. Parents should resist societal pressure and use common sense to make the right decisions for their family. Children might be better off with a parent who is accessible, rather than one who is working 24/7 to make tuition payments. Select public schools offer a top-notch education at a rock bottom price and parents who get involved in their child's school can really make a difference.

The public schools are experiencing a revitalization as a result of a number of factors: More families are making the decision to raise their children in the city, there is a budget surplus as a result of the recent Wall Street boom, the cost of a private school education is well beyond the reach of most families. Parents also say they select public school as a values choice; they don't want to raise children who are "precocious," and "entitled."

Clara Hemphill's book *The Parents' Guide to the City's Best Public Elementary Schools* (Soho Press 1998) reassures parents that the best school for their child might be the one right around the corner. Community School District 2 in Manhattan, for example, is a pilot district for the New Standards Project and boasts schools with the highest reading and math scores in the city. Recent announcements of multi-million dollar gifts from alumni to Brooklyn Tech and Bronx Science ensure that the specialized high schools can compete with the independent schools in their ability to attract the best and the brightest students.

The New York City school system, the largest in the nation, offers a truly diverse student body, enrichment programs for gifted students, magnet/option programs*, bilingual immersion programs, collaborations with the city's major cultural institutions, corporate grants for computer and science curricula—whatever is new and exciting in education is happening in New York City's public schools. Be aware that

*Option or alternative schools are schools of choice that are at the forefront of the educational reform movement. They are small, director-managed schools with a clear guiding vision and specific philosophical, thematic and curricular commitments. Although they are located in regular school buildings, they are autonomous. Staff, parents and students elect to attend these schools. They are magnet (TAG) schools with a mandate for ethnically, socioeconomically and gender-balanced populations. Admission is by application, which can be obtained from the schools. Parents must contact each school since application requirements and notification dates vary from program to program.

there is tremendous variation among individual schools in terms of philosophy, physical plant, magnet grants, enrichment programs, extracurricular activities and parent involvement. There are traditional schools as well as smaller "option" schools. Parents need to see with their own eyes how good public education can be.

The two questions parents ask most often concern class size and safety in the public elementary schools. For grades K–3 class size is "limited" to twenty-five students but can go to twenty-eight. For grades 4–6 the maximum class size is generally thirty-two, but can go beyond that. Student-teacher ratios vary from school to school because some schools have student teachers and parents often pay for extra para-professionals to staff classrooms. District superintendents say "there are fair, firm and consistent rules of discipline" in effect at all the elementary schools. Every elementary school has a guard in front who requests identification from visitors.

The standard time to preregister for the public school in your catchment area or zone (immediate neighborhood) is May of the same calendar year your child will be attending school (register in May of 2001 for fall of 2001). But be advised that many New York City public school gifted and talented programs require an application process that begins in the fall *prior* to the calendar year that a child would attend the school. Following the national trend toward a return to Middle Schools serving sixth through eighth grades, District 2 and 3 elementary schools now end after fifth grade.

How to Begin Finding Out About New York City Public Schools

1. **The Parents' Guide to New York City's Best Public Elementary Schools**, Clara Hemphill (Soho Press 1998) and **Public Middle Schools: New York City's Best**, Clara Hemphill (Soho Press, September 1999) and **New York City's Best Public High Schools** (Teacher's College Press, 2001)
   Everything you need to know about the best elementary, middle and high Schools in your area.
2. **The Board of Education Office of Zoning:** (718) 935-2000, press 1. Based on your address, they will tell you what school your child is entitled to attend.
3. *www.Publicschoolreports.org* is a website with information about specific public schools in all five boroughs. The website, directed by Clara Hemphill, is based at Advocates For Children, a Man-

hattan non-profit organization. There is a **Public School Hot Line** every Tuesday and Thursday from 10 A.M. to 1:00 PM, tel: (212) 947-9770. Parents can also have their questions about particular schools answered by e-mail at: info@publicschoolreports.org.

4. **Center For Educational Innovation/The Public Education Association (CEI/PEA)**, 28 West 44th Street Suite 914 Street, New York, NY 10036, (212) 868-1640,

   This one hundred year old organization which merged with CEI in 1999, is an advocate for highest quality schools for all of New York City's public school children. The CEI/PEA's Education Information Center provides timely and useful information to parents and the public about public schools. The Education Information Center publishes a *Consumer's Guide to NYC Public High Schools* and the new *Consumer's Guide to Middle Schools*.

5. **The 92nd Street Y, the Parenting Center at the Center for Youth and Family**, 1395 Lexington Avenue, New York, NY 10128, (212) 415-5611 (212) 415-5500 (to register) "Public School Options in District 2". The 92nd Street Y offers a very informative seminar on public school options in October. Call the 92nd Street Y for reservations. There is a $15 registration fee per person. The evening features a panel discussion and Q. and A.

6. **The Manhattan White Pages**

   In the center of the telephone book is a section called the Blue Pages that contains a directory of New York City government offices. Under the heading Education, you will find a listing of all the Manhattan public schools, elementary through high schools.

Manhattan is composed of six community districts. (The Upper East Side is in District Two. The Upper West Side is in District Three.) Call your community school district office for general information on alternative/option schools in the district (these include gifted and talented programs).

Call the elementary school or Middle School directly to request a tour. A representative of the Parents Association usually conducts these tours and can answer many of your preliminary questions. A school might have an excellent reputation but you should see the school with your own eyes and let the principal/teachers describe the school's philosophy to you. Some alternative/option schools *require* a parent tour before application.

Students who live within a zone (or "catchment") have first priority for enrollment in neighborhood elementary schools, followed by students who live outside the zone but within the district. A student may attend a school outside his zone only if there are "empty seats." Parents interested in sending a child to a school outside their zone or district need to obtain a variance. Children of a parent who works in another zone or district can receive a "working" variance so that they can attend a school near the parent's place of work. Contact the district office of the desired school for variance information.

Due to recent budget cuts, free busing on a Board of Education School bus to a school outside the student's zone is no longer provided; although busing *is* provided for students attending a gifted and talented school within the student's district. Students may obtain a bus pass for New York City buses.

PROGRAMS FOR GIFTED
AND TALENTED STUDENTS

Tracking (ability grouping) within grades at the elementary level, an educational practice familiar to many baby boomers, has fallen out of favor these days. However, many parents still prefer their "bright" children to be with other children of similar ability. In the past, many middle-class families made financial sacrifices to send their children to prestigious private schools where they would receive an enriched educational program. The burgeoning gifted and talented programs (also known as talented and gifted or "TAG" programs) within the New York City public schools are an attempt to lure white, middle class parents back to public education and it is working. Getting a child into Hunter Elementary is as prestigious as gaining admission to the most selective independent school. Like the private (independent) schools, most of the TAG programs require parents to apply on behalf of their children one year prior to the year of enrollment. While some of the public TAG programs still have a "cutoff score" (they will only accept students who score above a certain percentile on an I.Q. test; the Stanford-Binet IV is the most commonly used test) in District 2, a screening process (which includes an interview with the child) has replaced I.Q. testing. New York City public school TAG programs fill up quickly and waiting lists are maintained. All of these programs are free of charge.

Many of the programs for talented and gifted students are contained within the public elementary and middle Schools. A few programs are housed separately (The Laboratory School for Gifted Education, Hunter Elementary). Because the gifted and talented programs are not all alike—there are different models and different approaches—parents are advised to tour them.

Center For Talented Youth (CTY), Johns Hopkins University, 3400 N Charles Street, Baltimore, Maryland 21218, Phone (410) 516-0337, Fax (410) 516-0804, website: www.jhu.edu/~gifted. Parents who are seeking enrichment programs for a gifted child need look no further. The Johns Hopkins University Talent Search identifies students with exceptional mathematical and/or verbal reasoning ability in grades 2–8. These students (who have scored above the 97th percentile on nationally normed standardized aptitude or achievement tests) take above-grade-level tests through the Talent Search to provide an accurate evaluation of advanced talents. Test-takers receive recognition, guidance materials, and, if qualified based on above-grade-level test scores, the opportunity to participate in academic programs. CTY (Center for Talented Youth) offers three-week summer residential programs (approximate cost, $2,000). The Center for Distance Education offers Math and Writing Tutorials year-round (approximate cost, $400–500). Schools can form a team and join the on-line Math Olympiad. Students apply in the Fall and most test in December or January at test centers nationwide. Contact CTY for an application and brochure which lists deadlines and instructions.

I.Q. Testing

Hunter Elementary and some of the gifted programs require I.Q. testing, and the Stanford-Binet IV is the most widely used test. Testing must usually be done after July 1 of the year of application at an approved testing site. The results are shared with the parents and sent to the program. The usual fee is $125 but "accommodation can be made for families who are in need" we were told.

A good source on I.Q. testing for the various TAG programs is Victor Toledo, director of the **National Training and Evaluation Center**, 15 West 84th Street, New York, NY 10024 (off Central Park West), (212) 877-4480

Hunter Elementary provides a listing of approved testing agencies with the application.

The Programs

The programs highlighted below are only *a few* of the elementary programs for gifted and talented students available in Manhattan public schools. For information on TAG or alternative programs in your zone, contact your district office. (Keep in mind that the birthdate cutoff for public schools is December 31.)

The Hunter College Campus Schools:
Both Hunter Elementary and Hunter High School are located at 71 East 94th Street (94th and Park), New York, NY 10128
(212) 860-1262 (Pre-K and Elementary School admissions)
Hunter Elementary, Hunter Elementary is administered through Hunter College of the City University of New York. The school is tuition free and serves as a laboratory for the study of education. Admissions to nursery and kindergarten are open only to Manhattan residents. At seventh grade they take applicants from all five boroughs. Nursery, kindergarten and seventh grades are the only points of entry. However, there is an active wait list for kindergarten applicants. You must apply for your child one year in advance of enrollment—apply to the nursery school the year that he is three, apply to kindergarten the year she is four. Applicants to seventh grade are tested in sixth grade. Parents are advised to call or write for an application in September of the year prior to the year of enrollment. Parents must then make a testing appointment for the Stanford Binet IV at an approved testing center. (The usual fee for the Stanford Binet is $125 but it can be waived.) Students are interviewed in a group at Hunter Elementary. One recent year the cutoff for the Stanford Binet was 98th percentile and above but this score varies from year to year.

Hunter High School, Website: heimdall.hchs.hunter.cuny.edu (212) 860-1259 admissions, (212) 860-1261 for certification information.
    Seventh grade is the *only* point of entry to Hunter High School. Entrance is based solely on performance on the Hunter entrance exam taken in the sixth grade. Each year there are approximately 2,000 applicants for 240 places; there is a slightly lower cutoff for students of economically disadvantaged status and thirty places (of the 240) are reserved for these applicants. In order to sit for the January exam, sixth grade students must have the principal of their school submit a certification package to Hunter High by the first week of

November. To qualify, students must score in the top percentiles in reading and math on *any* standardized test taken in fifth grade. The cutoff varies from year to year. There is a $40.00 fee.

The Anderson Program, at Public School 9, 100 West 84th Street (at Columbus Avenue), New York, NY 10024, (212) 595-7193 Website: www.Andersonps9.org
Dr. Rachel Schnur, Coordinator

The Anderson Program accepts applications from all five boroughs for kindergarten through fifth grade. There are two classes per grade. Applications must be submitted the year before entering. Interested parents must send an SASE and they will be sent an application and a brochure describing the application process in full (or can pick up an application at the school during school hours). Admission is based on "very superior performance on a test of cognitive ability, an interview and screening, teacher recommendation, school records and social maturity." Call the following number(s) in the Fall to arrange for a group tour: (212) 678-2812 or 678-2813.

New York City Laboratory School for Gifted Education (Lower Lab), 1700 Third Avenue (between 95th and 96th Streets), New York, NY 10128, (212) 427-2798
Elizabeth Kasowitz, Principal

The Lab School "operates on the premise that gifted education need not be elitist." The Lab School serves kindergarten through fifth grades. There are two classes per grade. Applications must be submitted one year prior to enrollment. Call in early October for a group tour appointment. The tour is followed by an explanation of the school's philosophy and a question-and-answer session. Parents are then given an application and brochure. The application requires a preschool skills checklist and a teacher evaluation. When the file is complete, the child comes in for an hour-long performance based interview with four other applicants. Note: Students in Lower Lab must apply to the Upper Lab School as they would to any other gifted/option Middle School program. Admission to Upper Lab is not automatic.

New York City Laboratory School for Collaborative Studies (Upper Lab School), 333 West 17th Street, New York, NY 10011 (212) 691-6119
Rob Menken, Sheila Breslaw, Co-directors

The Upper Lab consists of grades six through twelve. Total enrollment is approximately 800. The Upper Lab School is rigorous and academic, but non-traditional; emphasis is put on collaborative and interactive approaches to learning. The Middle School has consistently scored in the top five in reading and math scores in the city. The majority of students come from District 2, but a small number are accepted from out of the district. Applications should be filed by mid-December of the year prior to enrollment. The largest point of entry is at sixth grade. Sixth and seventh graders are required to have an interview and to take a teacher-designed math problem solving test and a teacher-designed essay test; both are administered at the Upper Lab School. Ninth grade is the second largest point of entry. Applicants for ninth grade use the normal high school application process, but applicants must have a solid academic background and should have completed one year of Spanish. "We look at grades and courses." College courses are offered in the eleventh and twelfth grades and internships are available in eleventh. Students can take college level courses at area universities including NYU, Borough of Manhattan Community College, Hunter and Parson's School of Design. The school has an overseas and foreign exchange program funded by the Lauder Foundation.

Community Districts Two and Three

District Two is composed of Manhattan below 59th Street, East and West Sides (excluding the Lower East Side (District One)) and most of the Upper East Side.

Community School District Two Office, 333 Seventh Avenue, 7th Floor, New York, NY 10001, (212) 330-9400
Call and ask for the brochure "Choosing a Public School in Community District Two."
District Two gifted and talented and magnet program choice coordinator: Barbara Leventer-Luque (212) 330-9407. Jimmy Bueschen, Middle School choice, (212) 330-9473 will answer questions about the alternative programs, which include the gifted and magnet programs.
District Two Variance Coordinator: Beverly Herschkowitz, (212) 330-9406
There are six elementary gifted and talented programs in District

Two: P.S. 6, New York City Laboratory School for Gifted Education, P.S. 116, P.S. 11, P.S. 124, P.S. 130.

Community School District Three Office, 154 West 93th Street, New York, NY 10025, (212) 678-2800. District Three extends north from 59th Street to 122nd Street and east from the Hudson River to Central Park West.

District Three Gifted and Talented Programs, call Marilyn Carella at (212) 678-2897 for an application to Gifted Programs in District Three. School choice—grades 6–8

Office of Alternative Schools (Middle School information) (212) 678-2885

T.A.G. Programs in District 2

P.S. 6, 45 East 81st Street, New York, NY 10028, (212) 794-4772
Pam Fuchs, Liaison.
For a tour of P.S. 6 call the Parents Association in October at (212) 988-1029.

This popular East Side elementary school attracts many families who live in the zone. For the past several years P.S. 6 has not had any admissions except for in-zone families, with the possible exception of a very few places in fourth or fifth grades.

P.S. 116, 210 East 33rd Street, New York, NY 10016 (212) 685-4366
Eleanore Rubin, TAG Coordinator

The gifted and talented program at P.S. 116 serves kindergarten through fifth grades. Students are selected on the basis of a screening process. An interview and a teacher evaluation form from the child's current teacher are required for admission. There are two classes per grade.

P.S. 124, 40 Division Street, New York, NY 10002, (212) 966-7237
Nancy Jung, Gifted and Talented Program Liasion

The gifted program at P.S. 124, located in Chinatown, serves kindergarten through fifth grades. There is one gifted class per grade. The deadline for applications is December 1st previous to the year of enrollment. Admissions decisions are based on a screening process. For a tour call the Parents Association at (212) 274-0263. Parents can send a self-addressed, stamped envelope for an application.

P.S. 11, 320 West 21st Street, New York, NY 10011, (212) 929-1743
Fran Delmonico, Interim Acting Principal

The Gifted and Talented Program at P.S. 11 serves kindergarten through fifth grades. There is one gifted section per grade. Prospetive applicants should call for a tour.

P.S. 130, 143 Baxter Street, New York, NY 10013, (212) 226-8072
Lily Din Woo, Principal

P.S. 130 is located between Little Italy and Chinatown. The gifted program, created in 1998, serves grades kindergarten through fifth grade. The schoolhouse recently received a $32 million facelift and boasts an art room with a kiln, a science room, and a media center in the library. Applicants are admitted based upon a screening process and interview.

T.A.G. Programs in District 3

Patricia Romandetto, Superintendent, (212) 678-2880
Marilyn Carella, Director of Gifted and Talented Admissions in District 3: (212) 678-2897 (Grades pre-K through five.) Parents must call Ms. Carella for information about all of Distric 3's G. and T. programs. District children have priority for P.S. 166 and P.S. 9 G. and T. programs.
Jay Hecht, Director of Middle School Choice, District 3: (212) 678-2950, for selective middle schools
For admission to all District 3 gifted and talented elementary school programs, applicants must score in the superior range on the Stanford-Binet IV. ERB scores are also accepted and will be interpreted by the district office.

P.S. 145: 150 West 105th Street
(212) 678-2858
One class per grade, pre-kindergarten through fifth grade.
Tours are given beginning in mid-October.

P.S. 165, 234 West 109th street
Irma Marzan, Principal
Dual language gifted and talented program, beginning in 2001 with kindergarten and first grade and eventually serving K through 5.

P.S. 191, 210 West 61st Street
Elena Nassereddin, Principal
Dual language gifted and talented program, beginning with pre-K and kindergarten and eventually serving grades K through 5.

P.S. 163: 163 West 97th Street
(212) 678-2854 general, (212) 678-2926 for tour dates
K–5
P.S. 163 has a dual language (Spanish) Talented and Gifted Program, a magnet G and T, and a learning disabled G and T, kindergarten through fifth grades.

P.S. 9: 100 West 84th Street
(212) 678-2812
Diane Brady, Principal
P.S. 9's Program for Gifted and Talented students is a magnet program, for grades K–5. There is one class per grade. A teacher evaluation and scores from standardized tests in reading and math are required for admission to third, fourth and fifth grades.

P.S. 166, 132 West 89th Street, New York, NY 10024, (212) 678-2829
Jack Regan, Principal
The gifted program at P.S. 166 serves kindergarten through fifth grade. The program is very popular so parents should call Marilyn Carella at the district office (678-2897) the first week of October for applications, which are first come, first served. Check out the school's website which was set up by a P.S. 166 parent.

P.S. 185, 20 West 112th Street, New York, NY 10026, (212) 678-2841
Norma Genao, Principal
The G&T program at P.S. 185 serves kindergarten through second grade. P.S. 185 is a sister school to P.S. 208.

P.S. 208, 21 West 111th Street, New York, NY 10026, (212) 678-2882
Corine Pettey, Principal
The gifted program at P.S. 208 serves grades three through five. There is one gifted class per grade. P.S. 185 feeds into P.S. 208.

M.S. 54 The Delta Honors Program, 103 West 107th Street, New York, NY 10025, (212) 678-5855
Frederick La Senna, Program Coordinator

Students can apply to this top-rated Middle School at grades five or six. Entrance is based upon superior reading and math scores plus an interview. The school does not usually accept students from out of the district. Parents looking for a Middle School should call the district office for the "Middle School options book" in late October of the year prior to enrollment.

Mott Hall II: at P.S. 165, 234 West 109th Street
Alisa Berger, Coordinator
A new honors Middle School serving grades 6 through 8
In its first year, this program got as many applications as the popular Delta Honors program.

Alpha Honors Program, 215 West 114th Street, (212) 749-5800, at Wadleigh Secondary School, serves grades 6–8.

T.A.G. Programs in District 4

Community District Four Office: 319 East 117th Street
(212) 828-3500
Ben Waxman, Director of Option Programs, Coordinator of TAG/ alternative programs in District 4: 828-3555

P.S. 171, Patrick Henry Prep, 19 East 103rd Street
(212) 860-5801
Karen Marino, Director of Gifted Program
The TAG program at P.S. 171 serves kindergarten through sixth grade.

The Bilingual, Bicultural Mini-School (BBMS) at P.S. 83, 219 East 109th Street, Room #300
(212) 860-6031 or 6032
Miss Lourdes Arroyo, Director
The dual language (Spanish) TAG program serves kindergarten through sixth grade.

J.H.S. 117, 240 East 109th Street
(212) 860-6003
Janette Cesar, Director
The TAG program is part of the alternative complex within Junior High

School 117. The program serves children in seventh and eighth grade. Applicants are tested at the school.

Manhattan East, 410 East 100th Street,
(212) 860-6047
Lillian Sarro, Director
Outstanding Middle School for grades 6-8.

T.A.G. Programs in District 6

The Discovery School, P.S. 98, 512 West 212th Street
(212) 927-7870
Odile Santiago, Coordinator
The Discovery School's dual language Program for Gifted and Talented Students within P.S. 98 serves kindergarten through fourth grade.

Mott Hall, 131st Street and Convent Avenue, (212) 927-9466
Dr. Miriam Acosta-Sing, Director
Mott Hall offers a very demanding academic program for grades four through eight. The program is over ten years old. Eighty percent of the students are bilingual in Spanish but only one of the classes is bilingual. Applications must be filed one year in advance of enrollment. Applicants must live in District 6 and score 85% and above on citywide reading and math tests; students are also tested at Mott Hall. Teacher recommendations and grades are also considered for admission.

THE PUBLIC HIGH SCHOOLS

The board of education publishes a yearly *Directory of the Public High Schools*, which will be sent to you upon request, free of charge, if you call the Office of High Schools Admissions: (212) 481-7358. The directory provides detailed information on over 150 public high schools, including the thirty new "theme" schools that opened in 1994. The directory describes the admissions process and requirements for each school.

The Public Education Association (PEA) publishes a guide to city high schools consisting of statistical information and rankings.

The Specialized High Schools

There are four specialized high schools. These schools require an entrance examination or audition. *The Student Handbook for the Specialized High Schools* (which describes the individual schools and their admissions process and includes two sample admissions examinations) can be obtained from the Division of Student Support, 110 Livingston Street, Room 512, Brooklyn, NY 11201, (718) 935-3415.

Stuyvesant High School, Bronx High School of Science and Brooklyn Technical High School, known as "the science schools," emphasize mathematics and science studies. New York State Education Law requires a written examination for admission to the science schools. The three schools are different from one another so applicants must take the entrance exam at their first-choice science school. In addition, there is the Fiorello H. LaGuardia High School of Music and Art and the Performing Arts.

In 1998 alumni of Brooklyn Tech pledged to create a $10 million endowment fund. Three months later, Leonard and Ronald Lauder, both Bronx Science alumni, pledged $1 million to launch a campaign seeking to raise $10 million for their alma mater.

Timetable for admissions to the specialized high schools:
September: Call for a handbook and application
November: Applications are due in early November
December: Exams are offered to students in either 8th or 9th grades one year *prior* to the year of enrollment. The exam is taken at the candidate's first-choice school.
March: Notification of acceptance

THE MATH/SCIENCE INSTITUTE
345 Chambers Street
New York, NY 10282
(212) 312-4816
Fax: (212) 312-4815
e-mail: ravageb@stuy.edu

Bruce Ravage, Director

In March 1995 former Public Schools Chancellor Ramon C. Cortines announced the creation of an 18-month preparatory program designed to groom able seventh graders from diverse backgrounds for admission to any one of the three specialized science high schools. Participating students attend various parochial, public and independent schools. Originally housed at Stuyvesant High School, the program has expanded to four sites. Recommendation to the program must be made by the student's school principal. The Math/Science Institute has a post-grade 6 summer session, a Wednesday/Saturday grade 7 school-year program, a post-grade 7 summer session and a fall grade 8 session. Over an 18-month period approximately 1,000 students participated. In addition to test preparation, students take courses in literature, writing, math, science and research skills.

Bronx High School of Science

75 West 205th Street, Bronx, New York, NY 10468, (718) 817-7700
Vincent Galasso, Principal

Total enrollment: 2,600 students. Students come to Bronx Science from every borough. The Bronx Science yellow school bus can be seen travelling up and down Manhattan's avenues. The school population is 40% Asian. Bronx Science students have opportunities for independent research. There is a Holocaust Study Center and Museum, nine foreign languages are offered, and there are partnerships with NASA, The Bronx Zoo, Rockefeller University, Stevens Technology and so on. The handbook says, "Bronx Science is the nation's all time leader in the Westinghouse Science Talent Search." The school has five alumni Nobel Laureates. Extracurricular activities include over 60 clubs, numerous school publications, orchestral and vocal music programs, and 30 athletic teams; a nationally acclaimed speech and debate team, Mock trial, and a full-scale theatrical production each year.

Brooklyn Technical High School

29 Fort Greene Place (South Elliot Place at DeKalb Avenue), Brooklyn, NY 11217, (718) 858-5150, Dr. Lee McCaskill, Principal

Total enrollment approximately: 4,000 students. The student body is diverse. The brochure states that Brooklyn Tech excels in the areas of engineering, math and science and computer science. During ninth and tenth grades students take an academic core of studies and are introduced to engineering, computer science and lab science through hands-on experiences in well-equipped laboratories. At the end of sophomore year, students select a major area of concentration which they begin in eleventh grade. All tech students are prepared to follow any course of study at the college level, but are particularly well versed in their major area. Brooklyn Tech has over 100 clubs and fields varsity and junior varsity teams in handball, fencing, football, swimming, baseball, soccer and basketball.

Stuyvesant High School

345 Chambers Street, New York, NY 10282, (212) 312-4800, website: www.stuy.edu Stanley Teitel, Principal

Total enrollment: approximately 3,000 students. Stuyvesant High School occupies a brand-new high-tech building in lower Manhattan. In addition to advanced courses in mathematics and the sciences, students can select from a wide range of electives. Advanced Placement classes in biology, chemistry, physics, foreign language, mathematics, English and social studies are offered. Stuyvesant's extracurricular offerings are broad. There are over 100 clubs, a symphony orchestra, dance band, choral and ensemble groups, thirty-two athletic teams, fifteen student publications and an active student government. The school has an Olympic-size swimming pool.

Fiorello H. LaGuardia High School of Music and Art and Performing Arts

108 Amsterdam Avenue, New York, NY 10023, (212) 496-0700, Dr. Paul R. Saronson, Principal

Total enrollment: 2,500. LaGuardia is the high school featured in the movie *Fame*. It is the only public high school in the world that offers a complete academic program along with professional-level training in the arts. Because of the dual nature of the program, LaGuardia students can expect to put in very long days. Admission to this high school is based on an individual audition in dance, drama, instrumental music, vocal music or art. Only New York City residents are eligible. The handbook describes what is needed for the audition.

AFTER-SCHOOL ATHLETIC
AND OTHER PROGRAMS

There are a number of organized after-school athletic programs such as **Joe Espinoza**, **Cavaliers**, and so on, which feature quality coaching and team play and provide door to door bus transportation from your child's private or public school to the program and home. Your child's school probably has an established relationship with one of these programs. Both boys and girls are welcome to participate. Fees vary but since they provide transportation these programs are costly. As an alternative, we have listed below some of the most popular city athletic programs.

Westside Soccer League: (212) 479-7791 to register. Website: www.WSSL.org. Open to children from around the city, ages 5-16.

CYO Manhattan Youth Baseball: Bobby Hoffman, Coordinator, 156 William Street, 8th floor, New York, NY 10038, (212) 233-2370. CYO Baseball is the Manhattan version of suburban Little League. Priority is given to returning players and there is a wait list for new members. Call in September to register for spring.

Ice Hockey at Chelsea Piers Sky Rink: Pat Murphy, coordinator (212) 336-6100 x6172 Boys and girls teams, school leagues, travel teams

Yorkville Youth Athletic Association: Arlene Virga, Director, (212) 876-4976. Yorkville Youth Athletic Association offers a Saturday basketball league that plays from December to March. Teams play at four East Side locations. Kindergarten through tenth grade, co-ed, girls' and boys' teams. Volleyball in September, Tennis December through April. Baseball (K–8) begins in March; played at Asphalt Green and Central Park. Fees are very reasonable ($75.00 for a season of play) and there is space for new players.

Big Apple Sports Club: Tel: (212) 987-9853 or 9865, Fax: (212) 987-9764, a coed youth organization whose main purpose is to maintain and promote the teaching of fundamentals of sports. (Programs are based at P.S. 6 and other public schools/locations on the East Side) A very popular after-school program, Saturday competitive sports leagues, soccer and basketball travel teams, Holiday sports camps and school transportation services.

City Sports for Kids at Asphalt Green: Bob Glover, Shelley Lynn-Florence, Coordinators, (914) 366-4175. Track and field program, for a very reasonable fee.

Isaacs Center Beacon: at P.S. 198, 96th Street and Third Avenue, (212) 828-6342, after 6 P.M. open gym, Girls' gym night, swimming on Sundays at Asphalt Aqua Center, Saturday Football and basketball leagues, Softball/baseball leagues. All programs are free of charge; sponsored by the department of youth and Community Development.

The After School Workshop, 45 East 81st Street (at P.S. 6), New York, NY 10028, (212) 734-7620, Mrs. Sheila N. Bandman, founder and supervisor. Located in the "penthouse" at P.S. 6, the After School Workshop, now approaching its 25th year, is one of the best kept secrets on the East Side. In a relaxed and low-key atmosphere, children can choose from a variety of creative and recreational activities (crafts, dance, board games, sports, homework help, and computer). The attentive staff keeps things humming along, 3:00 to 6:00 P.M. weekdays and on vacation days. Children can attend from one to five days a week and regular Workshop children can bring a playdate free of charge.

OTHER
RESOURCES

1. **The National Association of Independent Schools (NAIS)**, Office of Public Information, 1620 L. Street NW, Washington, D.C. 20036, (202) 973-9700, website: nais-schools.org. The website has a database of over 1,000 schools.

    NAIS is a voluntary organization to which accredited independent schools may apply for membership. The primary function of NAIS is to serve its over 1,100 member schools. NAIS does not accredit independent schools but does issue guidelines, chart trends, sponsor workshops and publish information on issues relevant to the independent school community from diversity to boarding schools. Many of these publications are available on the school's websites.

    Also available from NAIS publications is JoAnn Deak's readable and informative book: *How Girls Thrive: An Essential Guide for Educators (and Parents)*.

    Parents who are interested in learning more about boarding schools can call The Association of Boarding Schools (TABS) Answer Line, (202) 966-8705,

2. **Educational Testing Service (ETS)**, Rosedale Road, Princeton N.J., 08541, (609) 921-9000.

    The Educational Testing Service publishes informational pamphlets on many issues related to independent schools.

3. **Reading Reform Foundation of New York**, 333 West 57th Street, Suite 1L, New York, NY 10019, (212) 307-7320, Fax (212) 307-0449, e-mail: readingreform@mindspring.com.

    The Reading Reform Foundation of New York, founded in 1981 by a group of reading specialists and interested citizens, is a nonprofit literacy organization based on the belief that almost every child, regardless of social and economic background, can learn to read, write and spell if taught by effective methods (with an emphasis on the use of phonics). Reading Reform Foundation offers graduate level courses all year 'round in the teaching of reading, writing and spelling, holds an annual fall conference, conducts workshops for parents and sends skilled teaching consultants into public schools throughout the city to work with classroom teachers.

4. **The Council for Spiritual and Ethical Education**, (404) 355-4460 1-(800) 298-4599 website: www.csee.org

    The Council for Spiritual and Ethical Education (CSEE) is a nondenominational organization composed of 425 member schools the majority of which are secular coed day and boarding schools located in the northeastern states.

CSEE is independent of any religious body and does not impose any one point of view. According to the brochure "It is the only national, interfaith, professional organization meeting the moral and religious needs of independent schools." CSEE conducts workshops and directs conferences on values, ethics and religion education.

CSEE has been actively promoting community service in schools for many years and sponsors conferences that feature community service workshops.

New York City Independent Schools That are Members of CSEE:

The Allen-Stevenson School
The Browning School
The Buckley School
The Caedmon School
The Cathedral School
Collegiate School
Convent of the Sacred Heart
Grace Church School
Horace Mann School
Marymount School of New York

The Nightingale-Bamford School
The Packer Collegiate Institute
Saint David's School
St. Hilda's & St. Hugh's School
St. Luke's School
The Spence School
The Town School
Trinity School

5. **The Catholic Center,** Office of Superintendent of Schools, Education Department, 1011 First Avenue (between 55th and 56th) (18th floor), New York, NY 10022, (212) 371-1000
   For $8, The Catholic Center will mail its complete directory of elementary and secondary schools. A list of Catholic high schools only will be mailed to you free of charge.

6. **The National Coalition of Girls' Schools,** Meg Milne Moulton or Whitney Ransome, Executive co-Directors, 228 Main Street, Concord, Massachusetts 01742, (978) 287-4485, Fax (978) 287-6014, website: ncgs.org

   The National Coalition of Girls' Schools has 98 member schools in North America (both public and private). Its members share a commitment to the values and advantages of an all-girl's school. They conduct research, gather data, and sponsor forums for leading girls' and womens' groups; NCGS publications, including: *Choosing a Girls' School, Raising Confident, Competent Daughters*, and *What Every Girl in School Needs to Know*, and *Girls and Technology*, are available by mail order.

7. **American Association of University Women (AAUW)**, 1111 Sixteenth Street N.W., Washington, D.C. 20036, 1(800)326-AAUW (2289) (membership information and to locate a local branch of AAUW), (202) 785-7788 (general) or 1(800)225-9998 (for a copy of *How Schools Shortchange Girls* and *Separated by Sex: A Critical Look at Single-Sex Education for Girls*). Members' Help Line 1-(800) 326-2289.

In 1992 the AAUW Educational Foundation released the report *How Schools Shortchange Girls* which challenged myths about the education of girls in the public schools and uncovered disturbing evidence of new barriers to their learning. In March 1998 the AAUW released a report that finds separating by sex is *not* the solution to gender inequity. *Separated by Sex: A Critical Look at Single-Sex Education for Girls* is controversial and well worth reading. Recently, AAUW published *Tech-savvy: Educating Girls in the New Computer Age*. The AAUW has been working toward eliminating the educational, financial and legal barriers faced by women and girls for over 125 years. Parents can request free of charge useful guides for assessing gender bias in their children's schools—the *School Assessment Guide* and *Growing Smart: What Works for Girls in School.*

8. **The Association of Teachers in Independent Schools in New York City and Vicinity, Inc. (ATIS)**, (212) 472-3572 e-mail address: atisny@aol.com

ATIS was found in 1914 to ensure that teachers in private schools were properly paid and protected. Today the incorporated, non-profit organization continues its support of educational professionalism and increased opportunities for private-school teachers. ATIS sponsors several workshops for teachers throughout the year as well as the annual conference—book exhibit. ATIS publishes *The Bulletin* twice a year, which reports news of schools represented by the association, and in the spring contains a list of school positions available. Yearly dues are $25.

9. **The Interschool Faculty Diversity Search**, (212) 501-0031 Annette Lieberson at the Collegiate School.

The Search is a newly created organization whose purpose is to enlarge the pool of talented candidates of color for faculty and administrative positions in participating schools. Although the Search is administered by Interschool (a consortium of eight Manhattan independent schools) many more schools (over 25) participate. Peter Clifton, who with his wife also runs Clifton Associates (a beginning teacher placement agency), is the Search's full-time recruiter.

10. **The Guild of New York Independent Schools**, Ms. Dorothy Hutcheson, The Nightingale-Bamford School, 20 East 92nd Street, New York, NY 10128 (212) 289-5020

The guild is an informal association of approximately fifty-two heads of school (from schools located in all five boroughs) who meet three times a year at the Cosmopolitan Club to discuss common concerns within the independent-school community (such as medical benefits for faculty) and to coordinate their calendars (vacation schedules, opening and closing dates). They do *not* discuss tuitions. The guild does not provide information to parents about individual schools.

11. **NYC-Parents in Action Inc.**, P.O. Box 555, Lenox Hill Station, New York, NY 10021, (212) 987-9629

Rumors circulate that certain schools have more drug and/or alcohol abuse than others. The truth is that a portion of the student body at all the New York City independent high schools (and boarding schools) does experiment with alcohol, drugs and/or sex. NYC-Parents In Action, Inc. is a nonprofit, voluntary organization that was incorporated in 1979 as a response to growing alcohol, marijuana and other drug use among minors and their parents. In support of the belief that "Good parenting is substance abuse prevention," NYC-PIA provides information, parent education, seminars and workshops and provides trained facilitators for parent-organized discussion groups. The Parent Representative program provides a link to the parent body within the independent schools. NYC-PIA publishes *FOCUS* and a newsletter. In cooperation with the Parents' League, NYC-PIA sponsors the annual Teen Scene—a candid discussion of teen life in the city by a panel composed of students from various independent and boarding schools.

12. **New York State Education Office of Non-Public Schools**, New York State Education Department, Non-public School Ser-

vices Team, Room 481 Education Building Annex, Washington Avenue, Albany, New York 12234, (518) 474-3879

New York State Education Office of Information, Reporting and Technology Services, (a division of the State Education Office that compiles statistical information), Room 863, Education Building Annex, Albany, New York 12234, (518) 474-7965

Upon request, the Department of Information, Reporting and Technology will send a statistical breakdown for each school based on an extensive questionnaire. Information includes the number and type of computers the school owns, which foreign languages are taught and the ethnic and religious composition of the student body and faculty. (Most of this information can be obtained more easily from the school's brochure or directly from the school.)

ACCREDITING ORGANIZATIONS

The New York State Board of Regents authorizes both the New York State Association of Independent Schools and the Middle States Association to accredit schools. According to the National Association of Independent Schools, "Accreditation is a process of peer evaluation that certifies that schools meet certain generally accepted standards of educational quality defined by an independent entity." Each of the independent schools sets forth its accreditation in its brochure. Tradition determines which organization accredits the school. NYSAIS deals primarily with the independent schools in New York State, whereas Middle States accredits many independent as well as public schools in the Middle Atlantic states. Note: NYSAIS and Middle States do not provide parents with information about specific schools—do not call them to find out which school is the best for your child.

How does it work? Both NYSAIS and Middle States evaluate a school based on its philosophy (or mission) and how well the school puts its philosophy into practice—is the school doing what it says it does? This evaluation process takes place every ten years or so. The first step in the reaccreditation process is a year-long self-study. Next, the school is evaluated by a team of recognized evaluators, which often includes heads of other independent schools. The evaluating team makes recommendations for improvement, and the school is requested to provide an action plan for implementing these changes. Accreditation is granted if the self-study, evaluation and planning reports reveal that the school meets the standards for accreditation. Accreditation is granted for a period of ten years. After approximately eight and a half years, the school begins another self-study and the cycle is renewed.

1. **New York State Association of Independent Schools (NYSAIS)**, 12 Jay Street, Schenectady, NY, 12305 Tel (518) 346-5662, fax (518) 346-7390 website: www.nysais.org, Executive Director: Fred Calder

   NYSAIS is a voluntary association of 155 independent nursery, elementary, middle and secondary schools in New York State whose enrollment is 59,000 students. NYSAIS publishes a useful pamphlet entitled "Choosing a School: A Guide for Parents." One of its main activities is advocacy for independent education.

2. **The Middle States Association of Colleges and Schools (Middle States)**, 3624 Market Street, 2nd Floor Annex, Philadelphia, PA 19104, (215) 662-5600 or 5610

   Dr. F. Laird Evans, Executive Director, Commission on Elementary Schools, Dr. Joseph DeLucia, Executive Director, Commission on Secondary Schools.

   The Middle States Association established standards that are administered by the three accreditation authorities under the auspices of the Middle States Association: the Commission on Elementary Schools, the Commission on Secondary Schools and the Commission on Higher Education. The Middle States Association is a nonprofit organization established in 1887 to set standards for American education. Middle States publishes information on school standards and the accreditation process.

Index of Schools and Programs

491